DEGREES OF DECEPTION

2ND EDITION

DOD SERIES
BOOK 1

KIMBERLY THACKER WEBB

EMERALD PEN

COPYRIGHT

Emerald Pen books may be ordered through booksellers or by contacting:

Emerald Pen Publishing

5000 Eldorado Pkwy Suite 461

Frisco, Texas 75033

www.emeraldpen.com

ISBN: 979-8-9922955-0-4 (sc)

ISBN: 979-8-9922955-1-1 (hc)

ISBN: 979-8-9922955-2-8 (e)

Library of Congress Control Number: 2013920834

Cover Design by Rebeca Covers

Printed in the United States of America

Emerald Pen rev. date: 1/ /2025

❀ Created with Vellum

In school, you're taught a lesson and then given a test. In life, you're given a test that teaches you a lesson.

— TOM BODETT

ACKNOWLEDGMENTS

Ten years after the publishing of Degrees of Deception, I had an idea to develop a second edition. The second edition of this book has been a joyful and rewarding process. I want to thank the many people who pushed me forward toward my dreams.

First, I have to thank God for giving me a purpose and having patience with me. Thanks for helping realize that nothing is impossible – You hold me in your hands.

I want to give special thanks to my husband, Steven for his tireless efforts in motivating me to finish and publish this book. Thank you for spending endless days and nights editing and helping me rewriting paragraphs to make them stronger. I love you more and more every day!

Thanks to my children, Kendal and Kaleb for all their prayers and support. I love you so much!

Thanks to my Mom, my Dad and my sister Kelli who are not here with me on earth, but are watching down from heaven.

Thanks to my sister, Michelle Collier for her love and support.

Thanks to my editors, Michelle Chester and Camille Hays of EBM Professional Services and Steven Jarrett Webb. My marketing team, Scott O'Reilly, CEO of OBOY! Productions, Kevin Walker, CEO and social media expert of Culture Lab, Damon & Warni Flournoy of CEO of NoysTech for my website.

Thanks to Tracey Dubose, my lifelong friend for dreaming with me and reminding me of our song, "Make It Happen."

Thanks to Patryce Young Curtis for over 20 years of friendship and constant encouragement in all my endeavors.

Thanks to Darren & LaVonne Allen who are our friends, but more like family for providing love, support and encouragement.

Special thanks to Deborah Bolden, one of my best friends, may she rest in peace. Thanks to Sherri & Norm Williams, Monica Hayes, Rechelle Pace, Carole Shannon, Loretta Barr, and Alveta Herbert for words of encouragement that help to move me forward toward my dreams.

To all the many readers and book clubs who have read the original Degrees of Deception, thank you for your kind words, accolades and support throughout the years.

UNTITLED

PROLOGUE

"Come on...come on, aw man, I keep losing her." Nick placed the pads on her chest and told Pete to charge the defibrillator again. He did, and then Nick blasted her body with another electric shock. After a few seconds of struggling to find a pulse, Nick said, "Wait... its back, let's go." The two paramedics rushed to load the gurney carrying the young girl's bloody body into the ambulance. Nick climbed in to apply pressure, seal the wound, and monitor her vitals. He yelled up front to Pete, "Her blood pressure keeps racing and then bottoming out; she has a weak pulse, and it's unsteady. We need to get to the hospital, stat. Step on it!"

"Already ahead of you, partner," Pete said, as he swung the ambulance into motion heading out of the parking lot. With the lights flashing and the sirens blaring, they raced down the street. "Wow, I wonder what happened. She's messed up bad; they all are. I lost count of all the paramedics back there."

"I don't know," Nick said, as he picked up the phone. "I'm calling ahead to let the hospital know they need to prep the OR because it looks like she needs surgery now."

❧

Hours later Jackie opened her eyes to the gentle burn of fluorescent lights bouncing off the sterile white walls. She tried to speak, but her throat dry and scratchy felt like someone used a knife to scrape at her vocal cords. She saw Eve and Lydia sitting in chairs across the room, talking to each other. She also heard a beeping noise above her head. Sluggish, she turned her head trying to take in her surroundings while fighting the effects of whatever was making her so sleepy. She turned toward the beeping noise and saw a monitor flashing a top and bottom number with squiggly lines running across the screen. Next to it, an IV bag hung on a tall metal pole. Thin tubing snaked down the pole and the end of it hooked into her arm. Jackie felt cool air pumping into her nose, so she wiggled it around, wondering where it was coming from. She stretched her mouth down from her nose and felt thin plastic tubes in both of her nostrils. At that exact moment realization set in, and her eyes bulged open. She took a deep breath as it sunk in that she was in the hospital.

Jackie felt groggy and dazed, so she closed her eyes to clear her head. After a brief rest, she opened her eyes halfway and lifted her left arm to get Eve and Lydia's attention, but it fell back onto the bed.

Out of the corner of their eyes, they saw Jackie's motion, heard the soft thud, and rushed over. Eve leaned down and said, "Jackie, try not to talk. Everything's going to be fine. Are you in pain?"

That one movement of Jackie's arm drained the only energy she had left in her body, but she mustered up everything she could and nodded. Her body felt like a Mack truck hit her and tore off part of her back and shoulder.

Lydia showed Jackie a button that she could push to release pain medication, and then pushed it for her.

Jackie gave Lydia a slight smile and prayed that the increasing pain would soon end. Within seconds of pressing the button, Eve, Lydia, and the room all became blurry as Jackie drifted into a pain-free abyss. As the induced slumber slowly pulled her under, and the weight of her eyes sent her deeper and deeper, she could still hear Lydia talking to Eve.

"This should have never happened to her. Jackie's such a nice person, a little lost sometimes, but she was just starting to get herself together."

"Are you serious? She's a big girl just like everyone else. And, she knew what she was getting into when she started."

The women continued to talk but Jackie only heard parts of their muffled conversation. She played tug of war with the looming slumber and willed herself to stay awake long enough to hear all they had to say. They talked about how long she would be in the hospital and the physical therapy she would have to go through to get full use of her right arm again.

Lydia watched Jackie wrestle, then bent down and whispered in her ear, "Your parents are coming in today on the first flight from Dallas. They'll be here soon. Close your eyes and get some rest. Our secret is safe."

To that, Jackie roused from the sleep that had been pulling at her. Her eyes popped open as she realized this wasn't a dream. It was her very real nightmare. She now remembered the police, the bodies, and the blood everywhere.

Her head felt so heavy that raising it was almost impossible, but she did it anyway, and it fell back onto the pillow like dead weight. The whole room spun around her, and she couldn't focus. Dark spots, shadows, glimpses of an abandoned building, and guns flashed before her. Panic pulsated through her body just as it did before. Jackie's heart raced and she broke into a sweat from the fear of that woman and what she would do to her. She tried to recall all that happened, but she couldn't concentrate; she could only see cinema like images flashing before her. She struggled to run, but her legs were too heavy. The hospital monitors beeped faster and faster. Nurses and techs rushed into the room, pushing Eve and Lydia out of the way.

Hoarse, Jackie screamed, "Ursula, where is Ursula?"

A tech restrained her while a nurse injected a clear fluid into her IV line. The flashes continued, and she saw a crowd of people gathered near the blood and the bodies. Jackie envisioned herself standing in the middle of them as they pushed and shoved, creating an unbearable uproar. She looked for a way out, but there wasn't one. She gazed down at her bloodstained hands and thought, *Oh God, what did I do?*

A wave of calmness washed over her and one by one, the images faded. She heard the nurse say, "I've given her a sedative to relax her. What did you say to her?"

Eve and Lydia looked at each other surprised, but said nothing.

The nurse eyed them from beneath her black rimmed glasses and said in a sharp tone, "Get out, visiting hours are over!"

PART I

SOPHOMORE YEAR

1

TWO YEARS EARLIER

Brittany got out of the Uber and paid the driver for her trip from the airport to her new college home. As the driver removed her bags from the trunk, Brittany glanced at her paper detailing the address and then at the house in front of her. Puzzled by its appearance, her British accent took hold as she blurted out, "Oh bloody hell! You've got to be kidding me. This is absurd."

Although deeply disappointed with her surroundings, Brittany couldn't wait to see Jax. They had become lifelong friends since their junior year in high school. Brittany was the first and only exchange student that Jax's parents hosted. Although originally from Africa, most of Brittany's education occurred in London, England. Recent events prompted her parent's insistence that she return to America to finish her college degree.

Brittany again studied her environment as she stepped onto the sidewalk from the street. She was almost knocked down by children riding their bikes, laughing, and yelling as they blew right by her.

Although, perturbed by their rudeness, her attention quickly diverted to the sounds of loud rap music playing from a car burning rubber and speeding down the street. Brittany then questioned, "My God, where am I?"

With a slight smile of thanks to the driver, she picked up her bags and walked toward the house. The reddish brick row house was three stories high, with dark brown awnings covering some of the windows. From her vantage point, at least one window on each floor had an air-conditioning unit hanging from it. Throwing her head back in disgust, she said, "No central air? Oh, dear God, how am I supposed to live here?" Remembering her plush and roomy high rise flat in London, complete with an entertaining lobby for guests, maid service, and a doorman, she was already beginning to feel like she was being reduced to live like a peasant instead of the daughter of a diplomat.

Brittany stared at the five steps to the house and spotted the chipped paint that coated each step—an image that reminded her of her own broken heart. She thought about her parents, and then closed her eyes, attempting to control her anger toward them. Moving from London to D.C. was one thing, but if her parents thought that moving her away from Charles was going to stop their relationship, then they were sadly mistaken. She would never leave him; he was her soul mate.

With bags in hand, she moaned and then leaned on the black iron railing. Gazing at the green indoor/outdoor carpet covering the porch, she longed for the baby she lost but strove to put it out of her mind. She took a deep breath, looked up, and shook her head, sighing at the dilapidated house as Ike, an off-balanced drunk, stumbled behind her.

Through his booze-slurred speech, he tapped Brittany on the shoulder and said, "Hhhhheeeyy, I need to catch a bus to see my sick momma, can..." As he spoke, he struggled to keep his balance, rocking from side to side, "...ouuuu spare some change?"

Brittany rolled her eyes and turned to him, amazed that he was bold enough to approach and talk to her. No drunks in London had ever been so brazen. Smelling the stench of cheap liquor and musty body odor, she said in a very sharp tone, "I have no such thing. You, dear friend should get a job!"

She moved forward, but he stepped in front of her, almost falling on her. She stepped back to avoid physical contact with him.

His head swayed with his body half slumped over. He gave her a strange look and said, while pointing his dirt-laden finger at her, "You ain't from around here. Where you from?"

"If you must know, I am from South Africa."

"Oh... You here to go to school?" He stood upright, putting his hands on his hips. "You college girls, you all the same. You think you betta' than us. You think I ain't ever had a job."

Quick to spout off, Brittany said, "I did not say that you have never had a job. I merely said get a job and quit begging people for money." She shrugged her shoulder and turned her nose up at him. "It is most embarrassing."

"Embarrassin'?" he asked with his eyes down and mouth wide open. He lifted his head and looked her in the eye. "Let me tell you what's embarrassin'. Workin' and tryin' to take care of yo yo yo family and never makin' ends meet."

He staggered as he talked and grabbed Brittany's bag for balance. She jerked it away from him, almost causing him to fall forward. He held onto the black railing to steady himself while he finished his speech. He stepped closer to Brittany, attempting to make eye contact. She waved away the stench with her hands and backed up again. Brittany looked at him and then glanced at the front door of the row house. She wondered, *What kind of a con is this fool trying to play on me?* Pointing his crooked finger behind him, he said, "Givin' up, 'cause you can't find no job that pay worth nothing. Lookin' at your eighty-year-old mother who can't get her diabetes pills and watchin' her foot hav' to get cut off, cause I can't get no help fo' her. Now that's embarrassin'." With confidence, he managed to stand tall and hold his head high.

Brittany heard Ike's plight, took another deep breath, and with a somber attitude, she said, "I am sorry for your trouble." She put her bags down, reached in her purse, pulled out a twenty-dollar bill, and handed it to him.

"I hope this can help you catch your bus." Brittany rolled her eyes, not just at Ike but also at the despair and laziness of many Americans.

Ike stared at the money and said, "Oh yes... this sure will, thank you, thank you so much." He smiled as he walked back down the walkway.

She picked up her bags and rushed up the stairs, once again eyeing the house. She shook her head in disbelief that she would make it her home for the next three years. Before ringing the door-bell, she paused in front of the weather worn door with its rustic doorknob and sighed.

Jackie opened the door and said, "Hi, Brit. How was your trip?"

As she crossed the threshold, Brittany peered back at the drunk, wanting to forget the exchange. She set her bags down and said, "It was a bit bumpy, but other than that, I am here."

They hugged each other, and of course, Brittany gave Jackie the double kiss, one on each side of her face.

"Here, let me help you with your bags. I see you met Ike," Jackie said as she moved Brittany's bags from the foyer and placed them by the stairs.

"Thanks. You... know him?" Brittany said with a squeamish smirk.

"Yes, everyone in the neighborhood knows Ike. He's good people."

With a half-hearted laugh and a grim look, Brittany said, "Jax, you can't be serious." Even though Brittany heard Ike's story, she still thought he could be doing more with his life than panhandling.

Jackie ignored her. "So, how are your parents doing?"

"Oh, you know the usual; Dad's at home doing his diplomat thing and Mummy, of course, busies herself with the boutique in London, or planning the next dinner party. That is, when she is not in my business."

Brittany and Jackie had one thing in common—their parents. Their fathers were always gone, and their mothers were usually busy entertaining friends and watching their daughters' every move.

"Well, let me show you around the place. This is the den and dining room. Feel free to hang out here with your friends. As long as you are not disturbing the rest of us, we don't care."

Brittany studied the lounge with a scowl on her face and finally said, "Oh, I don't think you have to worry about that."

"Oh yes, I'm supposed to tell you no overnight guests, no drugs, and no parties. Of course, these are my parents' rules, but we don't always follow them. Besides, they never come up here anyway."

"Well, that's much better. I have never done well with rigid rules."

They both laughed, and Brittany walked past the lounge into the kitchen with Jackie following.

"This is the kitchen." Jackie opened the refrigerator and said, "We mark all of our food with our names, so we don't get it confused. If you want to cook, that's up to you, but we all mainly go out to eat except for LaJuana, who sometimes cooks." Jackie whispered to Brittany even though no one was in the house but them. "Oh, and I wouldn't put anything in the fridge that you really want, because most of the time, it's gone the next day. I think LaJuana eats the leftover food."

They both chuckled as Jackie opened the cabinets to show Brittany where the pots, pans, and plates were kept. "Do you have any questions?"

"Jax, you know I don't cook, but who is LaJuana?"

"Oh, she is one of our housemates, and she lives on the other side of the kitchen, right down this hallway." Jackie pointed down the hallway.

"What kind of name is LaJuana?" Brittany asked. She had always been amused at the ridiculous names Americans gave their children.

"I don't know, but she is a nice girl. Kind of fat, but she stays to herself."

Brittany turned up her nose again and then pulled Jackie out of the kitchen and back into the lounge. "Listen, show me around later. I want to get some new trousers in Georgetown. I heard they have charming clothes."

Brittany walked into the hallway and up the stairs, leaving her bags resting at the bottom.

"Okay, let's at least take your things to your room." Jackie picked up her two bags and walked up the stairs behind Brittany. "Your room is on the second floor, the third door on the left." Jackie set the bags down, took the key, opened the door, and walked in. "Feel free to put in a TV and whatever else you need."

A bed and a desk were the only furniture in the room. Brittany simply stood still with her mouth wide open.

"Are you okay?" Jackie asked.

She paused and then responded, "Uh...I...I do not know."

Jackie ignored her stammering and continued, "There are two phone jacks, one behind your bed and the other is by the window. You will have to contact the telephone company and have your phone turned on, but we mostly use our cell phones." Brittany's expression didn't change, so she kept going. "We pay for the water, electricity, gas, and trash pickup, so you don't have to worry about that. Here's the door to your closet."

Brittany opened the closet door and her eyes bucked open. She said, "Dear God. This is so tiny! How am I going to get all of my clothes in here? I just packed a few things to get me through the next couple of days." She buried her head in her hands and said, "This is crazy. Several trunks of my clothing are being shipped here next week. How am I supposed to make this work?"

Jackie replied, "It's a row house, not the mansion you are used to living in. Look, my room is down the hall from you, and in between your bedroom and mine is the bathroom." Jackie walked down the hallway, motioned her to follow, and opened the bathroom door. "It's quaint but functional. You are responsible for your own towels and toiletries, including toilet paper."

Brittany faced her friend, placed her hands on her shoulders, and shook her. "How do you live here? This is so..." She frowned. "...basic. Your home in Dallas is nothing like this." She looked around and said, "I was really expecting a lot more."

Jackie glared at her and shrugged out of her grip.

Turning to look at her surroundings, Brittany said, "I hate to say this, but this is barbaric. It looks like a peasant lives here."

Jackie raised her voice. "Brit, this is not the Ritz Carlton! This is the real world. In case you didn't know, this is how most college students live. In fact, we probably live better than most college students do. Where did you live in London?"

"In one of London's premier flats with a doorman and maid service. I think you call it a high-rise apartment building."

Jackie shook her head and focused on the floor.

Brittany said, "I know, I know. It is going to take me a moment to adjust. It just seems so primitive." She took a deep breath, closed her eyes, and said, "I can do this, I know I can. Let me unpack a bit and figure out how I am going to make this work. Then we can go to the mall. It will help me get my mind off this place."

Jackie said, "Okay. Let me know when you're ready, I'll be in my room."

Thirty minutes later, they took the subway headed for the mall. Only a couple of people were on it, as most people were still at work and it was only the middle of the day. They got off at their stop, and Brittany said, "I heard that everyone at Karrington University looks like they stepped out of a premiere of New York's Fashion Week. Is that true?"

"Well, it's not quite Fashion Week. Most of the people who dress like that are in the business school. Friday is the one day out of the week when everyone's on the yard, and it looks like a fashion show then."

"Well, I still need some new rags," Brittany said, almost skipping toward the mall door with Jackie following behind her.

"Okay," Jackie said, "But I really don't have any money for clothes."

Inside the mall, they saw everything from hip hugger pants to the latest Donna Karen shirts. They went in and out of the stores, trying on clothes and buying a few must-have items. Brittany had two bags and Jackie had one of her own, but somehow Jackie was carrying all of them.

Brittany stopped and said, "Ostentatious? We must go in here."

Jackie followed Brittany into the store. Down the center of the store was a long red carpet leading to the cash register. It caught their eyes. They looked at each other and in unison said, "Love it!"

Jackie and Brittany rushed around in opposite directions looking for their favorite designers. As they searched, they marveled at the color scheme in the boutique. It was black and white with hints of deep purple swirled in designs all over the walls. Sporadic splashes of purple material swooped down from the ceiling. The black and white checkered marble floors gave the boutique a clean and sleek look.

Brittany yelled, "Jax, I love this store! We should have come here first."

Jackie said, "I know, I've never been here before," as she thumbed through the clothes in the Versace area.

They both found outfits and headed to the fitting room.

Brittany slipped on a pair of Gucci pants and said, "I love the way these trousers feel."

She came out of the fitting room and spun around to see herself in the mirror. Jackie peeked out and saw Brittany's outfit. She said, "It's so cute. You've always had such style. I wish I had that."

Brittany then said, "Stop it. Let me see yours."

Jackie came out of the fitting room. "Oh, Jax that is it, you must get that! Wow! You are fierce. Who is the designer?"

"The jacket is Nicole Miller, and the pants are Donatella Versace."

Brittany said, "Wait." She walked out of the fitting room toward the cash register, picked up some Armani sunglasses, came back to the room, and handed them to her.

"Here Jax, try these on with it."

Jackie put the sunglasses on. "I know I like it, but I've never seen this combination of colors before... black, teal, yellow, and pink? It's almost like a shirt and a jacket together. But I can't buy it."

"Yes, you can, you have to! Look how the jacket accentuates your waist, and the trousers hug your curves. It was made for you. Besides, these must be the new colors for the fall season. They go well with your eyes. Turn around. Aw, it's magnificent! You simply must get it."

Jackie looked in the mirror, "You know this would look a lot better on me, if I had a tan." Jackie sighed. "Brit, I can't. My parents gave me two-thousand dollars to buy all my books plus a little spending money. It's supposed to last me until Thanksgiving.

Besides, I just spent a bunch on books plus some stuff for my bedroom. If I buy this outfit, I'd be dipping into my spending money and the rest of my book money. I still have to buy two more books."

Brittany said with a flippant expression, "So, use that."

"Are you crazy? How am I going to study? I can't do that. My parents warned me this year that they were not giving me any extra money. Anyway, I need those two books, because both classes start on Monday and Tuesday. The bookstore was out of them earlier this week, but they will have a shipment on the first day of school. I don't want to be irresponsible."

Brittany admired the outfit and pled her case. "Think about it this way. It would be irresponsible not to buy this outfit because it looks so good on you. How many times do we go shopping wishing something fit better here or there? Or, we see an outfit we like, and decide not to buy it. Later we come back to the store, and 'ta da' it's gone."

Jackie shook her head, seemingly unsure of what to do.

Brittany said, "Okay, this is what you do. Go to the library and check out the textbooks you need. Then get a part-time job and use the money from the job to buy the books. Thereafter, quit."

"But where am I going to get a part-time job?"

"No worries. Get online when you get home and search for jobs."

"What do you know about searching for jobs?"

"My boyfriend finds jobs on the internet all the time." Brittany smiled and said, "That's what I like about him, he's so resourceful."

"Maybe you're right. Who knows when I'll find something that looks this good on me again. Good looking out, Brit!"

They took their outfits to the cash register, where several sales associates were mingling. Brittany paid for her outfits first while Jackie watched them. Whispering to Brittany, Jackie said, "I wonder if they are all models."

"Sh...h they can hear you," Brittany replied.

Jackie laid her items on the counter and the lady at the cash register said, "I see you chose the color blocking jacket. We just got them in. They're bringing this back as the new trend for this season, but it's very pricey for such a young lady. Is this for a special occasion?"

Jackie replied, "No, just to college. But you're right, it's expensive. Maybe I should wait to get it."

Brittany chimed in, "Jax, how many times do we have to go through this? You have a plan. You are going to borrow the books from the library and get a part-time job."

"Okay, you're right, but something just doesn't feel right."

"That's because you are not used to making adult decisions." Brittany told the cashier to ring it up.

The cashier listened to the conversation and said, "Your total is nine hundred forty-six dollars and fifty-three cents."

Jackie screamed, "What! How much are the glasses?"

Brittany puckered her lips because Jax was embarrassing her. "Stop worrying and acting like a pauper. Just pay it. You're worth it."

The cashier said, "These are the Armani logo stemmed sunglasses, and they are three hundred twenty dollars. Did I hear you say you need a part-time job?"

"Oh my God, I had no idea the glasses were that expensive."

Brittany said, "Poppycock, they're Armani. What do you expect?" She turned to the cashier and asked, "Ma'am, are you hiring?"

The cashier said, "Well, the store is not. But I have a side business, and I can use some help on a part-time basis." She smiled and said, "Here is my card. Call me if you want to make some real money."

"Okay, thanks. "Jackie took the card from the cashier.

Brittany had to admit something about the cashier seemed out of place. All the other sales associates were drop dead gorgeous and the cashier was just average and a bit eerie.

Brittany grabbed their bags and said, "Thank you, ma'am. Jackie, ta ta, let's go."

As they left the store, Brittany said, "See, you already have a prospect for a part-time job. Aren't you glad you bought the outfit?"

"Yeah, I am, but that was a big chunk out of the two thousand dollars my parents gave me."

Brittany patted her hand and said, "Jax, don't worry, you're getting a job."

They both remained quiet while riding the subway home, until Jackie broke the silence. "So, my mom told me what happened with your boyfriend and everything. Are you okay?"

"Yeah, I guess. My parents are not fond of him."

"Why? What did he do?"

"He does not come from the right background. But I really love him, and I do not care where he is from. I wish my parents could see him the way I see him, but they refuse to give him a chance."

Brittany imagined Charles and smiled. "He's different from the other fellows. He's charming, warm, and polite. My parents think he is only after the family fortune, but I know he's not. He loves me."

"Well, did he give them the wrong impression when he met them or was it because of the baby?" Jackie asked.

"Seriously, do you think my parents would meet him or talk to him? Remember, I am not supposed to be dating him. But you're right; my disgracing them with a bastard baby didn't help."

"Awe... I don't want to say that I understand, but I can see that it really bothers you."

"At first, I was hurt that my parents would not let me keep the baby. But I thought about it, and maybe they were right. I am not ready to be a mother. I still have so much I want to do."

Brittany didn't want Jackie to know how she really felt. The truth was, she thought about the abortion a lot, and it hurt because she knew it was wrong. She resented her parents for forcing her to destroy her gift, and she planned to make them pay for it. After all, it was her baby, not theirs. No one had the right to take it away.

"I'm so sorry. When Mom told me, I wanted to call, but I thought that maybe you needed some time to yourself. I figured that you didn't want to talk about it."

"You have nothing to be sorry for. I did need a little time to process the whole thing. It was my fault because I got careless. However, we are still dating, and we are getting married when I graduate. What about you? Who are you dating?"

"Nobody, I am happier by myself." Then Jackie quickly changed the subject. "Our stop is the next one."

Brittany said, "Do you know what my mum had the audacity to tell me before I left home?"

"No, what?"

"She told me that there were two things that she expected me to get while I am at Karrington University."

"What?"

"First, a degree and second a 'Mrs.' in front of my name from a Karrington man. Apparently, there are many successful businessmen, doctors, and lawyers who graduate from Karrington. Can you believe that?"

"Yes, there are actually some mothers who send their girls to Karrington just for that very reason. Karrington men are considered a hot commodity."

The subway stopped and they got off. Jackie suggested, "Let's stop and grab something to eat, it's getting late." They agreed to continue their conversation once they took care of their fierce appetites.

Finally, back at home, they walked into the foyer of the row house and Brittany said, "The barbeque was good, but not like your home-town in Texas. At least I am not famished anymore."

"Of course, D.C. barbeque can't compare to Texas."

Brittany stirred their conversation back up. "So, did your parents express the same sentiment as mine regarding Karrington men?"

"No, my parents just want me to graduate. Speaking of graduating, what's your major?"

"Well, I transferred in with a major in international business, so I will probably keep that, since I will need it to run the businesses back home. But I must tell you, I wanted to come to Karrington all along. So, when they proposed this as their option, I loved it, even though I know they are trying to get me as far away from Charles as possible."

"I'm sorry to hear that. It must be hard."

"Don't be." Brittany yawned. "Oh, pardon me. I am afraid I am a little tired from my journey. It could be a bit of jet lag. I'm going to pop upstairs and get some rest."

"Okay, I'm gonna get on my computer and start looking for a job."

After an hour or so, Brittany lightly knocked on the door and opened it, "Jax, how's it going? Did you find anything?"

Sitting at the vanity, Jackie replied, "No, not yet. I thought you were going to get some rest?"

Brittany said, "I can't sleep. Hey, I see you haven't put away your outfit yet."

Jackie got up from the vanity, walked over to the bed and pulled the plastic away from it, accidentally tipping her purse over. The business card the lady gave her at the mall fell on the floor. She picked it up and it read: *Lockheart Enterprises, Nita Lockheart, CEO.*

Brittany said, "Is that from that lady?"

"Yes, I guess if I get desperate, I'll give her a call. I'm just not into selling beauty products or anything like that." Jackie picked up the card and pushed it back into her bag. "You know, with the first day of classes only a couple of days away, I'm going to have to do something soon."

2

IT was the first day of school, and Jackie headed to her class in Hughes Hall. She saw a girl she met last year, Ursula Mendez, who motioned Jackie to sit next to her.

"Hey, what's up?" Jackie said, glad to see her.

"Nothing much, Jackie. What's up with you?"

"Not a lot. How was your summer? Did you go back home?" Jackie asked.

"Girl, please. I have a job up here, so I stayed in D.C., but I did miss New York. What about you, did you go home?" Ursula asked.

"Yes and listened to my parents lecture me the whole summer about managing my money better and being more responsible. It's just the same ole same ole."

Just then, the professor walked in and Ursula said, "We'll talk after class."

She seemed so cool, kind of the way Jackie wanted to be. They had a class together last semester and studied for a test at Ursula's place. She lived in a huge apartment with a 60" flat screen TV, a bar, and very posh furniture. On top of that, she wore kickass clothes and drove a 3-series BMW. Jackie's parents wouldn't dare let her bring her car to school.

Ursula and Jackie caught up after class, reminiscing about last year and swapping stories about their summer escapades. Jackie joked about how happy she was to live off campus. Her brother, Jarrett, graduated last year and now that he was gone, she was in charge of managing the row house.

"Jackie, where's your book? I noticed you didn't open it when he gave the assignment."

Jackie admitted, "Well, I kind of got in a bind with my money. I'm short on two of my books, American Lit and Local Government. I've been looking for a job so I can buy them, but I haven't found anything yet, plus the library didn't have any available to check out. Hey, the place where you work, are they hiring?"

Ursula paused but said, "As a matter of fact, we are hiring. But why do you need a job? I didn't think rich kids worked."

"Uh... whatever, I just need something for a while." Jackie pulled out a piece of notebook paper and a pen. "Give me the name and address?"

Ursula paused again and shook her head, "Actually, it's a home-based business. I only work a couple of hours a week."

"Wow that sounds perfect. How much does it pay?"

"It's a sales position, so it depends on how much you sell. But it pays well."

Jackie continued to press the issue, "Okay. Where do I go to apply?"

"We don't work with applications. It's strictly on a referral basis."

"Oh, then in that case, refer me!"

Ursula laughed and said, "Girl, you're a trip. I will. I think you'd be good at it."

"Really, what do you sell?"

"We prefer to keep that a secret until all of the clients arrive," Ursula said.

"Well, how am I going to sell something if I don't know what I'm selling?"

"Simple, I'll invite a few friends over for a party. You provide the place, a little alcohol, some heavy hors d'oeuvres, and whatever else you want. I'll bring the product and the people, and let's see how well you do."

Jackie contemplated this because it sounded weird, like one of those pyramid businesses, the kind her parents always told her to stay away from. She really needed to buy her books, so she decided to do it, and at the same time she decided not to tell Ursula that as soon as she made enough money, she planned to quit.

"Okay, heavy hors d'oeuvres and alcohol?" Jackie's eyebrows rose a bit. She wondered what they sold and to whom.

In response to Jackie's expression, Ursula explained, "Our clients are very high-end people with exclusive taste. Just pick up some upscale hors d'oeuvres from one of your favorite restaurants. I usually provide some Grand Marnier, Cognac, and maybe a little champagne. How about we start this Saturday evening, say around seven o'clock? Will your house be empty?"

"Yes. Most of my housemates are gone on the weekends, so I'll have the house pretty much to myself." She didn't let Ursula know it, but she thought it was crazy to serve hors d'oeuvres and alcohol for some sort of beauty product party. But she needed a job, and it was not like she'd done this before. She took on an 'oh well' attitude and figured maybe Ursula was right. Maybe it was more of a high-end business than Jackie thought.

"Okay great. I'll leave my local government book with you, so you can read the next assignment, but don't forget to bring it to class next week. And remember the party's a secret, so don't tell anyone."

Jackie agreed to their plans and wrote her address and phone number down on the piece of paper and gave it to Ursula.

"Thanks. See you Saturday."

It was Friday. The first week of school was finally over, which meant it was party time! Jackie called her girlfriend, Trina, to see if she was ready to party, and of course, she was. They called a cab and headed over to Chicago's, the hottest club in D.C. The music was jumping when they arrived.

As usual, Trina and Jackie competed against each other to see who could get the most telephone numbers in a night. Sometimes Jackie won, and sometimes Trina won. It was all in the game. Regardless of who won, they decided a long time ago that as soon as they left the club, they had to throw the numbers away. Jackie had been known to keep a couple, just because the guys were so fine.

The club was crowded, with almost no room to stand. They danced until they couldn't stand up. A man and a woman got up from the bar, and Jackie and Trina took their seats.

Trina said to the bartender, "I'll have a Long Island iced tea."

"Make that two of them," Jackie shouted over the music. She handed the bartender her parents' American Express card, and yelled, "We need to start a tab!"

Trina said, "Isn't that card supposed to be used for emergencies?"

"Yes. This is an emergency. I need a drink," Jackie said with a straight face and then laughed.

Trina laughed too. "Look at that guy right there. Where do you think he works?"

"I don't know, maybe a bank. He's kind of stiff necked."

"That's what I like about this place, it's not just students who hang out here," Trina said, as she watched the bartender make their drinks.

"Yeah, real men with jobs hang out here, not that I've ever had any luck in that area."

"Jackie, you just haven't met the right guy. You'll know when you meet him."

"Maybe you're right, but I'm not holding my breath. Some people are meant to be single, and maybe I'm one of them."

"Girl, drink! Stop with the drama."

Jackie took a sip and said, "It's easy for you to say, you've had boyfriends. What have I had? Nothing."

"Jackie, it will happen. Quit being pressed about it," Trina said lightheartedly.

"Okay, let's change the subject. How did you know you wanted to be a microbiologist?" Jackie asked as she took the red cherry off the small plastic green sword and stirred her drink.

"I always knew I wanted to do something in medicine, but I didn't always know what. Just like you knew you wanted to major in political science."

"I didn't know that that's what my parents chose for me. Truth is, I don't know what I want to do. I really can't think of anything that I'm passionate about."

"You will. College isn't over for another couple of years. You've got time to find out what you want to be."

Trina and Jackie continued to drink well into the night. One of Jarrett's friends came in and saw them. Jackie motioned for him to come over to the bar and they talked for a minute. When Trina and Jackie decided to leave, they tried to help each other up from their barstools and both fell to the floor. Too hammered to be embarrassed, they looked at each other and laughed. Jarrett's friend failed to find the humor in them falling down drunk, and decided it was time for them to go. So, he walked them to his car and took them to the row house.

Early the next morning the sound of her cell blared in Jackie's ear, abruptly waking her up. Grimacing, Jackie blinked her eyes to focus and pushed the green button to answer, "Um...uh...Hello."

It was her brother, Jarrett, on the phone.

"Jackie, what the hell were you doing last night? I got a call at a quarter to three this morning about you at Chicago's. I thought Mom and Dad talked to you about being responsible."

"Jarrett." Jackie hesitated so she could get her thoughts together. "Like you and your friends never went out to Chicago's for drinks."

"Yeah, we went to Chicago's many times, but we weren't drunk off our asses falling off bar stools. Do you realize anyone could have taken you and Trina home and raped you, or even killed you? He told me you were so drunk that you passed out as he was helping Trina upstairs to your room."

Jackie had a hard time focusing on the words he was saying. But, sure enough, he was right. She looked down at the end of her bed, and there was Trina, spread out with her legs hanging off the edge.

"Okay, maybe we drank too many Long Island Teas." Jackie coughed because her throat was so dry it felt like cotton was stuck in it. "I didn't know they were that strong."

Jarrett took a frustrated breath by Jackie's naivety and yelled, "You don't know what a Long Island Iced Tea is? Of course it's strong! What would you have done if my friend hadn't been there?"

Jackie wanted to yell back, but her head hurt, so she whispered, "Catch a cab." Then she thought better of her plan to ask him for money. She realized he was just like their parents, maybe even worse.

"Jarrett, can I call you back? I think I'm about to be sick." Jackie threw the phone down and fought to hold down the vomit that was rising up her throat. She bumped into the wall as she raced down the hall and reached the toilet just in time. She decided the Long Islands were good, but they weren't that good. After cleaning herself up and changing her clothes, she walked Trina to the door, so she could sleep off the rest of her hangover at home. Once her friend was gone, Jackie went into the kitchen in search of something to drink that would settle her stomach. But before she could get there, she bumped into Bijon, an Indian medical student. Out of all the house-mates she could have run into this morning looking a mess, she had to run into the one she hated the most. He took one look at her and laughed.

"Hi, Jackie. How was your summer? Oh, looks like you had a blast, or is this hangover only from last night?" His words dripped with sarcasm as he laughed.

Jackie didn't say a word, ignoring him. She walked to the kitchen and looked in the refrigerator. Deep down, she couldn't stand him. Every time she came to visit Jarrett last year, he was rude and sarcastic to her.

He yelled from the den, "Let me guess, you're celebrating the new school year?"

Jackie snarled. "Shut up!" She found a 7UP, went back upstairs and climbed into her bed, reflecting on how much Bijon got on her last nerves. But she couldn't worry about him. She needed to get a little rest, so she would be ready for her new job. Maybe she could make enough for her books tonight and quit. Brittany had a study group tonight at seven o'clock, so she would be out of the house, and the other house-mates would be nowhere to be found. Jackie couldn't believe there was a study group the first week of school. Nevertheless, Jackie had to focus on getting lots of sales and recouping her book money.

She slept until five o'clock, then rushed out to pick up the items for the party. She had no other choice than to use her parents' credit card again. It was obvious the $53.47 she had left in her account was not going to cover this. If they asked, she decided that she would tell them that she wanted to have a party to start the school year off right. She thought they would buy that. She sure hoped this job paid well, because she needed the money.

The biggest room in the house was the den, which fed into the dining room. At half past six, Jackie set up the dining room table with the food and drinks. Everything was ready; she just needed Ursula and her friends to arrive. She sat on the couch to wait but ended up taking a thirty-minute nap.

The doorbell rang, and she got up with a cheerful smile and checked her breath. Jackie invited Ursula in, and then went upstairs to freshen up. While she brushed her teeth and touched up her makeup, she heard the doorbell continue to ring. Jackie came back downstairs and found that the guests were mingling. She didn't know anybody, but it looked like a great party. Jackie saw Ursula and walked over.

"Hey, there's a lot of people here, looks like a good turnout."

"Yeah, it is. Here's my local government book. Remember to bring it on Tuesday." She handed the book to Jackie. "I want you to meet a friend of mine. This is Nita."

"Thanks. Hi." Jackie stopped mid-sentence. The lady looked very familiar. Jackie asked her, "Have we met before?"

"Actually, we have. You came into Ostentatious boutique a week ago and bought a very cute outfit." Nita looked Jackie up and down, which made Jackie a little uneasy because she felt as if she was judging her.

"That's right." Jackie remembered her. She seemed nice, but something about her was shady. As Jackie eyed Nita up and down, she observed that her clothes were fierce and decided that she had good taste.

Nita walked around, admiring the place. "Is this your house, or do you rent a room here? It's very nice."

Jackie answered, "Uh... it's okay," as she looked around the house and wondered what it was that she saw, because the house wasn't that nice. "My parents own the house. I just manage it while I'm in school."

Nita carried on, "And of course, it's close to campus. Do you walk to school?"

"Yes, unless I catch a ride with friends." Jackie replied but wondered why this woman cared how she got to school.

Nita adjusted her clothes and brushed imaginary lint off her outfit. "I was hoping that you would call, but I never heard from you. And then Ursula told me about a girl she knew wanting to make some extra money. Once she described you, I knew you were the same girl that came into the store that day."

"Okay, yeah. So, now what do you sell?"

"Be patient, you'll see. We are about to place the product out in just a minute. Is it okay to use this buffet table?"

"Sure, let me move the plants and candles." The buffet table opposite the dining room table would be a good place to display her products. Jackie guessed she should have thought of that.

While the guests were enjoying the drinks and hors d'oeuvres, Nita asked for everyone's attention. As she talked to the group, Ursula set up the buffet table behind her. Jackie was curious about why they were being so secretive about whatever it was they sold.

Nita said, "I know many of you have busy lives and don't always get a chance to unwind and relax. Jobs and families can cause a great amount of stress in your life. Well, I want you to sit back and enjoy, because we have a product that is guaranteed to remove all your stress. Who would like to try it first?"

A young woman stepped forward and Ursula moved away from the table so everyone could see the product. She then handed the woman a long, thin, clear plastic tube. Ursula pointed to the buffet table as if she were some sort of product model on a game show. There were fifteen thin tubes and fifteen lines of white powder on a large square mirror. Nita instructed the woman to sniff the white powder through the tube in one slow motion, and she did.

Jackie shouted, "Wait a minute! Is that cocaine? You can't sniff cocaine here. This is the product?"

Ursula pulled her to the side and said, "Jackie, relax, everyone does it. It's no big deal."

Jackie yelled at the top of her lungs, "Are you kidding me? That's illegal! I don't want to get arrested." She pointed to the door, and said, "You need to leave and take that stuff with you. Are you crazy?"

Jackie noticed that while she was arguing with Ursula, each person took a tube, leaned down, and snorted the cocaine like it was no big deal. At the same time, Nita collected money from them. One by one, they sat back on the chairs and couch in ecstasy, while others waited their turn.

One of them said to her friend, "I didn't know this was going to be a coke party. Thanks for the invite."

Her friend responded, "I told you I had a surprise for you."

Jackie screamed at Ursula, "This is not supposed to be a coke party! I thought you were selling beauty products or something! You can't sell drugs here!"

Ursula guided Jackie into the kitchen because she was making a scene. "Jackie, chill out. The coke will be all gone before you know it, and there will be no evidence for the police to seize. In the meantime, think about the money you're making. Each person gets at least two lines of coke, and we charge two hundred dollars per line. You had a good turnout, so let's see how much money you made."

"Money? I can't take that money." Jackie walked away from Ursula to the other side of the kitchen, and then started to pace back and forth.

After Nita checked with each client to make sure they're happy with their high. She calmly walked into the kitchen and overheard the tail end of the conversation. "Well, technically, this party is Ursula's, so you'll only get a small percentage of the total sales."

"What do you mean Ursula's? You brought this stuff to my house." She shook her head trying to process what just happened. "Wait. I'm not even concerned about the money. Ursula, how could you do this to me?"

Ursula snapped back, "You said you needed money to buy your books. I was just helping you out!"

"By recruiting me to sell drugs?"

Nita walked over to Jackie, adjusted her clothes, brushed the imaginary lint off her outfit, and said, "Jackie, this isn't like selling drugs on the streets. Coke parties are done every day, and our clients range from heads of state and CEO's to doctors and lawyers. All of them rave about our product. Cocaine is seen as a recreational drug. It's just something people do every once in a while. We don't deal with crack heads or people strung out on drugs. We are so far above that. Coke is a source of entertainment. All it does is add life to a party, that's it."

"What? Are you serious?" Jackie said in disbelief. She couldn't understand how this lady convinced herself that she was performing a service to her community.

Nita said, "Yes, I am. There's one other thing I need to tell you. This is not something that you want to tell anyone about. After all, the party was at your house, which means you would go to jail if you mention a word about it."

Jackie's mouth flew open as being behind bars was never in her realm of possibilities.

Nita remained calm, "Relax, Jackie. No one has ever gone to jail in my group. We protect each other, and we are very careful. But, if you don't want to do it, you certainly don't have to but think about it. You really would be perfect. No one would suspect you at all, but I have to caution you again, no one must know about this party. Do you understand?"

Jackie fearfully answered, "Yes, I do."

"Because if this gets out, then you will have to deal with me." Nita stepped closer to Jackie and let her eyes explain that she meant business. She then smiled and said, "Oh, and I calculated the sales tonight, you earned three hundred dollars, but I'm deducting two hundred because of your attitude."

She handed Jackie the money as LaJuana and Lindsey walked into the kitchen. Jackie looked at them and then at the money. Nita said, "Go on, take it. You need to buy your books, and think about what I said."

Lindsey said, "Who are all those people in there? And why do they look spaced out?"

Reluctant and shocked at the nerve of this woman, Jackie took the money and ignored Lindsey.

LaJuana stared at Jackie, Nita, and Ursula. She asked Nita, "Do I know you?"

Nita took a quick look at LaJuana and said, "Honey, I don't think so." Her tone was condescending and sharp. LaJuana left the kitchen with a puzzled look and went to her bedroom. Lindsey opened the refrigerator, took a soda out, and headed back to her room as well.

Jackie stood in the middle of the kitchen holding the money. She now had $153.47 to her name. At least, now she could buy her American Literature book. The book cost $99, but she wondered what was the real cost?

"Please, DeMarcus, please. I'm sorry. I'll never do it again!" Marissa shrieked as she clutched her stomach and braced herself on DeMarcus' bed.

"I know you won't do it again, because I'm gonna make sure you never do it again!" DeMarcus yelled and without hesitation, he raised his leg and thrust his foot into Marissa. "Despite how you talked to me tonight, I'm proud of myself...that was an award-winning kick I just plunged into the small of your back."

Marissa let out a piercing scream and fell to the floor.

He asked her, "How dare you correct me in front of my friends. Who do you think you are? You dumb bitch."

As she crawled across the floor toward the desk, he screamed, "You don't correct me on the elements of the alter ego theory. I'm the Criminal Justice major, not you, and I know what I'm talking about!"

She reached the desk and used the chair to stand up. She turned to face him, tried to hug him, and with tears rolling down her face said, "I'm sorry, DeMarcus, I didn't mean it like that. I love you, please stop."

He pulled away from her embrace and walked away, facing the door.

"Girl, you should have thought about love before you embarrassed me tonight." He then turned around and side-kicked her in the ribs causing her to fall over the desk, knocking down all the books and papers sprawled across it.

"I've told you before about disrespecting me, haven't I? Especially in front of your little white friends." DeMarcus exhaled and backhanded Marissa across the face, sending blood gushing from her nose.

Terrified, Marissa picked up DeMarcus' pillow for shelter against his blows. She squealed, "Please, please, please stop, I love you!"

It was almost midnight and Jackie lay, listening to this girl getting her butt kicked—again. School just started, and they were already fighting. In fact, until that moment, she wasn't sure he was back because he was the only housemate she hadn't seen. The last time she saw him, it was nice. He was nice—gentle and caring, the kind of man she could fall in love with one day. She forced herself to stop thinking about it because she could feel her cheeks blushing. DeMarcus and Jackie shared a wall, so they could hear everything going on in each other's room. *Bam!* Just then something that sounded like glass smashed against the other side of the wall. Jackie heard these same sounds almost every time she visited her brother,

Jarrett. She had asked Jarrett about DeMarcus and Marissa, and he said it was best not to get involved. Jackie couldn't understand why they were always fighting. She really didn't want to get involved in their drama, but she felt like she couldn't let Marissa get hurt. She agonized about what she should do. Call the police or confront him herself.

"You think because you're dating a brotha you can treat me any ole kind of way. Well, Barbie, somebody told you wrong!" DeMarcus used a turning kick to land a direct hit to Marissa's left shoulder, which caused it to separate. Bloody, exhausted, and defeated, Marissa fell against the shared wall and panicked. "Somebody, please help me! Please!"

Jackie's picture crashed to the floor and shattered. She jumped out of bed and said, "Damn, I just put that up there yesterday." She ran out of her room and banged on the brown wooden door right next to hers.

No one answered, so she screamed, "DeMarcus! It's Jackie. Answer the door! I know you're in there! Marissa, are you okay?"

DeMarcus yelled back, "Who? Jackie?"

"Jackie Jones." She sighed because he should remember her. "Jarrett's sister."

"What are you doing here?"

"I live here now, and I'm managing the house since Jarrett graduated. Open the door!"

In an aggressive tone he said, "Jackie, this has nothing to do with you. This is between me and Marissa, so leave us alone."

"DeMarcus, if you don't open the door, I'm calling the police." She silently reprimanded herself for fantasizing about this maniac just two minutes before.

On the other side of the door, DeMarcus whispered to Marissa, while tightening his grip on her arm. "Get up and tell her you're okay."

Jackie banged harder on the door and yelled, "She is not your punching bag! Open the damn door or I'm calling the police. I'm serious, DeMarcus, I will."

DeMarcus stomped across the floor and opened the door. Marissa stood next to him, bruised and bloody with tears streaming down her face. In between her sobs, she managed to say, "I'm... okay," then leaned against the wall holding her arm.

"You don't look okay. Open the door all the way," Jackie replied.

Marissa murmured, "No, Jackie. Please, I'm fine. Please, don't call the police. You'll only make it worse."

Jackie reached out for Marissa, but before she was able to touch her the door slammed almost catching her arm.

Jackie yelled, "Hey, you almost got my arm, and you owe me a picture frame."

DeMarcus shouted back, "Jackie, she is fine. Now leave us alone!"

Jackie went back to her room. She knew one day; he was going to kill her if this continued. She knew she needed to do something, but didn't know what. She called her friend Trina to talk it over with her.

"Hey."

"Hey. What's up with you?" Trina said.

"Trying to get some sleep, but I can't. Remember last year I told you about one of the housemates, DeMarcus and his girlfriend, Marissa?"

"The kick boxer? The one that beats his girlfriend?"

"Yes, and he's at it again."

"What?" Trina yelled. "Call the police."

"I can't do that. He'll know that I called. Besides, Marissa asked me not to. She said it would make things worse."

"Okay, seriously?" Trina said.

"I know, but I don't want to make it any worse on Marissa than it already is, and I don't want DeMarcus coming down on me for getting in his business."

"Jackie, are you kidding me? If he's beating her, you have to call the police."

"I know I probably should, but I just don't know if I should get involved."

"You're the landlord. How can you not get involved? If you hear anything else, please call the police."

"Okay, I will. I'll catch up with you tomorrow."

Jackie hung up the phone, still worrying about Marissa. She heard him continue to scream at her and pondered what to do. Maybe Trina was right, she should call the police. Or maybe she should leave it alone like Jarrett said before. In the end, Jackie chose Jarrett's way and decided to do nothing because not getting involved seemed easier after all. Seeing the mess on the floor, she went downstairs and got a broom to sweep up the glass.

3

J ackie couldn't sleep at all. Her body felt awful because of the partying she did on Friday night, and her mind was sick because of the party she had on Saturday night. She spent the whole week contemplating what happened. She made $300 Saturday night in three hours, but only got a hundred of it.

Jackie was glad she bought groceries because she would be eating in a lot. The great thing was that she was wearing her new outfit, and it looked so cute on her. She felt good despite her lack of money and her fears related to the coke party. With this outfit, she would be the talk of the yard. Even though she didn't have all her books, at least she looked good. The money she made on Saturday would only cover one of her books, so she had been searching the internet and applying for jobs all over D.C. American Lit started at nine o'clock in Marshall Hall, and she didn't have the book. As she walked in and found a seat, a couple of girls complimented her on her outfit. She said, "Thank you" and smiled.

Professor Alcorn was a tall, slender woman with glistening vanilla skin and a shoulder length, strawberry blonde Cleopatra bob. She walked in, and immediately gave them a writing assignment.

She asked the class to write a paper on the social issues that literary giants such as Emerson, Thoreau, and Orwell wrote about in their time. She would like them to compare and contrast those with the social issues present today.

Jackie raised her hand and asked, "I don't have my book yet. Is that where we can find information on these authors?"

Professor Alcorn replied, "Stand up and state your name."

Jackie stood and said, "Jackie Jones."

She said, "Well, Ms. Jones, where are you from?"

"Dallas, Texas."

"And you don't know anything about the contributions of these authors?"

Jackie felt very uneasy standing in front of everyone, so she tried to direct the focus back to the professor. "Well, yeah, I do. But is this assignment in the syllabus, because I didn't pick one up?"

Professor Alcorn said, "No, the assignment isn't in the syllabus, and I handed those out on the first day." She checked her roll and said, "I have that you were here on the first day."

By this time, the other students in the classroom were gazing at Jackie as if these were authors that everyone should know. Jackie bowed her head down because she didn't know them as well as she should.

Professor Alcorn asked Jackie to be seated and gave her a long lecture on each author and their literary offerings. Jackie didn't hear a word she said, because she was so embarrassed.

After her classes, she planned to go the Allen Rollings Library and find out more about them. But first, she would meet with her academic advisor and drop this class. She felt like this little mishap was a blessing in disguise. Dropping the class would solve two problems, save her the embarrassment of returning, and she would have one less book to worry about.

Jackie finished her morning classes in Hemingway Hall and stopped by her academic advisor's office in Marshall Hall to make an appointment. But the earliest he could see her was four o'clock, so she finished her afternoon classes and returned to his office.

Dr. Thomas was the dean of the political science department and taught some of the elective courses. He was a 50-year-old, brown skin man with a thick, black mustache and black rimmed glasses. "Hi, Jackie. What can I do for you today?"

Jackie hesitated and said, "Well, I need to drop a class."

He opened her academic file, perused her course load, and asked, "Oh really? What class do you want to drop, and why?"

"I want to drop American Literature with Professor Alcorn."

His eyebrows rose, as he peered at her through his glasses. "Why?"

Jackie had to come up with a good excuse, or else he wouldn't let her out. Unable to come up with anything, she told him the truth.

"Well, I don't fit into that class very well, and I don't think Professor Alcorn cares for me that much. We didn't hit it off very well today."

"Fit in?" Dr. Thomas looked down at the paper again and then up at Jackie. "What happened?"

She told him about the literary authors saga and blamed her high school for her lack of literary knowledge and failing to properly prepare her for college.

Dr. Thomas stopped her and said, "Wrong. Every high school in America teaches about literature. You never read Dickenson, Fleming, or Hughes?"

"Well, yes, I guess I just didn't pay that much attention. I didn't think it was that important."

Jackie knew the moment those words came out of her mouth that she would regret them. She immediately wanted to take the statement back.

"I bet you think it's important now, don't you? I have a mind not to sign this request and make you stay in that class, so you can learn. What did you think the class was about?" he asked then stood up, took off his glasses, walked to the front of his desk, and sat on the edge.

"Jackie, there comes a time in your life where you must face the unknown. You can't run away every time something doesn't go your way, or you don't understand something. You have to confront each challenge and learn from it. How will you grow if you never give yourself an opportunity to learn?"

"I know, but I really want out of this class."

Dr. Thomas looked at Jackie, paused, and then continued as if she was committing a heinous crime by dropping the class. He put his glasses back on and walked back to his seat. "I can't force you into an introspective self-discovery. You have to want it and go after it yourself. So, I'm going to sign your request and hope that you spend some time thinking about this conversation and what your next course of action should be in discovering the unknown aspects of your education."

He signed the form.

Jackie thought about what he said. "I really appreciate you signing my drop request, Dr. Thomas. Thank you so much." Assuming that she was now home free and had one less book to buy, she picked up the drop request and walked toward the door. Just as she reached for the doorknob, she heard him say, "Oh, I forgot to tell you, you will need Professor Alcorn's signature as well."

Jackie turned around and yelled back, "What?"

He looked at her and raised his eyebrows.

Jackie adjusted her tone and then said, "I'm sorry. What, sir?"

He explained, "Those are the rules." Jackie sighed in complete disbelief. He looked at his watch and said, "If you hurry, I believe she is still in her office."

Jackie left his office, dejected. *How could this have happened?* She had hoped that she would never have to see or talk to Professor Alcorn again. She got herself together and decided what she was going to say to Professor Alcorn, then went down the hall to meet with her.

She reached her office door and knocked. Professor Alcorn answered from inside, "You may come in."

Jackie walked in and closed the door.

"Jackie. How is your research coming for your literary paper?"

"Hi. Well, that's what I wanted to talk to you about. I'm planning on doing the research, but I would like to drop your class." Jackie placed the drop request on top of Professor Alcorn's desk. "I have Dr. Thomas' signature, and I just need you to sign right here." Jackie pointed to the signature box, hoping for a quick response, so she could be on her way.

"Wait a minute. What do you mean? Why do you want to drop my class?"

"Frankly, Professor Alcorn, I was embarrassed today, and I feel to prevent myself from further embarrassment, it would be best to drop your course."

Professor Alcorn laughed. "And you should have been embarrassed. Jackie, I can't believe you were unable to discuss the *Tale of Two Cities* by Charles Dickens or *Animal Farm* by George Orwell. By the time you get to college, you should have read these books—they are part of the required college preparatory curriculum."

Without listening to Professor Alcorn, Jackie said, "My point exactly. I think it's over my head, plus I don't have the money for the book. So, if you'll just sign the drop form, we could save both of us a lot of time, effort, and frustration."

Professor Alcorn said in a firm tone, "I'm not signing that form."

Jackie's mouth fell open.

The professor explained, "Do you know what a disservice that would be to you? I'm sure your parents don't want you to drop a class because you don't know someone or something. That's the whole purpose of pursuing a higher education, to learn what you don't know."

"But even if I wanted to stay and take the class, I don't have the money for the book. So, you would really be doing me a big favor if you let me drop the class."

"I'm sure we can work something out, dear. I can refer you to a work study program, and you can work to buy the book. Sit down while I look this up." She turned to her computer and started typing. "Let me pull up your file. What's your student ID number? I'll call the work study group and set you up for a job. I think we still have a few available."

"I don't think I'll qualify for work study," Jackie said as she put her head down, knowing this conversation was going downhill fast.

"Oh, don't worry. We have several students on our work study program. As long as your parents meet the economic parameters for acceptance into the program, you should be fine."

"Ah... Umm, I know that they won't."

"What do you mean?" said, Professor Alcorn.

"I'm sure they make *way* over the economic parameters."

She gave Jackie a curious look. "What's your last name again?"

"Jones."

Professor Alcorn looked at her again. "You have a striking resemblance to a young man who I taught a couple of years ago. Are you related to... Ah, what was his name?" She scratched her head and looked up at the ceiling as if the answer was up there somewhere. "Oh, now I remember, Jarrett."

Oh no. Jackie simply shook her head, then whispered, "Yes, ma'am. He's my brother."

"A very sweet young man, and if I recall, you're right; your family won't meet the financial parameters for a work study program."

"No, ma'am."

"Then if that's the case, you had money when you signed up for the class. Why didn't you buy the book?" She looked Jackie up and down and said, "Um... I'm sorry dear, this conversation is over." She sneered and handed Jackie the form back. "I suggest you get to the library and start on your research for your paper. Oh, by the way, that's such a beautiful outfit."

Flattered that she noticed, but upset that she wouldn't sign the form, Jackie stood up and headed for the door.

Jackie hesitated, and said, "Thank you, I bought it in Georgetown."

Professor Alcorn said, "Maybe you should take your outfit back, and then you'll have money for your books."

Jackie's mouth flew open. This was the second time today that the professor had insulted her.

After leaving Professor Alcorn's office, Jackie went to the KU bookstore to buy her American Literature book, but they were out of the new and used books again. She checked online for the book and found it at several local colleges in the area. She planned to catch a cab over there after her classes tomorrow and buy it. Walking home, Jackie lamented about how this day had been the worst day she had ever had at Karrington. The only thing that went right was her new outfit. Everyone thought she was the bomb, except Professor Alcorn. *But she doesn't count, because she doesn't know what real style is anyway.*

Once she arrived home, she was thankful to find the house quiet. Jackie went straight to the kitchen to get a wine cooler to unwind from the day. She twisted it open and took a sip. The door to the kitchen opened, and there was Bijon again, this time wearing a faded Dolphins jersey. For the first time, Jackie noticed that he was not bad looking. He just wasn't her type.

"Hi, Bijon," Jackie said, reluctant to speak to him because of his usual attitude toward her, and in particular her drinking.

He looked at her outfit, and the wine cooler in her hand. He said, "Hey, Jackie. I see you're at it early today." He pulled a glass from the cabinet.

"Don't start, I had a horrible day. So, the way I see it, I deserve a little treat. Besides, this isn't even hard liquor."

"You must deserve a treat every day."

"Okay, don't act like I drink every day, because I don't. I only drink when I'm stressed or on special occasions, or if it's the weekend."

He laughed. "I can only judge by what I see."

"Whatever, Bijon! Not everyone can be perfect like you. Study and work, study and work, that's all you do. What's wrong with relaxing and having a little fun?"

"Nothing. Have at it." He opened the fridge, pulled out the orange juice, and poured it in a glass.

Jackie watched him and thought to herself, *He needs to do something with himself, like comb his hair.* She decided to strike up a conversation with him.

"Bijon, can I ask you a question?"

"Go for it."

"Why are you so serious all the time? Don't you get tired of studying so much?" She took another sip of her wine cooler.

"Nope. Unlike you, I have a real future. I'm going to be one of the best orthopedic surgeons in the country. How do you think I got a scholarship into Karrington's medical school? It was because I studied. I sacrificed. But you, Jackie, you'll never know about any of that."

"I'll never know what?" Jackie sighed.

Bijon didn't answer, he just looked at her like she knew what he was talking about.

"You're right. I'm not planning to go to medical school, but I plan to do well in life too. But it doesn't mean I can't have any fun. You don't even have a girlfriend." She took another sip, and asked in a judgmental tone, "Have you ever had a girlfriend?"

He stepped closer to her and asked, "What are you trying to say? You think I'm gay?"

"Look, I'm not saying you're gay, I'm just saying—"

He cut her off and retorted, "Jackie, you don't know anything about me. I don't have it like you. I bet that one outfit you got on cost more than all the clothes in my closet. My parents don't have money to just send me to school and buy a house for me to live in. That's why I have to work to supplement what my scholarship doesn't pay for."

"I get that, but there is more to life than studying. What about having some fun?" She frowned and added, "At least sometimes?" She threw her hands in the air to make her point.

"Fun is what cost my father his college education. Because he wanted to have fun, he now works two jobs. He's a mechanic during the day and a pizza delivery man at night."

Bijon's voice got louder and louder. Jackie was a little alarmed at his sudden anger.

"Fun is how he got my mom pregnant and had to drop out of school. We took his dream away. That's what fun does for you."

Bijon paused, and his eyes began to water. There was silence.

Jackie didn't mean to upset him. Lowering her tone, she said, "I'm so sorry. I guess everyone has to do what's best for them. I'm just trying to help you."

Bijon immediately composed himself again, then raised his voice even louder. "Jackie, how in the hell is that trying to help me? By reminding me that I can't enjoy life, because I might make the same mistakes my father did. Telling me that you think I'm gay because I'm not partying every night like you? Do me a favor, don't help me out anymore!" He dropped the glass on the countertop, left the kitchen, and slammed the door to his room. He put on his running shoes and ran out the back door.

Jackie thought, *Oh God, what drama*, as she took her wine cooler and headed toward the stairs. The front door opened and LaJuana walked in.

Jackie stopped and said, "Hi, LaJuana. What's up?"

LaJuana gave her a strange look and said, "Nothing much, I left my biology book. I need to study at work tonight."

"Hey, are you guys hiring down there? I need a job."

"You need a what?" LaJuana laughed. "What are you going to do with a job?"

"Work. What do you mean what am I going to do? What do most people do at a job?" Jackie didn't understand why no one thought she could work.

"Okay, you don't have to get all defensive, but didn't I see that lady giving you some money the other night?"

Panic welled up in Jackie and she thought of a quick lie. "Uh... that wasn't for me."

"Oh really? Who is that lady? She looks familiar to me."

Jackie looked at LaJuana and was afraid that she knew about the cocaine, so she attempted to sound natural. "Uh... um, her name is Nita. She is a friend of my friend Ursula."

"Nita? Hmm... interesting." LaJuana said.

"Well, is your company hiring or not?"

"Jackie, have you ever had a real job? And working for your parents' doesn't count. "

"Look, LaJuana, everyone has to start somewhere. You had to start somewhere."

"Yeah, and I know why I have to work, but why do you want to work?" LaJuana said as she rolled her eyes at Jackie.

It pained Jackie to admit. "I need the money."

"Really? You need money! For what? You got everything." LaJuana looked at Jackie.

"That's not true. I need the money to buy a couple of books."

"I know your parents gave you money for books. You didn't spend it. Or did you?" LaJuana looked at Jackie's outfit. "Did you buy that outfit with your book money?"

"Look, what I did with the money is beside the point, I need a job. So are they hiring or not?"

LaJuana said, "No, Jackie, they're not. Poor little rich girl in a bind, now that's funny."

Jackie turned, walked up the stairs, and unlocked her door. She sat on the bed wondering what she was going to do. She opened her purse and looked at the card that Nita gave her; maybe it wasn't such a bad idea. She took her cute outfit off, hung it up, jumped in the shower, and got ready for bed. She drank the rest of her wine cooler and struggled to fall asleep. She worried about finding a job, and the fact that she had a coke party at her parents' house. Before she knew it, daylight peeked through the windows, and she was awakened by her phone.

"Hello."

"Jackie how are you, honey?" asked the familiar voice of her mother.

"Fine, Mommy. How are you?"

"I'm fine. How are your classes going, and how is your money?"

Jackie hated to lie but she didn't have a choice. "Everything is fine."

"Good, I'm glad to hear that. Listen, your dad and I will be traveling this week to look at some properties in San Diego, so call us on the cell phone if you need to reach us. Love you."

Jackie's mind wondered back to the coke party she had and knew that her parents would be furious if they found out.

"Okay, love you too."

After she hung up, she had to hurry and walk to campus. Once on campus, Jackie walked into Hughes Hall and heard someone calling her name.

"Jackie... Jackie wait up."

She turned around and saw Ursula, so she kept walking toward the building, not wanting to engage in conversation with her.

Ursula called out again, "Jackie, come on... wait."

Jackie sped up her stride, but before she reached the building, Ursula stumbled in front of her, breathing heavy.

"I can't believe you made me run," she took a deep breath, "to catch you."

Jackie looked at her, but said nothing. She thought she knew her better than that.

"Oh, so you're not gonna talk to me?"

Jackie still looked at her with no expression on her face.

"Jackie, I'm sorry. I didn't think it would be that big of a deal. You seemed cool, like you're up for anything. I'm sorry if I was wrong about you."

"Ursula, you knew I wasn't up for that. Oh, and here's your book."

"Okay, you were in a bind, and I was just trying to help you. I know what it's like to be in a bind, unable to pay for this or that. Not sure how you were going to make it."

"Ursula, yeah, I'm in a bind. But selling drugs?" Jackie looked at her and shook her head. "Why are you doing that? I'm sure your parents would be upset if they knew."

"What? I don't even have any parents. In fact, my family doesn't have anything. My mother worked during the day as a waitress and a prostitute at night to make ends meet. And, my father left her before I was born."

Jackie was silent. She didn't really know what to say next. She never would have guessed in a million years that Ursula grew up like that.

"I know, Jackie. It's hard for you to believe. I studied hard in high school because I wanted to get out of that hellhole. I applied to Karrington and got accepted. It was the happiest day of my life. I moved here from New York with the clothes on my back and spent six months stripping until I met Nita. She gave me money to enroll in classes at Karrington."

Unable to register all that she heard, Jackie asked, "What about financial aid or a scholarship?"

Ursula shook her head, upset. "I didn't want to apply for financial aid. I'm tired of handouts, tired of welfare, and tired of being on the free lunch program. Do you know how embarrassing that is? My grades were good, but not good enough to get a scholarship. I wanted to go to college, but I wanted to do it on my own."

Jackie pled with her, "But, Ursula, the coke parties are illegal. They're wrong."

"Jackie, how can you say it's wrong? You don't know the first thing about being wrong. You haven't lived wrong! My mother used to leave me at home all night by myself while she was out prostituting. My older brother would come home drunk and rape me. How dare you talk to me about wrong. I spent most of my life in wrong!"

Ursula talked about her childhood, and how her mother treated her once she was in high school. Sometimes, she made her prostitute herself and make her pay for her food and clothes.

Jackie's head hung low, and her shoulders slumped down. She said, "I'm so sorry. I don't know what to say, I had no idea." Jackie reached for Ursula's arm to comfort her, and Ursula snatched it away.

"No, you don't. So don't tell me about what is and isn't wrong. Our coke parties aren't hurting anyone. No one is being raped or murdered. We are just adding a little pop to a party."

"I guess I never thought that you would do something like that."

"Well, I did and still do. I met Nita after work one night and she told me I didn't have to strip anymore. She gave me a job hosting coke parties. She has been the mother I never had. The apartment, the car, and the clothes are all from Nita. But I'm only doing this to get through school and once I graduate, the coke parties will be over for me. I won't need them, because I'll have a degree."

"So, this is just temporary?"

"Yes, Jackie. I'm not doing this forever. Oh, and I'd really appreciate it if you didn't share my personal life with anyone. It's my past, and I want to keep it there."

"I wouldn't dare tell anybody. Where is your mother? Does she still live in New York?"

"I guess, I don't know. The last time she asked me to prostitute, I gave her the money and left and haven't seen or spoken to her since. If it wasn't for a counselor at my high school and Big Mama living across the hallway encouraging me to keep my grades up and graduate, I wouldn't even be at Karrington now."

The clock on Allen Rollings Library sounded, and students rushed past to get into the building.

"We better go, class is starting," Ursula said with an attitude.

They both walked into the class, each in silence, wondering what the other was thinking.

4

Jackie woke up still remembering yesterday's conversation with Ursula. She wondered about her housemates' lives. How did they grow up? Did they have a family like the one she had or were their lives more like Ursula's?

Trina knocked on the door. "Hey, Jackie. Are you ready?"

Jackie grabbed her backpack and said, "Almost." She opened the door, still thinking about Ursula. "Hey, what's up?"

"Nothing much. It's raining, get your umbrella."

Jackie picked up her umbrella and closed the door, locking it. Trina and Jackie always walked to class together on Tuesdays and Thursdays; their morning classes were around the same time.

They walked downstairs and Trina asked, "Why are you so quiet this morning?"

"I don't know. I was just doing some thinking."

"Thinking about what?"

"Life in general, I guess." She paused. "It's just amazing how some people have such different lives. You never know what someone else's childhood was like or the problems they've had to deal with."

"Ooookay? But everyone is different, Jackie. So who are we talking about?"

"No one in particular, it's just interesting and sad at the same time."

The gray sky gave way to rain that had been falling on and off all morning. Trina and Jackie raised their umbrellas as they left the row house. Just as they walked down the stairs, all of a sudden, they heard the *pop, pop, pop* sound of gunshots and saw a silver El Camino speed around the corner.

Frightened, Trina and Jackie dropped to the ground and ducked behind the bushes in front of the porch. Trina closed her umbrella and gestured for Jackie to do the same, but Jackie didn't move. Her heart pounded so hard she could hear it, and it felt like it was about to come out of her chest. They both looked at each other in fear. There was silence on the street, so Jackie got up to see what was going on, but Trina pulled her back down.

"What are you doing? Are you crazy?" Trina whispered in a harsh tone.

"No, I'm just trying to see. I think it's over," Jackie whispered.

"Do you want to get shot? Get back down and close your umbrella."

"Okay." Jackie did as Trina asked.

After a moment or two of hearing people screaming and crying, Trina peeked above the bushes. She squatted back down and said, "I think the shots came from the end of the street."

"What? That's on our way to campus," Jackie pointed out.

Holding their breath, they looked out over the bushes hoping it was over. All they could see were blurs moving in different directions because of the rain. At the end of the street, they saw a young man lying on the ground with people running toward him.

They got up, still shaken, and walked down the sidewalk. It was filled with puddles of water and their drenched shoes squeaked as they walked. As they got closer to the end of the street, Jackie's heartbeat faster and faster. They walked up to the crowd as screams reverberated throughout the block.

Jackie looked at the young black man lying on the ground. Bright red blood and pieces of brain matter oozed from his head onto the concrete. She grimaced at the horrible sight covering the sidewalk.

Trina pulled Jackie's arm. "Don't look, let's go." But it was too late; Jackie had already laid her eyes on the gruesome sight.

The sound of sirens from ambulances and police cars drew closer as the paramedics and cops rushed to the scene. Trina pulled on Jackie's arm again and this time Jackie reluctantly moved on, although it took every ounce of her will to walk away.

"My God, Trina; what has this world come to?"

"Drugs and fast money. People are caught up in the hype of having things, so they chase drugs to get dollars and that usually ends with someone dying. I don't know how many times it has to happen before people wake up and realize that it isn't worth it."

Trina's words stung, sharp and intense. Jackie played back the events of Saturday night, and she felt a sharp pain in her stomach. As she continued to listen to Trina, it only got worse.

Jackie changed the subject and asked Trina about her boyfriend. But it was hard for them to forget about what they witnessed moments before.

Once they got to school, they went their separate ways. Trina's classes were close to the entrance of the school, while Jackie headed across the campus toward the back of the school. Jackie made all her classes except the last one, because she was unable to concentrate. She couldn't get the images of the shooting out of her head. For the first time since she enrolled in Karrington, she realized that where she grew up in Dallas was worlds apart from D.C.

Jackie caught a cab to the one of the local universities. after class, which cost her eight dollars and seventy cents. She found her American Lit book and waited in line for the next available cashier.

"That will be ninety-five dollars," the cashier said.

Jackie opened her purse, gave her the cash, and then for another eight dollars and seventy cents, caught a cab back home. Once there, she climbed the stairs to her room and laid down on her bed wanting to sleep the rest of the day away. In fact, she wanted to sleep the past three weeks away. But she didn't have time; she was behind in American Lit, and she didn't want Professor Alcorn on her case anymore. On top of that, she still didn't have her Local Government book.

There was a knock at her door. Jackie yelled out, "What?"

"Hey, it's Brit. What's the matter with you?"

Jackie opened the door and sat back on her bed. "Oh hey, I'm just tired."

Brittany walked in and closed the door, "Tired from what? School just started."

"It's a long story." Jackie didn't want to go into it, so she changed the subject. "I haven't seen you in a while. Where have you been?"

"Oh, you know, just around." Brittany sat on the bed beside Jackie and smiled.

Brittany bounced up and down on the bed and said, "Okay, I'll tell you. I paid for my boyfriend to come up and visit me."

"You did what? When?"

"Actually, the first weekend of school."

"I thought a study group the first week of school sounded funny. Why did you lie?"

"Well, I wasn't for sure that it was going to happen, but I got him here."

"How did you do that?"

"I told my parents about how janky this flat was and how I needed more money to spiff it up. They agreed and sent me a ton of money. So, I flew Charles here. We rented a car and drove to New York."

Brittany looked up at the ceiling dreamy eyed before she continued detailing her romantic get-a-way. "We spent the week at the Waldorf on Park Avenue. It was wonderful!"

"Brit, are you serious?"

"Yes, you know me, Ms. Resourceful. I paid cash for everything. My parents will never know."

"You missed classes for a week?"

"Well, actually a week and a half. Oh, Jax, I love him now more than ever. We visited a couple museums, took long walks, and talked for hours. We even saw a Broadway play. It was most delightful! And on his last day in America, we ordered room service and stayed in bed the whole day. It was so romantic."

"You missed a week and half of school?"

"Yeah, but they don't cover much the first couple of weeks."

"Brit, this is Karrington University. Don't underestimate them. They cover a lot in the first couple of weeks to prepare you for what's coming ahead. You may be like ten chapters behind in all your classes by now."

"Oh, I don't care, I'll catch up."

"The hotel must have cost a fortune."

"It did, but with the money they sent me, I had more than enough. Oh, my parents thought redecorating the flat was the least they could do, with the rent being so cheap. They are forever indebted to your parents for providing a place for me to stay. They consider it a gift to them."

"First, the Row House is not that bad. And second, our parents' talk. What are you going to say when my parents visit, and they don't see any changes?"

"Jax, you told me your parents never come up here."

"Yeah, but what if they do?"

"Don't get your knickers in a twist. It's fine. Let me tell you what else I told them."

"Brit, you shouldn't have done that."

"Listen, I told them I really like Karrington and that I am glad that they sent me here. I explained how I am already learning so much, I even mentioned part of the orientation speech, diving into the intellectual waters of academia, and how it resonated in my soul. I explained how wrong I was about Charles and that he's a bad influence on me. Then I apologized for the shame and anguish that I'd put them through."

Brittany laughed so hard that tears filled her eyes, and she fell back on the bed. "My mum was crying on the phone and my father was so proud of me. They bought it as you say, 'hook, line, and sinker.' Overjoyed at my change of attitude, they were willing to send me whatever I needed to make my transition easier. They wired the money into my account the next day."

Jackie was in awe of Brittany. She would never have the guts to do a stunt like that. Her parents would kill her.

"Brit, I get lying to your parents about seeing your boyfriend, but missing a week and half of school; how are you going to explain that to your professors? Because believe me, they are going to ask. And redecorating my parent's row house, I can't believe they bought that."

"Well, Jax, they did. And when your mom talks to you, you have to cover for me."

"What? Oh no, I'm not getting in this."

Brittany looked at Jackie with her puppy dog eyes and begged, "Please, please."

Reluctant, Jackie said, "Okay."

"What am I supposed to do? I needed to see him. I needed to be with him. My parents had us separated for months. I missed him!"

"Okay...I'm just saying that was a bold move. But I can't talk. I've got my own issues."

"What's going on? What have you been doing since I've been gone?"

"Well... I'd rather not talk about it right now," Jackie said, hoping Brittany wouldn't press it.

"Okay, but you know I'm always here if you need me." Brittany got up and walked toward the door. "As you can imagine, I actually have lots of homework I need to get to, so I'll see you later."

"Okay, me too. Just close the door on your way out."

The next day Jackie went to her State and Local Government I class. The instructor, Professor Gupta, was a short man from India with dusky olive skin and jet-black hair. He entered the classroom and with a thick accent said, "Alright everyone, I trust that you're ready to proceed with the simulation of our political system. Who would like to be first and impress us with their record sheet?"

Everyone in the room looked around, but no one raised their hand. The room was silent.

"Well, I guess you have forced me to choose." Looking at his class roll and scanning the names, he said, "Jacqueline Jones, stand and give us your record sheet for your political system, including the name of the community, region, population size, growth pattern, years of incorporation, racial composition, age range, industrial base, income distribution, and principal issues."

Jackie was stunned that he was able to recite all of that without looking at his paper and even more without taking a breath. She also had no idea what he was talking about. Hesitant, she stood to her feet and tried to think of something to say, but nothing came to mind.

"I'm sorry, sir. I didn't read that part in the book."

"Well, of course you didn't. This assignment was in the simulation workbook that accompanies the book. I gave the assignment out last week. You didn't hear the assignment?"

"I'm sorry, sir, I didn't."

"This is most disappointing, Ms. Jones. Have a seat. Is there anyone else who would care to share their findings?"

A student stood up, and Professor Gupta asked him to state his name.

"Broderick Banks. With all due respect, sir, I believe the assignment was to begin preparing our simulation, but I'm ready, sir. May I proceed?"

Professor Gupta looked puzzled and said, "Perhaps, I wasn't clear in my communication. I apologize, and by all means, let's hear your record sheet."

With assurance, Broderick recited his record sheet almost from memory, complete with every fact Professor Gupta asked for and then some. Jackie had never seen him on campus before, but that didn't mean anything. With the thousands of students on the Karrington campus, there were many people that she had never seen before. Broderick had light brown skin and curly brown hair, and he wore smart boy glasses.

After class, Jackie grabbed her bag and headed for the door. Professor Gupta stopped her and said, "Ms. Jones, may I see you?"

Jackie braced herself. *Oh God, here it comes.* "Yes, sir. I'm really sorry about the mix-up."

"Oh, Ms. Jones, there was no mix-up. I suggest you listen in class, read the assignments, and complete them on time. Your friend stepped up and saved you some embarrassment, but next time I won't be so kind. I expect you to treat my class like it's the most important class in the world. When you fail to complete assignments, it shows a lack of respect for me and your education."

"Yes, sir, I understand." She turned and walked to the door. She swore last year was much easier. She didn't know what had happened, but she had to get back on her game. She went around the corner and then heard a voice behind her, "The proper response is 'thank you.'" She turned, and it was Broderick.

She offered him a slight smile and said, "Hi, and thank you." She sighed. "Of course, he knew it wasn't a mix-up."

"So, he cut you some slack," Broderick stated as he extended his hand out to shake hers. "I'm Broderick."

In turn, although she thought the whole handshake thing was kind of lame, she stuck her hand out and said, "I'm Jacqueline, but most people call me Jackie."

He shook her hand but held it for a moment letting her know he was interested.

Jackie was flattered and pulled her hand away in a slow motion.

"Well, I'm not most people. So, Jacqueline, where are you from?"

"Dallas, Texas. What about you?"

"Des Moines, Iowa."

Jackie eyeballed him, because she had never met anyone from Des Moines, Iowa. She checked out his clothes. He had on a tan suit coat and tan pants with a white collared shirt. She was not sure who the designer was, but she knew it was not made of cheap material. She smiled, liking his taste. She knew that he must be in the business school because they were the only students who wore suits on campus.

"You wanna get something to eat?"

"No, I can't. I have a class," she said, but she liked him. He was nice looking, and he smelled like an ocean breeze, as if he just got out of the shower.

"Oh cool, I understand, maybe another time."

"But...uh...maybe I could skip it," she blurted out.

"Yeah, it's the first month, it wouldn't hurt, but I wouldn't make it a habit." Little did he know everything about him was convincing her by the minute. She didn't notice him in class before, but she was grateful for the distraction today. She knew that she needed to go to class, but she also wanted a man. So, she skipped the class.

"Okay, where do you want to go?" she asked, excited that she finally had a date.

"Well, I'm hungry, so I was thinking Mongolia's Chinese Buffet. But I'm cool if you want to go to Mr. Lee's."

"Oh, I don't live in the dorms. I don't have a meal plan at Mr. Lee's."

"Okay, Mongolia's it is. My treat."

They walked a couple of blocks to Mongolia's and as usual, there was a crowd. After they ordered, they ate and talked for hours. Jackie missed both of her afternoon classes, and so did he. They talked about everything—their lives, their majors, their families. Afterwards, they exchanged numbers, and he walked her back to campus.

Jackie thought that maybe she had a boyfriend. She walked back to the row house on cloud nine, not remembering when she had been so happy. She could hardly wait to see if he called that night. No matter what, she promised herself she wouldn't call him first. Well, unless she thought he forgot her number. No, she'd better play it cool, he would have to call first. One thing Jackie knew for sure, she couldn't be embarrassed again in Local Government, especially since her new beau was in the class.

Recalculating her money in her head, she had $58.77 left over after buying the American Lit book. Of course, that didn't include the money for the cab to and from the school, which cost her $8.70 each way. She thought she was down to somewhere around $40. When she got home, she would sit down and come up with a plan.

As soon as Jackie walked into the house, she plopped on the couch, pulled out her notebook, and perused the information on State and Local Government I. The book was $85, and the workbook was $35. She wished that she hadn't bought that outfit. She blew over $1000 in less than two hours, all because she let Brittany talk her into it.

The next assignment was due in a week, and it looked intense. She had already checked the library, and they didn't have the books. How was she going to get the money to buy them? Calling her parents was out of the question. She'd been looking for jobs but couldn't find one. She was at a loss. She contemplated whether it would really be so bad to have Ursula throw another coke party. She couldn't believe she was even thinking about it, but maybe if she did one more party and never did it again, it would be okay. That way she would have the money she needed for her books.

She called Ursula, but there was no answer. Instead, the voicemail came on. "This is Ursula, I'm not in. You know what to do after the beep. Peace."

Jackie waited for the long beep. "Ursula, this is Jackie. Give me a call when you get this message."

She then started working on her political science paper while she waited for Ursula to call. But instead of focusing on the topic, she daydreamed. She thought about her life when she was younger, about her parents, and how things were before they started investing in real estate.

She and her mom always had time for long talks. As a family, they spent time together going to the park and feeding the ducks. Those were great days. She remembered going to church on Sundays and praying every night before she went to bed. After the corporation took off, they stopped doing everything together as a family. Her parents didn't have time.

She couldn't blame them. After all, their lives were full—a new house, new cars, and any and everything else they wanted. They stopped going to church, and she figured they didn't really need God anymore. In fact, she now questioned if there really was a God. How could God let a boy get shot in the street like that? What about Ursula and how she grew up? Jackie didn't understand it, and she didn't understand God.

Her cell rang and seeing who it was, Ursula answered on the second ring. "Hey, Jackie," there was a pause, "it's Ursula. What's up? I got your message." Ursula sounded like she was in a bad mood. Jackie could tell she really didn't want to talk to her. Things were a little tense between them since their last conversation. Plus, Jackie still borrowed Ursula's book sometimes, and she could tell it was getting old.

Jackie tried to sound upbeat. "Yeah, I wanted to ask a favor."

Ursula hesitated before she asked, "Um...what?"

"Could I borrow your book again? I promise I will have my book soon." Jackie knew Ursula took assignments seriously.

Ursula remained silent for a moment.

"Jackie, I can't keep letting you borrow my book. I'm behind two chapters and one project."

Jackie pleaded with her. "I know, me too. I'm behind five chapters and two projects. I've been submitting applications all over D.C., but nothing has come up yet. My parents don't know what's going on with my money, and I can't tell them. I know you're going to call me a hypocrite, but I need to make a little extra cash. Can I borrow some money from you?"

"Oh...no you didn't call me! Uh-uhn, after you gave me the Mother Teresa speech. Oh, no, I can't help you. I'm sorry."

"Ursula, please. You know I wouldn't ask unless I really needed the money."

"Jackie, you acted all self-righteous about the whole thing, and now you have the audacity to ask me to borrow some money? Where do you think I get the money? You bitched and moaned about how terrible it was. And even after I told you how Nita helped change my life so I could go to Karrington, you still looked down on me. So, the answer is *hell* no!"

"I'm sorry, Ursula. I didn't mean it like that. I was just shocked. Please forgive me." Jackie sighed realizing that Ursula was her last hope. "I really need to buy my Local Government books. I've already been called out in class. You saw what happened last week."

"Yeah, and I also saw Prince Charming come to your rescue. Why don't you ask your little boyfriend for the money?" Ursula laughed.

"Ursula, you know he's not my boyfriend. Besides I just met him. I can't ask him for money."

"Well, you can't ask me either, because if memory serves me right, I tried to help you before and I got screamed at. You need to call your parents."

Jackie started to cry. "There's more. I think my housemate Lindsey saw the coke. She keeps looking at me funny every time I see her, and I'm scared she might call my parents."

Ursula said, "Do you know what Nita would do if someone snitched on her to the police? Okay, stop crying. Did she say anything to you?"

Jackie sniffled, "No, she just looks at me weird."

"Okay, we'll worry about Lindsey if she becomes a problem. You let me know if that skank says anything to you."

"Okay. But, Ursula, can you please help me?"

"Alright, but you're going to have to have another coke party."

"If I have this party, do you think I will make enough to buy my books?"

Ursula responded, "That depends. I'm throwing a party at the Wellington Rome Hotel this Friday night in the penthouse suite, and I'll introduce you to some of my friends. We are having a meeting at five o'clock. If you are gonna do this, you'll need to be there at four-thirty and then we will have the party around seven. Before you can do your second party, Nita requires that everyone attend one business meeting. You can mingle and then setup your own party."

"If the meeting starts at five o'clock, why do I need to be there at four-thirty?"

"Jackie, the meeting starts at five, but you need to be at the hostess orientation at half past four. Okay? So don't be late."

"Okay. Hostess orientation? That sounds formal."

"Jackie, do you want to work or not?"

"Yes, I'll be there. Will Nita be at the party too?"

"She will be there for the meeting, but not the party."

"Good, she is kind of creepy."

"Jackie, she is cool. She is just all about the business."

"Okay, I'll see you Friday at four-thirty, and thanks so much for helping me." Jackie was relieved that she was finally going to solve her money problems.

"Don't thank me yet, because I want 50 percent of whatever you make."

"What! Ursula, I can't give you 50 percent of what I make. I need the money to buy my books. If I give you 50 percent, I won't be able to buy them. How much am I supposed to get anyway if the charge is two hundred dollars a person?"

"Jackie, it's not two hundred dollars a person, it's per line. Then I guess you'll have to have another party until you have all of the money."

"That's not fair."

"No, it's not. It's business. I've helped you out a lot, first letting you borrow my book, and then giving you money from the first party. Now it's time for me to benefit."

Begrudged, Jackie agreed and hung up the phone. For the first time, she wished that she'd never met Ursula.

5

T he cell rang, and startled Jackie. She answered, "Hello."

"Hey, it's Trina. Whatcha doing?"

"I'm working on my political science paper, or at least I've been trying to work on it for the past three hours. But I'm really daydreaming. What time is it?"

"Around eleven o'clock."

"You're kidding?" Jackie looked at her alarm clock to make sure. "Hey, I met someone."

"What? You mean a guy?" Trina said.

"Of course, I mean a guy," Jackie said, insulted that she would assume anything else.

"Well, when did you meet him and what's his name? I need details. Tell you what, meet me out front and let's get a Philly cheesesteak at Sandra's."

"Okay, give me five minutes," Jackie said, happy to go hang out and tell her girlfriend about her new man. She was not doing anything anyway, plus Sandra's had the best Philly cheesesteaks in D.C. She threw on her Juicy Couture hot pink warm up suit, the one that made her waist look thin and fit her rear perfectly. Jackie made sure she always looked good, because she never knew who she might run into. She headed out of the house and met Trina who lived one house over.

"Okay, tell me about your new boyfriend," Trina said as they walked to Sandra's.

"Well, he's not my boyfriend, at least not yet. I just met him today, but we talked all afternoon, and I like him."

"What does he look like?"

"He has light brown skin, brown eyes, he's tall and slim. Perfect."

"What? That's not your type," Trina said.

"It is now."

"When have you ever gone for someone that looks like that?"

"Okay, I'll be the first to admit, he's not the kind of guy I typically like, but no one is sweating me right now except Broderick."

Trina gave Jackie a skeptical look and sighed. "Cool with me, I'm just saying. I know what you like, and you know what you like."

"Okay, I gotcha. And, I have to confess, I still have feelings for DeMarcus." Jackie reminded Trina what happened with DeMarcus last year, but she didn't tell her everything.

"Okay, let's see. DeMarcus vs. Broderick." She paused, "But, I don't understand why you have feelings for someone you know you can't have."

"What?"

"Talking about, thinking about, and daydreaming about DeMarcus. He's trouble, and you know it. Besides, he has a girlfriend. In addition, you just called me a couple of weeks ago because he was using her as a punching bag. Forget about him. Trust me if you fall for him, you are going to wind up getting hurt and not just emotionally."

They continued their walk down the street, passing drunks, drug dealers, and young men in alleyways shooting dice. Jackie took the opportunity to change the subject, knowing Trina didn't understand DeMarcus like she did.

"Trina, do people hang out on the street this late at night in Jackson?"

"Nope. People are in their houses with their families or in the bed asleep."

Jackie looked around at all the people out on the street and said, "Just wondering. It seems like D.C. is jumping every night."

Trina laughed. "That's because these people don't sleep. They're too busy trying to get their party on. Speaking of parties, where are we going this weekend?"

"I don't know. I kind of wanted to leave it open in case Broderick called."

Trina moaned, "I know you are not going to sit around and wait for a man to call you. How do you know he's not planning a date with someone else as we speak?" she said in a condescending tone.

"Okay..." Jackie paused and took in the comment. "I'm not saying that I'm going to wait around, but what if he called? I want to be available. It would be nice to go on a date."

"I'm not trying to be mean, but this is Karrington University. Look around, all the women here are beautiful. You think he's at home doing nothing? Come on, girl. And you just admitted that he was cute," Trina said.

Jackie kept walking, but was a little upset that Trina thought that Broderick wanted to date other women when he was obviously interested in her. Just because Jackie hadn't had a man in a while, didn't mean that Broderick wanted anyone but her.

"Jackie, you're a beautiful girl, and I'm not trying to hurt your feelings, but this is college. It's okay to like someone, but I wouldn't get caught up. No one here is looking for a relationship. And, don't forget, he's really not your type. How long could it possibly last?"

They continued walking, but Jackie remained quiet.

"Here's what I would do if I were you. When he calls, don't go out with him right off. Make him beg. He needs to realize that you have a busy life with a lot of options, and that you might be on a date with someone else."

Trina was a good friend, but she didn't get Jackie at all. Jackie not only wanted a boyfriend, she needed a boyfriend. Besides, she saw plenty of people on campus in committed relationships, and they were happy. Wanting to take the focus off herself and put it back on Trina, Jackie stopped walking, looked straight at Trina, and asked, "What about you and Vincent?"

Trina answered, "Case in point. We've been dating since the end of last year and all I hear him talking about is himself and his major. I'm so tired of hearing about insurance and what he plans to do after graduation. I'd rather talk about other things. I just don't think he's into me anymore."

"What are you talking about? He seems into you every time I see him. He does talk a lot about his major and his future, but that doesn't mean he's not into you."

"Yeah well, I think he's into himself."

"Okay, say I take your advice, who would I say I'm out with?"

"I don't know, but he doesn't need to know that you aren't dating anyone."

Jackie knew Trina had a lot more experience in this area than she did, so she decided to get as much how-to advice as she could.

"So...what do I say when he calls?"

"Tell him you'll have to call him back because you're washing your hair."

"Now you know that's a lie, and he will too."

Trina said, "Can't you just pretend that you're washing your hair? He doesn't need to know what you're doing."

Jackie thought about it. She wanted a real relationship, but not one built on lies and deceit. "I don't want to lie to him."

They got to Sandra's at eleven-thirty, and the line was out the door. Ambulances and fire trucks raced through the intersection as they waited. In D.C. sirens could be heard every night, sometimes two and three times a night. To Jackie, Dallas was a much quieter city especially after dark.

After almost thirty minutes, they grabbed their cheesesteaks and ate them on the walk back. Neither one of them knew what made Sandra's so addictive, but they had a Philly from there at least once a week.

On their way back, they passed by some hookers on the street arguing. One shouted from across the street at the other, "Get your skinny white ass off this corner! It's mine!" She wore a black mini skirt that was so short her butt cheeks were hanging out and a turquoise halter-top that functioned like a bra instead of a top. Her boots were a bright canary yellow with some sort of red design around the sides and could be seen from a mile away. Jackie thought, *who in the world dressed her*? To top it all off, the hair from her long black wig hung past her behind.

The other hooker shouted back, "Look here, bitch, I'm always on this corner, so take your skank ass on!" This one had on a candy apple red dress with a low-cut V-neck that was almost at her waist. It was missing a hem at the bottom with frayed material sticking out.

Trina said, "You know, any minute one of her breasts is going to pop out of that dress."

Jackie laughed and said, "In Dallas, that's called a country sighting. It's just that nasty."

Then the hooker with the yellow boots started walking across the street toward the one with the red dress and said, "Don't make me come over there and cut you, because I got a blade, and I will!"

The other hooker shouted back, "I wish the hell you would! When I get through with you, you gonna wish your pimp beat your ass instead of me."

Trina walked faster and pulled Jackie with her. Of course, Jackie wanted to watch the action. She was curious because she had never seen hookers this close before, except on television.

Trina said, "Let's go, I don't want to be a witness to this." They both wrapped up the rest of their cheesesteaks and headed home.

She looked at Jackie and stated her observation, "Girl, you've changed. Our freshmen year, you didn't want to see anything. And now, you want to see everything! Wow, a year can really make a difference. Yelling and cursing used to bother you, but now you do it yourself."

"Hell, I guess D.C. changes you," Jackie said as she walked up the stairs to her house and waved bye to Trina.

~

The next day, Brittany came down to the kitchen looking hung over. Her final drink at the pub last night was not worth the headache she had this morning, so she decided not to go to class. She heated up some water for her tea and looked in the refrigerator for her milk marked with her name on it. She went to the pantry, grabbed the cheerios box and the biscotti container. She pulled one of the house-mates' bowls down from the cabinet and poured her cereal. Once the water was ready, she poured it over the teabag in her cup and then poured milk over her Cheerios and in her tea.

She missed her boyfriend and wondered what would happen with their relationship. She thought about the baby a lot and wondered what her life would be like if she had gone against her parent's wishes and kept the baby. As much as she tried not to focus on it, she couldn't help but be curious about whether her boyfriend would make a good father and husband. As she thought about all of this, Bijon came into the kitchen and greeted her.

"Hey, Brittany. What's up?" He pulled his orange juice out of the fridge.

"Nothing much, I just feel awful. I don't know if I caught some sort of cold or what," Brittany lied, not wanting the ridicule that Bijon always placed on Jackie for drinking. She placed one hand over her forehead and pulled biscotti out of its packaging with the other.

Bijon moved away from Brittany to the opposite side of the kitchen, and said, "Okay, well stay away from me, because I can't afford to miss school or work."

Brittany smiled and walked into the dining area to sit down and eat.

Bijon stood in the kitchen doorway watching Brittany. He asked, "So, what part of Africa are you from?"

"South Africa."

"How come you don't sound like you're from Africa?"

"Well, I was educated in the British system, so I guess I have picked up a bit of a British accent. And you, Bijon, where are you from?" Brittany could tell that he was interested in her, but she didn't know why.

"America."

Brittany blew her tea to help it cool and said, "America, by way of where?"

Bijon sighed and said, "My family is from Mumbai, India, but I was born in America. Most of my family lives in Tallahassee, Florida. It's not like they sent me here to be educated."

Brittany ate her Cheerios and gave him a strange look, not expecting to get all that information. She used a napkin to wipe the milk from her mouth and said, "Oh, so you are American. I was about to say you look Indian, but you don't sound Indian."

Bijon, a little perturbed changed the subject and said, "So, your family must have money?"

Brittany raised her eyebrows at him while she sipped her hot tea, wondering what his angle was.

"Sorry, I don't mean to get so personal, it's just that I don't see those starving kids in Africa on television going to school in the British system."

Brittany finished her cereal and wondered if he was trying to insult her or her country.

"Bijon, my father is a diplomat, and my mother owns a fashion boutique in London. So yes, you might say we have money. Is that a problem?"

"No, I was just asking." Bijon drank his juice. "I wondered if you were another student with a golden spoon in your mouth."

Brittany laughed and said, "I'm sure your parents have money too, or else you wouldn't be at Karrington."

Bijon said, "What? I'm here on scholarship. My parents don't have anything."

Brittany shook her head, turned her nose up at his response, and said, "Oh...I'm very sorry to hear that."

"Why? You think most Americans have money?" Bijon questioned.

"No, I think most Americans should have money," Brittany said in a cynical tone.

He laughed and said, "Brittany, don't you know that most Americans are broke? We come here for a better life, and it's supposed to be a better opportunity. Although, I'll let you know after med school if that holds true. But in no way are we rich, in fact, we are far from it."

Brittany dismissed his comment and said, "I lived in America my junior year of high school with Jackie, and I didn't see any 'broke' people."

Bijon sat down at the table and looked at her like she had lost her mind. He said, "Seriously, you've got to be kidding? That's because you were staying with Jackie. Look at D.C., it's full of broke people. Haven't you noticed the homeless people begging for money on the street?"

Brittany remembered the man she encountered walking up to the row house the first day she came here, but maintained her position, "Yes, I have seen that, but they all must be lazy, because America is the land of opportunity. You come and go as you please and the government doesn't stop you. You can be whatever you want, and no one says, 'that's not allowed' or 'we have enough people in that field, you'll have to pick something else.' We say in Africa, if you can't make it in America, then you can't make it anywhere."

Bijon yelled, "What? It's hard in America! You make it sound easy, but it's not that easy!"

Proud of herself, Brittany watched the look of dismay and anger that appeared on Bijon's face in response to her opinion. "Well, the rest of the world sees America as the land of ultimate opportunity. I'm not sure why everyone here isn't a millionaire."

Bijon rolled his eyes and raised his voice. "You can't be that naïve! You know what; I can't believe I'm having this conversation. The world thinks that? That's the farthest thing from the truth. I watch my family struggle day in and day out. America's not all it's cracked up to be."

Brittany sipped her tea and bit into a biscotti. She listened to his tirade and then imparted her wisdom further. "You've never been to India, have you?"

"No, and I don't plan on going," Bijon said.

"Well, I have. Maybe if you went for a visit, you would see life is not so bad in America." She eyed him waiting on his response. "Let me explain. Here children can go to school for free; I believe you call it public education. In Africa, children must pay to go to school, pay for their books, and their uniforms. Most children are unable to go, because their parents don't have the money. Going to school in Africa...it's a big deal because we recognize that education is power. It's the key to getting out of poverty. Children here see it as a burden and a governmental obligation they must fulfill. My father was fortunate enough to go to school and learn. But it took him years to prepare and position himself for greatness. It just doesn't happen overnight."

Bijon couldn't counter her argument, "Well, I can't believe I have to defend myself and every American who is not a millionaire. But you know, people have to work hard over here too. Nothing is handed to you in America."

Brittany responded in kind. "Really, what about housing? In America, those that are financially challenged get subsidized housing, do they not."

"Well yeah."

"In my country, no one gives us subsidized housing. There is no such thing. If you don't have the money for it, then you don't get it."

She used her hands to make her point. "And what about food stamps?"

"What about them?"

"Well, the government hands you money so you can go to the grocery store and buy food. In Africa, there's no such thing as food stamps. People stand in food lines and hope and pray that the missionary volunteers don't run out."

He raised his voice again. "Don't sit here and undermine my parents' suffering. What are you talking about? There are plenty of people who can't afford a house. My parents don't have their own house. They are renting, because they can't afford, nor do they qualify for their own house."

Brittany also elevated her voice. "And why is that?"

Bijon's eyes were like daggers aimed at Brittany when he said, "How am I supposed to know? Opportunities weren't there for them. My parents never made enough money to have a house. Even today, I have to send them money from time to time to pay the electric bill or to buy gas for the car. People think America is so great, but it's not."

Brittany saw the pain in his eyes. To diffuse the conversation, she placed her hand over Bijon's and said, "Bijon, I don't mean to hurt your feelings, but my father says it is not how much you make but what you do with what you make."

Bijon flicked her hand off and said, "Are you implying that my parents were foolish with their money, and that's why they don't have anything?"

In a delicate fashion, Brittany made her point. "No, I'm not saying that at all. But the opportunity to succeed in America is much greater. Do you realize that compared to some parts of Africa, your parents are better off than many people. The mere fact that they have food in the refrigerator for tomorrow deems them to be considered rich in my country. Most Africans live hand to mouth, sometimes never knowing if they will have food for the night, not to mention the next day."

Bijon listened as he watched Brittany.

She put her head down and said, "I'm sorry, I don't understand Americans. If I could take you to parts of Africa that are so impoverished, you would see that Americans have it easy. Africa's economy sinks at a steady pace while the American dollar continues to stay strong."

Bijon calmed down, and said, "Okay, I can appreciate that, but there are plenty of people in America that don't know where their next meal is coming from, but it's still hard."

Brittany drank the rest of her tea but noticed the change in his voice and said, "That may very well be so." She paused and sighed before moving forward. "Bijon, do you know what's wrong with Americans?"

He gritted his teeth, and in a stern tone said, "No."

"Americans are always looking at what they don't have, in terms of material things. The more money they have, the more things they can buy. But in Africa, we are taught to be happy in spite of our circumstances. You see little kids starving in Africa still running around playing. They understand that things do not dictate happiness. People, family, and community dictate it. Sure, we need things like food and shelter, but even when we don't have those things, we don't fall into a depression and give up. We continue, because we believe things will get better somehow. I hate to be blunt, but Africans are eternal optimists."

While Brittany educated him, Bijon looked down at the table as he listened.

She lowered her head down and leaned in to make eye contact with him. She looked deep into his eyes and said, "So pardon me if I don't have sympathy for Americans, when I've seen Africans suffering so much. I'm not trying to hurt you. I'm just stating the facts. And yes, my parents have money and sometimes I splurge, but I never spend more than what I have."

Bijon was moved by her sincerity, and they both saw something in each other that they hadn't seen before. Bijon's cell phone rang. He picked it up and said, "Hello," turned away and spoke in a soft voice, "Oh hi, I'm fine. What about you? Hey, listen, let me call you right back. Maybe we can meet tonight before I go to work. Okay, bye." He hung up the phone and turned back to Brittany, but she was gone.

Moments later, intrigued by their earlier exchange, Brittany came back to the dining room after putting her bowl in the sink and said, "Don't let me interrupt your conversation with your girlfriend. I'm going upstairs to lie down."

As she walked to the stairs, Bijon said, "No, that wasn't my girlfriend, but we'll have to continue this conversation."

Brittany looked back at him and said, "Anytime. You know where I live."

Bijon went back into the kitchen and smiled. He grabbed a pop tart, his books, and headed out the door.

Brittany returned to her room. Earlier, she felt nauseous from the cocktails she drank the evening before, but now she just felt pity for Americans because they couldn't see how rich they were.

LaJuana was down the hall listening to parts of Brittany and Bijon's conversation, as she got dressed. She was interrupted by the ringing of her phone. She knew it was either her grandmother or her job, because she didn't have any friends.

She answered, "Hello."

The voice on the end of the line, sweet and pure, said, "How's grandma's baby?"

LaJuana was excited to hear from her and said, "Hi, Grandma, I'm fine. How are you?"

"Fair to midland. You know my legs still achin'. Ain't nothing the doctor can do though. He said it's just old age and arthritis. I'm gon' be all right, I just keep plugging along. You coming home this weekend?"

"No, Grandma, you know I don't have any bus money for that. Besides, I have to work this weekend. It's hard to pay my rent and eat."

"Baby, I know. Grandma wishes she could help you, but I can't. Maybe the good Lord will see fit to send us some money down from heaven like He sent manna down to the children of Israel."

Saddened by their lack of money, LaJuana knew her grandmother shouldn't have to take care of her. That was what a mother did, not a grandmother. She despised her mother, Lisa, but even more, she detested the one that got her hooked-on drugs in the first place. She put the thought out of her mind. Instead, she smiled because she could always count on her grandmother to bring God into the conversation, "Grandma, I wouldn't bet on that."

"Well, you don't know. Honey, God is able. You hear me? Don't you never give up on God, okay? Now listen, I want you to come home. I got a surprise for you."

"Grandma, what is it?"

"Now, it wouldn't be a surprise if I told you, now, would it?"

"Grandma, can it be next weekend? I am covering someone else's shift this weekend. But can you give me a little hint?"

"No, I'm not givin' you no hint. I'll see what I could do about your bus money. See you next weekend. You take care of yourself, and I will talk to you soon if the Lord wills."

After they hung up, LaJuana wondered what her grandma was up to.

6

Jackie called a cab to take her to the Wellington Rome Hotel in downtown D.C. She chose a cab over an Uber because it was substantially cheaper, and she didn't have any extra money. She got dressed, walked downstairs, and waited on the porch. Ten minutes went by and finally a yellow cab showed up. She opened the door and got in and as soon as she sat down, she felt a sharp scratch on the back of her thigh. She slid over and saw that the black leather seats were ripped underneath her with pieces of the white cushion sticking up. Just as she was about to get over the seat issue, the smell of the driver overwhelmed her. Jackie had nothing against foreigners, but sometimes their body odor was so strong that it choked her. She couldn't tell if it was the cab or the driver that smelled like smoke, old hamburgers, and musty armpits, but if she had to guess, she would say it was the driver.

The Middle Eastern driver turned to her and said, "Where to?" as he slurped from a Styrofoam cup.

Thinking they told him that when she called, Jackie shrugged and replied, "The Wellington Rome Hotel."

He turned back around, pushed the meter down, and put the car in gear. As they drove off, she heard a clicking noise in the engine, and it sounded like something was not connecting.

She asked, "What's that noise?"

The cab driver said, "No problem, don't worry, it's nothing."

Don't worry? she silently questioned. She was wondering if they would even make it to the hotel. They hit a bump and parts of the dirty fabric on the ceiling of the cab pulled loose and hung down in front of her. *I've got to get my car up here. This catching a cab stuff is depressing.* Opening her purse, she checked to see if she had her Este Lauder perfume. Her mom always said, "It's a good habit to keep it in your purse because you never know when you might need it." And she was right, because Jackie needed it today.

Jackie tried to take her mind off the cab and the driver by focusing on Nita's business meeting she was heading to. She asked herself if she was doing the right thing. Should she go to this meeting, or should she call her parents and tell them about the mess she had created? Deep down, she knew she couldn't do that. Her mom warned that if she couldn't handle being away at Karrington, then maybe she needed to transfer closer to home, maybe even to a junior college. There was no way she was leaving Karrington for some junior college. So she decided that she had to start acting more like an adult. She could do this on her own. She just needed to get enough money for her Local Government book and workbook.

The cab pulled up to the entrance of the hotel, and Jackie couldn't wait to get out. The bellman from the hotel opened the cab door and greeted her. Jackie got out and looked at the hotel. It was a majestic site that resembled a royal palace with gold and glass everywhere. As she stood taking in the view, the cabbie yelled, "That'll be ten dollars and fifty-four cents." She retrieved a twenty-dollar bill from her purse and handed it to the driver. He took it and sped away.

Jackie ran after the cab and the bellman ran as well. She screamed, "Hey, give me my change! Wait, that's my last twenty!" Unable to catch him, Jackie hung her head low, threw up her arms, and tears began to roll down her face. She couldn't believe this was happening.

The bellman said that he would call the police. He walked her into the hotel lobby and showed her to the ladies' room where she could dry her face. He then said, "Don't worry, ma'am. I saw the whole thing, and I got the cab company's name and the cab number. What is your name so I can tell the police?"

Through her sobs and with her voice cracking, Jackie answered, "Jackie Jones" and went into the bathroom. She looked at herself in the mirror and cried, "Why is this happening?" Her mascara and eyeliner revealed the paths of her tears. She got a paper towel and wet it to wipe the lines from her face. Something inside of her told her, *It doesn't have to be this way.* After drying her eyes, she realized whatever reservations she had before were gone, because now she didn't have any money. Her cell phone rang, and she mustered up the energy to say, "Hello."

On the other end of the phone was Broderick, "Hey, are you okay?"

Still shaken from the cab thing, but excited to hear his voice, she tried to sound normal. "Ahhhh, hi. Ahh, yes, I'm fine, just not feeling well."

Broderick said in a concerned tone, "What's wrong?"

"Ahhh...it's just a little cold."

He said, "Aw, that's too bad, I'm so disappointed, I wanted to see you tonight."

"Oh, I wish I could, but I can't," she said, still upset by the turn of events.

"Hey, I understand. You sound like you need to take care of that cold. Well, I hope you feel better. Do you need anything?"

"No, thank you. I'll be fine."

She couldn't believe it, he called. She hung the phone up and reapplied her makeup. The time was now four-thirty, and Ursula urged her not to be late, so she would call Trina later. Her friend would be so proud that she didn't go out with him the first time he asked. Jackie was happy that he sounded so concerned about her cold and how she was feeling. He would make a perfect husband, but she could never let him know what she was doing.

She walked up to the concierge's desk and asked for directions to the penthouse suite. The bellman pointed to the elevators and told her that he had called the police. The good news was, they were in the area and were on their way. She thanked him and got on the elevator. There was a hotel employee waiting to take her up. The elevator walls were mahogany with classic swirl designs carved in the wood and mirrors on each side. She thought to herself, *now this is nice.*

He greeted her and asked, "Which floor, ma'am?"

She said in a quiet voice, "The penthouse suite."

"No problem." He took out a small key and inserted it into the opening next to the button marked "P". The elevator was so lavish, there was a flat screen TV in the corner that showed the hotel's many amenities.

"Here's your stop, ma'am. Have an enjoyable evening."

"Thank you."

Jackie walked to the penthouse suite and knocked. The black double doors were outlined in gold trim with gold door handles.

Ursula opened the door and said, "Hey, girl. I'm glad you're on time. We were just about to start. What's wrong?"

Jackie walked in and said, "Hi, nothing." Her eyes were mesmerized by the beauty of the room. She didn't pay any attention to Ursula. The floor was hardwood with a tan marble entrance. There was a bar adjacent to the entrance of the room with several bottles of champagne displayed on the merlot marble countertop. Next to the bottles were two large platters of food, and they smelled wonderful. Past the bar, the room opened into a very large living area. The overall design was very sleek. In the center of the room were twenty or thirty chairs arranged in rows, facing a pull-down screen.

Ursula said, "Jackie, are you alright?"

"Yeah, I'm fine, just having a bad day. The cabbie drove off without giving me my change." The room was filled with beautiful furniture, wall paintings, and fresh purple flowers, it was a sight to see.

Ursula said, "Awe...man, you got to watch the cabbies. You never know what they'll do."

Jackie said, "Yeah. This is a really nice place." On both sides of the room were sitting areas with rich brown leather sofas and loveseats. The room was immaculate. There were two guys sitting to the left. Ursula introduced her to them. One was a student from Smith Dash College and the other from Dickens University.

Ursula motioned for Jackie to sit down and announced, "Hi every-one. I'm Ursula and I've been working with Nita for over three years. This is a quick overview of your host/hostess duties while you're throwing your parties." She gave each of them a handout and asked that they read it to themselves. Jackie read it and waited for her to continue.

"By following these directions and rules, you should have no problem hosting and being successful in the business."

All of a sudden, the door opened, and Nita walked in. She inspected the two large platters of hot appetizers on the bar. Ursula stopped and asked her if the appetizers were okay. Nita nodded and walked over to where they were sitting. She greeted the two guys first, and then she greeted Jackie saying, "I trust that Ursula is answering all of your questions and being a good hostess."

They all nodded.

"Good. We'll give you more information during the business meeting."

She smiled at Ursula and said, "Ursula dear, please continue. I'll be in the bedroom." Jackie watched her as she walked away, still not sure what to make of her.

Ursula resumed her talk and gave each of them a small white piece of paper with a number on it. "This number tracks our progress and our sales. Sales reps are encouraged to provide a party atmosphere for our elite clientele, but never to indulge in the product ourselves. We are allowed to have one glass of wine or beer at our parties, but never hard liquor. All numbers are given and recorded in Nita's database. Your managers will give you tubes. Never have more than fifteen people at a party; and always have a minimum of ten.

Parties are held in inconspicuous locations, like at a house, an apartment clubhouse, or even a hotel. The cuts are different. As you know on your first party, you made 5 percent of the sales that night. Since you're coming up on your second party you will make 10 percent, your senior rep gets 15 percent, and the rest goes to Nita."

One of the guys said, "Okay, that's the part I'm interested in. So, can you give us an example of a good night? How much can I make?"

Ursula laughed and said, "Well a good night would be if everyone snorts three or four lines of coke, so if you have twelve people and they each snort three lines of coke, that's a total of thirty-six lines. Each line is two hundred dollars, so two hundred times thirty-six is seven thousand two hundred dollars. You'll get about seven hundred twenty dollars, the senior rep would get one thousand eighty dollars, and Nita gets her cut and then pays the supplier. But the 10 percent adds up quick if you are having a party twice a month or more and possibly helping your senior reps with parties."

The same guy asked another question. "So how much do the other reps make in a month?"

"That depends on how many parties they host, but I would say for beginners about twelve to fifteen hundred dollars. Also, remember you only work a few hours a month. Once you get the hang of it, a typical rep could average about three parties a month and maybe help with a couple more. You should make somewhere between two thousand and twenty-five hundred dollars after expenses. Some reps make a lot more than that. It depends on your party and your clients. However, you set the tone for your parties, so you can make them alive and hopping or not. Your senior rep will help you develop your clientele. Afterwards, you are expected to network and collaborate with others at your parties to gain new clients on your own. If you fall short, that affects your base and bonus, which means you may owe Nita money. Take it from me, that's the last thing you want to do."

Jackie thought about the money and said, "That's a lot of money."

"Exactly. Why do you think we want to do it? You'll meet the other reps at the meeting." Ursula looked at her watch and saw that it was almost five o'clock, and said, "Okay, I've got to hurry, because the meeting will be starting soon. Nita has worked hard to develop this business, and it has taken her years to craft it and make it her own. So, there are no conversations with the police whatsoever. And if anyone ever sold Nita out, there would be severe consequences, like your life. She doesn't like murder or bodily injury, but she is not above it either."

Everyone looked at Ursula and then at each other. Jackie only thought about the money. The possible consequences of being arrested or killed never crossed her mind.

Ursula rushed through the rest of her speech. "Nita works for very high-end people. The supply's great and the demand is even greater. She buys the finest quality cocaine. We have five or six minutes before the business meeting starts, so make yourselves at home. Let me have your handouts back, so I can shred them. Oh, all money that you collect is given to your senior rep and the senior rep gives you your cut. Do yourself a favor, never try to keep the money, it always catches up with you."

Ursula pulled Jackie to the side and said, "Let me give you a tour."

As she walked past the rows of chairs, Jackie noticed that there were two shredders at the front of the room. Ursula shredded the documents they read earlier. The shredders seemed out of place in the posh penthouse suite. They passed by the bar where the large plastic covered platters of hot appetizers were sitting. Jackie peeked to see what was inside. Chicken quesadillas, spring rolls, spinach and artichoke dip, smoked Gouda cheese, and grapes. All delicious look-ing, sitting in trays waiting on them to dig in.

After the tour, Jackie sat on the soft mahogany sofa and heard someone knocking at the door. Over the next few minutes, the door opened and closed as people arrived. Before she knew it, the room was filled with a diverse group of Nita's representatives—White, Black, Hispanic, and even one Asian. Nita asked everyone to mingle a little before the meeting started. Jackie introduced herself to some of the other college students; she found out that some were not in college. Two of the reps were secretaries at law firms, there was also a housewife, a couple of musicians, and an artist. Nita had an array of people working for her. They all seemed nice and none of them looked like drug dealers. There was a lot of laughter and chatter, and for a brief time, Jackie forgot the reason she was there.

Nita asked, "May I have everyone's attention? Please be seated, so we can start our presentation."

Everyone found a seat and a silent stillness followed as they all waited to hear from their leader. Nita stood before them smiling and speaking in her most proper tone. "Hello, everyone. I want to welcome our newest reps to our family. Would you stand and give us your names and where you are from?" Each new rep stood and did as she had directed.

After the introductions Nita said, "For our seasoned reps, I want to congratulate you on an outstanding quarter. Why don't you give yourselves a hand?" Everyone clapped. "I'm going to have Ursula pass out the handouts so we can begin our PowerPoint presentation. Some of you who have been with us for a little while will see that we are doing 46 percent better this year than last year, which of course makes our supplier happy, makes me happy, and will make you happy when it comes to bonus time."

Everyone agreed and laughed a little. Ursula passed the handouts to everyone, and Jackie read the material. Nita spoke again, but Jackie focused on the handout. The front page said, "Lockheart Enterprises." The next page had her mission statement and the purpose of the organization. It didn't say anything about cocaine or drugs.

The next page had a detailed organizational chart that showed the number 747 as the CEO and three sets of numbers reporting to the CEO, which were the managers. Thereafter was a tiered listing of numbers, first the managers, then the senior reps, and finally the reps. There were so many numbers that the chart filled the page. Jackie heard Nita explain the numbers and the names that matched the numbers. The next page divided D.C., Maryland, and Virginia into quadrants and regions, with special emphasis on Baltimore. She had numbers placed in each region and quadrants with the managers' numbers circled. No names were listed on the page; however, Jackie saw her number 214, which was the number Ursula gave her earlier and happened to be the area code in Dallas. So she guessed the number circled belonged to Ursula. Nita told the group to pay close attention to the D.C. quadrant.

There was a knock at the door. Nita gave an agitated look at her three managers and walked to the door, saying, "Who is it?" The voice on the other side of the door said, "It's the police."

The room fell still and silent. One of the managers ran over and turned the projector off while another manager rushed to pull beauty products out of the cabinets of the kitchen. She placed them on the center table. Nita motioned everyone to be quiet and calm. She adjusted her clothing, making sure there was no lint on her outfit, and then opened the door. With a pleasant smile, she asked, "Yes, sir. How can I help you?"

Two officers were standing at the door and one of them looked in the room and responded, "We didn't mean to interrupt your meeting. We are looking for Jackie Jones. Is she here?"

Nita paused and said, "Yes, she is. Let me get her for you."

Nita turned her long sleek neck and walked over to Jackie like a snake going after its kill.

"Jackie, these kind officers are here to see you."

Scared to death of Nita, Jackie stood and walked to the door where the officers were. Nervous, she faced the officers and said, "Sir, is there something wrong?"

The officer said, "Well, we got a call from the bellman about you being robbed by a cab driver. We need to get your story and a brief description of the man so we can file a report."

Jackie sighed with relief. "Oh yeah, I forgot about that."

The other officer walked into the room and picked up a container of blush and lipstick. He said, "This must be one of those beauty product parties. My wife sells this stuff."

Nita smiled and said, "Yes, everyone needs beauty products. You can never have enough."

He picked up a bottle from the bar and said, "Wow, look at all this champagne. You must be celebrating a big year in sales."

Nita put on a fake smile, and responded, "Yes, sir. Our reps did an outstanding job this year."

The officer nodded his head and said, "I'm sure everyone's legal."

Nita said, "Why of course officer. Please feel free to check their ID's." She turned to the reps and said, "Everyone get your ID's out so the officer can check them."

"That's quite okay. Everyone looks old enough to drink." He joined the other officer in the hallway. They got the description of what happened and Jackie's contact information and said, "You guys have a nice day."

Nita yelled back to them, "You too, be safe."

As soon as Jackie closed the door and turned around, she felt the sudden grip of Nita's hands around her neck, choking her. Nita's voice changed from the pretentious businesswoman to a ghetto girl from the hood. She screamed, "You stupid, stupid little bitch! How dare you bring the po po to my meeting? Are you crazy?"

Everyone was startled at Nita's actions and her voice.

Panic stricken, Jackie struggled to breathe and tried to pry Nita's hands off her neck, but she couldn't. Nita was too strong. "I forgot," Jackie said, gasping for air and crying. "I forgot the bellman called the police after I got robbed."

Nita released Jackie's neck and shook her head like she didn't know where she was or what she was doing. Jackie held her neck, coughing and trying to catch her breath. Ursula rushed to help her. In one motion, Nita turned to her reps and changed her voice back to the sophisticated businesswoman. She adjusted her clothes and brushed the imaginary lint off her outfit. She looked at her Rolex watch and said, "It's time for a five-minute break. Jackie and Ursula, in my bedroom now," Nita demanded.

They rushed to walk behind her, trying to catch up with her quick stride. After they got into the bedroom, Nita slammed the door and turned the radio up. She walked over to Jackie and slapped her so hard that Jackie fell to the ground.

Nita gritted her teeth and then yelled at her, "Get up. You stupid ho. Do you know how long it took me to build this business?" Jackie looked at her, but she didn't respond, afraid that Nita was going to kill her.

"Girl, you better answer me," Nita shouted at her.

Jackie sobbed hard as her heartbeat very fast. She stood up and answered, "No."

Nose to nose, Nita looked Jackie in her face and said, "No, what?"

Jackie felt Nita's hot breath on her face and said, "No, ma'am."

Jackie knew that whatever happened next it wouldn't be good. She looked to see if she could run to the door and escape, but decided against it, because Nita would catch her and snap her neck. Nita took Jackie's right arm, turned her body around, and pulled her arm behind her back, hard. Tears were running down Jackie's face, and she was shaking because it felt like her arm was about to break.

Nita said loud in Jackie's ear, "Not one time in twenty years have the police ever showed up at one of my meetings, until today. Who the hell do you think you are? You think this is a joke? This is my life, bitch. And if I have to kill you to keep it, I will!"

Jackie's arm burned and tears streamed faster down her face. She stood there hoping Nita wouldn't break her arm, then her legs buckled beneath her. Now, almost crying like a baby she uttered, "I'm sorry, I forgot they were coming. I'm so sorry; please don't hurt me... please. It will never happen again. Please stop, you're hurting me."

Nita ranted, "Oh it hurts? You haven't seen hurt." She kneed Jackie in her back, causing her to fall to the floor again. It felt like her spine had been bent. Jackie's neck, face, arm, and now her back were in excruciating pain, but she was thankful that Nita was not in her face anymore. Jackie's vision was blurry from her tear-filled eyes, but she could still see Nita's angry face. She raised up on her knees and Nita walked in front of her and backhanded her. Jackie fell backwards as her eyes rolled in the back of her head.

"How do you think I feel? I'm the one that's hurt. I run a successful business, and I'm not about to have some uppity bitch cause me to lose it, all because you can't think."

Nita jerked her neck around and stared at Ursula with contempt in her eyes. She walked toward Ursula who stood against the bedroom door trembling.

"Ursula, this is your fault." She pointed her finger in her face. "I thought you told me she was smart. You were the one who begged me to hire her. You said that she would be perfect, no one would suspect her."

Whimpering, Ursula said, "I know, I'm sorry, Nita. I didn't know she would do that." She pleaded with Nita, as she looked down. "Please don't do this. I've done everything right until now. Please give me another chance. I'm sorry."

Nita backed away and paced the floor for a few moments, prowling like a lion ready to devour its prey. She looked at Ursula like she was ready to pounce. She said, "You better not move." Suddenly, Nita balled her fist as tight as she could and punched Ursula in the stomach. Ursula doubled over, struggling to catch her breath. Nita then punched her in the nose and blood gushed all over Ursula's blouse and the floor. She stumbled to the side, but Nita caught her. She held Ursula's head in her hand, looked at Jackie, and then back at Ursula. She said, "Both of you disgust me." She bashed Ursula's head into the wall and Ursula fell to the floor.

Nita said "I can't believe that just ten minutes ago I was happy and excited about my new reps, the prospects of new business, and the third quarter profits. Now, thanks you two, all I see is your motionless bodies before me. If it weren't the fact that Ursula is my girl, Jackie you would be dead. It's nothing for me to kill. I've done it before, and I'll do it again."

Nita stood in front of the bedroom door. With her back facing them and her hand on the doorknob, she said in a dark and evil tone, "Let this be a lesson to both of you bitches. I will kill you if you ever do anything like this again. You have five minutes to clean yourselves up and get your asses back in this meeting."

Nita adjusted her outfit, brushed the imaginary lint off her sleeve, and regained her composure. She then turned the music off, opened the door, and walked out as if nothing happened.

7

Ursula got up and went into the bathroom to clean her blood-smeared face. Jackie followed behind her to help while her arm and back were throbbing with pain.

"Ursula, I'm sorry. I didn't mean..." Ursula put her hand up and stopped Jackie from talking.

"I'm not interested in your apologies, right now I want to get cleaned up and back to the meeting." Ursula sniffed and put her head down.

It was obvious that Ursula accepted her punishment and was going to try to get back into Nita's good graces, like a child who had disappointed her mother.

Sounding somber Ursula said, "Are you ready?"

Confused by Ursula's attitude and not sure what to say or do, Jackie frowned and said, "Yeah, I guess so."

As they walked out of the bedroom to re-join the group, Jackie was amazed by what just happened. She thought they needed to get out of there and call the police, but she didn't voice it out of fear. The room was quiet as they walked in. Everyone looked at the red hand-print on Jackie's face and the blood on Ursula's clothing. The evidence was clear that something bad had happened.

Nita broke the silence by saying, "Okay, come, Ursula and Jackie, you both sit up front where you can see." They looked at her in complete astonishment. "Come on, I won't bite."

Jackie and Ursula moved slow and sat down in the seats as Nita suggested. Jackie was cognizant that one wrong word or move could turn this nice, polite person into an uncontrollable and enraged madwoman.

Nita, in a festive tone, said, "Now everyone turn to page five of the handout and we'll go over a few of the highlights of my presentation."

Jackie looked down and turned to page five, listening to the upbeat tone in Nita's voice. She asked them to look at the excel spreadsheet which showed the line items titled *"Cost of Product."* Jackie read the pages, and nothing on the spreadsheet said anything about cocaine or drugs. She only half listened, because she was thinking about getting up and running out of there. Her thoughts were interrupted by laughter and applause for the outstanding work the team had done. Nita instructed them to turn to page seven where there was a diagram that revealed each representative's number, region, and his or her sales for the month. There was also a column for those that had been in the business for over a year, representing what they did this month compared to last year. She called each number, and they all were celebrated for their achievements. It was amazing how Nita managed the coke parties like she was running a major corporation.

Nita said, "I want to make sure I explain for those who are new, the list of clients' names are never used. I have the master list, and we use telephone numbers. They are divided by type of profession, and then sub-divided into frequent or occasional customers. Further, a last digit is added to every number that tells of their social status. As you create your client lists and host your parties, you will be able to determine what will make them more enjoyable. On page eight you will find a list. Page nine shows a pie chart of projected sales for the next year."

Jackie followed along as Nita guided them through her presentation. The last two pages covered the performance measurements and goals for the year. Nita ended with a motivational speech on having extraordinary success in the business and her vision for the future. She explained the job assignments for the month along with the numbers of the clients to be invited. She then told them that each representative's list would be left at the table. Nita invited them to eat, drink, and socialize for the next thirty minutes because Ursula was throwing a party, and everyone would have to leave.

The managers collected all the presentation packets and shredded them. While everyone mingled, Jackie and Ursula sat still, and Nita didn't speak to them at all. She carried on as if they weren't even in the room.

After about fifteen minutes of mixing with her staff, Nita went into the bedroom, closed the door, and sat on the bed. She hadn't thought about her childhood in years, but while choking Jackie it brought back memories. It was a part of her life that she had buried, or so she thought, but today she couldn't shake the nightmares of growing up in the projects. She remembered the little room where she spent hours trying to take care of her family.

Old, dingy, light blue walls filled with smudges of dirt and faded paint, roaches crawled across the floor, and the stale smell of spoiled food in the refrigerator. It made her sick to her stomach just thinking about it, but the images were forever imprinted in her mind. She remembered all too well the small green fabric couch in the center of the room with little black holes all over it. Her mother's friends used it to put out their cigarettes. The three smallest kids slept on the three thin, green cushions. She could remember the wooden table where she sat each day, trying to do her homework. It wobbled because one of the legs was broken. One day, Nita decided to fix it. She stole glue from school hoping to glue the leg back to the table, but it didn't work, just like most things in her life. Instead of giving up, she sat at an angle with the broken table leg straddled between her legs, holding it so she could finish her homework.

She remembered everything, one day in particular, like it was yesterday. The youngest kids were running around the table and throwing small rocks at each other while Nita sat at the old crippled wooden table trying to study for her freshman language arts test. The older kids were outside playing while she kept the younger ones inside. Before her mother started having babies, Nita used to play outside too. Her mother would always tell her, "Nita, go play in the traffic." So, that's what she often told her siblings who were old enough to go outside. She knew what her mother meant by it, and her siblings knew what she meant by it too. She yelled at them when they cried, because her mother yelled at her when she cried. She beat them when they didn't listen, because her mother beat her when she didn't listen. Feeling imprisoned by her brothers and sisters made her hate them. It was because of them that she decided early on, she never wanted to be a mother.

Being the oldest of the nine kids, Nita was responsible for taking care of them. She had to feed them, put their clothes on, and take the older kids to school while the younger ones went to the neighbors. She had to do so much because her mother spent her time at the military base in Aberdeen, Maryland trying to land an army man. She often succeeded, just never for long. Her mother never married any of their fathers, so Nita didn't know her father, nor did she care to know him.

One specific day she remembered, her 5-year-old sister throwing rocks at the other two kids hitting one in the face and one in the eye, causing them to cry. The two younger kids picked up the rocks and threw them back at their 5-year-old sister, causing her to cry. All of them were hurt, crying, and screaming at each other. Nita tried to control them by screaming at them to stop. Yelling at them didn't work, so she chased them and the older two ran outside, but Nita caught the 2-year-old and swung him around pinning him against the wall. She remembered being so angry and frustrated that she put her hands around his little neck and lifted him off the ground choking him.

She yelled at him. "Stop crying! You rotten kids! Stop crying!"

The more he cried, the more she choked him. He tried to scream, but he couldn't. He pushed her and kicked her with his little arms and legs. He did everything he could to fight her.

She told him, "Be still and listen to me. I'm sick and tired of you crying, all of you. You want something all the time. I'm tired of it. Stop it!"

The little boy stopped crying. Nita heard a gurgling sound, each time he tried to catch his breath. Instead of letting go, Nita tightened her grip and said, "This time I'm going to stop you for good."

After two or three minutes, the little boy turned blue. While Nita held him up against the wall, his eyes stopped blinking, and no more sounds came from him. After she realized that he wasn't moving, Nita let him go and his small lifeless body slid down the wall and fell to the ground. His eyes remained fixed on Nita, and she stood frozen, looking at him for more than twenty minutes. Instead of sadness, she felt a sense of relief, almost like a brick had been lifted off her shoulders. She knew things would never be the same from that day on. In fact, she was delighted and thought that maybe now her mother would listen to her about watching the kids. With the boy lying still on the floor, Nita calmly stepped around him and went to a neighbor's house to ask for help.

That same afternoon, all the children were removed by CPS and put in different foster homes. Nita spent two years in a youth detention center where she received counseling each week, and later she was placed in foster care until she was eighteen. Once the police completed their investigation, charges were filed against Nita's mom, and she was convicted of negligent homicide and supervision as well as child endangerment because she left a minor to watch her children. The day Nita's mom went to jail was the last day Nita saw her as well as her siblings. Today was the first time in years she thought about killing her younger brother. Nita shook her head at the memory of her brother's death. She thought about how all she wanted to do that day was study. Nevertheless, because of her mom's irresponsibility, her brother had to die.

She stood up, adjusted her suit, and dusted off the imaginary lint from her clothing. She picked up her bag and headed for the door. As she exited, she didn't look at Ursula or Jackie. She slammed the penthouse door behind her.

～

Jackie walked over to the table and looked at the job assignment sheet. She and Ursula had another party next weekend. Ursula said very little to Jackie, she gave Jackie brief instructions to call the numbers on the list and invite them to her party next weekend. Jackie did as she said, and Ursula didn't say anything else to her.

Jackie watched Ursula during the party. She wasn't her usual self. Ursula laid a glass mirror on the table and cut the cocaine with a razor blade. She then arranged it in thin lines and placed thin tubes in front of the coke. Each client was given up to four lines during the party. They all enjoyed the hors d'oeuvres, liquor, and coke. Jackie counted fifteen people at the party, so the total for the night should have been $12,000. Ursula collected the money from the clients.

After the party, they left the hotel and got into Ursula's car in silence. Ursula drove to Jackie's house and parked in front.

Jackie got out and said, "Bye."

Ursula didn't open her mouth; she just drove away.

Jackie stood there on the sidewalk feeling awful, but she also realized that she helped her and didn't get paid. Although she couldn't really say she expected to, after what happened with Nita. She went up to her room and fell on the bed, exhausted from the day's events. That night she tried to sleep but tossed and turned. Finally, she got up and ran downstairs for some water. Jackie stepped into the kitchen and turned the light on to see dirty dishes piled in the sink. She walked past the mess to Brittany's cabinet. In it, she found a complete bar with all the liquor her heart could desire. She picked out a bottle of Grand Marnier and poured herself a glass. She had never tried it before, but Brittany said it was strong yet smooth, and she needed something like that. She took a sip and coughed, hoping it would take the pain away from her arm and neck. Jackie flipped the light switch off and took the glass with her to the couch. She sat in the dark, with a faint glow of the streetlight outside that pierced through the front door window. She sipped her Grand Marnier and worried about the mess she had made for herself and now for Ursula. She couldn't do this. She couldn't be a part of any more parties.

Multitudes of thoughts flooded her mind. She thought about that poor guy that was shot in the street at the beginning of school. She was confused and scared because she still didn't have the money for the Local Government book. She liked Broderick, but didn't think she could have a relationship until she solved her money problems. Not to mention, she was already behind in at least four of her classes. She had hit rock bottom, and no one knew it but her.

After several moments, she heard a noise from upstairs. Someone came out of their bedroom and walked downstairs. She could see the figure, but she couldn't make out the face. She didn't really care about who it was, so she sat and sipped her drink. The intruder turned the light on, and it momentarily blinded her. Once she was able to see again, she realized it was DeMarcus.

"I thought I heard someone down here. What are you doing sitting in the dark? It's three- thirty in the morning."

Perturbed and in no mood to be questioned, Jackie responded, "I could ask you the same question. What are you doing up at three-thirty in the morning?"

"Sometimes, I can't sleep, so I come downstairs to get some water and clear my head. Uh, I mean I just get thirsty."

Jackie thought what he said was strange, but she didn't express it because she had her own set of problems.

DeMarcus went into the kitchen and retrieved his glass of water. He walked back in the den, looked at her as she sat on the same couch where they made love last year.

Jackie wasn't focused on him because her mind was on other things, but she asked, "Can you turn the light off when you go back upstairs?" She kept her head down trying not to make eye contact with him since she still had feelings for him. She also knew that what happened last time with them was an accident, and it couldn't ever happen again. Trina was right, he was trouble.

"Whatever." He walked toward the stairs and then stopped. "Jackie, I can't leave you down here in the dark by yourself. Besides, you might need me tonight." He smiled.

Jackie looked up at him without a smile, and asked, "Can you please leave me alone?"

DeMarcus walked over and sat down beside her. He changed his voice to a more serious tone and said, "Okay, what's wrong? Do you want to talk about it? I'm sure it can't be that bad."

Jackie thought, *He has no clue what bad is.* Surely, he didn't think that she was going to open up to him, and she didn't even really know him. They had sex a year ago and that was it. It was a mistake, and now she just wished he'd go back upstairs.

"No, I don't want to talk about it. I'm fine, I just need to think." Annoyed with him, she said, "I'm sure Marissa's waiting on you."

"Na, she's fast asleep. Let's just talk?"

Jackie couldn't believe that he was that dense. She sighed and asked, "About what?"

"About you. Do you know what your problem is?"

"No, I don't. The problem I'm having right now is you. Can you please go upstairs and let me think in peace."

"Jackie, look at you. You're beautiful and smart. But you don't even know it. Your problem is...you. I watched you over the past year with Jarrett and with Trina. You always let others talk you into what they want you to do."

Her eyes filled with tears because she couldn't believe that he was saying this to her, especially right now.

"You know the difference between me and you? I'm my own man. I make my own decisions, and no one can sway me from them. That's the difference between leaders and followers, and if you don't get it together, you will always be a follower."

Her self-esteem was already low, but DeMarcus managed to push it all the way in the ground. She put her head in her hands and started to cry. She was so tired of people telling her this. She was trying to change, but it wasn't happening fast enough.

DeMarcus attempted to console her by putting his arms around her and holding her. "Jackie, I didn't say that to make you cry. I just want you to see yourself the way others see you."

Still sore from her earlier beating, she winced from the pain. As she looked up at him, the light from the front door shone on his brown eyes allowing her to see the sincerity in them. DeMarcus placed one hand under her chin and used the other to wipe away her tears. He said, "Your skin is so soft. It's like it's never been touched before."

And for a moment, she became lost in his eyes and unable to move. He smelled so good, like some sort of masculine cologne. She didn't know the fragrance, but his smell aroused her. He slowly leaned in for a kiss. She closed her eyes and received his lips. DeMarcus held her head in his hands and her problems with Nita, the drugs, and school all suddenly vanished away. The pleasure she felt was indescribable. It was like she was floating, drifting farther and farther out to sea with DeMarcus as her lifeboat. Before she knew it, they made love all over again, right on the very same couch.

Realizing this shouldn't have happened a second time, Jackie sat up, looked down at her nakedness, and said, "I can't believe I keep letting you do this to me." She rushed to put her clothes back on.

DeMarcus responded in a very soft, serine tone. "Nothing happened that you didn't want to happen." Then he slid on his pajama pants and walked back upstairs.

In turn, Jackie was left with her thoughts. She asked herself how she kept getting into these predicaments. While DeMarcus' girlfriend slept upstairs, Jackie made love to him downstairs. It had happened again, and this time, they didn't even use protection. She wondered about DeMarcus. From the outside he appeared to be unavailable and abusive, but there was more to him. He was a very loving and compassionate man.

Before long, Jackie dosed off to sleep on the couch, thinking about DeMarcus and the time they shared last year and the love they made tonight.

8

LaJuana called her grandma to let her know she was leaving for Baltimore later than planned. She hoped her grandma would give her a hint about the surprise; although, LaJuana didn't get too excited because the surprises were never anything major. It could be a new sweater, movie tickets, or a homemade pie. But maybe this time was different. Maybe Grandma won the lottery, or, maybe one of the people that her grandma worked for died and left her some money. Just thinking about it made LaJuana smile. Deep down she didn't want anyone to die, but on the other hand, if it would get them out of the circle of poverty, then she would be okay with that.

Grandma picked up after the second ring.

"Hi, Grandma. How are you?"

"Fine, baby. How you doin'?"

"I'm okay. Listen, I'm catching a ride with a friend from work, but she isn't leaving until five o'clock this evening, so I'll be a little late for the surprise."

"Oh, baby, that's fine. It'll be here. You got money to help pay for gas?"

"Yes, ma'am, it's taken care of."

"Okay, then I'll see you later on this evening."

"Alright, bye."

Driving to Baltimore gave LaJuana mixed feelings. On one hand, it reminded her of her sweet grandma, but it also stirred up anger toward her mother, Lisa. LaJuana hated Lisa because she chose drugs, alcohol, and men over her. In addition, Baltimore brought back memories of more than just the mother she never had; it also caused her to think about the person responsible for all her suffering —Lisa's drug dealer. Ever since LaJuana was a little girl, she vowed that one day she would find that person and make them pay.

They drove into Lochearn, a town west of Baltimore where LaJuana's grandma lived. As they drove onto LaJuana's street, she saw cars parked up and down the block and in the driveway. LaJuana thanked her friend for giving her a ride then grabbed her bag from the back seat. As she got out, she wondered what was going on. Before she could close the car door, she heard Mrs. Gray call her name from across the street.

"Hi, LaJuana!"

She turned and said, "Hi, Mrs. Gray."

Her friend asked, "Hey, what time do you wanna leave tomorrow?"

"I don't care. Whenever you need to. Call me and let me know."

"Okay," and her friend drove off.

Mrs. Gray sat in her rocking chair on the porch wearing a light green and yellow flowery housecoat with pink furry slippers. She asked, "How's school?"

"It's fine. How are you doing?"

"You know, fair. As long as the good Lord keeps me here, I'm going to keep on keepin' on."

A boy walked on the sidewalk behind LaJuana and bounced a basketball. Mr. Keeler, her grandma's neighbor, rolled his wheelchair up the wooden ramp that led into his house.

Mrs. Gray said, "Hi, Mr. Keeler. How you doing?"

He replied, "Doin' fine," but he didn't turn around.

Mrs. Gray steered her attention back to LaJuana and said, "I know your grandma sure is proud of you, and I am too. You know you the first person I've ever known to go to college."

"Uh...Thanks."

LaJuana got an uneasy feeling when her grandma or anyone from the old neighborhood made college a big deal. She didn't like the pressure, because her grades were average at best. She was not some sort of brain and that was the main reason LaJuana hadn't declared a major. For one, she was not sure what she wanted to do and two, she didn't want to let anyone down by picking the wrong one.

Mrs. Gray looked at the cars parked out in front of Grandma's house. "Everything okay over there? I see a lot of cars. Nobody died, did they?"

"No, my grandma called me and asked me to come home for some kind of surprise, but I don't know what's going on."

Mrs. Gray turned her nose up and rocked in her rocking chair. "Oh, she didn't say nothin' to me about no surprise. Um..."

"Ah, now you know you're always welcome to come over any time," LaJuana said to Mrs. Gray, knowing that she got upset anytime someone had something in the neighborhood and didn't invite her.

Mrs. Gray laughed. "I know you right. Tell your grandma I might come over later. I got to let my beans finishing cooking."

"Okay, see you in a little bit."

LaJuana fixed her eyes on a mother and daughter next door to Mrs. Gray's house. The little girl yelled, "You can't get me," and stuck her tongue out and ran. Her mother chased after her and caught her. They both fell on the grass. The mother tickled her daughter and said, "I got you now," and the little girl laughed.

LaJuana thought, *it must be nice to have a mother to play with, one that cares about you.* She sighed and wished she could erase her mother and the drugs from her memory.

She walked up the short driveway. Her grandma had a yard that looked like a beautiful green rug. She cut and maintained it herself, but occasionally, she let her friend, Tree Man, do it for her. He trimmed the two trees in the front yard, and she paid him when she could. When she couldn't, he took a hot meal for payment for his services.

Neatly planted around the two trees were her grandma's favorite violet flowers, which were flowing back and forth in the breeze. LaJuana remembered playing hide and go seek as a child behind those trees, being careful not to step on the violets. Her grandma always said, "You may not have much in this world, but you should take care of what you do have." LaJuana had never forgotten those words.

She stared straight ahead at the one-story white frame house. It showed its age with chipped paint and pieces of worn wood exposed. Maybe she and her uncle could paint the house this summer, because she knew her grandma didn't have the money to pay someone to do it. The 780 square foot house was all her grandma had to her name, but it was filled with love.

Walking up the two concrete steps, LaJuana noticed one of the steps had several big cracks in it and the other step wobbled when she put her weight on it. She opened the screen door and walked in. Her grandma kept her door open during the day, so people felt welcome to stop by and visit.

"Hey, baby." Grandma's smile brightened as she limped over to hug LaJuana.

"Hi, Grandma," LaJuana said, eager to hug her back.

The smell of fresh greens, pig feet, and hot sauce flooded the room. LaJuana's grandma was the best cook in town. Many people told her that she needed to do catering or open a restaurant. However, she always said, "I don't cook for money; I cook because I like to see people eat and enjoy themselves." Candied yams were LaJuana's favorite, and no one could cook them like her grandma.

Inside the house were little keepsakes that white people gave her grandma when she cleaned their houses. Miniature pieces of furniture, small porcelain dolls, or pictures of Jesus lined small shelves affixed to the walls. Grandma saw these unwanted items as treasures, and LaJuana viewed them as reminders of the warmth and love in her grandma's heart for little things thrown away.

LaJuana scouted the room and saw relatives and friends that she hadn't seen in a long time, and for a moment, she wondered if someone had died.

"Hi, Kelli. Hey, Alan. What are you doing here?" LaJuana asked, puzzled to see them because they were good friends of the family, particularly with Lisa. They all hugged each other and LaJuana strolled in the kitchen, wondering who else was in there. She greeted the other guests and found out what else her grandma cooked. To no surprise, there was a mouthwatering dinner complete with hot water cornbread, candied yams, macaroni and cheese, and a sock-it-to-me cake. There she hugged her cousins, Sherri and Marc.

Sherri said, "Do you know what the surprise is?"

"No," LaJuana said, hoping that it was really a surprise since all these people were there.

Just then the doorbell rang. Unable to contain her excitement, Grandma announced, "Okay, everyone, my surprise is here!"

The door swung open, and in walked Lisa.

LaJuana's mouth gaped open. She didn't remember the last time she'd seen Lisa, but she was amazed because Lisa looked decent and healthy. LaJuana watched Lisa as she greeted her friends and family, but she wasn't prepared for what happened next. Her mother walked over to her and without a word hugged her for a long time.

LaJuana stood stiff, and did not return the hug. The embrace felt like a needle piercing her skin inserting pure hate through her veins.

Everyone clapped, happy to see the mother and daughter reunited.

Grandma was the first to speak while holding back tears. "I've been waiting for this day for a very long time and now it's here." She hugged both LaJuana and Lisa.

"Everyone, I wanted you to see Lisa. She has been clean for over six months. We are so very proud of her. This celebration is just for her. Do you have anything you want to say, Lisa?"

"I don't know where to start. I know that many of you have seen me clean before, and that I've disappointed everyone in this room." A manufactured tear fell, before she continued. "It's been a long, hard road, and I know many of you have your doubts. But this is the longest I've ever been clean. And I just have to take one day at a time. I'm so happy to see all of you, but I'm especially happy to see my daughter who's in college. I'm very proud of you, LaJuana."

LaJuana didn't respond but thought, *she's got to be kidding.* She was taken aback at how Lisa stood there and gave a victory speech as if she was Mother Teresa and only had a quick trip to the Betty Ford Center.

Grandma interrupted her thoughts and said, "Let's say the blessing and eat. We've got plenty of time to catch up."

After they blessed the food, everyone moved toward the kitchen while trying to catch up with Lisa and wishing her well on her journey.

The doorbell rang again, and a tall white man entered. Lisa ran over and hugged him. "Everyone this is my fiancé, Brian."

The man standing at the door sucked the air right out of the room. Disappointment set in as they listened to Lisa.

Lisa said to her mother, "I wanted to surprise you."

LaJuana smiled and thought to herself, *See, nothing has changed. She may have given up drugs and alcohol for a quick minute, but not men. Same old Lisa.*

Lisa introduced LaJuana to her new man and said, "Brian, this is my little girl, LaJuana. Although, she's not so little anymore, she's my college girl now." Lisa smiled at her new man. "She goes to Karrington University."

LaJuana remained silent. *How dare she stand there and brag about me going to college. This bitch has some nerve.*

Brian extended his hand and said, "Nice to meet you."

LaJuana gazed at Lisa and her boyfriend. Lisa nudged LaJuana with her elbow and said, "Say hi, LaJuana."

LaJuana shook her head, rolled her eyes at both, and walked back into the kitchen.

Lisa sighed, and her new friend comforted her.

Everyone ate and talked to Lisa about her plans and her new life. LaJuana remained quiet the whole evening, wishing the charade would end.

After a couple of hours, the guests said their goodbyes one by one and wished Lisa the best. LaJuana decided to go into the kitchen to wash the dishes.

Grandma approached LaJuana. "Need some help?"

LaJuana was curt when she said, "Nope, I'm fine."

Grandma persisted and initiated a conversation with LaJuana. "I want you to take my gun back with you to D.C. A lot of bad things happen in that city, and I want you to feel safe."

LaJuana said, "Okay," knowing that wasn't what her grandma wanted to talk about.

Grandma cut to the chase. "LaJuana, aren't you happy to see your mother?"

LaJuana didn't answer; she kept washing the dishes.

Grandma sighed and said, "I thought you would be glad to see her clean and starting over."

LaJuana took a deep breath and then said, "It's hard to start over when you constantly have a man in your bed. But yeah, I'm happy for her."

Grandma took a breath and said, "I have to admit, I wasn't expecting her to bring a man. But at least she is clean. She is trying to do right this time."

LaJuana looked up to the ceiling, closed her eyes, and tried not to be disrespectful. She finally said in a nonchalant tone, "I'm happy for her."

Grandma placed her hands on LaJuana's arms and positioned herself, so she was facing her. "Look, I know you have a lot of anger towards your mother, but you are going to have to get over it. She has made some mistakes, some awful mistakes, but you must learn to forgive and forget. Honey, that's what the good Lord would want you to do. We all make mistakes, and no one is perfect. And I know she has a lot of making up to do but give her a chance."

Not wanting to upset her grandma, LaJuana said, "Okay. I'm kind of tired. I think I'll go to bed." She walked to her room and slumped on her bed. She called her friend and told her she would be ready to go at nine o'clock in the morning.

All week LaJuana had been secretly hoping that grandma's surprise would be a boat load of money to make up for her miserable life, but now she was more disappointed than ever. Lisa was back, but as far as LaJuana was concerned, nothing had changed.

9

————

Jackie gathered her dirty clothes and detergent, then headed down the stairs to do her laundry. She hadn't washed clothes in two weeks. She had so many clothes in her arms that she could barely see the stairs below. Careful not to trip, she walked down each step looking over the side of her arms at the stairs. DeMarcus came up the stairs and cleared his throat. "Eh-hem. Do you need some help with those?"

Surprised and pleased to see him, she said, "No, I'm fine, thank you."

He leaned closer to her and said in her ear, "You sure are! Why don't you come to my room after you take those down to the basement?"

Jackie glanced up the stairs and said, "I'm not doing that. Isn't Marisa up there?"

"No, I sent her home last night. I've been thinking about you all week long."

"Now I know you're lying, because I heard Marissa talking to you this morning."

He stepped back and said, "Okay, she was here, but she is gone now. In fact, she'll be gone all weekend. I'm meeting a buddy of mine in Norfolk today, but I'll be back early in the morning," He stroked Jackie's cheek and said, "But I can stop by your room when I get back?"

Jackie giggled, liking the special attention. "Look, DeMarcus, I don't want you to think I'm your little play toy because I'm not."

"Baby, I'm not thinking about you as my play toy. I'm thinking about much more. You know I been sweating you for a minute. All those times you came to see Jarrett, and then that day we spent on the couch...Wow. Then the other weekend you were off the chain. Um... we need to do that again. You can't tell me you're not feeling me, cause I'm feeling you."

He sounded like a thug, but Jackie liked men with a little thug in them.

She smirked and said, "Maybe a little, but I'm not trying to break up you and Marissa."

He came closer, wrapped his arms around her waist, and looked in her eyes. Some of Jackie's clothes slipped and fell over the railing. He kissed her behind her ear and said, "Trust me, Marissa will understand."

Jackie pulled away and said, "Whatever! Look, I have a lot going on right now, and I can't afford to make any more mistakes." Jackie tried to be stern, all the while she was smiling at him. "So I'm glad that you find me sexy and believe me, the feeling's mutual. But we just can't. My life's already too complicated."

"Are you still worried about whatever was bothering you the other night? I told you; you can talk to me. Whatever it is, I got you."

And just like that, he turned from nasty boy to a kind and gentle man looking to rescue a damsel in distress. His handsomeness and his words once again lured her in, and before she knew it, he was kissing her again and she was in ecstasy.

LaJuana walked in with her groceries and gasped as if she witnessed a crime. She said, "Oh...my God."

Surprised and stunned by LaJuana's sudden appearance, Jackie pulled away from DeMarcus and said, "Oh, no ...I can explain, it's not what you think...Wait."

LaJuana sprinted to her room carrying her groceries. She said, "You don't wanna know what I think."

Embarrassed, Jackie hurried to pick up her clothes and screamed at DeMarcus, "Don't ever do that again!" She ran downstairs past the kitchen and into the basement, leaving DeMarcus staring after her.

He continued up the stairs and mumbled, "Whatever, girl. You know you want me."

Jackie threw her clothes on top of the washing machine and headed back upstairs to LaJuana's room. She knocked on the door and pleaded, "LaJuana, open up. I want to talk to you."

LaJuana opened the door, and Jackie walked in.

"I want to explain what you saw."

LaJuana replied in a sarcastic tone, "You don't owe me an explanation. You're grown. You do what you want to do. But let me ask you this, are you planning to reduce his rent in exchange for sex?"

"What? No, we're not having sex. Look, LaJuana, what you saw was an accident. That's it. I don't want him, and I don't like him." Jackie sighed because she didn't want anyone to know about the kiss. "Please don't tell anyone."

"You mean Marissa. Cool, you know me, I keep to myself. It's just nice to know who you can trust and who you can't." LaJuana walked over to her nightstand and took chips and soda out of the bag. Lackadaisically, she said, "Although, I never trusted you anyway. You don't have to worry about me, I couldn't care less about what you do or don't do. Now, can you shut my door?"

Jackie exhaled loudly before she asked, "LaJuana, do you have plans tonight?"

She answered, "Yes, why?"

"I just need the house to myself."

"Oh, I see. So, you and DeMarcus can be alone?" She folded her arms and tilted her head ready for some juicy gossip. "What do you have planned? A candlelight dinner? A little wine? A little nasty? Are you dressing up like a nurse or something?"

Jackie yelled, "What? Are you crazy? No! What do you think I am?"

"The jury is still out on that one."

She sneered, irritated that LaJuana thought so low of her. "I just need the house to myself. It has nothing to do with DeMarcus."

"Well, no problem here. I have to work tonight and won't be back until after 2 a.m. Is that long enough for you?"

"Thanks." Jackie closed the door before LaJuana could say anything else. She could be such a bitch sometimes, but Jackie hoped she didn't say anything to Marissa.

The doorbell rang and Jackie rushed to answer it hoping it was Trina. She peered through the dingy off-white curtain and saw that it was.

"Hey," Jackie said, opening the door.

Trina came in as always with a bright smile on her face and said, "Hey, girl. What's up?"

"Not a lot. We need to talk."

"Okay." Jackie took Trina's hand, and they ran upstairs to Jackie's room.

"Close the door, you are not going to believe this, but I've got to tell you. I slept with DeMarcus last weekend."

Trina's mouth flew wide open. "You what? I know you like him, but what about Marissa? Forget that what about him beating her all the time?"

"I'm not planning on dating him. It just happened."

Eager for details, Trina said, "Okay, tell me everything. When? Where?" She sat on the bed beside Jackie, waiting for the juicy tidbits.

Jackie told her about their night and the kiss in the stairwell.

She put her hand up and stopped Jackie. "Okay, wait a minute. How come you sound all in love when you talk about him? And, how are you sleeping with him when you're supposed to be dating Broderick?"

"I don't know."

"Um...I've never heard you talk about Broderick or anyone for that matter like this. Sounds serious. But I've got to tell you, I don't think it's a good idea. DeMarcus is dangerous."

Jackie tried to offset Trina's opinion of DeMarcus. "He's not that bad. It's just when he gets upset."

"Are you justifying his behavior?" Trina stood up and put her hands on her hips.

Jackie stood up and said, "No! No, I'm just saying there's more to DeMarcus than that. He has another side that's very calm and sweet."

"Are you serious? This is the same guy that beats Marissa until she is black and blue." Jackie gave Trina a look. Trina said, "Okay I give you this, he's fine. But Jackie, he's got some serious problems."

"I know. Don't worry, it'll never happen again."

"What are you talking about? I know you guys are attracted to each other, but um…" Trina shook her head as if it would never work.

Dissatisfied with Trina's response, Jackie now wished she'd never told her anything about her and DeMarcus. "Trina, let it go. I said it won't happen again."

"Okay cool, I won't say anything else, but matters of the heart are serious and that's a triangle that I wouldn't want to be in. What are we doing tonight? It's Saturday, time to party."

"Oh, I can't. I have to work." Then she started to plan on how she would get the other housemates out of the house in time for the party.

"What, you got a job? That's great, where do you work?"

"Ah…Well, I throw parties in different homes of clients."

"Oh, okay, parties for what? Don't tell me, you had to start selling beauty products?"

"Yeah…" Jackie didn't want to lie to her, but what else could she say. "But I don't want you to tell anyone."

"Oh, girl, don't worry, your secret's safe with me."

10

Jackie looked through all of her purses, hoping to find some money in one of them, but soon gave up. Tonight was it. It would be the last party for her. She planned to get the money and buy her books. If she ended up without enough, she would call her parents and ask for the rest. As soon as Ursula got to the house, she planned to tell her. Besides, they both had some time to think about how Nita hurt them. She was willing to bet that Ursula wanted out too.

Since Jackie didn't have any money for appetizers and drinks for the party tonight, she planned to ask Brittany to give her a loan. Hoping maybe Brittany would help her, she knocked on her door. Brittany answered wearing a black and pink Japanese robe with a matching scarf over her hair.

"Hey, what's up?" Brittany said after she yawned.

"Nothing much. What are you doing tonight?" Jackie hoped she had plans, so she didn't have to explain the party.

"Nothing, I'm exhausted I stayed up late working on my T bill for accounting. Somehow, I can't get my expenditures and revenues to add up right. I'm telling you; accounting is most disturbing."

"I'm sure." Jackie sat in the chair at Brittany's desk.

"Jax, is something wrong?" she asked after watching Jackie's strange behavior.

"No, I just have a lot on my mind. I got robbed last weekend."

"Bloody hell! Are you okay? What happened?"

"I took a cab to...ah downtown and when I got out, I gave the cabbie twenty dollars, and he took it and drove off."

"Oh my God! Did you call the police?"

"Unfortunately...yes." As she thought about the events that happened after the police arrived. "But I haven't heard anything yet."

"What do you mean?" Brittany looked puzzled. "Did you give them the cab company and the cab number? They'll track him down and arrest him."

"Yeah, but in the meantime, I don't have any money. I managed to make it through this week on my groceries, but that was my last twenty dollars."

"You know, I don't believe in lending friends' money, but this is a most unusual and dire situation. How much do you think you need?" She opened her brown and tan Coach bag and pulled out the matching Coach wallet. Will two hundred dollars do until you get your allowance for the month?"

"Oh Brit, yes! Thank you!" Jackie hugged her friend for dear life, because she felt like she had saved hers. "Thanks so much!"

Brittany pushed Jackie away and said, "Okay, okay. Now remember it's a loan, and I want it back."

"As soon as I can, I will pay you back. I promise. I have a job." Jackie stared at the two bills.

"You do? That's great! Where?"

"Well, it's kind of selling...well I'd rather not say. I don't want anyone to know."

"Oh, no problem. Did you have to take that job selling beauty products?"

Jackie dropped her head in response. She hated lying to both of her best friends.

"Don't worry, Jax, I won't tell anyone. Besides, it's temporary, just until you get your book money, and you'll have that in no time.

Then you can quit the beauty business, and no one will ever know."

"Thanks. I'm having a party here tonight, so I'd appreciate if you could stay in your room."

"Oh, the last place I want to be is at a cheap beauty product party." Brittany looked at Jackie. "Ah, bloody hell, I'm sorry, that didn't come out right. You know what I mean, but I can't be seen at one of those parties. Old women arguing over lipstick and all."

Jackie dove deeper into her lie said, "No, it's okay. It's embarrassing, but I have to do what I have to do."

"You'll be alright."

"Well, I guess I better go and get ready for my party. Thanks again."

Jackie closed the door and held the money in her hands breathing a sigh of relief. She went back to her room and placed the money in her pocketbook. She then headed up to Lindsey's room and knocked on the door, but there was no answer. Jackie wondered where she was and when she would be back. In the meantime, she decided to go out and get the stuff she needed for the party. She spent $185 at the restaurant and the liquor store. At the grocery store, she spent $15 on ramen noodles, tuna, bread, and lunchmeat for herself, after which she had no money left. Everything was all set—the food, the alcohol, the music, and Ursula was bringing the cocaine. Jackie wondered who would show up and how much she would make. Well, whatever she made, it would be more than what she had.

Now, just as she got to her room and was about to freshen up, Bijon knocked on the door and said, "Jackie, can I come in for a quick minute?"

She opened the door, irritated that he'd come up to her room. She turned around leaving the door open and sat down on her bed. In a sarcastic tone she said, "What is it?"

Bijon had never been to Jackie's room. "Look, I wouldn't come to you unless I had no other choice." He paused and whispered, "I need a favor. Can you talk to your parents? My rent is going to be a little late this month. My mother had an operation two months ago, and the insurance isn't covering all of it. So, my dad had to borrow some money from me to make one of the payments, which will make my rent a little late. I've never been late before, so I'm hoping that your parents will cut me a little slack."

"Oh, okay. I'll let them know." Jackie's attitude changed and she said, "I'm sorry about your mom. How's she doing?"

"She is much better now, but I don't want to lose my housing. It took me a long time to find housing, and I can't afford to pay another first and last month's rent."

"Oh, don't worry. I will call them now. When do you think you'll have the rent?"

"No later than the end of next week."

Jackie paused and said, "Tell you what, why don't you give me the money, and I'll take care of everything with my parents. Don't forget to add the late fee." Her parents taught her one thing about business. It was still business, even if you were helping a friend.

Bijon looked at Jackie in a strange way, "Okay...so bring it to you instead of sending it to your parents?"

"Yes."

"Alright, I appreciate this."

Jackie said, "No problem."

Bijon left her room, then went downstairs and out the front door for a quick run.

By the end of next week, Jackie would have all of the money she needed to buy her last book, and some left to save. She would call her parents and tell them that Bijon and his family had fallen on hard times, and he wouldn't be able to pay the rent for the month. It was the perfect solution to her money issues. Now she could have this party and have extra money for emergencies. Then, she would be done with Ursula, Nita, and the coke parties.

Before she could call her parents, the doorbell rang, and Jackie rushed down the stairs to answer it. It was Ursula.

"Ursula, we need to talk."

Ursula walked past her on her way to the dining room with a bag in one arm and a briefcase in the other.

"No, we don't. We need to get ready for the party," she responded.

Jackie followed her and could tell from her tone that she was still upset about last weekend. "Ursula, this whole thing isn't for me. I can't do any more parties after tonight."

She twisted her head around and gave the impression that she knew something Jackie didn't. "What do you mean you can't do anymore parties?" She laughed and shook her head. "You must be crazy. You can't stop. Once you're in, you're in."

"No, I'm not in. This is my first party, and this is it for me. I'll do the party tonight and then I'm out."

Ursula set the coke down on the buffet table. She grabbed a cracker with smoked salmon and cream cheese on it and took a bite. "You should have thought about that before you attended the business meeting. Now you know how the business works; Nita will never let you out. But she'll be stopping by after the party, so feel free to discuss it with her."

"What! Why is she coming here tonight?" Jackie panicked. "Is she going to do something to me? I'm calling the cops." She walked toward the phone and Ursula grabbed her arm to stop her.

"You don't want to do that. Relax, she felt like you misunderstood her last week, and she wants to set things straight."

"Oh no, there was no misunderstanding. She was quite clear. You don't have a problem with what she did to us?"

"Jackie, that's the first time that I've ever had a problem with Nita. She treats me more like her daughter than her employee. That was, until you came along." Ursula rolled her eyes at Jackie and shook her head as if Jackie disgusted her. "I suggest that you listen to what she has to say. Oh, and I wouldn't mention the fact that you don't want to do anymore parties."

The doorbell rang again, but Jackie didn't move to answer it because she couldn't believe what Ursula was saying. Ursula answered the door as the guests arrived one by one. Many of them mingled with each other around the buffet table where the appetizers were. Ursula poured rum and coke in a cup and took a sip.

Jackie leaned over and whispered in her ear, "Ursula, I thought we couldn't drink hard liquor at the parties." She was surprised to see her break one of Nita's rules.

She glanced at Jackie and said, "We can't. But who's going to tell?"

"I guess no one." Jackie poured herself a drink and Ursula snatched it out of her hand.

"I said we can't. That means you can't."

Jackie stared at Ursula and walked away, ticked off that she was treating her like this.

Ursula opened the product, laid it on the mirror, and cut it with a razor blade. Before long, the party had started, and everyone was enjoying themselves mingling with one another. Most of them already knew one another so Jackie's part was easy; it was as if the coke sold itself.

Ursula introduced Jackie to the clients and told her what they did. She pointed out three military colonels. They walked in kind of stiff-necked, which made Jackie think they might have been at the wrong party. But once they snorted a line, they saluted each other and laughed until they were crying. One of them was cute and he flirted with Jackie by complimenting her on the house and the party. It made her feel good, so she smiled at him.

A very tall and exotic looking young lady stood in the corner. Jackie initiated a conversation with her while admiring her outfit and wondering who the designer was. She later found out the woman modeled and worked for Nita as well.

Jackie was introduced to a couple of pro football players at the buffet table. They drank and snorted coke like they have been doing it all their lives. In fact, they were the first ones to start snorting the coke. Jackie talked with them for a little while and discovered they were linebackers. One of them offered her two tickets to their next game, and she took them. That's cool, two tickets from professional football players. Jackie thought, *Broderick would love this*. The other football player had Ursula on his lap. The rum and coke must have gone to her head.

Next, Jackie saw the owner of a global architecture company who asked her a million questions about the row house. What year was it built? Did she know much about the builder? He asked about all sorts of masonry stuff that she didn't know about, nor did she care to know. He introduced Jackie to his assistant who he was sleeping with, because she spent most of the night curled up in his lap kissing him after her lines. Jackie looked at his finger and saw that he was wearing a wedding ring, but his assistant's finger was bare. Jackie mentioned to them twice that they may need to leave and get a room.

Ursula was cool with it, because she already had their money.

Sitting on the couch near the door were two lawyers from a multi-million-dollar law firm. Both were dressed in Armani suits and were very quiet at first. But after their first line, they each came alive. One seemed cool, but a little weird. He snorted and sat by himself in a daze. The other recited arguments for court cases and told Jackie about the millions they made from a case this week.

Jackie was amazed at how cocaine affected everyone. For some people, it made them very mellow, like they were thousands of miles away in some far away land. And for others, it made them less serious and full of laughter. Yet for some, it caused them to talk about every-thing—their life, their dreams, their deepest darkest secrets, and even fantasies. You name it, and they said it. The lawyers told Jackie if she ever needed any legal advice to let them know, and they would represent her "pro bono." Of course, Jackie didn't know what that meant.

She stood back and watched the party. Part of her felt bad about having the party, even though everyone was so nice to her. Some of them told her they were her friends for life. Jackie thought it was kind of cool, since a few of them offered her perks. This was a completely new life for her. She now had a bunch of new friends, which she never had before.

Jackie mingled with all her guests, but some wanted to be left alone to enjoy their high. She was cool with that, because it was less work on her, if she didn't have to mingle with people she didn't know.

One of the well-known jazz musicians kept asking her if she knew whether Snoopy the dog from Charlie Brown was dead. She reas-sured him that she didn't think so, but he wanted her to ask around and find out if anyone knew. Jackie thought that maybe he didn't need to get high anymore.

She asked Ursula about him, and she said, "He always says weird stuff when he's high. Just ignore him. The high will wear off, and he will be normal again."

While the jazz musician worried about Snoopy, his friend spent all his time singing a melody that was in his head. He was singing so loud that Jackie turned the music up to drown him out.

Jackie saw a nicely dressed lady standing near the alcohol and went over to meet her. She could tell the lady didn't want to talk about what she did, so Jackie didn't push the issue. After she snorted her first line, she gave Jackie a fifty-dollar tip. Surprised by the gesture, Jackie took it, unaware that they could get tips. Ursula immediately snatched it out of her hand. That's the second thing today that she had snatched from her, and it pissed Jackie off.

"Ursula, why did you do that? She is giving me a tip."

"Again, Jackie, she is not tipping you, she is tipping me."

"Okay, then why is she tipping you?"

"Because she is a franchise owner of a chain of restaurants around the world and feels that it's very important to tip for good service."

"Oh, so does she tip after each line?" Jackie got excited and thought she could really get paid if she did.

"Yes, she does."

"So that's an extra two hundred dollars." Jackie stated.

"No, that's an extra two hundred dollars for me."

The more Jackie listened to Ursula the more she disliked her. Jackie said she was sorry about last weekend, but this was going too far.

"How do you figure that, if I'm throwing the party in my house?"

"I figure that this is the least you can do for me after last week."

"Ursula, you made three thousand dollars last weekend and twelve hundred was mine, but you didn't give me any of it. And I worked the party just like you. Since I didn't get paid, I thought that was the least that I could do for you."

"Well, you thought wrong," Ursula said as she stuffed the fifty-dollar bill in her pocket.

"Oh, so I'm not getting paid tonight either? If that's the case, everyone can leave right now."

"Don't be stupid, Jackie. I'm sure Nita wouldn't like that. You'll get your money tonight."

"So, does Nita know about this extra tip money?" Jackie asked, curious about what else Ursula kept from Nita.

Ursula pulled Jackie into the kitchen, raised her voice, and pointed her finger in her face. "Look, you work for me! Don't ever question me on how I pay you or what Nita knows or doesn't know. Besides, if I were you, I wouldn't be in Nita's face talking about anything that she didn't bring up to you. You aren't on her good side." Ursula shoved Jackie toward the kitchen door and said, "Now, go and mingle with your guests, like a good little hostess."

Jackie rolled her eyes and walked away. She knew she was going to have to watch Ursula. She was not giving Jackie her cut of the money and she couldn't be trusted.

Nita arrived at the house after one o'clock in the morning. All the guests were gone except for the two lawyers. They were having their last drink. Overall, the party was a success; everyone enjoyed themselves. The guests asked her to place them on her list, but she wasn't planning to have another party, even though she had to admit, they were a lot of fun.

Nita came over to Jackie and said, "Why don't we sit down here and have a little chat." She pointed to the sofa and Jackie followed her but sat as far away from her as possible. She didn't want anything to do with Nita after their last encounter.

"Now, I know things got a little heated last week, but I want you to know that I realize this is all new to you. You're still getting comfortable with your new job responsibilities."

Jackie listened as Nita talked in her proper voice again, acting like this was a real job. If Jackie didn't know any better, she would think that it was.

She declared, "You have to think smarter. After all, you're a businesswoman. If you think about it, it's like having your own business. And I'm sure you understand why the police can't ever be involved."

Jackie felt a large lump in her throat, not knowing if she was able to speak, but said, "Uh...Nita, about that...I wanted to talk with you too. I don't think I'm cut out for this kind of work. I think tonight should be my last party."

Nita looked surprised, adjusted her skirt, and dusted the imaginary lint off her jacket. "Well, I had no idea you were so unhappy with our little business arrangement. What is the problem? Is Ursula not helping you?"

"Oh no, Ursula's great," Jackie lied because she didn't need any more problems with Ursula.

"Then, what's the problem? Please," she put her hand on Jackie's leg, "you can talk to me." Nita seemed sincere, almost caring, but Jackie remembered what she did to her last Saturday. She was the personification of evil, so she wasn't fooled by Nita's fake compassion.

Not wanting to look at Nita, Jackie put her head down.

"I don't like it. I'm afraid I will mess up again." She looked up at Nita and said, "It's just not for me."

Again, Nita adjusted her clothes.

Jackie wished she'd stop doing that because it made her nervous.

"I see," Nita said, dissatisfied with Jackie's response. "You do realize that you don't get to make the decision to leave or to stay, right? You see dear, once you work for me, I make the decisions about the future of your employment, not you, and I'm not ready to release you yet. Besides, we wouldn't want an anonymous note to reach the university president about one of the students named Jackie Jones and her coke parties. Last I checked, Karrington has zero tolerance for drugs." Nita stood, picked up her purse, and walked to the door. "I'm glad we had this little chat." She turned and smiled at Jackie. "Now, we understand each other, right?"

"Nita, please, I'm begging you. Please, I don't want to do this anymore."

"Jackie, I don't care. Now, Ursula will have your next assignment to you soon. And remember, Karrington is a very prestigious university. I'm sure they won't mind making an example of one student to send a message to the rest of the student body." She smiled and said, "Have a wonderful evening," as she walked out the door.

Nita walked to her black Jaguar and drove off.

Jackie stood in the doorway, amazed by how mean and evil Nita was. Ursula walked behind her and said in an upbeat tone, "Told you so," and handed her the money she made for the evening— $800.

From that night on, Jackie had coke parties at her parents' house twice a month, and sometimes, she helped Ursula and the other reps host their parties. Her parties grew and so did her list of clientele. Before she knew it, she made a lot of money in a short amount of time.

Jackie hosted as least twenty-six parties for the school year. She averaged between $1000 to $1200 a party totaling over $26,000 in earnings all from working a part-time job. She put it all in a safety deposit box at the bank, because she didn't want anyone to see the money and question why a college student would have so much cash. It was sad to say, but more than half of her entire sophomore year was spent dealing drugs and sneaking to the bank to deposit her cash. She bought her last two books for State and Local Government I, but she didn't buy anything else. She didn't get a chance to spend a lot of time with her new boyfriend either.

Jackie couldn't wait for summer. Nita never made any of the college reps stay over the summer unless they wanted to. She saw it as an unpaid vacation for those who wanted to take it. Jackie wanted to get as far away from the row house as possible. She also wanted to get far away from Nita and Ursula, because they reminded her of what she was becoming—them, drug dealers.

PART II

JUNIOR YEAR

11

Lindsey was sorting her laundry in the basement when Bijon came down the stairs with a basket of dirty shirts under his arm. He saw her, turned around, and went back upstairs, but not before Lindsey stopped him to ask a question.

"Bijon?"

"What?" he asked mid-way up the stairs, surprised that she was saying anything to him, because they haven't spoken in two months.

"How long have you and your family been in America?"

"Are you serious?"

"I just wondered what made you move to America."

"I was born in America," he said in a matter-of-fact tone.

"Oh, so you are here legally?" she said, "I didn't know."

Amazed at her ignorance and upset by the insult, he said, "Yes, I am."

"I thought maybe you were here on a Visa or green card."

Bijon shook his head. "You've got some nerve asking me that. I don't have a Visa or a green card. I am a US citizen, just like you."

"So do you plan to stay here once you graduate or are you planning on going back home?"

"Lindsey, are you deaf? I just told you I was born in the US. This is my home. Are you really that racist?"

"Look, you don't have to be ugly. I just know a lot of terrorists come over here, get an education, and use it against us."

"Did you just call me a terrorist?" He threw his arms up and said, "Conversation over. I liked you better when you weren't talking to me." He continued up the basement stairs.

Lindsey yelled, "I'm just asking, I wasn't calling you a terrorist!"

Bijon went to his room and called his friend to vent about Lindsey.

"You're right. I don't know why I'm letting that bitch bother me." He paused listening to his friend's helpful advice and longing sentiment. "Yeah, I miss you too." He pondered the request. "Tonight? Uh, I don't know. Lindsey's so damn nosey it's unreal. I really don't want her in my business." He paused and then said, "Yeah, I know. Okay, come over after midnight. Call me first, and don't ring the doorbell."

He ended the call and put his running shoes on. Running helped clear his head and made him feel better about life. He hoped that running would help him cope with Lindsey's narrow-mindedness.

Ursula called Jackie to get her flight information so she could pick her up at the airport. Jackie heard her voice and dreaded seeing her. Being back at home in Dallas with her family and away from the hustle and bustle of D.C. warmed Jackie's heart and allowed her to breathe. She had a great summer working at her parents' company, and for the first time she didn't complain because she was happy to be doing something legal. But just hearing the sound of Ursula's voice made her feel as if her airway was being restricted. She hated to leave, but she knew she had no other choice.

Last year, Jackie did what she was told, but she felt so bad lying to everyone. She knew that this year something had to give, but she didn't know what to do.

Jackie flew into Washington D.C.'s Dulles International Airport for her junior year at Karrington and saw a man and woman hug and kiss for what seemed like an eternity. She heard him say, "I missed you so much." Next, she watched a little boy smiling as he ran toward his father screaming, "Daddy, Daddy," and jumped into his father's arms.

Jackie continued her walk toward baggage claim to collect her bags. She then heard someone call out, "Hey, Jackie, over here." Looking around, she saw that it was Ursula motioning her over to where she was. At this point, Jackie realized the ease of the summer break was over.

Hesitant to move, Jackie's steps were slow and deliberate, like an inmate on death row, walking to their final doom. She offered Ursula a somber, "Hi."

"What's wrong? You didn't have a good summer vacation?"

"No, I had a great summer." Jackie halfway smiled, but thought, *I just don't like coming back to you and Nita.*

"Uh... looks like somebody got a tan. I like it."

Jackie replied, "I'll be lucky if it lasts until October."

"And what did you do to your hair?"

"I cut it. I needed a new hairstyle."

"Okay, I don't get you. Why are you always trying to change the way you look?"

"Whatever," Jackie said. Obviously, Ursula didn't understand. She was Puerto Rican, and everyone could see that, but that was not how it was for Jackie.

Ursula changed the subject and smiled. "I've got good news. You got a promotion. Now you're a senior rep, and you know what that means. You'll get to have one VIP party a month at the penthouse."

Jackie's face fell. She walked back over to baggage claim and yanked her bags off the belt.

Ursula watched Jackie and shrugged her shoulders. They then walked to the exit, crossed the street, and entered the parking garage in silence.

Jackie raised her voice, "Ursula, you know I don't want a promotion! I want out of this business. Why would you let Nita do that?"

"I can't tell Nita what to do, you know that."

"You could have persuaded her that it was a bad idea, just like you told her I would be good at this."

Ursula rolled her eyes and popped her gum. "Well, you might as well forget about that, because what's done is done."

Ursula pointed to her car in the second row and said, "I parked over there."

They got in Ursula's three series black BMW, and she told Jackie all about her summer, how much money she made from her coke parties, and how well her reps that stayed for the summer did.

Jackie didn't say anything; she just listened and stared out of the car window wondering if any of this would ever end. She heard a siren, saw an ambulance rush up Georgia Avenue to an emergency, and thought, *It's probably a drive by.* They drove into Jackie's neighborhood where all the houses were three stories with brown lawns. In Dallas everything was different—big houses, big yards, big everything. She thought about her yard at home, where her chocolate Labrador Retriever, Pixie, had plenty of room to run and play in the lush green grass. She missed her already. She had never seen anyone in D.C. with a dog.

Ursula interrupted her thoughts by asking, "Hey, are you listening?"

Jackie said, "What?" The interruption disturbed her cozy thoughts of home, which ticked her off.

After a stint of awkward silence and the agitated frown on Ursula's face, Jackie tried to make peace and change the subject from drug dealing to something much lighter. She asked, "Hey, do people in D.C. have dogs? I've never seen a dog here."

Ursula smiled and said, "No. Are you serious? People are trying to feed themselves. Nobody has money for a dog. Listen, I need to tell you this before I forget. Nita's called a back-to- school meeting for next Saturday night at seven o'clock at the Manchester Isis Hotel. It's mandatory that everyone attend."

Jackie sat in silence but thought, *Hell, as if I want to go to that. Thank God these meetings are only once a quarter.*

They finally reached the row house. Jackie got out, took her bags, and closed Ursula's car door. As she began to walk up the stairs, Ursula pushed a button to roll her window down and yelled, "Uh... you're welcome for the ride," then she drove off.

Ursula can kiss my ass. They used to be tight, but things had changed. Mainly, Jackie had changed.

She unlocked the door, dropped her bags, and plopped down on the couch. Quiet and peaceful, she sat alone in the house. She remembered her fun summer. Her mom cooked almost every night. Jackson and Jarrett came over to the house, just like old times. Her parents told her how proud they were of her and how she handled her sophomore year, but if they only knew. Jackie put it out of her mind, not wanting to think about her parents finding out about her secret life.

Over the next week, she listened as her housemate's shared stories about their great summer vacations. She went to all her classes, but felt out of touch, like the world was passing her by. Nothing seemed to excite her. She still wasn't sure what she was going to do. On the one hand, she felt like she couldn't keep having the parties. On the other hand, maybe she could, if she could learn to enjoy and embrace the parties like Ursula did, since it was only temporary, and she didn't plan to live in D.C. after college. Moreover, Jackie had to admit there were some inherent benefits. The coke parties made her feel powerful and in control, plus for once in her life, she had more friends than she ever had before.

Around nine o'clock that night, she heard a gentle knock on her door. She opened it, and it was DeMarcus leaning against the inside of the door studying her from head to toe with seductive and inviting brown eyes.

"Hey, gorgeous." He stepped in like he was supposed to be there and closed the door.

Jackie put her hand forward and objected, but he kissed her on her neck and said, "I've missed you so much. I thought about you all summer."

Jackie enjoyed his kisses, her hand fell, and she asked, "Then why didn't you call?"

"You know me. I was working."

Jackie laughed a little as he moved in and grabbed her around her waist. It was hard for her to resist DeMarcus. His touch made her feel so good.

She turned away from him and sat on the bed. "DeMarcus, we need to stop this. You have a girlfriend, and I have a boyfriend." At least, she hoped she had a boyfriend. She and Broderick never spent a lot of time together last year. They saw each other off and on because of her work schedule. She hoped they could have a real relationship this year.

"Yeah and...haven't you heard of friends with benefits? That's what we have, a friendship, and some serious benefits." He gave her a mischievous smile and sat on the bed beside her.

"Yes, about that. Your girlfriend thinks you're being faithful and so does my boyfriend."

He nestled close to Jackie's neck and said, "I'm glad you brought that up. I think you should let him go. I don't like this sharing thing." He gave her a soft kiss on her lips.

"Uh...Whatever!" She pushed him away. "I'm not letting my boyfriend go for you."

He laughed while he took off his shirt. "I bet you will, once I put this on you."

"Ah...no." She scooted further away from him toward the head of the bed but noticed his sculptured body.

"Okay, how about I end it with Marissa, and you end it with what's his name," he said as he eyed her body and moved closer to her.

"DeMarcus King!" She couldn't believe him. "No, no. We have to stop this. We both know this is just about the sex."

"Come on, Jackie, that's what people do in college. They have sex. Let's just have fun and enjoy it."

DeMarcus got up and squatted on the floor. He took her socks off and gently massaged her feet. She loved when he did this. He then moved his hands underneath her night shirt and onto to her legs and thighs. And before she knew it, he had taken her to cloud nine once again. She loved his smooth chocolate skin. He had a way of making her forget about the outside world and her problems.

Jackie woke up around eleven-thirty to the sound of her phone ringing.

"Hello," she said, still groggy from her peaceful ecstasy.

"Hey, Jacqueline. Are you asleep?" Broderick asked in a quiet tone.

Jackie heard his voice, sat up in the bed, and looked over at DeMarcus lying beside her. "Ah. Hi, no, I'm good. How are you?"

The sound of the phone awoke DeMarcus too and he turned over facing Jackie. He watched Jackie squirm in the bed and then smiled listening to her conversation.

She motioned for him to remain quiet. He nodded, but instead started caressing her back and kissing her neck while she was trying to talk. Jackie could hardly control herself. She pushed DeMarcus away.

Broderick asked, "Is everything okay? You sound distracted."

"No, I was just watching a story on the news." With haste, Jackie scrambled to turn on the TV and increased the volume at the same time.

DeMarcus pulled her down by her shoulders and climbed on top of her, kissing her breasts. She pushed him as hard as she could, but she couldn't get him off. Part of her wanted to enjoy DeMarcus without alarming Broderick, but the other part wanted him to stop before he blew her cover.

"Well, I didn't mean to interrupt, I'm about to turn in myself. Call me when you wake up in the morning. I want to see you," Broderick said.

"I miss you too. And I'll call you. Have a good night."

Jackie hung up the phone and yelled, "What are you doing? I don't want him to find out."

DeMarcus said, "But I do."

He kissed her; at first, she hesitated, but then they made love again.

12

Jackie forgot to call Broderick, and it had been over a week since she heard from him. She was embarrassed and ashamed about being with DeMarcus. She was also afraid that he overheard DeMarcus the night he called. She wanted to hear his voice, so she dialed his number, and he picked up on the second ring.

"Hello."

Wow, he sounded so handsome. Jackie wasn't sure what to think about their relationship, especially with DeMarcus in the way.

"Hello," he said again.

"Oh, hi, Broderick. It's Jacqueline."

"Hey, how are you?" She could tell he was smiling and glad to hear from her.

"I'm doing okay. I was just thinking about you," she said as she smiled too.

"You know, I was thinking about you too."

"Really, what were you thinking?"

"Just wondering if you're going to have time to date me this year. We didn't see much of each other last year because you were always working."

"I know. I feel so bad. I'll have more time this year," Jackie said, lying because she knew she wouldn't have more time, in fact, she would probably have less.

"Then how about we go and have an early dinner today?"

"How early?"

"How about I pick you up in thirty minutes?"

She loved his spontaneity. He sounded like he couldn't wait to see her. Jackie was already thinking about what she was going to wear. She wanted to wear something sexy and cute, but nothing slutty. She debated whether she should show cleavage or not.

"I'll be ready." She rushed to her closet and tossed all sorts of clothes in the air in search of the perfect outfit. After pulling half of her clothes out of the closet, she found a cute little black Spiegel dress that crisscrossed in the back. She wanted to show a little skin. It fit tight around her waist and accentuated her behind. She crimped her hair with her large crimping iron. She used a lot of hair spray, because the texture of her hair wouldn't hold the crimp otherwise. Jackie spread the crimps apart, and it made her hair look shorter but wild. She examined herself in the mirror. Satisfied, she grabbed her black leather jacket and sprinted downstairs to wait for him.

Something about Broderick calmed her. It was like he was the exact opposite of Jackie. She loved how he was so sure of himself and deep down she hoped that by spending time with him some of that would rub off on her.

They went to a Jamaican restaurant in DuPont Circle called Fish, Wings, and Tings. It was a quaint spot that a lot of Karrington University students supported. The server came promptly with two glasses of water and gave them menus.

Broderick thanked the server, then asked for a few minutes to look over the menu.

He turned to Jackie and asked, "What's on your mind?"

"What do you mean?"

"You seem like you're a little anxious. What's going on?"

She thought it was romantic that he could read her so well. She liked that he cared enough to ask. Maybe he was the knight in shining armor that she had been waiting for.

"Well, I was thinking about the news last night. Did you see the story about the lady that overdosed, and her kids were found wandering the streets alone and hungry? It's so sad."

"Yeah, well, Jacqueline, anyone that gets themselves mixed up with drugs is sad. A lot of times we want to blame others, but sometimes we do things to ourselves that have nothing to do with anyone else." He took a drink of water.

Jackie nodded in agreement and said, "That's true."

She could tell he felt strongly because he continued talking. She didn't mind because she liked hearing his voice and watching his lips move.

The server came back with a basket of rolls. They ordered sodas and two Caribbean dinners.

"A lot of the time, we keep ourselves down. And the main reason is drugs, guns, and gangs. All three contribute to the decline of African Americans as a people and this great nation." Broderick put butter on a roll and took a bite.

Jackie watched him chew and thought about what he was saying.

The server brought their sodas.

Broderick said, "I'm sure our ancestors both in Africa and America are turning over in their graves. Look at how we have pissed away opportunities that they never had by selling, smoking, and snorting drugs."

Jackie sipped her soda, not knowing what to say to him. She hadn't even thought about how their ancestors must feel. She thought, *this brother is deep.*

He took another sip and looked at her. "Jacqueline, have you ever tried drugs?"

Jackie coughed a little as her soda went down wrong. Her eyes wandered from side to side, and she said, "Uh... no." She lied again because she didn't want to the truth to come out, besides Jackie didn't really count marijuana as a drug.

She cleared her throat and said, "What about you?"

He said in a laid-back tone, "I tried marijuana back in high school, but that's it. And as soon as I figured out what a complete waste of time and money it was, I never tried it again. Besides, I don't need anything altering the chemicals in my brain. I'm not trying to be strung out on some drug for the rest of my life. I've got a plan for my future."

Jackie wanted to know more about his plan and if there was any room for her in his future. She said, "Really, what's your plan?"

"I'm going to develop my own law firm."

"Well, that sounds nice. My brother is a lawyer."

Broderick said, "See, I bet he couldn't have done that if he was high on drugs."

What Broderick didn't know was that Jackson did drugs during law school but cleaned up his act once their parents threatened to take him out of their will. Jackie didn't want to discourage Broderick, so she kept it to herself.

Jackie said, "Okay, but what about the people who do drugs just for fun? Look at some of the celebrities and athletes. Haven't you ever wanted to spice up a dull party with a little coke?"

Broderick frowned and his eyes narrowed in on Jacqueline.

She knew she had said too much.

He said, "Uh...No. Is that what you guys do in Dallas when a party is dull?"

Without hesitation, Jackie said, "Of course not, I'm just saying."

"Well, I hope not." He gave her a suspicious look, then continued to share more of his knowledge.

Jackie liked hearing him talk; however, the conversation was getting a little irritating.

Broderick went on, "Anyway, you show me a person that does drugs and thinks there's nothing wrong with it, and I'll show you a person who's fooling themselves. People like that will end up strung out, losing their life, and/or in jail. That quick temporary feeling is not worth all of that." He pointed at her. "That's a person who has no future and no purpose."

Jackie concentrated on every word, as he gave her a verbal dissertation on the victimization of African Americans on drugs. She said, "Okay...well, obviously you feel pretty strongly about it."

The server brought their food and asked, "Is there anything else I can get for you?"

Jackie said, "No, everything looks great. Thank you."

The server said, "Your eyes are so pretty."

Jackie said, "Thanks," and picked up her fork to try the brown rice.

The server stood there and then said, "Do you mind if I ask you a question?"

Jackie knew the question; it was always about her race. She dropped the fork back on her plate, and it made a loud clanking sound, as if she slammed it down. She glanced at Broderick, and he looked at her, using his eyes to try to encourage her to answer the question. Jackie thought, *he probably wants to know too.*

Unenthusiastic, Jackie said, "Sure."

The server asked, "What color are you? Well, I think I know, but what are you mixed with?"

With disgust in her tone, Jackie raised her voice and answered, "Frustration!"

The server said, "What?" Amazed at Jackie's rudeness, she walked away.

Broderick, upset at Jacqueline's response, said, "Why didn't you answer her question?"

Jackie said, "I did."

"No, you didn't."

Jackie was so tired of this question but felt bad about the way she acted. She called the server back over and said, "I'm sorry, I'm mixed with African American and Israeli."

With a guarded look, the server said, "Oh, that's different."

Jackie said in a gloomy tone, "I know." She looked down at her food. The jerk chicken smelled great. She cut it and took a bite. It had a little too much seasoning on it for her, but it was good. The jerk chicken sat next to a mound of brown rice and gooey looking plantains. Jackie didn't touch the plantains.

The server left to take another order two tables over.

"What's up with you? Why are you so touchy? She complimented you and you got an attitude. In fact, the minute we started talking about drugs you got an attitude. What's your problem?"

"I didn't get an attitude. I called her back and said I was sorry. Aren't you happy?" Anger set in and Jackie asked, "Can we talk about something else, please?"

"Sure, we can. So why don't you think doing drugs is wrong?"

"I didn't say doing drugs was okay." Jackie couldn't believe that he was pushing all her buttons, trying to make her angry.

"You didn't say it was wrong, so I assume you think it's okay."

"Are you listening to me? I'm just saying some people do it for fun."

"I got that, but I don't think you see how drugs are killing our people. Instead of our children having role models like lawyers and scientists, their role models are the neighborhood drug dealer, pimp, or gangbanger. Black on black crime is real, and drugs do nothing but perpetuate that travesty."

"Okay, didn't I bring up the lady that overdosed and how sad that was? If people want to do drugs for fun, I don't see anything wrong with that." Jackie sighed and changed the subject, "How's your jerk chicken?"

"It's fine. How's your moral compass?" he asked.

"What? Look, of course I see a problem with drugs. I just know that some people use them, and they don't see anything wrong with it. And, I guess I hadn't really thought about it that deeply."

"Well, Jacqueline, if you are going to be my girlfriend, you've got to look at the whole picture, not just a few details here and there."

A long pause filled the air and the space between them, as it registered that he called her his girlfriend. So now, they were officially an item. Sure, they went out some last year, but nothing like this. She'd been calling him her boyfriend, but now it was official.

"Jacqueline, did you hear me?"

"Yeah...I guess I got caught up on the girlfriend part."

He smiled and laughed a little; Jackie did too. He looked at her and caressed her hand.

She pleaded, "Broderick, I didn't come here to fight or to discuss the social ills of our society. I came here to spend time with you. So can we just do that?"

"I guess we can for now, but I do want to talk more about this." He reached for both of her hands and held them across the table. It was like no one else was in the room, just Jacqueline and Broderick. It felt like a romance novel.

He said, "Well, we both know that we like each other. Last year we didn't have a chance to really date as much as I would have liked, but I think this year is different for us. I'm not into dating a whole bunch of women. Let's just date each other and see what happens. You game?"

Jackie was still caught up on him grabbing her hands and holding them. She looked at him and said, "Definitely."

Jackie couldn't believe it. She actually had a boyfriend.

13

Jackie heard the doorbell ring. She went downstairs to answer the door, but first peeped through the peephole. It was Marissa standing with her arm in a sling wearing sunglasses and a scarf.

The door creaked as she opened it. "Hi Marissa. Is everything alright?" Jackie said, focusing on the sling Marissa's arm was resting in.

"Yes, I'm fine," Marissa responded. She walked in and sat on the couch, placing her bag on the floor, like she always did when she waited for DeMarcus.

Jackie's mind reverted to all the time she spent with DeMarcus. If Marissa only knew what she and DeMarcus had done on that very same couch, she would never sit there again. There was a long pause of silence between them, mainly because Jackie tried to get the image of her and DeMarcus out of her head.

Jackie broke the silence and asked, "I'm not trying to get into your business, but why do you keep letting him use you like a punching bag?"

Marissa sighed. "Jackie, I really don't want to talk about this. You have to understand, DeMarcus loves me. He's just under a lot of pressure. It's his senior year. He has to make some decisions as to whether to continue at Karrington for graduate school or get a job. He's stressed out because he's not sure what he's going to do."

Jackie couldn't believe Marissa was making excuses for getting her ass beat. She felt sorry for her and wondered when she was going to ever wake up. Jackie shook her head as she admitted, *I'm weak but Marissa takes the cake.*

"Okay, but what about my freshman year and, more importantly, last year? Just about every time I came by to visit Jarrett, I heard him yelling and beating you."

Marissa dismissed her argument by waving her hand and sighed. "Jackie, you're young. Relationships are difficult. They're not happy-happy all the time. DeMarcus and I have been together three years. Every relationship has its ups and downs." She lowered her head and sighed again. "He's had a rough childhood. No one can expect him to be perfect. You don't know DeMarcus like I do."

Jackie thought, *I know DeMarcus well, especially every inch of his chiseled body.*

"So, are you saying that if someone had a bad childhood, it's okay for them to beat their girlfriend?"

Marissa exhaled hard and shook her head. "Have you ever been in a relationship before?"

Jackie thought, *What nerve! What does that have to do with anything? I was only trying to help.* She then replied, "Not really, but I'm in one now."

"Well then, you know there are good days and bad days. The goal is to focus on the good days, because they always outweigh the bad ones. That's what I have to keep reminding myself."

"Maybe you're right, maybe that's why I haven't been in very many relationships."

Who did Jackie think she was kidding? She hadn't been in any relationship until now, but she knew they didn't start and stop with someone getting their butt kicked.

Marissa explained, "He doesn't mean to hurt me. He just gets frustrated and doesn't know how to channel his anger. And, when he does hit me, he apologizes and makes it up to me."

Jackie directed her attention to Marissa's arm. "Is your arm broken?"

"No, it's just a hairline fracture, nothing to be worried about." Marissa dug in her bag for a magazine. "Don't let me keep you. He should be here soon, so I'll just wait here and read this article."

Jackie guessed that was Marissa's way of telling her to go to her room because she didn't want to talk anymore. She looked at her with concern, but wondered what it was about DeMarcus that made her keep letting him abuse her.

Sure, he was six feet tall and had milk chocolate brown skin, hypnotic ebony eyes, and teeth that sparkled like white pearls. Jackie beamed as she envisioned him. His smile lit up the room and then there was his hair. Black coarse dreadlocks fell beautifully below his shoulder with a small white shell attached to the end of one dread. She loved it when he pulled part of his hair back into a ponytail and let the rest hang down. It was so badass sexy.

What could Jackie say? The same things that caused her to sleep with him probably caused Marissa to ignore his cruelty. She felt like such a hypocrite.

"Jackie, really, I'm fine, don't worry. He's on his way. I'll wait here."

Jackie snapped out of her trance and said, "Okay." She went upstairs to her room and thought to herself, *He's fine, but not that fine.* The beatings crossed the line.

Jackie heard the front door open, and it was DeMarcus, so she walked back down and stopped halfway on the stairs to listen to their conversation.

"Hi, Marissa. I missed you so much. Come here. How are you?" DeMarcus walked in and rushed to her.

"I'm fine," Marissa said.

"I'm so sorry, I got so upset." He looked at her arm.

Marissa touched his face and said, "Don't worry, it's okay."

He was so persuasive. Jackie looked down from the second-floor stairs and could see his desperation. He hugged Marissa with such intensity, careful not to touch her arm. He planted a soft kiss on her cheek as if a couple of nights ago never happened, and she melted in his arms. Jackie melted too as she imagined herself in Marissa's shoes, feeling the coolness of his lips on hers. He had a certain *je ne sais quoi* about him that she couldn't resist.

But his face had regret written all over it. "I need you so much. I feel so drained when you're not here." He looked past her and shook his head. "This is all my fault. I hate when we fight. Please forgive me."

She held his face in her hands and said, "I do forgive you."

He looked deep in her eyes and in the most tranquil voice asked, "How are you, really?"

Marissa responded, "I'm fine, now that you're here."

Jackie watched him soak up every fiber of Marissa's being with his eyes. He took in each word from her mouth as if it were a flower about to bloom and he didn't want to miss any part of its creation. He was sensual, even when he was begging for forgiveness.

"Marissa, I can't say how sorry I am. Really, I mean it this time. I'll do anything for you, just tell me that you love me and you won't leave me."

Marissa wiped her tears away and said, "I'll never leave you. I love you with all my heart. I don't care what happens, I'll always love you, and I'll never leave you."

Again, he hugged her as if his life depended on it.

Jackie had never seen this kind of passion between them before. Maybe he was sorry.

Out of the corner of his eye, DeMarcus saw Jackie staring at him and released his embrace.

"Oh. Hi, Jackie."

Jackie nodded at him.

"Marissa let's go upstairs so we could talk. Do you want something to eat or drink? How about we go out to dinner tonight?"

"No, DeMarcus, I'm not hungry. I'm fine, really. I just love you so much." She proceeded up the stairs with DeMarcus behind her.

They passed Jackie on the stairwell. He reached out and squeezed

Jackie's behind and smiled like a sneaky snake. Jackie moved away from him. She couldn't believe that he was doing that when Marissa was just a couple of steps in front of him. All the flirting and sleeping together had to stop. She had a real boyfriend now, and she was not going to mess it up with DeMarcus.

But she was kidding herself, because she was into DeMarcus. Something about him drew her, almost the same way she was drawn to Broderick, but different.

Jackie couldn't resist feeling good about herself. DeMarcus liked her and Broderick liked her too. She knew it was wrong, but it felt good to be wanted by two men.

14

___

LaJuana rose early Saturday morning to go to the supermarket. She put on a pair of no- name faded jeans that were so tight that they looked like she pushed a watermelon into a pair of panty hose. She pulled a pink fuzzy sweater over her head; it was one of several her grandmother bought at the swap meet.

LaJuana went into the kitchen, emptied DeMarcus' box of cereal into a bowl, and poured Lindsey's milk over it. She rushed back to her room before anyone could see. She didn't feel bad about eating her housemate's food. After all, they could afford it, and she couldn't.

She performed the same ritual every day and every night. She got up before everyone else and scouted for food in the fridge. Late at night, she went back for any goodies left by her housemates. But she never ate Bijon's food, first because she didn't like Indian food, and second, he never had any. However, if he did, she wouldn't do that to him.

She finished her cereal and put pink lip-gloss on to match her top. She believed in natural beauty. She combed her short hair back and put on a white baseball cap. LaJuana looked in the mirror and hated the image that projected back at her. She was fat, and she was ugly. She needed to lose at least fifty pounds. Even turning to the side disgusted her because the mirror showed her bubble butt. Disappointed, LaJuana sighed and drooped down on her bed. She silently asked, *how am I going to catch Bijon's eye with the way I look?* She was not like the other Karrington girls. She didn't have the perfect figure for designer clothes, nor the money to get her hair done every week. She was just a plain, ordinary girl.

She decided a long time ago that everything her mother loved she would hate—drugs, alcohol, and black men. That's one of the things that drew her to Bijon; he was none of those things. He was Indian and nice to her.

She knocked on his door. "Hey, Bijon. It's me."

"Uh...just a minute." She heard Bijon fumble out of the bed as he sloshed across the floor.

When he got to the door, she heard him whisper, "Pull the covers over your head, and don't say anything."

Bijon opened the door and walked out, wearing blue and green pajama pants.

LaJuana wasn't expecting this little treat, she was surprised to see him without a shirt. He tried to close the door as quick as he opened it, but she peeked in and saw clothes and a crushed pizza box on the floor, an open Chinese food container on the desk, and a lump under the covers.

"Oh, I didn't know you had company," LaJuana said with her head hung low.

"Oh, that's alright." He rubbed his eyes. "What's up?"

"I'm just going to the store and wanted to know if you need anything."

"Naw, I'm cool. Thanks."

LaJuana, a little heartbroken said, "Alright," and walked away.

Bijon turned to go back into the room, but stopped and asked, "Hey, you, okay?"

"Yeah, I'm fine."

"There's something different about you today. You look nice." He smiled at her.

That was all LaJuana needed. She changed direction and walked back to face him. Tilting her head and batting her eyes, she hoped for a little more conversation. She grinned and said, "Thank you."

Bijon smirked a little, "Alright, I'll see you later." He went in the room and closed the door.

Little did Bijon know, his compliment made LaJuana's day. She liked him more than any of the other housemates, mainly because he didn't grow up with a silver spoon in his mouth. He had a simple life, like hers. However, LaJuana wanted a little more with him, other than sharing groceries. She wanted him to notice her, like a girlfriend, but she hadn't been able to turn his head, until today.

She skipped toward the front door, smiling because Bijon finally saw her beauty. She stopped and looked around the den. She still couldn't believe she lived here. It was so much nicer than her home in Lochearn. Her life in the row house made her feel like a princess in a castle. She opened the door, just as Lindsey put her key into the lock.

Lindsey walked in and said, "Hey, girl. Where are you off to so early in the morning?"

LaJuana said with sarcasm, "I could ask you the same question. Where are you coming from so early in the morning? But I won't, because I don't care."

"Whatever, you don't have to be so nasty all the time."

LaJuana sneered and closed the door behind her. She couldn't stand Lindsey. She reminded her too much of her own mother. Since Lindsey's twins didn't live with her and she didn't take care of them, LaJuana saw her as irresponsible and selfish. She harbored the same hatred and resentment against Lindsey that she harbored against her own mother, and she wanted nothing to do with either of them.

Lindsey walked into the kitchen and opened Brittany's cabinet. She stood there twisting her long, blonde locks trying to decide on her choice of alcohol for the day. Lindsey had been sneaking Brittany's alcohol for weeks. She poured herself a tall glass of rum and drank it slow, while walking up to her bedroom on the third floor. This would help her sleep the day and night away.

Lindsey thought about the guys she was sleeping with. None of them saw her for anything other than a piece of tail. Although she loved men, alcohol, and occasionally drugs, she was lonely. This fake life didn't drown out her longing to be with someone who valued and loved her. She acted like she didn't care, but inside she did. Sure, they brought her gifts, and some took her on trips, but it was always temporary. Lindsey put all of that out of her mind and chose to enjoy the ride while it lasted. She constantly repeated to herself, *they can't buy my love, but they can sure rent it.*

She unlocked her bedroom door, saw the light blinking on her answering machine, and pressed play. She heard the voice of her ex-husband saying that the twins wanted to come for a visit. Lindsey was so excited because she hadn't seen the twins in forever. She couldn't believe they wanted to see her. She didn't hesitate. She put the rum down and dialed his number.

Eager to talk to her children, Lindsey said, "Hello, Paul. It's Lindsey. Can I talk to the girls?"

He didn't sound happy to hear from her, so she paused before saying anything.

Lindsey repeated, "Hello."

Sounding cold and bothered he replied, "Yes."

"Well...I got your message about the girls wanting to come up for a visit."

"Yeah, about that, can you hold on?" he said.

"Yeah...okay," Lindsey said, not sure why his voice sounded so different from earlier on the answering machine.

She heard him close the door and pick up the phone. He snarled at her. "I only called you because the girls wanted me too. I didn't expect you to call back. In fact, I had hoped that you wouldn't."

Confused and a little angry, Lindsey said, "Well I did, and if they want to see me, I want to see them too. For God's sake, it's been almost three years. How long are you going to keep punishing me?"

He responded in a callous manner, "I know how long it's been.

You don't have to tell me. And no one is punishing you. When you left, you punished them."

"Look, I'm sorry. I've said that a hundred times. I don't want to play games. I just want to see my girls."

He said, "I really don't think that's a good idea. They have a lot of good role models in their life, and their grades are good." He paused and then sighed. "I don't want them seeing you and messing that up. I seem to remember that whatever you touch, you destroy. Look, I gotta go."

"Paul, please, please let me see them. I miss them so much." Tears formed in Lindsey's eyes and rolled down her cheek. "Can I see them, please?"

He screamed, "No!" And then whispered, "I've already told them that you didn't call back because you're too busy with your life."

And before Lindsey could say anything, she heard the dial tone on the other end of the phone. She called back several times, but there was no answer. She figured that he unplugged the phone. Lindsey picked up an old picture of the girls and pulled the frame to her chest, hugging it for dear life. Lindsey finished her rum, laid in her bed with the picture frame, and cried herself to sleep.

15

———

Jackie felt a chill in her room. She grabbed her robe and slippers before heading downstairs to turn up the heat. Once downstairs, she peeked out the window and caught a glimpse of snow falling on the D.C. streets. She seldom saw snow in Texas, so she opened the door and stepped onto the porch. It was a cold and balmy Sunday morning in late October. Her eyes took in the scenery as she absorbed the quietness and beauty of the snow. She looked up at the sky and closed her eyes; soft, cold snowflakes one by one landed on her face. She took a deep breath and inhaled the tranquility the snow brought as it fell. It was pure and peaceful, everything Jackie wanted in her life.

The flakes melted as soon as they fell, and the frostiness of the air made her body shiver. The wet, cold white flurries caused her face to become numb and her teeth to chatter. It was yet another reminder that her world was anything but pure and peaceful. Sighing at the mess she had created; she felt the stress of her life creeping in on the serenity she just experienced. Jackie rushed back inside, turned the heat up, and headed back up the stairs.

She grabbed the remote and flipped through the TV channels,

wondering about her existence. She was bored and didn't feel like studying. Her phone rang and she turned the TV down.

She answered, wondering who would call so early on a Sunday morning.

The voice on the other end of the line sounded somber. "Jackie, it's Mom. I've got some bad news."

Her heart dropped and she swallowed hard not knowing what her mom was going to say. "What's wrong?"

"Well, late last night, your Aunt Ruby died."

"What! What happened?" Jackie said in complete shock.

'Well, I don't know all of the details, but they think she OD'd on cocaine."

"What! Are you serious?" Jackie knew her dad's sister liked to party and have a good time, but she had no idea that Aunt Ruby was into drugs. Jackie didn't expect or need this blow, especially since she was selling the stuff herself.

"Mom, are you sure? I know she liked to drink a little, but drugs?"

"Jackie, you never know what people do in their private time. You think you know someone, and then you find out that you really don't. They do things right under your nose and you never know about it."

Jackie didn't move, she sat still, totally silent. Her mom's words cut to the core.

Her mother said, "Jackie, are you alright? I knew this would really hurt you, especially since she was your favorite aunt."

"No, I'm okay. I'm just surprised, that's all."

"Well, honey, we are all surprised by this."

"How's Daddy?"

"Daddy...well he's doing. He's still in shock, trying to figure out how something like this could have happened. We still don't know all the details, so pray for him. Ruby was found in her condo on the couch with lines of coke left on her coffee table."

It wasn't often that her mom told her to pray, so when she did, Jackie listened. Her Aunt Ruby had a wonderful life. She was a successful single woman who lived in Chicago and loved traveling all over the world.

Then, an even scarier thought popped into Jackie's head. *What if her aunt had shown up at one of her parties?*

"Honey, I know you are speechless. We haven't decided for sure when the funeral will be, but we are thinking about next Saturday. Do you want me to get you a plane ticket for Friday night?"

"Um..." She didn't want to go to the funeral because of the guilt. Besides that, Nita rescheduled the Back-to-School business meeting for that weekend, and Jackie had to attend, it was mandatory. Nita had already cancelled it several times because she was having issues with the supplier.

"No, Mom, I think it would be too much on me to come. Besides, I have a lot of studying that I need to do before next week." Which really wasn't a lie.

"Okay, sweetie, I understand. Oh, my other line is ringing. Jackie, let me call you back."

"Alright, Mom. Tell Daddy I'm really sorry."

"I will, dear."

Jackie sat on her bed trying to process the awful news. She loved her aunt and really looked up to her. Aunt Ruby enjoyed life to the fullest. Jackie's thoughts were interrupted by a voice in her head that said, *And maybe that's the problem.*

She dismissed the thought and aimed the remote at the TV. She turned the volume up and sat on her bed in a daze. She wondered if her aunt was going to coke parties. As a regional vice president for a technology company, she definitely hung out with many influential people. Was she someone's client?

Jackie remembered what Nita always said. "Coke parties are done in every state. They are the in-thing, and everyone with any sense is doing them and making money." Did Aunt Ruby have a coke rep?

So many unanswered questions flooded Jackie's mind, so much so, she couldn't keep up with all of them. Then she heard someone on the TV say, "Yes, of course there is social injustice in the war on drugs." She listened further and the anchor talked about the money that was being made by dealers at the expense of human lives and their families. The guest speaker said, "No one is immune, it affects all of us."

That was all Jackie could take. She picked up the remote and switched the TV off. She grabbed her clothes and went into the bathroom to take a shower, hoping to take her mind off her aunt, the TV news, and her life.

Jackie tried to enjoy the shower, but she couldn't. She turned the water off, dried her body, and put on her robe. She looked in the mirror at herself but heard the drip of the shower. She walked back over and tightened the knob, but the water continued. The sound of the constant dripping reminded her of all the lies she told. Drip... drip...drip...were the lies one by one falling from the faulty faucet. Too many to count and too many to catch. The sound made her nauseous. She turned the knob clockwise and then counterclockwise and back again, but it didn't stop. She walked back to the sink, clutched it, and hoped to stop the sound of all the lies running through her mind, but nothing helped.

16

Jackie had another rough week at school. She was behind in most of her classes and didn't see how she would catch up. Depressed and mourning her aunt's death, she skipped her Thursday and Friday classes, because she hadn't read the assignments and didn't feel like being embarrassed.

She went to Nita's meeting and hoped it would be short, so she could crawl back in her bed.

All the reps were excited to get together and brag about their quarters, especially those who had been working longer than a year. But the only thing Jackie could think about was her Aunt Ruby whose funeral was that same day.

Jackie looked around the room and saw some new reps that she had never seen before. Nita made the introductions of all the new reps and the areas of town they serviced. She informed the group that if things continued to progress in a positive direction, they would all have bigger Christmas bonuses than they had last year. Nita pointed to the gifts she had for each of her senior reps and managers and asked them to take two each.

After the meeting, Jackie walked up to Nita and asked to speak with her, albeit not in private. Jackie tried to be nice to Nita, even though she hated the sight of her.

Nita said in her most sophisticated voice, "Of course. Let's sit down at the bar." Nita picked up a plastic straw and chewed on it.

Jackie sat down beside her and took a deep breath. She began, still thinking about her Aunt Ruby. "Well, Nita, I know we talked about this before, but I was wondering since you have so many new reps that maybe you really don't need me anymore."

"Nonsense, of course I need you," Nita replied as she sipped on her Glenlivet Whisky.

Jackie lied to Nita, "Well it's just that my grades are getting really bad, and I don't want to lose my scholarship. I'm already on academic probation. I could really use the time to study instead of doing the parties."

One of Nita's managers brought her dinner to the bar and handed her a rolled white cloth containing her utensils. The plate had a healthy portion of seasoned prime rib, braised garlic shrimp, broccoli lightly drizzled with Hollandaise sauce, caramel-glazed carrots, and a slice of lemon along with a sprig of parsley for color.

"Ah...that's a shame. Perhaps you should spend more time studying when you are not working." She smiled. "Look, Jackie, everyone has time constraints. You just have to find a way to make it work." She patted Jackie on the back like a puppy, opened the white cloth, and picked up the knife and fork to cut the prime rib and took a bite.

Jackie thought to herself, *Nita is so pretentious. She speaks proper, wears designer clothes, eats fine foods, but none of that will ever change who she really is, a demon.* Jackie got a little frustrated just thinking about Nita and her greed. Without even realizing it, she raised her voice and said, "Nita, you're not listening. I want out!"

Nita's expression suddenly changed. She chewed her prime rib and used the napkin to dab her mouth before speaking. She turned to face Jackie and raised her steak knife to Jackie's throat. "Don't get it twisted; you work for me! Who do you think you're talking to?" Nita stuck the knife in just enough to break the skin causing blood to trickle out. "I'd like to hear an apology."

Startled and frightened by Nita's sudden aggression with the knife, Jackie squealed, not knowing what Nita was going to do next.

Nita pushed the knife in a little more, realizing that she needed to teach Jackie a lesson.

Jackie could feel the cold blade of the knife in her skin. Trickles of blood soon turned into a steady stream flowing down her neck.

"I'm sorry."

"I'm sorry, what?" Nita pressed the knife in.

"I'm sorry, ma'am for being disrespectful," Jackie said as she held back tears. She was afraid to move, thinking Nita could slit her throat at any moment.

"That's much better." She paused, "Jackie, do you know where the jugular vein is?" she said in her low ghetto tone as she kept the knife inserted into Jackie's skin.

Jackie said trembling, "No, ma'am."

Taking the knife out, Nita used its tip to scrape over the vein in Jackie's neck. She answered her own question, "It's right here. With one cut of this vein, you'll instantly die." Nita paused, letting this reality sink into Jackie's mind, and then she said, "Jackie, do you want to die today?"

By this time, everyone in the room watched them in silence.

Nita noticed all eyes were on her and glared at the managers. One of them redirected the reps and said, "Let's go over the future projections for next quarter while Nita finishes her conference with Jackie."

Jackie heard her and thought, *Conference, what the hell? She is threatening to kill me. How does that amount to a conference?* But she stayed still, trying to remain focused on the questions Nita asked.

"Jackie, I'm going to ask you again, do you want to die today?"

Quick to respond, Jackie cried out, "No, ma'am."

"Now let me make myself clear, I don't give a damn about your grades. All I care about is my money. But I'm starting to become concerned about your lack of loyalty to me. You've done a horrible job of showing me your appreciation."

Nita pulled the knife away from Jackie's neck, leaned closer so that she was eye to eye with her, and said, "There's no out. If you get out, you do so in a pine box. Do you understand?" She backed away and returned to her jovial self, proper accent and all.

Thankful, yet still afraid, Jackie responded, "Yes, ma'am," and began to cry.

"Ursula, come get your rep. Take her to the bathroom and clean up this mess." Ursula moved without hesitation and escorted Jackie from the bar.

Using the same bloodstained knife, Nita sliced another piece of prime rib and put it in her mouth. Nita yelled, "Ursula."

Ursula rushed back to the bar. "Yes, Nita."

"Tell Jackie that since she made my blood pressure go up, I'll need all her profits for next week's party. That includes your share as well."

Ursula looked in the direction of the bathroom and said, "Damn, I already had that money spent."

It was Sunday morning, and the doorbell rang. Lindsey went downstairs to answer it.

"Hi, Trina."

"Hi..." Trina looked at Lindsey's tight, see-through black and red lace negligee and her black furry stilettos. She avoided looking at her by staring at the floor.

"Is Jackie up? I want to see if she wants to go to church." Trina said.

Lindsey noticed Trina's disapproving look. Then she said, "Good luck with that. I think she's still sleeping."

Just then, Brittany came down the stairs. "Hey, Trina." She paused when she saw Lindsey, "Uh... hey, Lindsey."

Lindsey ignored her and said, "Where's your friend? Trina's looking for her."

"Who, Jax? You know she is still asleep." Brittany laughed a little. "Lindsey, I don't mean to intrude, but do you think you should put on some trousers and a shirt? I'm sure you don't want the chaps to come in and see you looking like that."

"I can't help it because I'm sexy, and the two of you aren't." Lindsey slung her long blonde hair and sashayed into the kitchen.

Trina asked, "Are you serious?" She waved a hand dismissing Lindsey and ran upstairs to Jackie's room.

Brittany followed Lindsey and said, "Lindsey, this has nothing to do with being sexy or plain. It is about having some dignity and decency."

Lindsey said, "Whatever." She grabbed the orange juice from the fridge and poured herself a glass. She probed Brittany. "Why is Trina trying to get Jackie to go to church?"

Brittany filled her tea kettle with water and placed it on the stove to heat, trying to ignore Lindsey's attire. "I don't know. Jax has been a little down since she got back from Dallas."

"What? I didn't know that," Lindsey said. "She's been back more than three months. Did something bad happen in Dallas?" she asked, poking around for dirt on Jackie.

"No, I think she misses home," Brittany said.

Lindsey said, "Is that all? Jackie is such a child."

"So, what's up with you, Lindsey? What have you been up to?" Brittany said.

"Well, I've been traveling a little, spending time with my boyfriends, and just hanging out."

"Sounds like fun."

"It would be more fun if I had my settlement from my job. If I don't get it soon, I'm going to be out of money."

"Yes, Jax told me about your lawsuit."

"She can't keep her mouth shut at all. What did she tell you?" Lindsey was upset that Jackie told people about her money problems.

"Nothing really. Just that you had a lawsuit against your company. Why don't you find another job? That way you're making some income while you wait on your settlement."

Lindsey turned her nose up and flipped her hair.

Brittany ignored her, put a tea bag into her cup, and poured the hot water over it. "Would you like a cup of raspberry tea? It's good. It is from London."

Lindsey wanted to say no, but then she heard the word London and of course, she wanted to try it. "Oh...London? Yeah, I want some. And, just so you know, my lawyer said that I can find another job, but it might damage my case. See, if I can prove that I haven't been able to find a job making the same amount of money, then they would have to pay me what I was making and maybe a little more."

Brittany eyed Lindsey. "Okay, and how are you supposed to eat until they pay you?"

"That's a good question. I still have a little money that my mom hid away before she died," Lindsey offered. "I'm so glad that I didn't spend all of it in Europe, while I was there mourning my mother's death."

Brittany said, "Please, do not take this the wrong way, but it seems that some Americans are always looking for a handout, when they could create their own means to support themselves."

Lindsey was offended. "I'm not looking for a handout. I was wronged and they should pay for how they treated me."

"You were wronged, but who is going to take care of you until that wrong has been rectified? Think about it, you are sitting here waiting for a settlement that may or may not materialize. When in the meantime, you must pay rent and eat."

"Materialize? What are you talking about? That's one thing I can't stand about you college students, you're always trying to show someone how smart you are. Do you mean it may or may not happen? Because my lawyer assures me that it will."

Brittany said nothing, instead she placed a teaspoon of sugar into each coffee cup and stirred. She walked into the dining room and placed the cups down on the table. They both sat and sipped their tea in silence. Brittany opened her book and started reading.

"Lindsey, do you like poetry?"

"No, I'm not really into poetry."

"Really? You should read some." Brittany flipped through the pages to a poem, "Read this poem and tell me what you think."

Lindsey looked at Brittany puzzled but read the poem to herself. "Okay, that's interesting," she said, wondering what the big deal was.

"Really? How did it speak to you?"

"What are you talking about?"

"Lindsey, read the poem and let it speak to you."

"Let it speak to me, are you kidding? Is that what you do in Africa, read poems, and let them speak to you? Nothing I have ever read has ever spoken to me. That's just crazy." She drank her tea and said, "Don't get me wrong, it's a good poem, but it's not speaking to me."

"Lindsey, just read it line by line, and apply it to your life. If you read it closely, you'll see the message that the poet is sending."

"Well, I don't know what the message is. Maybe I need to read it a couple more times."

"Okay, Lindsey. Feel free to keep the book if you like, just please return it once you are finished."

"Alright."

Brittany shook her head, finished her tea, left the book on the table, and headed back upstairs.

Lindsey picked up the book and opened it to the poem again. At first, she stared at the title. All her life, it had been her and her mother enjoying years of fun and laughter. But now, her mother was gone, and Lindsey was alone.

She decided to read the poem again. This time, the poem resonated with her like nothing ever had in her life. She got up, picked up a piece of paper from the buffet table, wrote the poem down, and then took the paper and the book upstairs. She sat on her bed and read it repeatedly while she thought about her life.

While reflecting on the poem, Lindsey discovered something about herself. She had been a victim of her husband, a victim of her job, a victim of alcohol, and a victim of the men she slept with. She decided that she was going to turn her life around and make a change. First, she was going to call her attorney and see if he could help her with custody of her twin girls. She may not get custody, but maybe she could at least get visitation. Lindsey had to face the cold hard truth; besides the row house, they were all she had left in this world.

17

Bijon stared at his books, wondering if it was all worth it—the long days and nights of studying. He wanted to experience the American dream once he finished medical school. He was not sure, after all he'd been through, if he could even enjoy it. His life seemed to spin out of control, but in slow motion. As he scanned the room, he saw bills on his bed. Part of him wanted to throw them all in the trash, but he knew he couldn't do that. Somehow, no matter how hard he worked and how much he made, he never had enough money to cover all his expenses. He was so tired of this circle of poverty and on top of all of that, he had lost the one person he ever truly loved.

The doorbell rang, and Bijon hoped one of his housemates would answer it. He needed to find the energy to go to work tonight, but he was exhausted. The doorbell rang again and this time he answered it. It was Marissa. They both just stared at each other, not sure what to say or what the other was thinking.

Marissa smiled and walked in. "I'll just wait here for DeMarcus."

Bijon watched her as she walked by. She took her usual spot on the couch and placed her purse on the floor beside her. Sean looked so much like her. He could see him, smell him, and even taste him when she was around. He loved that man so much.

"Okay."

He walked into the kitchen with his head hung low and his shoulders slumped. He couldn't take his mind off Sean. After about two minutes, he came back into the den where Marissa sat thumbing through her psychology book.

He asked, "How is he?"

Marissa acknowledged the pain in Bijon's eyes. "Sean's fine. How are you?"

Bijon sighed. "I'm hanging. It's been three weeks, but I'm dealing." He put his head in his hands and took a breath. "Look, I don't want anyone here to know, so..."

Marissa held her hands up and interrupted him. "Don't worry, your secret's safe. The whole-time you guys have been together, I've never told anyone, not even DeMarcus. But I know my brother misses you too."

Bijon took a deep breath and exhaled. "I do miss him, but Sean, he's so demanding. He wants me to come out of the closet, but I can't do that." He rubbed his head, torn between his allegiance to Sean and to himself. He loved Sean, but he was not sure about his sexuality, because he also had feelings for women. He contemplated if maybe, he made a mistake getting involved with Sean.

Marissa stood facing Bijon. She comforted him by reaching up, pulling him close, and giving him a hug.

It was the first human contact Bijon had had in three weeks. He relaxed in her arms and allowed her care and concern to envelope him. He lingered because he had so much weight on his shoulders, and he was grateful for her tenderness.

She whispered in his ear, "Sean is spoiled, he needs to grow up. Maybe you two can work it out later. Just give it some time. You guys have been together for two years. This is just a rough spot. I'm sure you'll work through it."

Bijon listened to her reassurance and somehow it made him feel better. He was still not so sure about their relationship or the whole gay thing. Although, he couldn't deny the past two years with Sean had been the happiest of his life. When he was with Sean, his life had meaning and everything was balanced in his world.

DeMarcus walked through the front door and saw Bijon and Marissa embracing.

DeMarcus yelled as he threw his suitcase down and marched toward them. "Marissa, what the hell are you doing?"

Startled by his appearance, Marissa stepped back from Bijon, and said, "DeMarcus, it's not what you think. Bijon was—"

"I go out of town, and here you are playing me. Hell no. Bitch, are you crazy?"

Marissa pleaded, "No, no he's upset, and we were, we were just talking."

Bijon laughed a little at the obvious misunderstanding. "DeMarcus, dude you got this all wrong."

DeMarcus screamed, "Fool, I know what I saw! You got something going on with my girl?"

Without waiting for Bijon's explanation, he turned to Marissa and said, "You stupid ho. Are you sleeping with this terrorist?"

"No, you don't understand."

Angry at DeMarcus for his inaccurate portrayal of him, Bijon said, "How many times do I have to tell you, I'm not a terrorist! I'm from America!"

DeMarcus got in Bijon's face, grabbed his collar and shouted, "I don't give a damn where you're from. You don't step to my girl!"

Bijon jerked away from DeMarcus's grip. "I wasn't stepping to your girl. We were just exchanging a greeting." Bijon looked at Marissa praying that she didn't reveal what they were really talking about.

DeMarcus caught the look and said, "Well then, why don't you greet your ass back to your room, and Marissa greet your ass upstairs." He pushed Marissa toward the stair rail, causing her to trip and fall on the stairs.

Bijon watched Marissa as she stumbled to get up. He yelled, "DeMarcus, there's no need for that!"

DeMarcus raised his fist at Bijon and said, "Fool, are you still talking to me? Man, I'm not in the mood. I just got back from my trip, and it didn't go well. So I suggest you get your faggot ass out of my face!"

Standing on the stairs, Marissa tried to change the subject, "DeMarcus, why don't I get you something to eat?"

He snapped, "Not hungry."

He turned back to Bijon. "The next time I catch you even looking at my girl, so help me God, I'll kill you."

"Man, there's nothing, and I mean nothing going on between me and Marissa," Bijon said, surprised that he would threaten to kill him.

In a brazen tone, DeMarcus said, "Oh, don't you think I know that? If there were, your head would be through that wall by now. Stay away from her!"

DeMarcus marched upstairs to deal with Marissa.

Bijon went to his room to put on his running shoes to jog. He would fight DeMarcus, but he knew he couldn't win. A quick run cleared his mind every day, but since the breakup with Sean, he ran twice a day. Today, he was running because he knew Marissa was going to be beaten because of his secret. He felt like a coward, but there was nothing he could do. He loved Sean, but he couldn't let love jeopardize his chance at an internship at Walter Reed Hospital, especially since love was the one thing that caused his father's dreams to fail.

18

Twice a month, Ursula drove four hours and twenty-two minutes back to her old neighborhood in New York. She usually spent a couple of hours in the city and then drove back to D.C. She liked driving, because it gave her a chance to think about graduating and moving to Colorado or Oregon. She really didn't care where she moved, as long as she could get as far away from drugs, Nita, and everything in her past. She would start over, and no one would know where she planned to call home except Big Mama.

She usually drove straight to the park across from the elementary school. Today she was a little early, so she went to the old apartment. Ursula parked her car in front of the apartment building, locked it, and hoped it would be safe. She walked up the sidewalk, glanced down the block, and saw nothing had changed. A group of guys huddled together shooting dice and throwing money on the ground. In the other direction, an old homeless woman pushed a shopping cart filled with stuffed green trash bags.

Ursula walked up to the door and a man left as she walked in. She went up the stairs to her old apartment and wondered if her mom still lived there. The light green paint on the walls in the hallway looked worse now than before. Ursula stared at apartment 2B where she and her mother once lived. The B on the apartment hung on by a thread. She stood there, thinking about her childhood.

Ursula remembered the first time she met Big Mama, a day she would never forget.

Ursula and Tracy went to the same school and rode the bus together. One spring day, Ursula took her key off her necklace to unlock her door, just as she did every day. Her friend, Tracy, knocked on the door across the hall from Ursula's. They looked at each other and said, "Bye."

Ursula went inside and closed the door. After a brief moment, she heard a thump at the door and opened it. An older black lady stood there wearing a yellow, green, and red flowered housecoat. She also had a light blue apron with a smudged reddish-brown stain on the front wrapped around her waist.

With her hands on her hips, she said, "Girl, don't you know better than to open the door without asking who it is first?" Ursula didn't say anything, she just looked up at her.

The lady leaned down to Ursula and said, "Where's your Mama?"

Ursula shrugged her shoulders. "I don't know."

The old lady peeped in the apartment and asked, "You here all by yourself?"

Ursula said, "Yeah."

She questioned her more. "Where's your Big Mama?"

Ursula stuttered, "Uh...um...uh," not understanding exactly what she was asking.

The old lady saw the sadness in Ursula's eyes, then bent forward to her and said, "Your grandmother, baby. Where's your grandmother?"

Ursula smiled and said, "Oh, in Puerto Rico."

"That's so far away. Are you hungry?"

Ursula nodded.

The older lady walked into Ursula's apartment, looked around, and said, "When was the last time your mama cleaned up around here?"

Ursula looked around the room and saw the mess. The older lady was right, the house needed to be cleaned.

Then she went into the kitchen and opened Ursula's refrigerator. It was empty, except for some jars of mustard, mayo, and a carton of spoiled milk. She closed the door quickly because the smell made her gag. She asked, "Did your Mama leave you anything to eat?"

"No."

"You wanna come to my house and eat?"

"Yeah."

The older lady walked out of the apartment to her own place across the hall and turned around because Ursula wasn't following her.

"Well, come on, baby. From now on, I'll be your Big Mama, and I'll get you something to eat. Now, we don't say yeah when an adult asks you a question. We say yes ma'am or yes sir. Just cause we poor don't mean we don't talk right. You understand?"

Ursula walked behind Big Mama and said, "Yeah."

Big Mama turned around and stared at her.

Ursula corrected herself and said, "Yes, ma'am."

"That's better. I'm going to write your mama a note and leave it so she knows where you are." Big Mama wrote the note and told Ursula to leave it inside, reminded her to lock the door, and put the key necklace back around her neck.

From that day on, Ursula spent more time at Big Mama's house then she did at her own. Big Mama gave her a snack, helped her with her homework, and fed her dinner every night. She treated Ursula like she treated her grandchild Tracy, who lived with her. She always hugged her and told her how much she loved her. It made Ursula wish that she belonged to Big Mama instead of her mother.

At night, before they went to bed, Big Mama talked about having a better life outside of the projects. Every night, she showed them a picture of Karrington University and told them to close their eyes and imagine themselves in college. Her grandson Jordan was already there and planned to graduate in a few years. She knew that once he did, their lives would be different. Big Mama said it was the best school in the world and told them if they asked the Lord then He would send them.

Now, Ursula looked back at the door of apartment 2A and missed the days with Big Mama and her family. She especially remembered the summers when Big Mama's nephew came to visit. They had so much fun together, and he was so nice. They talked about everything, including their dreams and their deepest secrets.

At the time they met, he was 10 years old, and Ursula was 12. She told him about her mom stripping and prostituting. He was the only person she told about her mom's boyfriend and brother raping her and how as she got older, her mom wanted her to have sex to help pay the rent. Likewise, he shared all his family problems with her and told her the real reason he spent the summers with Big Mama.

He was her first. Even though she'd been raped before, he was still her first. Her sophomore year in high school, after one of his summer visits, Ursula found out that she was pregnant. Big Mama scolded both for their actions. Later, she advised Ursula to put the baby up for adoption. Ursula told her mom about the pregnancy, and she screamed at her that she didn't have the money to feed another mouth. She told Ursula to get an abortion. Disgusted by her mother's attitude, coupled with the reality that Ursula's mom wasn't feeding the one mouth she already had, Ursula complied with her request. They managed to scrape together the money for the abortion. Weeks later, heartbroken, Ursula had the abortion. Big Mama consoled Ursula and told her that God would forgive her.

The next summer, things were different between Big Mama's nephew and Ursula. They both felt bad about the abortion. Big Mama reminded them of their mistake, so the nephew brought condoms to make sure there wouldn't be any more accidents.

Shortly after Ursula's junior year in high school, Big Mama moved and Ursula's summer romance with the nephew was over. Jordan graduated from Karrington and landed a major job. He moved Big Mama and Tracy out of the projects. Ursula hated that day more than any other, because Big Mama, her nephew, and Tracy were all she had in the world.

Big Mama stayed in contact with Ursula. She wrote to her and encouraged her to finish school so she could go to college. Throughout that year, Ursula thought about her summer love and wondered if he missed her as much as she missed him.

Ursula didn't see his face again until the spring of the following year, the end of her junior year of high school. That was the day she gave birth to his son, the spitting image of his father.

19

Ursula looked at her watch and sprinted down the stairs. She wanted to make it there in time for recess. She got in her car and headed for the park across town. Getting there just in time, Ursula sat on a park bench and watched the children play across the street in the schoolyard. She smiled when she saw her son. He looked just like Big Mama's nephew. Ursula wanted to hug him and kiss him, but she didn't want to meet him until after she graduated.

Adoption was the best decision. A white family on the Upper East Side adopted him. His adopted parents always sent her pictures of him and wrote letters about how he was doing in school.

Sometimes, Ursula sat for hours after recess was over, just watching the people and thinking about her life. She planned to contact Big Mama and invite her to the graduation. She knew Big Mama would be so happy to know that she was graduating from Karrington University. Maybe she would ask Big Mama about her nephew—where he was and whether he was married.

Even after all the years apart, Ursula knew that she was still in love with him. Years had gone by, but her love had remained the same.

～

Meanwhile, back at Karrington, a metamorphosis had occurred in Jackie's life. After her scary encounter with Nita, her attitude had changed and she decided since she couldn't get out, she would make the best of the coke parties. As a result, she was more confident and had more friends. She was not sure what happened, maybe it was because she had a boyfriend or maybe it was because she had matured.

As she walked across the yard she heard, "Jackie."

She turned around and said, "Hey, what's up?"

"Nothing much," Kyle said. "When are you and Broderick throwing the next party?"

"I don't know. I haven't talked to him this week."

"What? What do you mean you haven't talked to him? Aren't you his girl?"

"Yeah." Jackie liked the sound of that. She thought, *He's right. I am Broderick's girl.*

"Let's have it at your house. How about tonight?" Kyle said, eager to get together.

"Okay, I'll call Broderick," Jackie agreed before really thinking it through.

"Cool, let me know."

Since Jackie and Broderick had been dating, a few of his friends got together almost every month to have a party. At first, Jackie thought the parties were lame because they got together and talked instead of partying. But now, she found herself enjoying them.

At the parties, they talked for hours about the injustices in South Africa, world hunger, fraternity and sorority hazing, or mistakes that movie stars made. You name it, and they talked about it. Most of the time, right in someone's dorm or living room they solved world problems that had been plaguing the government for years.

Jackie got home, called Broderick, and of course, he was ready to party.

He said, "Great, I'll call everyone. How about seven o'clock?"

Jackie said, "Yeah, that's good." She paused wondering if he was going to say something about coming early. He didn't, so she did. "Are you coming over early?"

He said, "You know I am."

"Cool, I'll be waiting." She was glad she got to spend time with Broderick, because her next coke party was tomorrow.

Jackie and Broderick answered the door like they were married. Schooley and Max stood in the doorway.

"Hey, guys. What's up?" Schooley said.

"Hey, Jackie," Max said, and they hugged.

Schooley handed her a box of Captain Crunch, one bowl, and a bottle of Alizé. He gave Broderick the brother hug.

"Okay, now what am I supposed to do with this?" Jackie held the items up to him.

"That's all I had. You got some milk?" he said and walked into the den.

Jackie looked at him and laughed. "You're so crazy."

Max handed her some ramen noodles. He also gave Broderick a brother hug.

"Look dog, it's hard for me to give up my ramen noodles." He followed Schooley and Broderick into the den.

Jackie said, "Lucky for you, I picked up some appetizers myself." Before she closed the door, Kyle and Shaun walked up the sidewalk.

"Hey, what's up?" She was glad to see them.

"Nothing much."

Jackie noticed they didn't bring anything, but she didn't say a word. She just welcomed them in. Trina and Brittany came downstairs to join the group.

They all grabbed a plate and sat down to eat. Schooley opened the Alizé. But before they could start, the doorbell rang again and this time Broderick answered it. Wendy and Donnetta came in and said their hellos to everyone. Wendy set a foot long sub sandwich on the table beside Jackie's appetizers, and Donnetta laid a bag of chips down next to it.

"What are we going to talk about tonight?" Schooley said as he eyed the appetizers and picked up four hot wings. "I love when you guys host. You serve classy food." He looked over at Shaun and said, "Not like when we go to Shaun's."

Shaun fired back, "Hey, man, whatcha trying to say?"

"Aren't you listening? I just said it," Schooley replied in a sarcastic tone.

Shaun defended himself, "Man, whatever. You know I'm on financial aid. My parents ain't got it like your parents." He pointed to everyone in the room.

They each looked at him and continued talking, because he always had an excuse as to why he didn't bring anything to the parties. Shaun waited with his plate, while Wendy took a knife and sliced the foot long into individual pieces. She placed them on the buffet table beside the other food.

"I want to talk about rap music. Why does every song involve calling women bitches and hoes? I am so sick and tired of it. I mean, is it that hard to refer to us as women? Or how about just calling us by our names? And why does everything revolve around sex?" Donnetta spouted off with an attitude.

Brittany's cell phone rang, and she walked upstairs to answer it. Jackie knew this was going to get good, and Brittany was going to miss it.

Kyle said, "I feel you on that. Sometimes, I do think they get carried away with the names. But, if you listen to the music, it rhymes with the rap. So I think they throw it in because of that. Now the sex part, all I could say is, girl, you know sex sells."

Wendy said, "No, I'm not buying that. Rappers are poets. They can find another way to talk about women other than calling us out of our names and talking about our body parts."

"Jackie, am I right?" Wendy looked to Jackie, Donnetta, and Trina for moral support.

Jackie and Donnetta nodded yes.

Trina said, "That's true. She has a point."

"If you think about it, rappers have a platform where they can send positive messages to the world if they wanted to. I have to give credit where credit's due. Some of them do have positive messages, but those are few and far between." Wendy took a bite of her sandwich.

Shaun stood up to get a soda and said, "Again, this shit is getting blown way out of proportion. You guys know rap is my favorite music, and let's be honest, some girls are bitches and hoes, cause that's how they act."

"Hold up!"

"Wait a minute!"

"You know that ain't right!"

They all said at the same time.

Trina asked, "Shaun, you don't really believe that do you?"

Shaun raised his arms to calm everyone down and said, "Hear me out. Hear me out now. I'm not talking about you guys, Wendy, Donnetta, Jackie, and Trina. You don't fit in this category. But we have all seen some women with tight, tight, tight short skirts, and low, I mean, low cut tops where you could see all their goodies. To me, those girls are hoes. I would never take one of those girls home to meet my family. They got one thing on their mind, and that's all they want. Don't get me wrong, I'm okay with that. I mean, you know, I can accept that." He laughed a little, looking for support from his boys. They all laughed and one chimed in, "Yeah, man. I know what you mean."

Jackie looked at Broderick because he was smiling and joining in with them. He looked back at her and stopped smiling.

Donnetta came back, "Really? Well, what if guys were calling your daughter those names?"

Schooley said, "We don't even have to discuss that, because that's not happening. I'm not going to let my daughter dress like that. And I'm going to teach her the difference between nice guys and thugs." He shook his head. "I'm not raising a hoochie momma, that's just not happening."

Donnetta said, "Okay, let's move to the next subject. Did you see the news last night? About the guy they arrested for having fifty kilos of cocaine in his trunk. Can you believe that?"

Jackie spit her drink out and it shot across the room. Luckily, it didn't get on anyone. Broderick patted her on the back and asked, "Are you alright?"

Everyone looked at Jackie wondering what her problem was. Wendy passed her a napkin to clean the wine off her pants and the carpet.

"Yeah, I'm fine." Jackie said, embarrassed by her outburst.

Broderick said, "Yeah, let's talk about that. Jacqueline and I had this conversation awhile back. Tell them what you think, Jacqueline."

Jackie threw daggers at him with her eyes. How dare he embarrass her in front of their friends.

She said, "Obviously, drugs are wrong, but there are a lot of people that do them for fun."

Schooley was the first one to put his two cents in. "Let me school you on something, Jackie. People say doing drugs is just for fun. But you and I both know people who start out doing drugs for fun and eventually become hooked, if they are not careful. Not to mention the fact that I'm sure we all know someone who has gone to or was in jail because of drugs." He looked around the room and they all nodded their heads. "I got a boy right now doing ten to fifteen in the state penitentiary and he was just selling drugs for fun."

Everybody laughed except Jackie.

Jackie made her point. "I know, but let's just say that some people only do it to liven up a party. They're not hooked. They just do it for recreational purposes."

Schooley kept going, "Jackie, wake up! Nobody does drugs recreationally. They're hooked, and that's why they keep doing it."

Donnetta chimed in, "My sister was on drugs back in Ohio, and it started as something fun to do on the weekends. She lost her husband, her kids, and her house. Now she is homeless living on the streets. Sometimes we can find her and sometimes we can't." She put her head down, a tear formed in her eyes and rolled down her cheek. She paused and wiped the tear away. "It's really sad. She said she wants to quit, but she can't."

They were all quiet for a minute, realizing the extreme effect drug use had on the family attached to the person using. Jackie thought about how her family felt when Jackson ran with the wrong crowd and used drugs. They were worried day and night about him.

Max broke the silence. "Donnetta, I'm sorry to hear about your sister. But you mean to tell me, no one in this room has ever tried drugs?"

Everyone looked around at each other, but no one acknowledged their drug use.

He said, "Well I have. I used to smoke marijuana, and I've tried coke a few times, but I'm not on skid row."

Jackie replied, "See, that's what I'm talking about, not everyone gets hooked."

As soon as Jackie said it, she wished she could take it back because Trina looked right at her. In high school, Trina's brother was killed because he was at the wrong place at the wrong time. It was a drive by shooting, and he was caught in the crossfire. Trina put her head down, obviously disappointed in Jackie's answer, but she said nothing.

Donnetta said, "I guess it affects everyone differently, but you don't know how it's going to affect you until you try it. I'm not gonna lie, I smoked marijuana, but I never tried coke." She shook her head. "The way it did my sister, I didn't want anything to do with it."

Broderick said, "What about you Wendy, Shaun, and Kyle?"

Jackie figured that Broderick thought he was Oprah moderating the discussion like he knew what he was talking about. It was these times when Broderick really got on her last nerve.

"You know, back in the day, I think we all probably tried something at some point. I'll admit, I used to smoke weed all the time in high school. But you know, things change, you grow. I decided that it wasn't for me anymore, and I'm focusing on other things now," Kyle said.

Shaun remained quiet.

Wendy finally said something since everyone was looking at her. "My Dad's a cop, so I never tried it. I never wanted to get caught and have him embarrassed among his cop friends. But my dad said if they could clean the streets from drugs, cops would have nothing to do, because 90 percent of everything they do involves drug offenses."

Jackie sat in silence and listened to her friends' opinions on drugs. No one had anything positive to say, but then again, she didn't expect them to. The horrible irony of this whole discussion was the fact that they were sitting in her living room, talking about drugs, and tomorrow night she would be there cutting cocaine on the very same buffet table where Wendy cut the sub sandwich.

She felt lower than low, her whole being sank. Her life had completely changed. She was now a junior, had a boyfriend, and friends with social consciousness. She was choosing to suppress hers just to make money. It was a sad thing, because she had grown to enjoy the parties and the money.

Broderick said, "Jacqueline, Jacqueline. What's the matter?"

Jackie finally came out of her daze and said, "Nothing."

He said, "Something's wrong. You just zoned out."

She looked around, and everyone was back at the table getting more to eat and drink.

Trina joined Broderick and added, with an attitude, "Yeah, what's the problem, Jackie?"

Jackie halfheartedly said, "Nothing, I'm good."

Broderick offered, "Let me get her some more Alizé." He got up and went over to the table.

Trina said, "What's going on with you?"

"Nothing. This discussion is too heavy for me. Whatever happened to drinking and dancing at a party?"

They both heard Shaun talking and listened to his conversation.

Shaun said, "Well, if you notice, I don't even drink. My father is a recovering alcoholic. I always thought there was something in our DNA that caused us to be more addictive. One of my cousins tried crack and it tore his stomach lining out. Within a few hours, he died. So, I don't mess with it and can't understand anyone that does."

"Wow, I didn't know it could do that," Kyle stated as he poured some of Brittany's apple cognac he found while snooping through the kitchen cabinet.

Schooley said, "Man, that crack is potent. It's like poison in your system."

Just then, Brittany came downstairs and said, "Sorry, long distance phone call. What did I miss?"

Everyone looked at her like she was crazy. Schooley said, "Brittany, it's too much to go back over."

"Aw...bloody hell," Brittany said, disappointed. "I missed the exchange of ideas."

Schooley frowned at her and said, "You know hell got to be bad enough all by itself, why does it have to be bloody too?"

Brittany said, "Uh...it's something we say back home."

The party went on until after midnight. They continued to discuss issues facing not just the black community, but all communities. Jackie couldn't get it together; she was torn between her own conscience and what she was doing.

Broderick helped her clean up after everyone left. Jackie had planned for him to stay over, but now she wanted him to go. She needed to be alone to collect her thoughts and sort everything out in her mind.

He brought the last dish in the kitchen and said, "Alright, what's wrong?"

Jackie rinsed off the sub sandwich plate and said in a somber tone, "What do you mean?"

"I mean, after we talked about drugs, you checked out and you haven't been back since. Did I say something wrong? Are you upset that I told everyone about our conversation?"

She finished rinsing the plate and placed it on a towel to dry. She looked at him and said, "Yeah, I am a little upset. I thought that our conversations were just between us, not our friends."

He said, "I'm sorry, baby, you're right. That was wrong. It won't happen again. Forgive me?"

Jackie couldn't stay mad, because Broderick was so cute.

He hugged her and kissed her on the lips. "Let's go upstairs."

She, of course said, "Okay."

They walked toward the stairs, and the front door opened. DeMarcus and Marissa walked in.

DeMarcus looked surprised to see Broderick and Jackie on their way to her bedroom. With a smug facial expression, he said, "Well, what do we have here?"

"Uh...DeMarcus, this is my boyfriend, Broderick. Broderick, this is DeMarcus." She paused and said, "He's one of my housemates and this is his girlfriend, Marissa."

Marissa said, "Nice to meet you."

"I didn't know you had a boyfriend," he said in a smart aleck way. "Hey man, what's up?"

He said, "Nothing much, what about you?" Broderick stuck out his hand to shake hands with DeMarcus.

Jackie couldn't believe he did that.

DeMarcus laughed, looked at Broderick's hand, and said, "Man, are you serious?"

Broderick pulled his hand back and looked DeMarcus squarely in the eye. He said, "Forgive me, man, that's not how you do it in the hood, is it? I'm sorry, I forgot where I was."

DeMarcus walked closer to Broderick like he was about to clock him.

Broderick didn't move, but instead squared his shoulders as if ready for the challenge.

DeMarcus said, "Naw, that's not how we do it, dog."

Jackie stepped in between them and pushed them away from each other. She tugged on Broderick's hand and pulled him up the stairs with her. She looked at DeMarcus and Marissa and said, "You guys have a good night." Marissa looked confused as Broderick and DeMarcus stared at each other like they both were ready to fight.

When they got to her room, Broderick asked, "What the hell is up with your roommate?"

"Overlook him; he's crazy," she said, as she pulled the covers back from the bed.

"Is he?" he said, suspicious. "Or is something going on between you and him?"

Jackie turned around and stared at him, wondering if he really knew or if he was just fishing around. "What? Are you crazy? Did you see his girlfriend?"

"Yeah, I saw her, but I also saw how he was looking at you. And you didn't answer my question."

Jackie shook her head trying to act outraged that he would think such a thing. "No, there's nothing going on between us. DeMarcus is just like that," she explained, hoping he would drop the inter-rogation.

Broderick said, "Um..." as he looked in his overnight bag for his toothbrush and clothes, "Okay, where's his room?"

Jackie knew Broderick was going to freak out when she told him that DeMarcus lived right next door. After a moment, she said, "He lives next door."

"Next door...where?"

She hesitated and then said, "Next door to me." She sighed and said, "Please don't make a big deal about this."

Broderick frowned and raised his voice. "You gotta be kidding me?" He shook his head and found his toothbrush, opened the door, and looked at the entrance to DeMarcus' room.

Jackie held her breath and watched Broderick, hoping he would just let it go. He looked at her and said, "I'm going to take a shower." She quickly handed him some towels and a bar of soap. He then walked to the bathroom. When she heard the shower turn on, Jackie breathed a sigh of relief. She closed the door, sat on the bed, and wondered what DeMarcus was trying to do.

Someone knocked at the door, and thinking maybe Broderick forgot something, she jumped up and opened it. DeMarcus was standing there with a smirk on his face.

He stared at her and said, "I thought you were going to get rid of the boyfriend."

"What? Keep your voice down." She motioned him to be quiet with her finger. Whispering she said, "I never told you I was getting rid of him. Look, he's in the shower. Goodbye." Jackie almost had the door closed, but he pushed his way in.

DeMarcus walked into her room, closed the door, sat on the bed, and started looking through Broderick's things. Jackie picked up the bag and put it on the chair.

Perturbed he said, "You know I don't like this, and I don't like him."

"I don't care what you like. Get the hell out of my room. I don't want him to come back and see you. Get up and get out!" She raised her voice to just above a whisper, because she didn't want Broderick or Marissa to hear her. She pulled DeMarcus' arm to get up, but he was way too heavy.

DeMarcus smiled at her useless efforts. Pushing her arm away, he asked in an arrogant tone, "Does he know about us?"

"Are you delusional? There's no us, fool!"

"I don't understand, Jackie. Why did you have to pick someone so nerdy? You know who he reminds me of?"

"No, and I don't care," Jackie said with a great deal of frustration.

"What's that guy's name?" DeMarcus looked up to the ceiling trying to remember the name. "It was a cartoon. It used to come on when we were kids. Oh yeah, Poindexter. That's it. You know, he wore those little glasses."

"I don't care what you think. I like him. I may even love him."

"Come on now, you think I believe that. Besides you owe me!"

"I owe you what?"

"You brought this fool to our love palace. This is our place, Jackie."

"Are you serious?"

"Oh, yeah baby, I'm serious. Does your boy know we've done it on the couch several times, and in this bed? Do I need to keep going?"

Jackie thought about all the times and places they've had their midnight escapades. "Alright, what is it that you want?" Jackie asked desperate for DeMarcus to leave.

"You know what I want?"

"No...no!"

"Okay. I tell you what, I'll leave on one condition. Give me a kiss."

"No. I'm not giving you anything." Just then, they heard the shower turn off and she knew it was a matter of time before Broderick came back in the room.

DeMarcus stood up, leaned in close, and faced her. She could smell his cologne. It was a clean and sporty scent. She loved the way DeMarcus smelled. He said, "I'm waiting for my kiss, and make it good."

He was so close to Jackie, she was having a tough time maintaining her space, but she stepped back a little and said, "No, get out!"

"Okay, I guess Poindexter will have to catch me in your room with the door closed. I'll have to tell him that we're special friends with benefits. I don't think that's going to go over well with him. Do you?"

Jackie knew she couldn't explain that, especially since Broderick was already suspicious of her and DeMarcus. So, she did it, she kissed him hard and quick. DeMarcus' kisses always did something to her. They stopped her in her tracks and made her feel tingly all over. She didn't know why he affected her like that. She just knew that he did.

DeMarcus smiled and said, "Damn girl, I like it when you're feisty." He opened the door and walked into the hallway.

Jackie said, as quiet as she could, "You have a girlfriend and I have a boyfriend, deal with it. Don't knock on my door again."

She slammed the door in his face hoping he got the message. Twenty seconds later, she heard another knock. She prayed it was not DeMarcus. God must have heard her prayers, because when she opened the door, it was Broderick. He said, "Did I heard you talking to someone?"

Without a thought, she said, "No, that was the TV."

He looked at the TV and said, "But it's not on."

Jackie told him that she just turned it off because she heard him coming out of the shower. She opened her vanity drawer, pulled out a lighter, flicked the switch, and lit the candles in her room.

Afterwards, she kissed him on his cheek and ran her fingers through his hair. She asked, "Can you help me get undressed?" Hoping to get his mind off what he thought he heard. Jackie turned on the stereo to set the mood.

Broderick smiled. He was always so gentle and kind, never in a rush. He examined and kissed every inch of her body. She loved how he admired all her curves. He said that he loved her thighs because they were so smooth and creamy. They made love, and it was wonderful. Although, she felt a little guilty because a couple of times she imagined that he was DeMarcus. But she was careful not to call out his name.

Afterward, Broderick fell asleep, and Jackie was left alone with her thoughts. She was still not sure how she could be in love with two men at the same time, but she was starting to believe that she was.

20

Jackie felt uneasy about having her coke soiree, especially after the party she had with Broderick and his friends last night. But she didn't have a choice.

Jackie had most of her coke parties at the row house on Saturdays, because all her housemates were usually gone, except Bijon, who always stayed in his room. LaJuana worked as a waitress on the weekends at a jazz club. DeMarcus was either out with his boys, or he and Marissa were out with friends. Brittany usually stayed in her room on the phone with her boyfriend, or she was at the pub with friends. And of course, Lindsey was always out with one of her male friends.

Right before the party, Ursula dropped off the product, and Jackie got everything ready. That night, Jackie trained two young ladies, Lydia and Eve. They both arrived about 30 minutes before the party started, and Jackie walked them through the routine. It was hard for Jackie to believe that she had been promoted and had people under her. It was insane, but it was her life. They talked and got to know each other a little.

Lydia was a white girl studying history at Tomack University. She was a sophomore who needed money to get through school and pay for her tuition.

Eve was a black girl. She was a sophomore as well but majoring in Business at Swift Community College. Likewise, Eve needed money to pay for tuition, room, and food.

The guests arrived, and Jackie asked her new reps to sit and watch. She mingled with each of her guests before placing the product on the table. She gave her list a quick check and found that all were accounted for. She then took the product out of the briefcase and measured it. Jackie carefully cut the cocaine and set the lines on the large mirror sitting on the dining room table. Afterwards, she collected the money from Hal, one of her favorite clients.

Hal's cyberspace company just received a huge contract, and he was celebrating with some of his closest friends. At first, he didn't want to tell Jackie how much the new contract was worth. Jackie didn't press him, because she knew she would find out if she just waited. Cocaine was considered a truth serum at times. It had a way of allowing people to let go of their inhibitions. Just as she predicted, after a couple of lines, he told her everything.

Hal introduced Jackie to his girlfriend, Octavia. She was a tall, slender white girl with brunette hair. After her first line, she was the life of the party. She kissed every person in the room, including the other girls. Jackie didn't talk to her much. She was a little too flirty, maybe even bisexual.

Jackie walked over to the table, and there she met Sophia. She seemed a little shy and quiet. Jackie could tell she was not used to doing coke or any drug for that matter. But after her first line, like the others, she was cool. She told Jackie that she was the executive director for the Justice Department, and that she really needed to find a way to relieve stress. She was happy that she came and wanted to be placed on Jackie's client list.

Hal interrupted everyone and announced, "Now, I invited you all here to celebrate my big contract, but this has to be our little secret, because if I go down, we all go down."

Jackie had heard that phrase before and knew that he was good friends with Nita, because that was what she always said.

She went over to a young man sitting on the couch. He looked to be in a daze, but he only had one line, so she knew he was just relaxing and taking in the feeling. She sat down next to him and asked, "What's your name?"

"Matthew."

She could tell right away that he wasn't very talkative, but she pressed on. "So, Matthew, what do you do for a living?"

He responded in a laid-back fashion, "I work for Hal. I run the IT department for him. I'm the reason he got the big contract."

"Oh, wow, that's amazing. Congratulations."

"Hal said I can have all the coke I want." He leaned back on the couch, placed his arms behind his head, and rested on a pillow. She let him cruise for a minute so he could fully enjoy his high. She went back to her new reps and asked them what they thought.

Eve said, "You make this look so easy." She pointed to Matthew and asked, "Are they supposed to look like that?"

Jackie said, "Yes."

Hal rushed over to Jackie with a CD in his hands. He wanted her to play some music. Jackie took it and placed it in the CD player. He told her to play the second track, and she did. The track played and everyone in the room got up on their feet and did the hand motions to the song. Jackie even joined in. During the song, Jackie turned around and saw Lindsey dancing with Hal. She was shocked to see Lindsey, but more than anything, she was amazed at what Lindsey had on. She was wearing a short white and pink teddy outlined in black with hot pink stilettos. She looked like a hooker.

Jackie rushed over to her and called her name while trying to pull her away from Hal.

Lindsey brushed Jackie away. "In a minute, Jackie. Don't you see I'm dancing?" Lindsey seduced Hal with her eyes and her body movements.

Jackie walked to the other side of the room and watched them.

She looked over at Hal's girlfriend and saw that she was flirting with another guy. Jackie waited for the song to end. But, before she could get to Lindsey, she was at the dining room table leaning down using a tube to snort a line.

Jackie ran over to her and screamed, "What in the hell do you think you are doing?"

Lindsey looked at Jackie annoyed. "Enjoying the party. What does it look like I'm doing?"

Jackie pulled Lindsey by her arm and pushed her into the kitchen.

Lindsey snatched her arm back and asked, "What's your problem?"

Jackie yelled, "You! You're my problem. What are you doing here? And what do you have on?"

"Jackie, in case you forgot, I live here. I pay rent here, remember? I was going to bed, but I heard the music and decided to come down and join the party."

"Okay, look, it's not what you think," Jackie explained.

"Oh, it's exactly what I think. You're having a coke party. And I saw Hal," she pointed in his direction, "pay you two hundred dollars."

"Look, he didn't pay me two hundred dollars," Jackie said. *Lindsey obviously didn't see everything, because he's paid a lot more than two hundred dollars*, she thought.

Frustrated, Jackie said, "I need you to go upstairs and stay out of my business."

"Actually, this is my business, I live here, and I'm not leaving. Hal told me I can have all the coke I want because he's throwing the party. So the way I see it, I'm one of your guests now."

"Lindsey, please. I'm begging you. Leave."

"Beg all you want. I'm not leaving. I'm having too much fun, and besides, Hal's probably looking for me."

"He isn't looking for you. He's here with his girlfriend."

"Not for long." She put her hands on her hips, pushed her breasts out front, and posed. She licked her lips and said in a seductive tone, "Lindsey's here now." She walked back toward the dining room.

Jackie pulled her arm and said, "Lindsey, please don't say anything."

"Don't worry, I won't." She winked at Jackie. "I knew you were up to something, but I had no idea it was this. You know, you can trust me."

The last person Jackie could trust was Lindsey.

21

It was Monday morning, and Jackie was still thinking about her party on Saturday night. Deep down, she was a bit worried about what Lindsey would say or do. She knew what she was doing was wrong, but even though she hated to admit it, she had a blast! She had come to learn that the business had its perks. Many of her friends were famous and highly educated. If she ever needed a favor, say like from a city official, she could get it. The outgoing mayor had been to her parties, and they were now on a first name basis.

Jackie felt pretty good about herself, but then she remembered something that happened Saturday that had never happened before. Hal bought several lines of coke and convinced her to try one. After only a few minutes, she felt like she was floating. It was euphoric. She felt confident, like she could do anything, but at the same time she was much more relaxed than she had ever been.

For some reason, her body temperature went up and perspiration dripped under her armpits, so she took off her jacket, and then her shirt. She heard one of the guys tell her to take it all off, so she did. Before she knew it, she had stripped naked in front of total strangers. They encouraged her to give lap dances, and she did. It was weird because she knew exactly what she was doing, but didn't care. The feeling lasted about thirty minutes or maybe an hour. It was good, and she loved it. She'd always been curious about cocaine, and this was like nothing she ever imagined.

Jackie shook herself from her trance, took her shower, and got dressed. She was wearing her Guess jeans, a black, long-sleeved cashmere sweater, and her black, high heel boots. She grabbed her heavy coat and schoolbooks and headed out for criminology class. She continued to think about the cocaine knowing that she had to get it off her mind. She vowed to never to do it again, but secretly, she knew she was lying to herself. That feeling was so good that she knew she had to try it, at least one more time. It was almost like the cocaine called her name. Now, Jackie knew why coke parties were so popular and why people wanted to come. She tried to get herself to focus on criminology, although she had no interest in it. Her only interest now was cocaine. She walked across the yard to the Walker Center, one of the hangouts on campus. She looked around for someone she knew because she needed to get her mind off the coke.

"Hey, Jackie. What's up?"

Jackie turned around and saw Samuel. They took American Government together last year. He motioned for her to sit at his booth. She walked over, took her coat off, and sat down.

"Hey, Samuel," Jackie said cheerfully, still thinking about her high.

"How are things going?" he asked, smiling and looking her up and down.

"Pretty good, what about you?" She was not sure why he was staring at her like that. Samuel was not the most attractive guy on campus. He was skinny and bald, and that look didn't really appeal to Jackie. She liked him, but she was attracted to men who had some muscles, and some hair.

"It's cool. What did you do for the summer?" he said.

"I just went back home and worked for the family business. It was quiet and uneventful. I totally enjoyed it. What about you?" she asked, still not sure if she was dealing with the aftereffects of the cocaine, or if he was flirting with her.

"I interned in Indianapolis with a global company that distributes wireless devices. It was good. I may apply for another internship with them next summer. I learned a lot and had a blast."

"That's great. You're from Nebraska, right?"

"Yeah, but Indianapolis has got it going on!"

"I bet they do." She got up and grabbed her coat. "Hey, I got a class. I better go. See you later."

"Alright, take care," he said, while watching her as she walked away.

She walked across campus to Hughes Hall. After talking with Samuel, she thought maybe she should get a real internship next summer, instead of working for her parents. She sauntered into the classroom, still feeling peaceful, and saw the professor sitting at his desk.

"Good morning, Ms. Jones. How are you today?"

Surprised to see him there before class, she said, "Fine, Professor Talbot. How are you?"

"Doing well."

Professor Talbot was a thin, fragile looking white man, who was known to be a nice guy; although, he was a little nerdy at times. He encouraged his students and helped them as much as he could. He believed that if they failed, then he failed. Jackie liked that about him. Her classmates filed in behind her and found their seats.

Professor Talbot began his lecture by stating, "We are going to focus for the next couple of weeks on drug trafficking."

Jackie's eyes bugged out in surprise, and her heart started racing.

Oh my God, what have I gotten myself into now? Does he know about my coke parties?

She glanced around to see if anybody was looking at her, then she took a deep breath and convinced herself to stay calm. She checked the syllabus for today's lecture topic and there it was in black and white—Drug Trafficking.

Just then, DeMarcus came in and took his seat. Part of his senior internship involved being Professor Talbot's teaching assistant.

"Before we start, this week's homework will consist of reading The Fair Sentencing Act and the Anti-Drug Act. But today's assignment involves the original statute that birth these two laws.

Who is ready to dive in?" the professor said.

He looked at his roll and called, "Natalie Hines, can you tell me what you know about the Mandatory Minimum Sentencing legislation?"

Natalie was a lean, dark skinned girl with short hair. She was cute, and she knew it.

She stood proudly and said, "Yes, sir. The Mandatory Minimum Sentencing legislation is part of the war on drugs. If someone is convicted of a drug offense, regardless of how much or how little they're involved, they will serve a legislatively mandated number of years in prison."

"Good answer, but what if there are extenuating circumstances? Can the judge intervene and set his own sentence?"

Natalie really got on Jackie's nerves because she always had the right answer. She thought she was smarter than everyone else, which was probably true. She earned a National Merit Scholarship to come to Karrington.

Natalie displayed her knowledge. "No, sir. The judge in each case has zero discretion. He has to impose whatever minimum sentence the legislation requires. The larger the amount of drugs, the longer the sentence."

Jackie looked down and noticed that the palms of her hands were sweating. Her heartbeat rapidly, the sounds of the other students became muffled, her vision blurred, and the room spun in slow motion. She closed her eyes and took a deep breath, but her breathing became labored. Jackie inhaled and exhaled slowly to regain her composure.

Professor Talbot, pleased with Natalie's answer, said, "Good. Thank you." He scanned the classroom and asked Felix, "How serious do you think the legislature is on drug trafficking?"

Felix, a tall Hispanic male with curly black hair said, "Sir, they are very serious. As a matter of fact, I did some further research on the subject."

Here we go, show off. He too made Jackie sick. She couldn't stand him. Always reading more than the assignment required. It seemed like everyone in the class tried to outdo each other.

"And the US government expects citizens to call the police and turn anyone in that they think may be involved in selling or using drugs. If one person said that you participated or had knowledge of a conspiracy, then you are charged with a drug offense. Of course, there has to be some evidence."

What the hell! Jackie was horrified to hear this information. She thought that she was about to be sick. Her stomach churned like it did when she first rode the biggest roller coaster at Six Flags. Her body felt weightless. Out of the corner of her eye, she noticed DeMarcus looking at her. She flipped through her book and looked at the chapter titled "Drug Trafficking." She wished she had finished studying on Sunday instead of sleeping the day away.

"That brings me to my next question. There are many charges and counts for drug trafficking. Jackie, can you give me two examples?"

Jackie looked up from the book and took her time standing up. Still looking down at the page, she read the words out loud, "Solicitation of drugs." For a minute, Jackie felt like she was about to pass out, her legs wobbled as sweat dripped down her face.

"Uh..."

"Ms. Jones, you don't look well. Are you okay?" the professor asked.

"Yes, I'm fine. I think it was something I ate."

DeMarcus gave her a strange look.

"I'm sorry to hear that. Now, do you have the rest of the answer to the question?"

"Uh, no." She sat, and then slumped down in her seat, hoping that he would move to the next person.

"Can someone help Ms. Jones and give me a few more examples?"

Angelia raised her hand and answered, "To manufacture and/or possess with the intent to distribute. Engaging and profiting in an ongoing criminal enterprise. And, oh yeah, conspiracy." Angelia formed a smirk on her freckled face. She was usually quiet, but Jackie was happy that she was not quiet today.

"Very good, Angelia." Professor Talbot seemed pleased with her answer.

He looked around the class and asked, "Phil, is there any leniency for first time offenders?"

Phil was a husky brown complexioned country boy, who played football for Karrington. "No, sir. First time offenders face the minimum of 10 years in prison, just like everyone else."

"Isn't that astonishing?" Professor Talbot said as he got up and walked in front of the class, pacing back and forth. "One wrong decision can cost someone who has never been involved in criminal activity before, 10 years of their life."

From Jackie's perspective, he was looking right at her. Hardly able to control herself, she squirmed in her seat at the thought of serving 10 years in prison. Her heart dropped to her stomach and her head hurt more and more, until it felt like it would explode.

"I see that you all have been studying this topic. Now, who can tell me what three factors the federal mandatory drug sentences are based on?"

Immediately, Richard raised his hand, and Professor Talbot called on him. Richard stood and said, "The three factors are type of drug, weight of drug mix, and prior convictions."

Of course, Richard knew the answer. He was majoring in Criminal Justice. He was tall with mocha skin and short curly black hair. He was a cutie.

Professor Talbot asked, "Are judges able to look at other factors?"

"No sir. Factors like the offender role, motivation, and likelihood of recidivism aren't considered. The only way to reduce a defendant's sentence is by substantial assistance."

"Aw...very good. Who can tell me what substantial assistance means?"

No one raised their hand, except Richard again. Professor Talbot looked around ignoring Richard and asked the class, "What do you think it means? Just guess. I realize you have not covered that portion yet in your reading of today's assignment."

Again, no one moved, then DeMarcus got up from his stool and said, "It's information that is used by the government to prosecute other offenders, usually the ring leaders."

It was nothing for DeMarcus to watch Jackie during the class, but this time it was different. He looked at her and smiled like he knew what she had been doing. Jackie panicked. She tried to think. Does he know? Had he secretly been at the house during one of her parties? Could he have seen something that he shouldn't have?

Jackie sat in her seat, and it seemed like everything in the room had stopped. The four walls drew closer and closer to her, until she felt like she was being pushed, even squeezed by them. Jackie couldn't push back because the walls were too heavy, she felt like they were going to crush her unless she got out of there.

She could go to jail. This thought crossed her mind before, but never seriously, at least not until now. She felt like she had to do something, but she wasn't sure what. The mandatory sentencing guidelines were another effort to rectify the war on drugs and clean up society. Jackie knew she was only helping to make it filthier by having coke parties in her parent's house. She felt dirty. She had to get out now.

"Thank you, DeMarcus." Professor Talbot looked over at him, proud of his protégé. "Now, let's discuss the property associated with drug trafficking. Who can tell me what happens to the property?"

This time, Kenny raised his hand and Professor Talbot nodded at him.

Kenny stood and said, "The government can seize your house, automobile, and any other property connected with a drug offense."

They could take her parent's house! Jackie started coughing uncontrollably, tears began rolling down her cheeks. She grabbed her things and headed for the door.

Professor Talbot called after her and asked, "Jackie, are you alright?"

She managed to say, "Yes sir, but I need to go."

The professor said, "Okay, hope you feel better."

She ran to a water fountain, dropped her bag to the floor, and tried to stop coughing and catch her breath. She grasped the edge of the water fountain with one hand and pushed the knob with the other until water sprung forward from the spout and she drank. Finally, she was able to breathe. She told herself to stay calm. Everything was going to be fine. She had to get out of the business. She just had to think about how she was going to do it. She picked up her bag and headed home. She couldn't go to any more classes today.

As soon as she got home, she ran into Lindsey who was talking with one her male friends. They were sitting on the couch. Of course, Lindsey was dressed like a skank again, only this time, she was wearing a turquoise lace robe. Jackie walked past them into the kitchen for something to drink. And after the day she had, she needed something strong.

Lindsey said, "Hey, Jackie."

Jackie didn't answer. She poured some Grand Marnier and heard the front door close.

Lindsey came into the kitchen and asked, "So, when are you having another party? I want an invitation next time." She laughed.

Jackie stared at her but said nothing.

"By the way, I loved the spread. Shrimp, hot hors d'oeuvres, plenty of liquor, and I mean the good kind, not the cheap stuff. I know the difference."

Jackie said, "Look, you have it all wrong, I sell beauty products. Hal brought the drugs himself."

Lindsey said, "Like hell you sell beauty products! You must think I am a fool. Why are you selling coke...oh, I mean beauty products?"

Jackie looked at her, finding it hard to believe that Lindsey was so nosy. Jackie said nicely, because she needed Lindsey to leave her alone right now, "I'm sorry about what you saw, but I'm not selling drugs."

Lindsey persisted, "So, while we are talking about it, who do you sell for because I know you aren't smart enough to do this by yourself?"

"Lindsey, how many times do I have to say this, I'm not selling, okay?" Jackie walked out of the kitchen and ran upstairs to her room slamming the door. She looked around and said, "Damn! I left my drink. But I'm not going back down until Lindsey leaves."

Jackie sat on her bed, wondering how she was going to handle Lindsey. Then, there was a knock at the door. Already perturbed, Jackie answered it. Of course, it was Lindsey.

"Hey, Jackie. Can I talk to you for a second?"

Tired from her day and from dealing with Lindsey downstairs, Jackie couldn't be pleasant. Exasperated, she rolled her eyes. "What is it?"

Lindsey motioned for Jackie to let her in, so they could talk in private. Jackie did and again asked her what she wanted.

"You left in such a hurry downstairs; I didn't get a chance to talk to you about my proposition."

Jackie frowned and said, "Proposition? What the hell are you talking about?"

Lindsey started by expressing her appreciation. "Listen, I just wanted to really thank you for the party. In case you hadn't noticed, I've been doing a lot of traveling with some of my boyfriends. You wouldn't believe where they take me—Paris, Hawaii, you name it and I've been there. This has truly been some of the best months I've had in a long time."

Jackie looked to the ceiling letting her know that she couldn't care less about her sexual escapades and the destinations where she had them.

"Lindsey, I'm glad for you. Now what is it that you want? I have a lot of studying—"

"Okay, I'll just get to the point. How about you score me some coke on the side from your friend?"

"What! What friend? Are you dense? I just told you I'm not selling."

"You know who I'm talking about. Your older friend."

"I can't do that. First, she is not my friend. And second, I can't get coke for you."

"Oh yes you can, or our little secret will leak out to your parents. Now, we wouldn't want that to happen, would we?"

"Lindsey, are you blackmailing me?"

"Take it any way you want to. I just want a regular supply at least once a month. I don't think that's too much to ask."

"Are you crazy?"

"I saw you get paid. So don't act like you aren't selling. I'm not asking you for any money, I'm just asking that you to slip me a little coke here and there."

Furious, Jackie understood why Lindsey didn't have custody of her twins, and why she claimed she was being discriminated against at work. She was certifiably crazy.

"Lindsey, get out!" Jackie motioned by pointing at the door.

Lindsey walked out into the hallway. "Okay, well, you think about what I said. I'll expect my first supply on the fifteenth of next month. Oh, and since I'm waiting on my settlement—"

Jackie slammed the door in her face before she could complete her sentence and shook her head at Lindsey's nerve.

Lindsey yelled outside of Jackie's door, "Do you think you can let me slide on this month's rent as well?"

Jackie wondered aloud, "What am I going to do? She is blackmailing me for coke, and she wants me to let her slide on the rent. If I don't give it to her, she is going to call my parents."

Jackie called Ursula and told her about Lindsey as well as what she learned in her criminology class.

Ursula cut her off and said, "I don't care about the class, just tell me what that bitch said."

Jackie could barely get the words out, because she was crying so hard. "She just told me that I needed to have the coke to her, on a regular basis, by the fifteenth of each month."

"How dare she demand free coke. Who does she think she is? Tell me everything you know about her, where she is from, her family, her job. Everything, and don't leave anything out."

They stayed on the phone for an hour while Jackie did as she was told. She was so stressed out. She wished she had a little coke to help her relax. At her next party, she decided she would sneak some for herself, or better yet, she would just buy it because she didn't want to mess with Nita's money.

22

Nita woke up early in her beautiful three-story custom home in Silver Springs, MD. She got out of bed and walked over to the window. Her eyes watched the soft moving water swaying back and forth from the soothing Potomac River. She took a deep breath and sighed. The peace of the water brought her into total serenity. Her favorite part of the morning was when the sun made its way into view and peeled back its rays.

Her home was an all-white palace— white walls, white furniture, white fixtures, and white marble floors. She had it cleaned once a day by her maid.

Nita lived a good life managing the boutique as well as her side businesses. As she glanced around her room, she strolled to her sitting area where she caressed a cashmere throw that sat on top of a white Persian lounge chair. As she stroked the soft throw, it reminded her of two goals in life, never to be poor again, and to marry a wealthy white man. She then stared at the heavenly white bed where her handsome boyfriend, Chase Winters, lay.

Nita loved the fact that Chase was rich. He and his family owned a string of American cuisine restaurants in New York, Atlanta, Washington D.C., and Houston. He also dabbled in real estate here and there. Chase was married and lived in New York, but he frequently came up to D.C. on business as well as to see Nita. She adored him, his skin, his blonde hair, and his blue eyes. Everything in her wanted to be just like him, to look more like him, to have his confidence, and to live the kind of life he lived. She believed if she were lighter, she wouldn't have to work so hard to fit into elite white society. So little by little Nita began bleaching her brown skin, hoping one day to match his glistening, natural perfection. He was such a good man to her, better than any man she had ever been with. He paraded her around like a queen, and she loved every minute of it.

Nita daydreamed for years about the same type of life she now had. Sometimes, she had to pinch herself just to make sure it was real.

She watched him as he slept on her silk white sheets. It was nothing for him to whisk her to the Alps for a weekend of fun or fly her in his private jet to Hawaii for the week. She really didn't know what she would do without him. He was her knight in shining armor. She believed no two people shared a love like she and Chase had and she waited patiently for the day that he would ask her to marry him. Nita hoped she didn't have to wait very long. Even though it was almost like they were already married, because she saw him more than his wife did.

This high class, social elite life was very different from the way Nita was raised. She had been in so many foster homes that she lost count. Back then, she used to feel alone, abandoned, but most of all, furious. Nita thought back to her childhood, remembering the days when she walked to school and passed drunks hanging on the street. One day a man pulled her arm; she jerked away from him and screamed, "No!" The old drunk splashed her clothes with beer for talking back to him. Standing there in her beautiful white house, Nita could still smell the salty beer and feel the wetness from it on her clothes. She clearly remembered his words: "Bitch, look what yo' made me do. I spilled my beer all over yo' ass. Now come here and let me lick it up." He laughed and chased her. Nita ran as fast as she could away from him, away from the projects, and away from that life.

Her school counselor told her, "If life gives you a lemon, don't just accept the lemon, go and make lemonade." And that was exactly what she did. She started by doing a few petty thefts, then joined some friends and burglarized homes of the elderly at night while the owners slept. She was caught a couple of times, but nothing major. Now she had the best house, the best car, and the best of everything.

The phone rang and she rushed to answer it, not wanting it to wake her angel.

"Hello," Nita said in a soft sadity voice. And with a quick stride, she walked into the kitchen to start the cappuccino machine. Chase loved cappuccino in the morning.

"Hi, it's Megan. I didn't wake you guys, did I?"

"Actually, Chase is still sleep, but I'm up making his cappuccino." Nita spilled milk and wiped it off her white granite countertop with a towel.

"Well, I just wanted to see if you guys are free tonight. We have skybox tickets to the football game, compliments of Robert's firm. Are you guys interested?"

"Oh, I didn't know there was a game tonight."

"There's not in D.C. This game is in Chicago. We're taking the jet around three this afternoon, and we'll have a limo drop us off at the stadium. What do you say?"

"That sounds like a lot of fun. Let me check with Chase, and I'll call you back." Nita was trying not to sound excited, but she was. That was how white people did it. They just flew their private jet to a football game. Forget about airports or standing in line, they had jets and skybox seats.

"Okay, great. Let me know, because if you guys can't go, I need to call Paul and Sandy."

"No problem. I'll let you know as soon as Chase wakes up. Hey, I guess we aren't playing golf this morning. Isn't our tee time at ten?"

"I've already called the club and cancelled. We can reschedule next week. Find out about the game, and let me know," Megan said.

"Okay, I'll call you back."

Nita poured the cappuccino into a white coffee cup that had *Beau-*

tiful Diva written on it in black script lettering. She looked through her 12-foot sheer white curtains out at the Potomac River. It was her idea to build the house facing west, so she could see the river from the bedroom, den, and kitchen. The builder didn't want to do it, but Nita convinced him that it could be done. As she thought about her life, she decided at some point today, she planned to buy some lemonade and have a toast to her old school counselor.

Nita walked to the front door to pick up the morning paper. She smiled as she brought it in and laid it on the bar. She knew that Chase liked to read it while drinking his cappuccino. She returned to the kitchen and opened the cabinet to get another coffee cup for Chase. His cup was plain white. Nita put it down on the counter and poured the cappuccino. Just as she did, she felt a light kiss on the right side of her neck from behind her. She closed her eyes and took a deep breath. Chase wrapped his arms around her waist, held her gently, and said, "Good morning, beautiful."

Nita smiled. "So you're up. I'm making your cappuccino, just the way you like it." She lingered a little before she handed him the cup. She loved it when he kissed her.

He released her and walked around to the white cushion bar chair and sat down facing Nita. She handed him the coffee mug and he said, "You spoil me, you know that."

She smiled and said, "I know, that's what I'm supposed to do."

Nita reached for a small plate out of her cabinet and placed two cinnamon flavored biscotti on it. She set it down in front of him.

Chase dunked the biscotti into the cappuccino. "Thank you. I'm so glad today is Saturday. It's been a long week." He slid his hand over his face as he recalled the week he had and bit the biscotti.

He finished chewing and said, "I bought a house in Richmond. I want you to see it. I don't know if I'm going to flip it or if you and I can live in it when I'm down this way. What do you think?" He smiled at her as he took a sip.

Nita smiled back at him because she had been thinking of expanding her operation to Virginia and maybe into the Carolinas, but she couldn't do it living with Chase. On the one hand, the thought of moving in with him delighted her, but her hours were too crazy and she didn't want him trying to control her.

Besides, she would never be able to explain where she was all the time, with Richmond being so far away from D.C. She had been with Chase long enough to know that he was a powerful man who got what he wanted. So, she said, "But you know that my boutique is in D.C., and I thought you liked my house."

He said, "I do, babe, but that's just it. It's your house. Anyway, you have a manager to take care of things down there. You don't have to be there every week."

She raised her eyebrows a bit and said, "I didn't know you had a problem with it being my house." Nita took a sip of her drink and said, "I'm sure the girls can handle the boutique, but I would feel better if I'm there every week. I'm sure you understand."

Chase put his cup down on the counter and remained silent.

She continued to sip her cappuccino and pleaded with him. "It's my baby, Chase. Besides, I won't see you more than I do now, unless you plan on divorcing your wife."

He looked up and clasped his hands together, using them to prop up his chin. He peered at Nita.

She stared at him and leaned in closer, stroking his cheek. "Are you? Are you planning to divorce your wife?"

He pulled away from her. "Nita, we've talked about this before. You know I plan to divorce her, but I can't right now. She'd try and take me for everything I've got." He shook his head, closed his eyes, and sighed. "I'm hoping that she'll get tired and just leave."

He saw the newspaper sitting next to his coffee cup and picked it up to browse the headlines. Before Nita could say anything, he offered, "The kids are in college now, so there's no reason for her to stay in this marriage." He put the newspaper down as Nita rolled thoughts around in her head.

He said, "But I have to tell you, that's one of the things I love about you. You make your own money. You're not worried about mine. I love that you are so self-sufficient." They both smiled at each other. He said, "But I don't like that you work so many hours. I want more time with you." He winked at Nita and looked back at his newspaper.

If you only knew. Nita had enough money to buy ten of these houses. She just chose to stay below the radar. She was rich and had been rich for many years. Chase had no idea that Nita had money in banks up and down I-95 under at least fifteen different aliases.

She knew she couldn't spend less time in D.C. She was the only connection to the supplier, and she wanted to keep it that way. Therefore, she just listened to him and smiled, sipping her cappuccino.

"Chase, what if something happened to your wife?"

He was barely listening because he was so entrenched in the newspaper article, so he responded casually, "Something like what?"

"Like maybe there was an accident, and she died," Nita stated then smiled.

Chase paused, put the newspaper down, looked into Nita's eyes, and in a stern voice asked, "What did you just say?"

"I'm not saying anything would, but what if? I mean, if there was an unfortunate accident or something." Nita looked up at the ceiling, thinking of ways to get rid of Chase's wife.

"Nita, are you talking about killing the mother of my children? It infuriates me that you would think about doing such a thing."

Nita wished now that she'd never mentioned it. She picked up something in Chase's tone, something she had never heard before—care and concern for his wife. He sounded like he was still in love with her, and Nita felt like the enemy.

Quickly, she turned it around and said, "Well no, I'm just thinking out loud. I mean, you're worried about her taking all your money. I'm just trying to find a way for her not to."

"And you think murder is the answer?" He looked at Nita like she was a common criminal.

And Nita didn't like that look.

He continued, "I said that I wanted her to leave, not that I wanted her dead."

Nita realized that this conversation was getting out of control. She walked around the bar where he was sitting and cupped Chase's face in her hands. She said, "I just love you so much. I don't want anyone to make you unhappy. It just sounded like she could do that...that she could make you unhappy by taking all your money." She tilted her head and said, "I just want you to be happy. I'm sorry."

He looked deep in her eyes and pulled her hands down from his face. He said, "I know you could never be capable of anything like that, it's just that I've never heard you talk like that before. I know you are a shrewd businesswoman, and sometimes you can be a little cold. But I've never seen that side of you. It's almost like I don't know you."

Nita gave him an innocent look, as if she was harmless.

He held her hands, caressed them, and said, "I know you want me all to yourself, and you have me. I'm here almost every other weekend. With the way the boutique keeps you busy, isn't that good enough for right now?"

She answered, "Yes," almost in a whisper.

Chase hypnotized her, she found herself under his spell, as he stroked her hair. "One day, we'll both slow down. I'll sell the businesses, and you'll sell the boutique. But for now, let's just enjoy this moment, okay?"

In a docile move, Nita shrugged her shoulder and agreed. She walked back into the kitchen with her back to Chase. She thought, *I'm creating an empire. There's no way I'm selling anything, not for Chase, not for anybody.* And from now on, she would never mention murder or his wife to Chase ever again.

She picked up her coffee cup and changed the subject. She knew that she let the real Nita slip out, and she didn't want to lose him. She told him, "Megan called this morning."

He said, "I thought I heard you on the phone."

"She and Robert have tickets to the football game tonight in Chicago, skybox of course, and she wants to know if we're interested in going."

Of course, rich people never got excited over anything.

He said, "What do you think? Do you feel like going? Or do you want to spend the whole day in the bed with me?"

"Um, options. Well, I do have a business meeting this morning, but I suppose I could cancel it." She smiled. "I don't know which offer to accept, though."

"Okay, I'll help you. When was the last time you were in Chicago or better yet, when was the last time you were at a football game?"

Nita didn't have the heart to tell him that she had never been to Chicago a day in her life or that she had never been to a professional football game.

So, she responded, "Well, I have to say on both, it's been awhile."

"Okay, it's settled. Cancel your business meeting. We'll meet them at the airport, but before that, let's spend the morning in bed. What do you say?" He stood, picked Nita up, and carried her like it was their wedding night.

Blushing, Nita said, "But I need to cancel my business meeting and call Megan."

As he looked down at her he said, "Don't worry. I think they'll know it's cancelled when you don't show up. I'll text Megan now and let her know that we'll meet her at the airport." Then he whisked her to the bedroom and lay her on the white silk sheets like she was a piece of fine China. Their lovemaking seemed to go on for hours. She was so in love with this man. She never wanted this day to end.

23

Jackie arrived at the penthouse suite at three o'clock for her first VIP party. The party started at seven, but she wanted to get everything ready. Especially since Nita sent a text message cancelling their business meeting. That was one less thing she had to worry about. She hated seeing Nita; actually, she hated being in the same room with Nita. She would never understand why Ursula was so faithful to her, when they both knew Nita was a bitchy witch.

Once she got promoted to senior rep, she was required to have one VIP party a month. The only cool perk was that she got to spend the night in the hotel suite. She set her bags down, got undressed, and took a shower. After the relaxing shower, she sauntered back into the main room and opened the room service menu. She studied the mouthwatering appetizers and ordered the five trays of pan-fried gulf crab cakes with apple celeriac remoulade sauce, the prosciutto di parma, and the basil marinated buffalo mozzarella, along with a whole tray of shrimp cocktail. She then ordered five bottles of wine, because she only brought cognac, vodka, and scotch with her.

The party was a success as always. Jackie calculated her share of earnings and found that she did well. Of course, she knew that Nita made the real money, and they got pennies compared to what she earned.

Between the coke parties, late hours of studying, and juggling both Broderick and DeMarcus, Jackie had a hard time keeping her head above water. It was starting to weigh on her. So tonight, she saved a couple of lines to help her relax and forget all her problems. She dropped $400 in Nita's moneybag and pulled out the mirror and thin tubing. She laid the cocaine on the mirror and sniffed the line of white powder through the thin straw. Within seconds she was in ecstasy and once there, she took a deep breath and floated.

In the morning, she found herself slumped over on the coffee table where she cut the cocaine last night. She must have fallen asleep, because her second line of coke was still sitting on the mirror waiting on her. Since it was already paid for, she sniffed the second line and feelings of euphoria took over her body again.

She drove back to the row house, fully energized. Reality set in as she walked up the stairs after spending the night like a queen. She unlocked the front door. Unfortunately, she was faced with Lindsey sitting on the couch looking at her mail. She said nothing to her as she headed down to the basement to wash her clothes from the weekend. Once she loaded them in the washer, she slowly walked back upstairs to find Lindsey in the same spot on the couch.

Not wanting to acknowledge her, she said in a monotone voice, "Hi, Lindsey."

Lindsey responded, "Hi, yourself. Don't forget about the fifteenth. And did I get an okay on the rent for next month?"

Her high was gone and for some reason it didn't last as long as before. If she had known she had to face Lindsey, she would have taken a couple more lines.

"No, you didn't. Look, it's bad enough that I have to give you coke, but I'm not reducing the rent."

Lindsey shook her head as she walked halfway upstairs and stopped to looked down at Jackie. "Remember what I said."

Jackie couldn't believe Lindsey. She told Ursula about her, and she was sure it would be taken care of. When she picked up the mail left on the couch, she found several letters addressed to different people all with the row house address. She asked out loud, "What's this? Who are all these people? The postmaster made a huge mistake, none of these people live here."

Lindsey heard her and rushed down the stairs, snatching the envelopes out of Jackie's hands.

"Let me see those. Oh, these are mine."

Suspicious, Jackie looked at her, as she perused through the other pieces of mail. She knew something wasn't right. She found a letter addressed to herself from Karrington University. She opened it fast, not knowing why the university was sending her a letter. The return address stated the letter was from the Dean of Political Science Scholarship Committee. Her heart dropped. She had never gotten a letter from them before. She opened it and it said that her grades had dropped below the scholarship requirement and that she would be ineligible for her scholarship next semester. *Oh God!* She sighed. *How am I going to explain this to my parents?*

Lindsey watched her and said, "Are you okay? You look like you are going to pass out."

Jackie couldn't respond. She had been so busy with the parties that she hadn't had a chance to catch up on her assignments, and she had missed more than a couple exams. With the first semester almost about to end, she knew there was no way for her to make up the grades before finals. She would have to contact her professors and come up with a lie.

She rushed upstairs to cry on her pillow. She couldn't believe this. She didn't want her parents to find out. She would use the copy machine to change her grades and pay for her tuition herself. Jackie hated to use the drug money, but she had no choice. Her tuition had to be paid next semester.

She cried herself to sleep, woke up two hours later, and sat on her bed to lament some more. Her life was a mess. She had to do something; she couldn't go on like this. Getting out of the business was a must. Her grades were more important than a coke party.

Her mind wondered, and she thought about her party last night and the obviously pregnant woman who was there snorting coke. Jackie talked to the lady several times about it, but she said she had done it with her other two kids, and they turned out just fine.

Jackie was not sure what to do. Nita had already threatened to turn her into the university or kill her. For a minute she contemplated turning Nita into the police. Substantial assistance could be her answer, but that meant she would be turning herself in too. She knew the authorities would ask her how she knew about all the coke parties. The problem was, she didn't want to go to jail or cause her parents to lose the house. Besides, Jackie didn't even know the supplier. After thinking about it all, she now felt sick to her stomach. She went downstairs to finish washing her clothes. She poured herself a shot of cognac to help clear her head.

In the basement, Jackie took her wet clothes from the washer and put them into the dryer. She set the dryer knob to forty minutes. She sat in a chair and watched the clothes through the glass opening in the dryer. The clothes bounced around, flying without a care in the world. Her black pants joyfully sprung up and down while her tan pants leaped from side to side. For a minute, her clothes looked like they were dancing. She watched her black pants float above the tan pants and thought about DeMarcus and Broderick. They both bounced around in her life, and she didn't know which one to choose. She had reservations, but she liked both. She got up, left the clothes in the dryer, and headed back into the kitchen for her drink.

Jackie sat at the dining room table trying to come up with a plan to straighten out her life. She heard Marissa and Lindsey coming down the stairs, talking to each other.

"Hey, Jackie," Marissa said as she sat down next to her.

Jackie wondered if she should talk to Marissa about her problems. After all, she seemed a lot like Jackie, a little confused and a lot trapped. Jackie decided against it.

"Hey," Jackie said in a depressed tone, ignoring Lindsey.

"Hey, yourself. Why so down?" Lindsey asked, "Was there bad news in your letter?"

Jackie remained in deep thought.

She knew that Lindsey loved nosing around in the roommates' lives because it prevented her from thinking about the failures in her own life—her marriage, her children and her job.

Lindsey poured herself a shot of Brittany's cognac. "Marissa, want some cognac?"

Jackie listened and thought, *how dare she offer Brittany's liquor to someone else like it's hers.* As usual though, Jackie said nothing.

Marissa said, "No thanks, I'm just waiting for DeMarcus." Marissa looked at Jackie's glass and asked, "How can you drink in the middle of the day?"

Lindsey came back into the dining area with two shot glasses and the bottle of cognac.

"Really? It's never too early for a little cognac. Besides, it takes the edge off the rest of the day. Here, try some." Lindsey placed a shot glass in front of Marissa and sat down with her own glass.

"That's something I have to agree with." Jackie picked up her glass and took a sip.

"Oh, you're talking to me now?" Lindsey said, pointing out the obvious cold shoulder she had been given.

"No, I'm not," Jackie, said.

Marissa pushed the glass away and said, "No, I better not. DeMarcus doesn't like me to drink. He says it makes me silly, and he doesn't like silly white girls."

"What? Marissa, you let a black guy talk to you like that. It sounds like you have almost forgotten that you are white."

Jackie said, "Lindsey, you sound like a racist. Interracial couples are everywhere."

Lindsey continued a tirade. "Who does DeMarcus think he is? And why do you let him talk to you like that?"

Marissa defended DeMarcus. "No, but he's right. It does make me silly. And I don't like the way it makes me feel, like I'm out of it or something."

Lindsey took a sip and winced as the cognac burned her throat.

"Marissa, that's the way it's supposed to make you feel. I got a question; how do you feel when he's beating you? Don't you feel a little out of it then too?"

Marissa's mouth flew open, and so did Jackie's.

"He..." Marissa stuttered.

"Lindsey, that's enough," Jackie interjected and pleaded with her eyes to stop the interrogation.

Marissa spoke up on the verge of tears. "He doesn't beat me. We just sometimes have arguments."

Lindsey came back, "Like the argument you had a couple of weeks ago, when he gave you a black eye."

Jackie's eyes raised, because she didn't see the black eye, nor had she heard them fighting.

Marissa stood up and said, "I'm going to wait for DeMarcus in my car."

Jackie reached up for Marissa's arm. "No Marissa, you don't have to do that."

Marissa flinched because her arm hurt.

Just then, DeMarcus walked in the front door. He put his brown suede satchel down by the door and entered the dining room. "Hey, guys."

Jackie sat and watched him while he kissed Marissa on the cheek. Part of her was a little jealous, but in her heart, she knew they could never be together.

Marissa said, "DeMarcus, I'm kind of tired. Can we go to your room now?"

He said, "Okay, is everything alright?"

Lindsey said, "No, everything is not alright. Why do you keep beating her?"

"What?" He eyed Marissa. "I don't beat her. What are you talking about?"

"You know what the hell I'm talking about. You beat her until she is black and blue. We can hear you kicking and punching her," Lindsey said.

DeMarcus got angry and said, "Look, you need to mind your own damn business." He then pushed Marissa toward the stairs.

Lindsey stood up and said, "You need to pick on someone your own size."

DeMarcus yelled back as he and Marissa walked up the stairs, "Lindsey, go to hell!"

She screamed back at him, "I'll be waiting for you when I get there! I can't believe she takes that crap from you."

As soon as they were upstairs and the door closed, Jackie said, "Lindsey, why did you do that to her?"

"She needs to learn to take up for herself. The next time I hear him beating her, I'm calling the cops."

Jackie argued, "Leave them alone. Let them handle their own problems."

"Jackie, are you blind? Apparently, she can't handle her own problems. That's why she gets her ass beat all the time."

Jackie shook her head and finished her drink.

Lindsey said, "Now, let's get back to why you're so down? It doesn't have to do with me and the fifteenth, does it?"

"Lindsey, do you really think I would tell you anything?" Jackie headed back upstairs to her room. She put her key into the bedroom door and saw Brittany coming out of the bathroom.

Brittany said, "Hey, girl."

"Hey." Jackie unlocked her door and walked in. Brittany followed behind her.

"Jax, what's wrong?" Brittany sounded concerned, but Jackie remembered that she wasn't concerned when she forced her to buy that outfit last year. She was the reason Jackie was in a mess now. It was all Brittany's fault.

"Nothing, I just have a lot on my mind," Jackie said in a noncommittal manner.

"Really? Me too." She sat down in Jackie's desk chair. "Charles doesn't call me as much as he used to. Do you think he has someone else? Or do you think he's not in love with me anymore?"

"Who knows, Brit?" Jackie stared at her, because once again, she had steered the conversation to her own problems. Jackie sat and waited, knowing that eventually Brittany would catch on and ask Jackie about her issue.

"I'm sorry, Jax. This has just been a real problem for me. But tell me what's going on with you? Why are you so down in the dumps?"

"I don't think you'll understand. It's financial."

"You act as if I have never had a financial complication before. Go ahead, try me."

"Well, it's about my side business. I don't want to do it anymore." Jackie pulled out her purse and handed Brittany two one-hundred-dollar bills and several others fell onto the floor. Brittany took the money from Jackie's hand but paid more attention to the pile of money that dropped. Jackie scrambled to pick it up.

"What's this for? Uh, I thought you were having financial problems. It doesn't look like you're having any financial problems now. Where did you get all that money from?"

"My side business. Remember last year I borrowed two-hundred dollars, and I forgot to repay it? Thanks, it really helped."

"Oh, yeah. I forgot about that. You must be back on your feet. Is all that money from your beauty product sales?"

"Yes and no. I have people selling under me now. I just don't want to do it anymore."

"So, give two weeks' notice and quit."

"It's not that simple. You can't just quit once you start in this business. Plus, I've been doing it for almost two years."

"What do you mean? Its beauty products, not drugs. Just quit. Honestly, I don't know how you stayed in it this long."

Jackie's heart pounded fast. She looked at Brittany with eyes wide open, and silently questioned if she knew.

Brittany said, "Why are you staring at me?"

Jackie told herself not to give it away and to think of something quick to say. "Uh... No reason. You just make everything sound so simple."

"Well, Jax, it is simple. I hope I helped."

"You did. Hey, Brit, I need to do some research for my sociology class. Can we catch up later?"

Brittany stood and said, "Sure, I'm behind a little myself." She walked to the door and turned around.

"Jax." She paused.

"This problem had an easy fix. You didn't need me to solve it. You had the answer all along. You're an adult now, start acting like it." She then smiled and left.

24

The next morning Jackie sauntered into her political science class unenthused about it or anything else. She slid in just before the professor closed the door, she walked up the stairs in the lecture hall to the fourth row and took her seat. She had much bigger problems than what was happening politically in the world or in this class, so she was there to be counted towards attendance and nothing else.

Professor Brown, a short, stubby white man wearing black bifocals began his lecture.

"Good morning, everyone. I want to discuss the assignment that's worth forty percent of your grade. The city has made preparations for us to attend the town hall in the council chambers this evening at six o'clock. We will listen and observe the proceeding. When it's time for Q & A, I expect you to participate. Please come in professional dress, no jeans or sweatshirts. If you are questioning your attire, then it is most likely not professional. As we discussed last week, there are several forms of city government. As a refresher to last week's discussion, I'm going to write them on the board." He walked over to the digital white board and wrote the following: mayor-council government, council-manager, commission, general law, and home rule.

"Who can tell me what form of government D.C. has?"

No one raised their hand. Professor Brown continued to look for volunteers.

"Okay, I'm happy to pick a volunteer." Then an Indian young lady in the front row raised her hand.

Professor Brown pointed to her and said, "Yes, please stand and state your name."

"Good morning, my name is Jiya. D.C. has a mayor-council form of government."

"That's correct and can you describe it?"

"Yes, sir. The mayor is like the chief executive officer and responsible for the local executive branch. The council is the local legislative branch made up of thirteen members who pass acts and resolutions."

"That's good. One more question, Jiya. How do the mayor and council work together?"

Jiya smiled. "The mayor and the city council work together to pass budgets, draft legislation, and oversee city departments."

"Great work, Jiya. You may have a seat."

"Who can describe the council-manager form of government?" He looked down at his computer and called out the name, "Stanley."

Stanley, a white, lanky student wearing a Philadelphia Eagles sweatshirt stood up and said, "Is it a city that is self-governed?"

"No, Stanley, that's a home rule form of government."

"Sir, I'm sorry, I honestly don't know."

"Stanley, I believe you need to take some time before tonight's town hall and familiarize yourself with these principles."

Stanley lowered his head and took his seat. "Yes sir."

Professor Brown explained, "The council-manager form of government is where a city manager reports to the city council. The city council is usually small and elected at large. The mayor is chosen by the council and mainly performs ceremonial functions. Hopefully you see the difference between a mayor-council and a council-manager form of government. Is everyone clear on these concepts?"

The students nodded in agreement, and some verbally said, "Yes."

"Now, I think we have a couple of people in here from Texas. If you are from Texas, please stand."

Jackie looked up from her desk hoping someone in the lecture hall was from Texas. Her friend, Karly from the other side of the room saw her and said, "Sir, Jackie's from Texas."

Jackie's heart sank into her stomach, as she gave Karly a glare and closed her eyes.

"Thank you, that's right. Jackie, please stand. I have a couple of questions for residents of the great state of Texas."

Reluctant, Jackie stood knowing she hadn't studied for this course, and she likely didn't know the answer.

"Jackie, what cities in Texas have the council-manager form of government?"

She stood silent for a few moments before answering his question. Then she said just above a whisper, "Dallas."

"That's correct. What other cities in Texas have this form of government?"

"Uh...Houston."

"No, Houston is a mayor-council form of government. You should know this."

Jackie knew at this point that she was playing a guessing game. She thought about places she and her family had visited. There was no way she could remember all the cities in Texas.

"Well...Austin."

Jackie could tell from Professor Brown's expression that his patience was growing thin.

"Yes, Jackie that is one of them. We don't want to be here all day. We have to be at the Town Hall at six p.m. Can you just list them for us quickly?"

"Ah...sure... I said Dallas."

Professor Brown waved his hand in a circular motion for her to move in an expedient manner.

Jackie could feel all eyes on her as she struggled to answer his question.

"Okay, ah...San Antonio?"

"Jackie please have a seat. Some examples of cities in Texas with a council-manager form of government are El Paso, Fort Worth, Corpus Christi, and Laredo, etc. The only major city in Texas that does not have this form of government is Houston."

Jackie sat down dejected from his interrogation.

"Now, your assignment is in the syllabus. Please review before tonight and have questions for our mayor. Now, I want to discuss comparative politics and public policy before we end class."

Once again, Jackie felt lost in this subject and almost every subject. She kept her head down, careful not to make eye contact with her professor or anyone until the class was over.

Jackie gathered her things and headed to her remaining classes. Her last class ended at 4:30 p.m., which would make it tough to be at the Town Hall by 6:00 p.m., but she didn't have a choice— she had to attend. She couldn't afford to get a zero on this assignment. She walked home at a rapid pace, hoping to shower, get dressed, and catch an Uber to the mayor's office. Lucky for her, she was just a ten-minute walk to campus from the row house.

Jackie washed her face and took a deep breath. For several moments she stared at her image in the mirror. She did not want to go to this event. Everything in her wanted to stay home and sulk. She still didn't know what she was going to do about her scholarship. Finally, she reapplied her makeup and gave herself a quick pep talk. Then she put on a baby blue blouse and her black Jones New York jacket and skirt. Next, she put on her heels, sprayed on some perfume, and grabbed her Louis Vuitton crossbody bag before heading out the door.

The digital clock in city hall said 6:01 p.m.,— she'd made it just in time for the meeting. A few other students filed in behind her. She took her seat in the council chambers amongst the other students. Her professor complimented them on their dress and timeliness.

At 6:10 p.m., Mayor Goodson gave opening remarks.

"Good evening, everyone. I would like to welcome you all to our town hall. As many of you know, this is my first term as your mayor, and I am always delighted to stand before you and brag on our great city. I'm happy to answer questions about some of our service improvements as well as any approved construction; however, I will not answer questions regarding complaints, tax increases, or other concerns." He pointed to section where the students were sitting. "Today, I want to welcome the students from Karrington University. And Professor Brown, thank you for being with us today. We will have a question-and-answer portion of the meeting shortly. Typically, in our town halls are informal, but I do have certain requirements that apply to all my meetings. Pastor Daniels will now come up and give the invocation."

Pastor Daniels, a middle-age Black man, stood and walked to the podium. Everyone bowed their heads as he gave the invocation. The mayor nodded in approval and then called Ray Castillo, the city administrator a Hispanic, middle-aged man, to the podium. Mr. Castillo didn't move at first, but then made his way to the podium. He looked a bit disheveled and seemed bothered to be there. Jackie could tell right away that the mayor and the city administrator didn't get along well. She wondered what was going on between the two of them. Mr. Castillo cleared his throat in the microphone and led the group in the Pledge of Allegiance. Afterwards, he sat down with a frown on his face. Mayor Goodson ignored him and returned to the podium to provide updates on activities in Washington, D.C.

Jackie watched the mayor and how he conducted business. Despite Mr. Castillo, Mayor Goodson seemed as calm as still waters on the Potomac River. She'd seen him on TV before but never in person—until now. He was cute. She watched how he moved his lips when he talked. She examined how his suit fit snug against his arm muscles. She wouldn't mind getting to know him a little better. She thought to herself, *Jackie stop it! He's twice your age. What would he want with you anyway?* Around town, he was known to be a flirt, and now she knew why. His whole aura gave a powerful vibe, personable and pleasing to the eye, not to mention personality plus. Her mom always said you want to be with a man that not only looks good but has a personality. And he had all the above.

Mayor Goodson said, "We will now open the floor for the question-and-answer portion of our town hall."

A nice-looking white man stood at the podium, dressed in an expensive suit with gold cufflinks.

"Sir, before you open up with questions and answers, I would like to make a statement."

"Yes, sir. Please state your name."

"Thank you, Mr. Mayor. My name is Chase Winters, and I am the owner of Winters International, Incorporated. We are a restaurant chain offering American cuisine with a European twist. I want to take a moment to thank the mayor and the council for what they have done to help small businesses in the area. I am in the process of opening another restaurant here in the D.C. area and the permits, paperwork, and other requirements have gone extremely well. While I have five restaurants across the nation, D.C. has been the easiest to deal with in terms of permits, paperwork and assistance from the city. So, I just wanted to personally express my appreciation."

Mayor Goodson stood up, and walked from his seat to the floor where Chase Winters was standing, and extended his hand. They shook.

Jackie thought to herself, *Chase Winters? That name sounded familiar. Where had I heard it before?*

The mayor said, "We are so happy that you have chosen D.C. to open your sixth restaurant. We want to make sure our entrepreneurs are well taken care of and that the process is not burdensome on them. While I can't take full credit, I would like to acknowledge the Directors of Economic Development, Building Inspections, and Environmental Services for their roles in making sure our businesses get what they need. Please let the record reflect our appreciation for the departments involved."

Chase Winters said, "Mayor, I would be honored for you to come to our ribbon cutting ceremony. Once the restaurant is completed, please bring your wife and family and have dinner with us. For those that don't know, Winters International's next location will be on the D.C. Wharf. Thank you."

Jackie watched the two of them. Their features were both strikingly captivating. That's what money and power look like. She often heard her friends and others make these same references about her father. Then it clicked. Ursula had mentioned Nita's boyfriend's name was Chase Winters. But why would he want to be with Nita? She was average at best, and he was gorgeous. Jackie thought, *Is he selling coke too, or is he the supplier?*

Mayor Goodson responded, "I would be delighted to attend the ribbon cutting ceremony and dine with you. My assistant, Robin will have to check my calendar, but if I'm available, I would be happy to attend. Thank you so much for the compliment. Now, we will turn to our question-and-answer session. If you have a question, please step to the podium and state your name along with your question."

Jiya sprung up and headed for the podium. Jackie sighed as she watched her try to impress Professor Brown.

"Good evening, sir. My name is Jiya Kumar, and I am a junior at Karrington University. My question is, what challenges do you see with the mayor-council form of government? And how do you overcome them?"

Mayor Goodson stood at the podium and said, "Well, I think having the mayor as the CEO of the city presents the same challenges as a CEO in corporate America. You have to be able to present a vision and be flexible as others get on board with that vision, or as the vision changes due to circumstances. I find that communication is key. You have to be able to explain the 'why' behind what we are doing and strive to work together as a team."

Jiya continued, "Thanks, but what happens when they disagree?"

"Well, we are all human and disagreements happen. I am open to hearing their thoughts and ideas. There are times where I agree with them, and sometimes we change course. Then there are times when I don't agree, and we hold steady towards the intended goal. If we are focused on the best interest of the city and how we can help the city, then I'm open. My whole administration is about servant leadership. We are here to serve the people, and if we are doing that, it doesn't matter to me who comes up with the ideas, as long as we help our citizens."

The room erupted in applause for the mayor. He placed his hand over his heart acknowledging their sentiment.

"Great question, Jiya. But let me just say this: communication is something your generation needs to work on." He raised his hand to motion a stop symbol before continuing. "Now, I don't want you to take this the wrong way, but I know many of you spend a lot of time on social media outside of class. And while it has it's advantages, it also has some huge disadvantages. Having dialogue with one another is important not only to express your opinions, but also to hear the opinions of others. Face-to-face dialogue can be lost when text messages are your main source of communication."

He paused briefly, then said, "Next question?"

An African American young woman walked up to the podium. "Good evening, sir. My name is Hannah Davis, and I'm a junior at Karrington University. I would like to piggyback on what you just said. Social media is a part of our generation. How do we bridge that gap between our communication skills and your generation's communication skills? Let's face it, when we graduate, it will be you guys making the hiring decisions, and we don't want to be discounted because of our inability to properly communicate with your generation."

"Great question, Hannah. Just for the record, I don't want this to feel like an us vs. them mentality. There must be some sort of balance. Social media is fine but not at the exclusion of face-to-face contact. All of us need to be able to read a person's facial expressions or body language. You can't see that via text messages. Those external factors are just as important as oral conversation. So, practice having conversations face-to-face, using eye contact and shaking someone's hand with a firm handshake. All of that is important, no matter what field you go into. You must have some sort of people skills to make it in this world. I don't know if you've heard the phrase that 'deals are made on the golf course.' That's face-to-face interaction. One thing you can all do, and I know Karrington pushes this agenda forward, is to get an internship and work within a department. It's not hard and these skills can be learned, but you can't be afraid to practice them. Make sense?"

She replied, "Yes, thank you so much! I appreciate the advice, and I know we all needed to hear that."

"You're welcome. My goal is for everyone to win. We can't do that if we don't learn from each other and help one another along the way."

A thin, young African man stood before the podium with a pen and a notepad. "Good evening, sir. My name is Sonny Abara, and I'm a sophomore at Karrington University. "Thanks for that advice. What makes D.C. different from other states?"

"Ah...you are referring to statehood. Good question. I think our major differentiation is our vibrant urban economy. For example our budgets have been balanced year-after-year for the past 20 years and we have a AAA bond rating, a higher rating than other states. Not to mention we have a bigger gross domestic product than many states. And, we practically operate as a state while also performing functions of a city and a county. I could go on and on, but statehood is a touchy subject for us. Did you know that D.C. residents pay federal taxes that is more per capita than any state and more total federal taxes than twelve states?"

Sonny responded, "No, I didn't know that." He picked up his pen and began writing. "Could you repeat that?"

"How about let's chat after the town hall and I'll give you all the information you need."

"Okay, great. Thanks." Sonny grabbed his pen and notepad and returned to his seat writing feverishly.

"These are all great questions. You guys have been doing your homework. Next question?"

Jose, a short Hispanic young man, headed to the podium. "Good evening, Mr. Mayor. What are some of the most exciting projects for the city right now?"

The mayor said, "Great question, state your name?"

"Oh, I'm so sorry Jose Hernandez."

"No worries, we are all friends here. So, Jose, for me, exciting projects are bringing businesses to D.C., like Winters International. The more sustainable businesses we can bring to our city, the stronger our economy becomes. The stronger our economy becomes, the more affordable we can make it for our lower income residents. We have an initiative where a special tax is charged back to the businesses to provide services to our poverty-stricken individuals."

"Wow, so you are constantly giving back to the community through local businesses. That's smart."

"Thank you. That was one of my first initiatives when I became mayor, and we were able to get it passed without any opposition. I think we have time for one more question."

Jackie popped up out of her seat and headed to the podium.

He watched her as she glided to the microphone.

"Good evening, Mr. Mayor. My name is Jacqueline Jones, and I'm a junior at Karrington University. Thank you for all the wonderful advice, but my question is about you. What is your next big milestone for your life?"

He chuckled, "Well, we all have aspirations, right?"

She batted her eyes and said, "Right."

"Let's see, I want to finish my term as mayor with a high approval rating. I want to complete all the initiatives and see growth with those initiatives, and perhaps have them expanded after I leave office. And lastly, my goal is to run for governor."

"Wow...that's a lot."

He looked straight at Jackie and said, "I believe in dreaming big and getting what I want."

She laughed a little and tilted her head, twisted her hair with a small amount of flirtation, letting him know message received.

One student in the back of the room said, "She is so unprofessional."

Jackie ignored the remark and continued her conversation with the mayor.

"So, if you don't mind me asking, what state would you run for governor?"

"It would either be Maryland or Virginia."

"Okay, thanks so much for answering my questions."

Jackie went back to her seat, but she knew he was watching her walk without even looking back at him.

25

J ackie realized that even though she didn't keep her grades up, she'd made a ton of money. She had been busier than usual, working almost every weekend. She was resolved to the fact that she had to put what she recently learned in criminology class out of her mind. She would also have to pay for her tuition, because there was nothing else, she could do.

Now that it was the holiday season, Nita threw a wonderful Christmas party and gave them each a sizable bonus. Expecting that the house would be empty soon, except for Lindsey, Jackie set out to find out what her housemates holiday plans were. She knocked on DeMarcus' door, but there was no answer, so she headed downstairs. She saw Bijon coming into the dining room and asked, "Hey, Bijon. What are you doing for Christmas?"

Bijon responded in a gloomy voice, "The usual, going home, which is the last place I want to be."

Jackie went into the kitchen and poured a shot of coconut rum and eggnog.

She called out to him, "Why do you sound like that? Home should be fun. No school and no projects. I would think you'd be excited about that. Since you never take a break, this gives your brain a chance to recuperate."

He walked into the kitchen. "Yeah, holidays give all of our brains a chance to rest, except yours, right?" He shook his head and smiled. "Your brain has been resting all semester long, hasn't it?"

She turned her nose at him and took a sip of her drink. "Look, this semester has been a little difficult for me, I'll admit. But in the spring, I plan to get back on my 'A' game. Don't hate me because I have a life. It's not my fault that you don't." Jackie hoped her parents would understand the bad semester she had, seeing that they would get her grades in the mail soon. The university had already mailed them out by the time she found out that she had ended the semester with 1 B, 3 C's, and 1 D.

He looked at her drink and said, "Bringing in the holidays a little early?"

"As a matter of fact, I am. Care to join me?" Jackie was sick of him judging her.

"No, I think I would rather retain all my brain cells. Wouldn't want to be like you."

"He won't join you, but I will," DeMarcus said as he leaned against the frame of the kitchen door.

"Whatever, DeMarcus," Jackie said, surprised and annoyed that he was eavesdropping.

"Bijon, you not messing with my girl, are you?"

"Your girl?" Bijon said, "Are you guys dating?"

"You need to quit. I'm not your girl. Marissa's your girl."

"A brother can dream, can't he?" DeMarcus walked closer to Jackie and stroked her cheek with the back of his hand.

"Bijon, don't you think Jackie is fine?"

"Uh, I don't pay much attention to Jackie. She's not my type."

"Man, you must be gay. This girl is fi-zine."

"Whatever." Jackie batted her eyes at DeMarcus and then changed the subject. She asked, "Bijon, when are you heading out?"

He stood there with a strange look on his face.

"Tomorrow is my last final, so I'll leave tomorrow night. What about you?"

Jackie said, "I'm leaving on Sunday. I have a couple of things I need to do before I leave." Jackie had parties scheduled for Friday and Saturday night.

She left the kitchen and walked to LaJuana's room, and DeMarcus followed her.

Bijon stopped her before she knocked and said, "She's not there. She's at work. But if you want to know, she leaves tomorrow morning."

"Okay, thanks."

Bijon went into his room.

DeMarcus followed Jackie back to the kitchen. "Do you want to know when I'm leaving?" He smiled at her and leaned forward for a kiss.

Jackie stepped back and said, "Look, DeMarcus, I know I've said this before, but this is it. After Christmas break, we are not hooking up anymore. You're dating Marissa, not me, and I'm dating Broderick. Okay?" Although she and Broderick hadn't been together in a month or so, she didn't want DeMarcus to know that.

"If you say so, but I can drop Marissa tomorrow. Come on, Jackie. Let's give this a try. We've been playing with each other long enough." He licked his lips, pulled her near him, and said, "It can work. Our chemistry is off the chain."

"I'm serious, stop it." She pushed him away and raised her voice. "I don't want you!"

DeMarcus' demeanor changed. He grabbed Jackie's arm, squeezed it, and pulled her into his chest. He said, "Don't ever tell me you don't want me!" He held her tighter to make her listen.

Jackie looked at him, and it seemed as if he was looking straight through her, almost like he didn't see her at all. She took her other hand and tried to push him away, but his grip was too strong.

He shook her and said, "Do you understand?"

Frightened by his actions, Jackie screamed, "Yes, DeMarcus! Stop, you're hurting me!" He didn't respond so she kept yelling, "DeMarcus, stop! You're hurting me, you're hurting me!"

Finally, he asked again, "Do you understand?"

Jackie made eye contact with him, hoping to melt his heart. Tears formed in her eyes, and she whispered, "I do. I'm sorry. I'll never say that again."

DeMarcus took a deep breath, released her arm, and walked out of the kitchen.

Jackie leaned on the kitchen counter, massaging her arm. She couldn't understand how she could have ever fallen for that maniac. She knew for sure that she had to stop messing with DeMarcus. He was dangerous.

26

Christmas break was over, and the spring semester was in full swing. Jackie wondered what was taking Professor Lyons so long. School policy mandated that students give the professor fifteen minutes to arrive before a class could be cancelled. Everyone else was talking or looking over their assignments, but Jackie was thinking about her next party.

Broderick walked into the classroom. They hadn't spoken since the middle of last semester. Their relationship kind of fizzled out, because of her work schedule. But since school started back up, they had been eyeing each other in class.

He swaggered over, sat next to Jackie and smiled. "Hey, Jacqueline. What's up?"

"Nothing much. I've just been busy studying." Jackie was so proud of herself for playing it cool, even though she wanted to kiss him. She smiled and said, "What about you?"

"You know me I spend most of my time in the library."

She smirked. "I don't believe you've been in the library that much."

He laughed. "No, not exactly, but I've been around."

Seduction filled his eyes. "You look good, as always."

Jackie laughed. "Thanks." She hoped they could put their relationship back together this semester.

Just then, Professor Lyons walked in. "Good morning, everyone. Sorry I'm late. I had a faculty meeting that ran over." He placed his briefcase on the desk and took a stack of papers out. "The topic of our discussion today is the effect of politics on social programs. How many people in this class have taken part in giving back to the community through a social program?"

Broderick and others raised their hands, but most didn't, including Jackie. He asked those who had participated to stand and explain their involvement. Jackie sat in silence trying to remember at least one time she helped someone less fortunate. Her focus was Broderick. He was so fine. Maybe the third time would be the charm for them.

The professor continued to give a dissertation about the importance of the political climate on social programs and social awareness. He passed out an assignment to the class. The room was quiet as each student examined their own individual assignment.

Baffled by her assignment titled "Karrington University Hospital Boarder Babies," she thought, *what in the world is this?*

Seeing the shock of his class, and the uncomfortable silence in the room, the professor explained the assignment. "This project will represent your final exam. The assignment will consist of you spending at least two hours a week in the facilities listed on your sheets. It will take about three months to effectively study the social problem, the people affected, and possible solutions to the problem."

Professor Lyons made eye contact with each student as he walked around the room. "Your project will have three components; you are to first review the current programs that the state and/or federal government have already implemented so you can determine what role politics plays in the program. Then you will develop your own program addressing the identified failures of the existing state and federal programs. Finally, you will introduce two ways that the individuals affected can take on their personal plight and help themselves. Please include in your research the political nature of each program, demographics, etc. It is important to remember that politics affects every aspect of our life. Please do not exchange projects with each other, the project you have been given is specifically assigned to you."

No one said a word. Everyone attempted to swallow the concept of spending two hours a week in a government facility.

"Now, I realize this will take some time, effort, and a lot of research. You should have plenty of time, if you manage it properly. Now do you have any questions?"

Broderick raised his hand and stood. "Sir, what about the assignments in our syllabus? Are we doing those in addition to this?"

"Good question, Broderick. Yes, you will be responsible for those as well."

The professor heard the moans and groans from his class. He said, "This is Karrington University. We don't moan. When given an opportunity to learn and expand our mind, we do it!"

Broderick interjected, "Sir, with all due respect, I understand studying the social systems, but is it necessary to spend time in these facilities?"

Jackie admired him. He was such a take-charge man.

The professor responded, "Yes, Broderick, it is necessary. First, the name of this course is State and Local Government II, and what better way to learn about the government than through its programs. Secondly, many of you don't really know what life is like outside of the gates of your own little world and Karrington University. I realize that not all of you come from families with money, but a great many of you do, and you need to see how the other side lives." He peered at Broderick while he adjusted his toupee. "Broderick, do you have any more questions? I feel quite sure that I have sufficiently answered you."

"No, sir, thank you." Broderick sat down and bowed his head looking at his sheet.

Jackie felt sorry for Broderick. She would try to cheer him up after class. When class ended, everyone left in silence. Jackie wondered what in the world she was going to do with her assignment, and when would she have the time to do it.

She rushed up to Professor Lyons before he left and prepared her lie. "I'm really excited about this assignment, but I don't know what boarder babies are. I know you said that we can't exchange, but is there any way you can give me a new assignment? I really need to keep my grades up, and I don't want to fail."

Without looking up, Professor Lyons said, "No new assignment. Each assignment has been specially chosen for each student." He placed his papers in his briefcase and finally looked up at her. "Jackie, if you don't want to fail, I guess you will have to visit the hospital and do your research."

"Yes, sir. I guess I will. Thank you."

Jackie saw Broderick leaving. She hurried back to her desk, picked up her bag, and ran after him.

"Broderick, hey. What's your assignment?"

He started to answer, but Jackie cut him off. She stroked his face with her hand and said, "Let's talk about it tonight over dinner."

He stepped back and said, "Whoa, Jacqueline. I can't...I have a girlfriend."

Shocked and dejected, Jackie put her head down and said, "Oh... Okay."

He said, "I'm sorry. Things didn't work out with us, but I moved on. I thought you did to."

"Oh yeah, I definitely did," Jackie lied.

There was complete silence between them. Finally, Jackie walked away and said, "Well, I guess I'll see you in class." She was so embarrassed that she had practically thrown herself at him, and he had a girlfriend.

Miserable after talking to Broderick, she strolled home thinking about what might have been between the two of them. Once she arrived, she dropped her bag to the floor and plopped on the couch, upset that she blew her chance with him. She really thought Broderick loved her.

Lindsey came down the stairs with an envelope in her hand.

"Hi, Jackie," she said in a wary tone.

Jackie didn't pay much attention to her but spoke back. "Hi, Lindsey."

Lindsey sat on the couch beside Jackie.

She said in a defensive tone, "Have I ever shown you a picture of my twin girls?"

Jackie said, "No," still thinking about Broderick. She wondered how long he'd been dating his girlfriend, was she a new girlfriend, or was she someone he dated before her. Maybe it was someone he really didn't know.

"Well, I'm sure you've seen them before," Lindsey said in an aggressive and angry tone.

Jackie eyed her, trying to figure out what was up with the attitude. "No, I've never seen them before. Why?"

"Well, that's funny, because I haven't seen them in a while either. But your friends have seen them, and they sent me this picture."

"Lindsey, what are you talking about?"

Lindsey threw the note and the picture in Jackie's lap. The note said, *you better keep your mouth shut. You think you got problems now. You won't have any girls if you open your mouth to anyone about our parties.*

"Oh my God. Where did this come from?" Jackie said, shocked at the note.

"Since they are your parties, I thought you might know," Lindsey snapped.

"Well, you don't think I sent this, do you?"

"No, you don't have it in you to do this. This came from your friends. I want you to give them a message for me." Lindsey narrowed her eyes and lowered her voice. "If anything, and I mean anything happens to my girls, I will do whatever I have to do to make them pay, and Jackie that means you too."

"What? I didn't have anything to do with this."

"Jackie, they obviously don't want me telling the police about the parties, and you must have told them that you've been giving me free coke for the last two months."

"Yeah, I did, but I had no idea she would do something like this." Jackie thought Ursula would talk to Lindsey and maybe tell her to back off. She had no idea that Ursula would threaten Lindsey's children.

"Jackie, what's the lady's name that came to the house?"

"Who? Ursula?"

"Is that the old one?"

"Oh, you mean Nita?" Jackie still couldn't understand how Lindsey could call anyone old, especially with her tanning wrinkles.

"Yeah. Her."

"Are you sure? I don't think Nita would do this." Jackie thought, *If Nita knew, she would probably do something far worse than send a threatening note.*

Irritated, Lindsey said, "I don't know who did this, but it said if I open my mouth about the parties, they are going to do something to my kids. I don't know of any other parties that are supposed to be secret, do you?" Ticked off, Lindsey got up and stared at Jackie, waiting for an answer.

Jackie said nothing.

After a few moments, Lindsey headed upstairs, leaving Jackie with the note and the picture of her girls.

Jackie continued sitting in silence, amazed at the note and the picture. She realized that this had gone way too far. Something had to give.

roderick called Jackie shortly after their encounter in class. Since then, they had been talking on the phone a lot and studying together. Both were unsure of what to expect from their relationship, but they had a connection that was indescribable, almost like they were meant to be together. Last night, they met at the library, and Broderick worked on his State and Local Government project. Jackie listened as he described the political impact of his program. He also shared his ideas about what he would do to change it.

She felt bad because she hadn't even picked hers up, that was until today. Still unsure what boarder babies were, she decided to get started on her project, especially since final exam time lurked around the corner. She drove to the hospital in her three series silver BMW that she treated herself to after her promotion. When she got to the hospital, Jackie exchanged polite hellos with the hospital reception-ist. She was told that the boarder babies were on the third floor, so she took the elevator up to three. The smell of blood, urine, and bleach all mixed together made Jackie nauseous. She headed for the nurses' station, passing a patient care technician rolling a blood pres-sure monitor down the hallway.

She reached the desk and asked for directions to the boarder babies. The nurse didn't look at her, instead she continued writing in her checkbook. After a minute of listening to Jackie's sighs, the nurse finally asked, "May I help you?"

Jackie responded, "Yes, I'm trying to find the boarder babies."

"Are you here to volunteer or to see a particular baby?"

"Well, kind of...to volunteer and do research. I'm working on a project for Karrington University."

"What project?" The nurse snapped.

Jackie told her about the project.

The nurse asked, "What's your name?"

"Jackie Jones."

After flipping through papers on her clipboard and finding nothing, the nurse searched in a file cabinet and took out a folder. She said, "Yes, I have your name. I thought you were supposed to be here months ago?"

Jackie bit her lip and as politely as she could, said, "Yes, but I've been a little busy."

She hated when people got into her business. After all, she didn't ask her why she was balancing her checkbook at work.

The nurse said, "Okay, we need you to fill out this volunteer form and then I'll give you a tour." She explained that they would do a background check and blood work on Jackie before she was allowed to volunteer in the hospital. Jackie wondered why they needed to do that, but said, "Okay."

Jackie sat down in the small waiting area off to the right and completed the paperwork. She heard wheels creaking and saw an elderly black woman pushing an IV pole, wearing a blue and white hospital gown that was open in the back. She saw the woman's exposed behind and frowned. She thought, *now that's just nasty. I don't know why anyone would want to see that.*

After about 10 minutes, the nurse returned and asked, "Are you ready for the tour?"

Jackie nodded.

The nurse took her paperwork, and they walked down a long

white corridor. She showed her the clipboard where she had to log her hours when she came in. She explained that the hospital couldn't give credit unless hours were logged in. Jackie nodded.

They walked further down the hall, past several carts of dirty linen, and into an area where there were small babies in cribs. Many were just days or maybe even hours old. Jackie peeked inside the cribs. They all were so cute, but most of them were screaming.

She watched a baby boy crying uncontrollably and asked, "Why isn't someone picking him up?"

"Honey, we can't pick up every crying baby on this ward. We barely have enough nurses for the third floor period. You'll get used to it. Boarder babies cry all the time. That's why we need volunteers like you."

Jackie listened to her, and realized how mean she sounded. She asked, "What exactly are boarder babies?"

The nurse caressed the hand of a little girl in a crib and said, "Boarder babies are babies that have been left in the hospital by their drug addicted mothers, mostly coke addicts."

"What?" Jackie's heart raced and beads of sweat formed on her forehead. Once again, she found herself trying to catch her breath and she felt a knot forming in her chest. She couldn't believe what she was seeing.

The nurse said, "Some of them have to be medicated to reduce the shakes and constant crying."

The nurse walked Jackie to the center of the room and pointed inside a crib.

"See this one, we have her on Diazepam to help her. Her mom must have been using every day, because none of the medications are working on her so far."

"Oh my God. She needs a blanket, she is shivering," Jackie said, disturbed by the sight in front of her.

"No, she's not cold. She's having spasms. That's her body's way of going through withdrawal."

"How sad. She is so little. How old is she?" Jackie asked in complete shock.

"She is only two and half weeks old. I've seen this kind of addiction before. It's extreme."

The nurse touched the baby's little forehead, trying to quiet her down, but it didn't help.

"The sad thing is that drugs alter their little brains. She'll probably never be normal." The nurse sighed. "Most likely, she'll have emotional, behavioral, and maybe even learning difficulties for the rest of her life."

Jackie couldn't speak. A million thoughts ran through her head. The nurse talked, but Jackie could only hear parts of what she was saying. The crying and ear-piercing screams of the infants were drowning the nurse out. Jackie's head hurt, because it was so loud in the ward.

She walked over to a crib where the loudest crying was coming from. "Can I pick her up?" Jackie asked, looking at the baby and thinking maybe that would help her to stop crying.

"Well...hold on." The nurse walked into a closet inside the nursery. She came out with a gown to place over Jackie's clothes and a surgical mask for her face.

"Put this on. I'm not supposed to let you hold the babies until after your blood work comes back, but I will let you for just a minute."

Jackie placed the gown and mask on, and gently picked up the baby.

"She is so light. How much does she weigh?"

The nurse smiled at the baby. "She is premature, born a month early. She weighed just under four and half pounds, which is not bad for a crack addicted baby, but now she is only three pounds." The nurse caressed the baby's hand. "Aw...sweetie, it's okay."

She then walked in front of the crib and said, "Most babies lose a little weight, but they pick it back up in a couple of days. This one keeps losing because we've had some problems with her taking a bottle. She is doing a little better, but the doctor says if we can't get her to eat more, then we will have to insert a feeding tube in her stomach."

The baby still cried. Jackie tried to console her by holding her tight and rocking her. She told her it was okay, but the baby couldn't be still. She kept shaking and crying, so Jackie laid her down softly in the crib.

The nurse explained the volunteer duties, but all Jackie could see were rows and rows of cribs, each containing abandoned drug-addicted babies. The nurse tried to talk over the crying babies, but it was hard because each one needed their mother, and each one had no one in sight to help them.

They walked outside of the ward, and the nurse said, "And because their mothers have left them, they are wards of the government, meaning the District of Columbia is considered their parents. They have nowhere to go beyond this hospital."

Jackie couldn't believe what she was seeing or hearing. Innocent human beings that didn't ask to be born already operating at a disadvantage. *How can anyone do this to a baby?* Even worse, how could she contribute to this? She remembered the pregnant client that was at her VIP party. Jackie didn't feel so well. Her vision blurred and she felt faint.

They walked into another hallway, and the nurse helped Jackie to a seat. She asked, "Are you okay? After you put the baby down, you turned pale. I thought you were going to pass out."

"No, I'm fine. I guess I'm just in shock. I've never seen anything like this before."

"I know it's troubling. It makes you think, why would anyone do that to their own flesh and blood? Let me get you some water. When you're ready, there is another area of boarder babies I need to show you."

"You mean there are more?"

"Unfortunately, yes."

The nurse brought some water in a small paper cup, and Jackie took a drink, but she still felt lousy.

The next ward they walked into had four caged like cribs, one in each corner of the room. Each crib had a small mattress inside with a white sheet and a blanket. The walls and tops of the cribs were made of metal bars.

Each one contained a child and a toy. All four children were standing up on the mattresses holding the bars looking out at the nurse and Jackie.

"Oh my God! Are they in jail?"

"No, don't be silly. They are too big for baby beds, so we place them in these containers. It's the only way we can keep track of them and keep them safe. This little one is ten months old. We named her Jackie. Her mother left after she gave birth to her."

Jackie looked at the little girl and said, "Aw...that's my name. She has such a beautiful smile." Jackie reached for her hand through the bars and held it.

"She was born addicted to heroin. Poor thing. You would think that would be enough, but" the nurse paused and then whispered to Jackie, "she is HIV positive, too."

"What!" Jackie snatched her hand back and the little girl cried.

The nurse said, "You can't get HIV by touching someone."

"Oh sorry, I know." Jackie backed away from the little girl and listened to the nurse before she touched another baby.

The nurse then introduced Jackie to the next baby, "This is Zachery. He's such a cutie. He just turned one year old."

The nurse informed her that once they were detoxed, they were moved to different areas of the hospital because they really didn't have room for them. They stayed in the hospital until social services placed them in foster care.

"So, he was born here, and now he's a year old? No one from social services came to get him?" Jackie couldn't believe that she was meeting forgotten children that no one knew existed.

"That's right." The nurse opened the cage and picked him up. He immediately smiled at Jackie and reached for her. Jackie hesitated to receive him.

The nurse said, "It's okay, he's not HIV positive, but I'm not supposed to tell you who has HIV and who doesn't."

Jackie picked him up, and he played with her hair.

"He's so sweet." Jackie laughed at him, while he played peek-a-boo with her.

"They all are. However, I think social services leaves them here longer, because they know they are safe and well taken care of. Some foster homes don't provide any safety or care at all."

They continued to talk, and Jackie placed Zachery back into his cage. He cried and said "No," which made her heart break. It was so unfair that he couldn't play and go outside. The nurse introduced Jackie to the other children there, but Jackie's mind stayed on Zachery.

Feeling overwhelmed and guilty, Jackie left the hospital and drove home. She accidently ran a red light, and horns blared at her. She couldn't get the babies out of her mind. She realized that the very thing she was selling caused these children's lives to be changed forever. After being at the hospital for two hours, she got home and was in a daze. Every party, every meeting, every client raced through her mind, especially the pregnant one. It was all too much for Jackie, and she couldn't take it. She panted for air and her heart fluttered again. She had to find a way out, because she couldn't have the death of babies, or even the fact they were suffering from withdrawal on her conscience.

She picked up a book to study, but she couldn't concentrate. She turned on the stereo, but the music did nothing for her. There was no book, no song, nothing that could erase the memory of those babies caged and crying.

She walked like a zombie to the kitchen in search of alcohol. She found some Patrón Tequila and poured a glass. She drank it quick, and it burned her throat as it went down. She poured another shot and drank it. She then took the bottle upstairs to her room. Once in her room, she set the bottle on the desk and climbed into bed. She crunched her body into a fetal position and cried hysterically into her pillow. Jackie screamed as loud as she could, she couldn't believe that she had let her life get out of control like this. Babies were suffering, Nita was constantly threatening her life, Lindsey's kids were in danger, and she lost her scholarship. She was in hell, and she had no way out.

And to top it all off, confusion had become her best friend. On one hand, she liked the coke parties. In fact, she had grown to love them, because her clients loved her. On the other hand, people died because of the exact thing she was selling. The criminology class discussion, jail time, and the possibility of losing the row house all invaded her thoughts. But there was nothing that added more fuel to the fire than the suffering of innocent babies who didn't ask to be born.

Jackie stopped crying. She knew she had to act, but Nita would never let her go. She tried so many times before. In her heart, she knew she couldn't keep having the parties either. Death was her only way out because if she stopped the parties, Nita would kill her. Although after seeing those babies today, she thought that maybe that was what she deserved and at this point, she was ready for it.

She contemplated sleeping pills and taking her own life. Then again, she knew Nita might beat her to it. She felt trapped. With no options and no way out, it was like she was losing her grip on life. She threw her books across the room, pulled her clothes out of her closet, and destroyed everything in her sight. Falling to her knees in the middle of the floor, she screamed at the top of her lungs. She knew suicide was her only answer.

In the room next door, DeMarcus sat on his bed and remembered all the times he had gone back and forth to New York trying to find her. He talked to a schoolmate last week at the corner store, and he told DeMarcus that most of the people had moved out of the neighborhood. He, himself, hadn't seen her in years. Something in DeMarcus couldn't rest until he saw her and talked to her again. After all these years, he still thought about her and missed her. She was probably married and had kids, but DeMarcus just wanted to know. He wished he could forget her, but he couldn't. Panic, rage, sadness, and loneliness, all felt like steel weights holding him down.

Jackie's screaming disturbed DeMarcus' train of thought. He hoped she stopped, but she didn't. The sounds coming from Jackie's room were all too familiar to DeMarcus. As a kid, he remembered hearing his mother crying and screaming during one of his parent's many arguments. He grabbed his head and put his hands over his ears, hoping to drown out the sound, just like he did when he was a child.

He yelled at Jackie, "Shut up!" Then he thought that maybe someone was hurting her. He wasn't there for his mom, but he would be damned if he let it happen again. He opened his door, rushed out of the room, and banged on Jackie's door. "Jackie, open the door! Who's in there?" He took a breath and said, "Are you okay? Open the damn door now!"

A few minutes before, he had been thinking of his failed trip to New York, but now everything was different. Now he was being forced to hear screams from his past. Only this time, they were coming from Jackie's room. Instead of hiding under his bed, he decided he was going to man up.

He ran down the hallway to Brittany's room and pounded on the door. There was no answer. Jackie screamed louder and louder. So he ran up to the third floor to Lindsey's room, knocked, and again no answer. There was silence now, so he tapped on Jackie's door again and still got nothing. He used his weight to try to push the door down, but it was locked from the other side. He finally left and walked next door to find Trina.

After a while, Jackie heard another knock on her door, a much softer knock. She looked at the clock and it read half past ten. She wondered how long she had been passed out on the floor. Finally, she asked, "Who is it?"

"Hey, it's Trina. Let me in."

Jackie fell backwards, as she tried to get up from the floor. She eventually managed to stand and open the door, leaning on the chest of drawers for support.

Trina took one look at her, and it was obvious she knew something was very wrong. Eyeliner and mascara were smeared all over Jackie's face. Her eyes were red and swollen. Her hair was all over her head and the stench of alcohol flooded the room. Trina didn't say anything, she just looked at Jackie and the mess in the room. Trina walked into the room and helped Jackie to the bed, and then sat next to her.

After a few moments, Trina said, "Jackie, what's going on? DeMarcus came and got me. He said that you were in some kind of trouble."

Jackie said, "Yeah," as she picked up the bottle and took another swig of Patrón.

Trina took the bottle from Jackie and lifted her chin up. "Whatever it is, it can't be that bad. Talk to me. What's going on?"

"I can't. I have to take care of this myself," Jackie said, slurring her words a little.

"Jackie, we tell each other everything. You look like you have been to hell and back. Now, what's going on?"

Jackie held her head down, and hopelessly shook it. She said, "I know, but you can't help me."

"How do you know? I can't help you if you don't tell me," Trina said, with great concern for her friend. "Did something happen on campus?"

"No."

Jackie looked at Trina with tears rolling down her face, because Trina didn't understand.

Jackie thought, *Trina thinks she knows me, but she doesn't. She has no clue of the person I've had become.* It was at that moment that Jackie knew for sure that she had to commit suicide that night. Trina talked, but Jackie couldn't hear her. She was too busy thinking of a way to end her life. Suddenly, Jackie felt Trina shake her.

Jackie jerked away from Trina's grip. "What are you doing?"

"You're not listening to me, so I had to get your attention."

Jackie frowned and said, "I heard you, what?"

Trina said, "So you'll go?"

Jackie didn't hear anything Trina said. She wanted her to shut up and get out.

"Yeah sure, go where?"

"I sat here and talked to you about God and going to church with me tomorrow. You didn't hear a word I said, did you?"

Jackie got up off the bed and took another drink. "Trina, look, I know you are trying to help me. But believe me, you can't help, and church can't help me."

"I'm not saying church can, but God can," Trina insisted.

"You know, I don't know if I believe in God anymore. I'm not sure it's worth it. Besides, I haven't been to church since I was a kid. Lightning might strike me if I walk in."

"Quit tripping, you won't get struck by lightning. That isn't how God works. And as far as not believing in him, you should, Jackie. I learned a long time ago that he can help us out of any problem. I asked you over a year ago, and you said that you would go one day. Well, tomorrow is the day. I really think it will help you sort out whatever it is you are going through."

Jackie sat back on the bed and looked at her.

"Jackie, you will never know if God can help you until you try him."

Jackie wanted to believe her so bad, but she didn't. She thought, *If God was truly God, why hadn't he helped me get out of the business? I've tried so many times, and he's done nothing to help me.*

"Trina, let me think about it tonight," Jackie said, knowing that Trina wouldn't take no for an answer.

"Are you sure you're going to be okay tonight? Maybe I should stay with you."

Jackie said with tears rolling down her face, "No, I'll be fine." She knew this would be the last time she would ever see her friend.

"You know you my girl, and I love you." Trina smiled at her. "I don't want anything bad happening to you, and I don't like it when you're upset and won't talk. But I understand, you want to keep whatever this is to yourself, and I can respect that. Church starts at seven-thirty and ten-thirty in the morning. Which one do you want to go to?"

"I don't care. Either one is fine with me," she replied, knowing that she was not going with Trina. She picked up the bottle again and took another sip.

"You might care if you lay off the Patrón." Trina took the bottle from Jackie once again and put it back on the desk.

"Okay, sure." Jackie didn't know why Trina even said that, because she knew that wasn't happening either.

"Alright, girl. I'm going to let you get some rest. Bye."

Jackie told her friend goodbye. She hesitated then stumbled as she stood, faced Trina, and said, "Thanks for being such a good friend. I love you." Jackie hugged her tight.

"Oh, you're so sweet, but that's what friends do for each other."

Trina opened the door and left, but before the door closed, Jackie heard DeMarcus in the hallway talking to Trina. Then he stepped into her room wearing an undershirt and sweatpants.

"Hey, you alright?" He walked over to the desk where Jackie was leaning for support and touched her cheek.

Jackie rolled her eyes and moved his hand. "I'm good, thanks."

DeMarcus examined her face and said, "I don't think you are."

"I am. I just need to get some rest." Jackie staggered toward the door and said, "So if you don't mind, I need you to leave."

DeMarcus reached his arm out to help steady her. He stopped and stared at Jackie in a strange way again. "No, I'm not leaving. I don't know what's going on with you, but whatever it is, it's serious, and you need me."

Jackie closed her eyes and sighed hard. She flipped her eyes up at him and said, "DeMarcus, didn't you see Trina? I've already talked to her. So, I'm good. I don't need you to hang out. Please leave me alone."

"I'm sorry, I can't leave. Something is telling me not to leave."

"What? I don't know what you were talking about, but everything is fine. I'm sorry I worried you. Besides, you're right next door, so I really won't be alone."

"I don't know. I don't have a good feeling about this. I can't describe it, but it's familiar. The last time I felt this feeling, it was right before my mom was killed."

"What?" Jackie replied.

"I don't want to get into it. I'm more concerned about you."

"Okay, DeMarcus, whatever. I'm changing clothes and I'm going to bed." She stumbled to her dresser drawer.

"Okay, go ahead." DeMarcus sat in her chair in front of the desk.

"You got to be kidding me. Jackie looked at him like he was crazy. "If this is some kind of way to get me in bed, you are fooling yourself, because I'm not in the mood."

"I'm not trying to sleep with you. Not that I wouldn't like to, but that's not what I'm about tonight. Like I said before, I'm concerned."

He looked at Jackie, and for a moment, she thought he knew what she was planning to do. She didn't even try to reach in her drawer for the sleeping pills. Jackie figured he would question her, so she left them where they were, changed her clothes, and climbed into bed.

Meanwhile, DeMarcus turned on her TV and sat at her desk watching her. For Jackie, this was the strangest feeling. DeMarcus didn't make any remarks or hints about sex. He just sat there like an angel watching over her.

28

Jackie tossed and turned most of the night because she couldn't sleep. She was anxious to take the sleeping pills and write her suicide note, but she couldn't because of DeMarcus. She wanted her family and friends to know that she had no other choice. But every time she looked over at the desk, DeMarcus looked back at her.

After several hours of his annoying behavior, she said, "It's two-thirty in the morning. Aren't you going to your room so you can get some sleep?"

He said, "No. Jackie, I'm not. Why don't you go to sleep?"

Jackie became more and more frustrated, and tears rolled down her face again. "I just have a lot on my mind, and I need you to leave."

DeMarcus walked over to the bed, took a tissue, and dried her eyes just like he did two years before on the couch downstairs.

He said, "Do you think it would help if I held you like I did before?"

Jackie fought back the tears because she wanted to find out his true motive. She surrendered, realizing that she needed someone to tell her everything was going to be alright.

She said, "Yes, please."

All of a sudden, she burst into another uncontrollable crying bout. Jackie's body shook, and DeMarcus couldn't understand what she was saying. Jackie felt like she was having a nervous breakdown because she couldn't stop crying and she couldn't think.

Without hesitation, DeMarcus climbed into bed, got under the covers, and held Jackie for what seemed like hours. He helped her calm down by telling her that everything was going to be fine and caressed her hair. Before she knew it, she fell asleep in his arms and drifted deeper and deeper into a soothing and relaxing slumber. Her body finally felt at ease, and for the first time in many nights, it was without the help of sleeping pills.

Early the next morning, the ringing of the phone woke them up. Jackie answered, and it was Trina calling to remind her about church. Jackie was out of it and told her she would call her back.

DeMarcus got up, leaned in close to Jackie's face, and said, "Morning, babe. How do you feel?"

His morning breath turned her stomach, but she didn't care. "I feel sleepy and a little out of it," she said, realizing that he had been there all night. "I haven't slept like that in over a year."

He said, "Good. Who was on the phone?"

She rubbed her eyes because they were burning. "Trina, she is trying to get me to go to church with her this morning, but I would rather stay in bed." Jackie pulled the covers back over her head.

He pulled them back and asked, "Why don't you go?"

"I don't know." Jackie sat up in her bed and remembered yesterday and her plan.

She finally said, "I'm not really into church. What about you, do you go to church?"

"Well, not as much now. But when I lived with my aunt, I had to go every Sunday."

"So, you believe in God?" Jackie asked, wondering about his beliefs.

"Of course, Jackie. You really need to go if you are asking me that."

He got up and walked toward the door. He said, "You look and sound better this morning, but I want you to call me if you get in a bad place like that again, okay?"

Jackie nodded in agreement, got up, hugged him, and said, "Thanks so much. I didn't realize how bad I really needed you last night."

He opened the door and said, "You need to get ready for church."

Jackie said, "Alright," in a whiny tone. She closed the door and realized that she had not seen this side of DeMarcus in a while. Partly disappointed that she couldn't carry out her plan, she opened the drawer and debated whether to take the sleeping pills now. She was still not sure what to do, but something told her not to take them, so she closed the drawer and called Trina. Figuring she didn't have anything to lose, she went to church with mixed emotions, not wanting to let Trina down.

They drove to the church, and when Jackie got out of the car, it felt like weights were wrapped around her ankles. Walking up the church walkway, she felt weak and wounded, like a casualty of war, injured from all the lies, drugs, and money. Beads of sweat dripped from her forehead onto her shirt. She was tired of fighting. She had so many areas of her life that were messed up, but she couldn't explain it to Trina, because she was convinced that she wouldn't understand.

"I don't know Trina, something feels wrong." But deep down, Jackie knew it was guilt. Her thoughts turned to the boarder babies, what she had done, and who she had become.

Trina said, "Look, I don't know what's going on with you, but you need help. I promise, you'll feel better after you go in. It's just scary because you haven't been to church in a while." Trina turned Jackie so she was facing her and said, "Trust me."

Jackie felt like such a hypocrite. She had committed sin on top of sin, knowing it was wrong. She thought, *I know that God wants nothing to do with me. If I were him, I wouldn't want anything to do with me.* She walked up the stairs and inside the foyer, hoping that God would be merciful to her. The massive structure of the church overwhelmed her and took her attention from sin to the beauty in front of her. The choir sang and they sounded wonderful.

Trina and Jackie sat down, and a lady greeted them. Jackie smiled in return. She listened to the choir and almost believed the words to the song. They talked about people plunging into despair and God's ability to forgive.

Of course, Jackie wasn't sure how she was going to stand up to Nita, but listening to the song really did something for her. The pastor asked all visitors to stand, and Jackie hesitated but did as he asked. She was amazed at the number of people who welcomed her to the church. They walked over, introduced themselves and hugged her. She was so surprised because she didn't know any of them, but they all seem excited to see her, and she couldn't help but wonder why.

The pastor got up next and told the congregation the title of his message, "Faithful to the End". The pastor started by saying, "How long are you going to let life defeat you? How long are you going to let Satan win? Your God is bigger than you, and he's bigger than your situation."

Jackie thought about that for a few minutes, because her God wasn't very big at all. He had never really done anything for her, so she wasn't sure what his size had to do with anything. Jackie rested in her seat thinking, *this man has no idea what he is talking about, he hasn't met Nita.*

"But some of you want to put God in a box, and you want to make him less than God. You treat him like he's any ole man who handles problems. But what you need to know is God can instantaneously change your situation."

The instantaneous part caught Jackie's attention, because she knew she needed a quick answer to her problem. But she had never seen God work before, so she questioned why would he do it now.

The pastor preached and Jackie listened. "Think about it. If he created the universe, he must be bigger than the universe."

Jackie pondered the size of the universe. Moreover, how big would God have to be to create it?

Then the pastor said, "Let me tell you a secret. Do you know that everything you take to God is small? Some of you think your problems are bigger than life. Well, I tell you nothing in your life, no situation, no circumstance is bigger than God."

Jackie whispered to Trina, "Now that's pretty deep."

Trina nodded.

The preacher stepped out of the pulpit and walked in front of the congregation.

He lowered his voice and softly said, "I want you to know that God told me there's someone here who has given up. You've given up on yourself, and you've given up on life. You've just given up."

Jackie stared at the minster as tears streamed down her cheek.

He walked up and down the aisle, looking at the people and said, "Someone in this place contemplated suicide last night. Oh yeah, you had it all planned out. How you were going to do it, the note you were going to write, and everything, but God had a different plan."

He stretched out both arms and said in a soft voice, "This is what God did last night. He swooped down like an eagle, spread out his wings, and just in the nick of time, he calmed the raging storm that was in you." He clapped his hands and raised his voice. "Oh, God's a mighty protector. For someone last night, God did the ultimate. He protected you from yourself."

Jackie heard the members saying "Amen" all over the church. She started crying and could barely see the preacher through her teary vision. She felt Trina put her arm around her. The pastor stood in front of the area where Jackie and Trina were sitting and looked right at Jackie.

He raised his voice again and put his hands behind his back. "Someone needs to hear this today. He wants you to know you are a precious and priceless, and He doesn't want you to take your life." The pastor paused and his voice broke. Filled with emotion, he said, "He loves you. No matter what you've done in the past, God's not condemning you. He's saying repent, turn from your wicked ways, and follow me."

He turned to the choir, and they stood and said, "Amen, pastor, amen!"

He pointed his finger to the congregation. "Now listen to me and listen good. He says when a man lives and when a man dies, that decision is not yours."

Jackie felt like a spotlight was pointed at her. The man had to know God, because no one knew what she was planning last night or even what she was thinking. How else would anyone know about her plan?

"We are complete, lacking in nothing, we have everything we need to be everything God has called us to be. Seek God and He will provide for all your needs."

Now he was losing Jackie, because she had never felt complete.

Jackie dried the tears from her eyes and focused on what the pastor said. Right there she asked God for direction in getting out of the business. For the first time, she realized something. She hadn't asked for anyone's advice about her problem. But maybe it was time for her to stand up, trust herself and let God tell her what she needed to do.

While Jackie thought about her situation, most of the church stood on their feet, shouting and tossing their handkerchiefs at the pulpit. The atmosphere in the church was full of excitement. She heard a lady say, "Lord, I believe it! I receive your confidence by faith." Jackie repeated what the lady said to God.

After listening to the sermon, Jackie felt different, like she could do anything because she believed God was big enough to handle her problems. Besides, the pastor proclaimed, God was a forgiving God. This specially made her feel better. He said that God loved his children so much, that he didn't care what they had done in the past. Jackie took this to mean including dealing drugs. The preacher said to confess, ask for forgiveness, and seek God again and Jackie did.

Leaving the church, Jackie was on a high. She had never been excited about God before, maybe because she never needed Him as much as she needed Him now.

She and Trina left the church heading to the parking lot and a church member stopped them. "Hi, girls. Did you enjoy service today?"

Trina and Jackie both responded at the same time, "Yes, ma'am."

"Good, so I'll guess I'll see more of you. I'm Sister Taylor. I'm over the hospitality committee." She extended her hand for them to shake.

Jackie said, "Nice to meet you."

"You too. Oh my, you have beautiful eyes." She stopped and asked, "Do you mind if I ask you a question?"

Something stirred in Jackie, and she remembered that she was "complete, lacking in nothing."

Jackie said boldly, "Sure, ask away."

Sister Taylor smiled and asked, "What color are you?"

Jackie took a deep breath and then let Sister Taylor have it. She stepped to her face and said, "Well first, I'm at an African American church, and sitting with my African American friend. My skin, my eyes, and my hair may not seem African American to you, but have you seen my ass? It screams African American." Jackie promptly turned around and showed the lady her butt. Then she said, "Now do you know what color I am?"

Sister Taylor started fanning herself, amazed at Jackie's rudeness.

Trina shouted, "Jackie, apologize to this woman!"

Jackie looked right into the woman's eyes and said, "No."

Trina turned to the lady and said, "I'm so sorry. My friend has been under a lot of stress. I'm going to take her home." She grabbed Jackie's arm and pulled her towards the car.

"Jackie, what the—"

Jackie stopped her and said, "Trina, I'm complete, lacking in nothing. From now on, people who ask me stupid questions about my color are going to get answers that would never make them question it again."

Jackie hated what she did, but she had had enough. She said a prayer to God, "Please forgive me for cursing on holy ground, and please forgive me for being rude. Amen."

After church, Jackie rushed home and rummaged through her closet. She took out everything Nita had given her over the past two years, which was pretty much everything in her closet. She made piles and piles of clothes and shoes, all designer and all from Ostentatious. She remembered the way each piece of clothing made her feel when she wore it. She put all the clothes in trash bags for Goodwill.

She picked through her jewelry box where she kept her diamond rings and earrings. She loved them, but they were brought with drug money, so they had to go too. Jackie snatched the brown satin sheets off her bed along with the down comforter. She took everything, including her brand-new laptop and her new cell phone, and put it all in a pile by the door. Tomorrow she would debate on whether she should return the car to the dealership.

Jackie would do her best to complete the boarder baby project by semester's end and pray for a C. After seeing Zachery in the hospital, Jackie visited him every week until school was out. In one month's, time, she put in more hours than she would have in the three months. That little baby had stolen her heart.

A perfect way to end the year; Jackie returned to Dallas for the summer, and this time with the will and determination that she could conquer anything with God. She vowed to use this summer as a chance to figure out how to get out of Nita's business for good.

PART III

SENIOR YEAR

29

On Saturday, Nita invited Ursula to her house for lunch. Ursula naturally accepted, but she wasn't sure about the motive behind the invitation. She had only been to Nita's house a handful of times. Ursula knew it couldn't be about her performance because she was always on top of her game. All her reps were handling their territories, and the money was rolling in just the way Nita liked it.

It was a perfect summer day, bright and shiny. Ursula arrived at the entrance of Nita's house shortly before noon in her black convertible BMW with her music blaring. She rocked to the beat and popped her gum. White tulips lined the drive up to Nita's estate, and Ursula was reminded of Nita's wealth. Two gigantic lion statutes positioned on each side of the stone fountain caught her eye as she circled the majestic water feature in the driveway. She glanced up at the massive white French Country Chateau with large bay windows and admired the immaculately manicured green lawn. Each time she visited the estate, it looked more regal than the time before.

Ursula parked behind Nita's white Mercedes under the port de cache. As she walked up the stairs, she pressed the lock button on her remote to set her car alarm. She stood at the door and took a deep breath. She lifted the heavy bronze door handles carved with the face of Athena, the mythological Goddess of wisdom and war, and let them drop three times. The handles made a loud thud sound. Within seconds, Nita answered the door, wearing white linen lounge pants and a sleeveless white tank top that displayed her muscles.

Nita motioned Ursula to come in. She said, "So glad you could come."

Ursula walked into the white marble entrance, wearing Guess jeans and a BeBe designer turquoise silk halter with a peek-a-boo bust line. She was surprised to see that Nita's maid, Sulema, didn't answer the door. They hugged each other and Ursula said, "Thanks for the invite," but thought to herself, *it's not like I had a choice.* If Nita called, Ursula had to come running.

Ursula saw white everywhere, just like before, only it looked like Nita had bought a few more sculptures to complete her decor. The sculptures seemed to add more to an already beautifully decorated house. Nita said, "No problem. I am always happy to have you over. Join me on the terrace." They walked through the kitchen, and she saw Sulema put the finishing touches on their meal. Ursula and Sulema exchanged pleasant hellos, and Ursula dropped her gum in the trash.

A lovely table was set for two on the terrace with a white table-cloth, champagne glasses, and a violet Rhododendron floral center-piece. Ursula and Nita sat down, while Sulema poured the champagne and served a Greek salad with grilled chicken, pears, and goat cheese drizzled with a pink dressing.

Ursula tasted the salad and said, "This is amazing, I love the taste. What kind of dressing is this? It's like a cross between sweet and tangy, with a raspberry twist."

Nita responded, "I'm glad that you like it. It's a splendid salad for a spectacular person."

Ursula looked up at Nita and smiled. "Aw, that's sweet." But she knew there was something more to this than just lunch.

Nita said, "I mean it. I had Sulema create that dressing just for you."

"You didn't have to go to so much trouble for me. Any dressing would have been fine." Ursula wondered why Nita was being so over-the-top nice.

"No, any dressing wouldn't be fine. Not today." Nita raised her glass and saluted Ursula.

"Today is a special day for you and me. It marks five years that you've worked for me."

As Nita talked, Ursula grew even more uncomfortable, because she knew things would change once she graduated. She planned to walk away from the business and never look back, but she couldn't tell Nita that.

Nita gave Ursula a cunning look and said, "How does it feel to be the chosen one?"

Ursula paused, not sure of what to say to Nita, but finally responded, "What do you mean?"

"Well, you've been with me the longest. It's time that I let you in on my plans for your future. I have been looking forward to this day for a very long time."

Nita took a deep breath and exhaled. She said, "I am so proud of you. You have become a shrewd businesswoman but not just any businesswoman, my businesswoman."

Ursula sat silently, shocked that Nita had plans for her.

Nita said in arrogant tone, "Do you remember when I first met you? You were stripping, wasting your talents. I pulled you out of that sewage hole and gave you a better life." Nita took a sip of her champagne and smiled at Ursula. "You said you wanted to go to college, and I helped you get there."

Ursula nodded.

Nita continued, "We've done a lot together, haven't we? I want to make a toast."

They both held their glasses up and Nita said, "Here's to you, Ursula. You've accomplished what most people only dream of." Their glasses clinked, and then Nita said something that surprised Ursula. "You know, it almost feels like I'm graduating from Karrington too."

Ursula maintained a poker face. She couldn't believe that Nita was trying to take the credit for what she had done. She was the one who studied after each party into the wee hours of the night. She was the one who made the grades, and only she would graduate.

They both sipped their champagne. Then, Nita talked about Ostentatious and the other businesses she was involved in. Ursula had no idea about all the businesses that Nita had, or that all of them were fronted through Ostentatious. Ursula was speechless and wondered why Nita was telling her about them now.

Sulema came in with a purple and black striped box with a purple bow on top.

Nita said, "I know you don't have any family to celebrate your graduation, so I wanted to give you something to help you look forward to your next year." Ursula was surprised that Nita would give her jewelry, because she usually gave her clothes.

Ursula said, "I don't know what to say, I don't graduate until next May."

Nita said, "Oh, I know. It's an early graduation gift. Open it and say thank you."

Ursula untied one side of the bow and then the other.

Nita said, "Hurry up."

Ursula opened the small box, and inside was a gold key. She picked it up and looked at it, not sure what to do with it.

Nita said, "This is the key to my boutique, Ostentatious."

Puzzled and still unsure of what to say, or how to react, Ursula said nothing. She learned a long time ago to be appreciative of all that Nita did and the gifts that she gave. Therefore, she just smiled and finally said, "I don't know what to do with it."

Then, Nita dropped the bomb. "Of course you don't. You have no idea. When you graduate in May, I am going to make you the new manager of Ostentatious. You will run the whole operation. Of course, I will oversee it, but you'll be in charge of it and the other businesses. It's a lot of responsibility, but I know you can handle it. Your training begins the following Monday after graduation."

Ursula looked like she had seen a ghost. She did not even intend to be in D.C. on the Monday after graduation.

Nita asked, "Is something wrong? Aren't you excited about my gift?"

Ursula said, "No, nothing's wrong. I'm just a little shocked, that's all."

"Well, that's to be expected. This is a big promotion for you. You will be second in command to me, and of course, you know I'll pay you handsomely. Anyway, this will give me more time to spend with Chase. So see, it's a win-win for everybody."

Sulema came in and said, "Ms. Nita, telephone. It's Mr. Chase."

Nita got up and said, "I have to take this." She took the phone from Sulema and went into the house, leaving Ursula on the terrace by herself.

Sulema asked Ursula, "Is there anything else I can get for you?"

Ursula paused and then said, "Yes, Sulema. Can you bring me a scotch on the rocks?"

Sulema said, "Coming right up."

Ursula leaned on the table with her head bowed down in her hands. Nita never even asked what Ursula wanted to do with her life. Everything was all about Nita and making more money for Nita. Ursula was thankful for how Nita helped her, but she felt that she had more than paid her back for everything she had done. For the first time, Ursula saw Nita for who she truly was, another greedy drug dealer that used any and everybody to get what she wanted.

Nita came back out to the terrace and apologized for the interruption. Sulema brought Ursula her scotch, and she drank it quick. Nita watched her and said, "Ursula, it's kind of early in the day for scotch."

She answered with a straight face, "Not when you're getting a big promotion."

Nita smiled and they both finished their lunch.

30

Jackie walked into "Uniquely You," one of Dallas' hottest spa and beauty salons. She felt like a princess every time she came in the door. The floors were sleek with black shiny marble, and the waiting room had five large flower shaped mirrors that covered the walls. In the center was the receptionist desk decorated in zebra stripes. Jackie signed in.

The receptionist said, "Hi, Jackie. How's it going?"

"Actually, everything is great."

"Good, I'm glad to hear that." The receptionist admired Jackie's one-piece halter denim jumper and her brown strappy neo soul sandals. "Your outfit is gorgeous."

"Thanks." Jackie smiled, knowing she had good taste.

"Where did you get it?"

"I picked it up at a boutique in Uptown last summer, but I don't remember the name of it."

"Oh, I need one of those. Hey, your mom was in here yesterday."

"I know. We tried to get our appointments at the same time, but we couldn't make it work."

"Okay. When do you go back to school?"

"Next week," Jackie said as she looked through the magazines at the receptionist's desk. "Oh, I almost forgot, can I get my nails done today too? Is Ming Lei available?"

"Let me check her schedule." The receptionist looked at the appointment book and said, "She can do your nails about 10 minutes after your hair is finished. Will that work for you?"

"Yeah, that's fine."

"Wonderful. Do you want a glass of champagne?"

"Of course, and a couple of the chocolate covered strawberries, please."

"Coming right up."

Jackie sat in the waiting room while her stylist, Monica, finished a client. The luxurious zebra throws on top of the black leather armchair made her feel royally exotic. Jackie perused through a couple of hair magazines and saw a short hairstyle she liked. She turned the page down so she could show Monica. Jackie scratched her shoulder, and white flakes fell off her skin and onto her clothes, the Aloe Vera cream was not working.

The receptionist handed her a glass of champagne and a small zebra colored plate with chocolate covered strawberries on it.

Jackie took the plate and said, "Thank you." She took one bite and heard Monica calling her.

"Jackie, I'm ready."

Jackie picked up everything and headed over to Monica's chair. "Hey, girl."

Monica said, "Hey, yourself." She looked at Jackie's shoulder and said, "What's going on here?" Monica touched the top of Jackie's shoulder.

Jackie said, "I know. I stayed in the sun too long yesterday working on my tan."

"Only white girls get tans. Why are you doing that?"

"I don't know. I just want to get darker."

"Okay, you want to be darker, and we got some sisters bleaching their skin trying to be lighter. I don't think anyone knows what they want anymore. Speaking of that, what are we doing for you today?"

Jackie opened the magazine to the hairstyle she liked.

"What? I would have to cut all your hair off. I don't think so. And besides, that hairstyle is for natural hair, you don't have enough kink in your hair for that."

Jackie said disappointed, "Well, I want something different."

"Girl, every time you come in here, you want something different. Why can't you be happy with the way we did your hair last time?" Monica placed the silk zebra print cape over Jackie's clothes.

"I don't know," Jackie said, a little dejected.

Monica shook her head. "Okay, let's go to the shampoo bowl."

Jackie walked with Monica to the back of the salon. She sat and leaned her head back as Monica turned on the warm water. She closed her eyes and relaxed as Monica began massaging her scalp with shampoo.

Monica looked around to make sure no one could hear her. "Jackie, what's going on with you?"

Jackie opened her eyes and said, "What? Nothing."

"Then why do you still have this thing going on about your hair and your skin?"

"I know, I'm trying to work on that."

"You've got to do more than work on it, you need to move past it. How long have I been doing your hair?"

Jackie sighed and said, "Oh goodness, since before I started high school."

"Exactly, and we've talked about you trying to be someone else ever since then. I've been patient, but now I have to be honest. You can't change your looks. You are who you are. It doesn't matter how many curlers I put in your hair, or how much heat we use to blow-dry it. It's not going to puff up. Your hair is straight, long, and beautiful."

"But Monica, you just don't understand what it's like. People are constantly asking what color I am. They say, 'Where are you from?' I'm tired of it. I want people to see that I'm African American like everyone else."

"I know, but being African American is more than color. It's about your attitude. What counts is who you are inside, not what people see on the outside."

"Are you saying that the outside doesn't matter?" Jackie questioned.

"Of course not. I do hair. Image is everything. But look at what you're doing. Your skin is red, and it's peeling from being in the sun too long. You do this to yourself every summer. When are you going to learn?"

"After this summer, I'm not doing it anymore. I'm going to get spray tanned. It's less painful."

"Jackie, you're missing my point!"

"I know. Baby steps, girl, baby steps."

Monica finished washing and conditioning Jackie's hair then wrapped it in a towel. "Now, how are we going to style your hair today?"

"You choose," Jackie said as she thought about all the time she had spent trying to change her looks. In the end, nothing had really changed. She remembered what the pastor in D.C. said, "You are complete, lacking in nothing."

Concerned and remorseful over his actions, he told himself he must find a way to control his anger. He didn't understand why this one area of his life was so difficult to restrain. He wanted the beatings to stop because he was becoming like his father, and that was the one person on this earth he didn't want to be like. DeMarcus realized that he had to stop this vicious cycle. He was glad his dad was in prison serving a life sentence for killing his mother. Although he didn't know which was worse, being in prison or facing his own daily prison of a constant lack of restraint. The reoccurring nightmares about the day his mom died and the beatings that led to her death had caused enough pain for him.

It took most of the summer, but DeMarcus finally recognized that he had a problem with anger. He enrolled in a weekly anger management class where his counselor encouraged him to spend some time exploring the root of his anger.

Disappointed in himself and heartbroken, DeMarcus called Marissa. She answered on the second ring. He hesitated before forcing himself to admit that he had the problem in their relationship. "Hey...it's me."

"Hi." She said cheerfully.

"Listen...I need to talk to you." He knew he was about to break her heart, so he chose his words with tender care.

She said, "Okay, do you want me to come over?"

"No, I don't. Look, I have a problem," he paused, "...with anger. I think that's why we get into it so much, and I keep hurting you."

"DeMarcus, what are you talking about? I'm fine."

"Yeah, but most of the time, you're not." He took a breath and said, "And that's my fault." It killed him to admit that he was just like his dad. How did this happen?

"Well, okay." She took a deep breath and exhaled a sigh of relief. "We can work on it together. I'll help you."

"No, I need to do this alone." He frowned and tears formed in his eyes. "I'm just calling to tell you it's over." He tried to speed through his speech, hoping he could hang the phone up before she started crying. "I'm sorry for everything I've done to you. I hope you can forgive me."

"I do forgive you, but—"

He interrupted her. "I don't want you to call me anymore, and I don't want you to come over. Let me get myself together." He heard her crying and said, "I gotta go." DeMarcus hung up the phone, grabbed his gloves, and punched his new punching bag while his face crumbled, and teardrops fell onto his shirt.

31

Lindsey really missed her mom. It had been almost six years since she died, but she still thought about all the great times they had in the house. Deep down, she resented Jackie and her family for buying it from them, even though she knew that she and her mother couldn't afford to keep it with all the medical bills.

Lindsey walked downstairs, and for a moment, believed she smelled her mother's perfume. She skipped into the kitchen and remembered how happy they were when it was just the two of them. Lindsey's father died in a car accident when she was just 2 years old. And so it seemed, her mother did everything she could to try and make up for the loss, including showering Lindsey with gifts. However, through the years, they both learned that nothing really could make up for the loss of a father. Her mother took very good care of her while she was growing up. Lindsey thought about her own daughters. She didn't want anything to jeopardize her custody case. She thought back to Jackie and the picture of her girls. How did they find her girls? Leaving them had emotionally hurt them enough. She couldn't have anyone try to physically hurt them too. She was resolved that she would keep her mouth shut, because the children and the house were the only things she cared about.

As Lindsey reminisced about her childhood and thought about her own children, she envisioned her mom making her favorite dish, lasagna. In fact, she could almost taste it now. Lindsey went back upstairs to get dressed, and then headed to the grocery store to buy the ingredients. She planned to cook this meal as a tribute to her mom tonight.

During the summer, Bijon worked at a research institute doing molecular lab testing. He enjoyed the work of a scientist, and the money helped with his medical school expenses. But most of all, he got real pleasure from the quietness of the house in the summer months. The silence allowed his mind to think about the possibilities in his life. He worked from nine to five and cherished the time after work to do further research at home on his computer.

Lindsey and Bijon both returned home at the same time.

Bijon said, "Hello."

Lindsey responded back with a dry, "Hello."

Bijon sprinted to his room.

Lindsey set her groceries down on the counter and looked around the kitchen. Her mother would have been so disappointed that she had allowed dirty dishes to pile up in the sink and old food stains to cover parts of the counters. Lindsey picked up a sponge and cleaned. As she wiped the counters and washed the dishes, she felt at peace, knowing this would please her mom.

She sensed a presence in the room. With confidence that it was her mom, she said, "I miss you so much." She knew that she wouldn't get an answer but prayed for a sign. After several moments of stillness and silence, her hope vanished, and tears spilled over from her eyes unto the sparkling countertops. Lindsey looked up at the ceiling and said, "I'm going to start taking better care of this house, like we used to. Soon it will be ours again."

After she sanitized the sink, she sautéed the ground meat, onions, and green peppers in a skillet. She realized how much she loved the smell of them, along with her mom's special seasoning. The scent made the kitchen feel like home. While the meat sizzled, she spotted the old CD player in the corner of the kitchen. She opened it and there it was, after all this time. A CD filled with instrumental music her mom used to play while she cooked. Lindsey loved the combination of guitar and violin. She turned it on, closed her eyes, and listened to the calming melody.

Her mom always said, *Music soothes the soul. It transports you from where you are now to another place.*

The music struck familiar chords in Lindsey's spirit. It caused her to long for the touch of her mom, but the whiff of ground meat burning interrupted her daze. She rushed over to turn the heat down on the meat, and then boiled the water for the pasta. On accident, she dumped the whole box of pasta in.

Making a quick check of her ingredients, Lindsey realized that she had almost forgot her mom's favorite ingredient—spinach. Frantically, she looked in the pantry for a can of spinach to layer in between her lasagna mix. She found one, and then carefully laid the meat, sauce, pasta, spinach, and cheese in a glass pan.

Lindsey placed her meal in the oven and made her salad. Soon the room was filled with the aroma of her mom's cooking. She reminisced and then set two place settings on the dining room table, just like she did with her mom. She didn't care that she was alone.

Next, she poured a glass of wine for her mom and tea for herself. She then picked up the fresh flowers she brought from the store and placed them in a vase. All she needed now was her mom, because the table was set perfectly. She sat looking at the empty place setting.

"Lindsey, Lindsey?" She heard a soft voice that sounded off in the distance. "Lindsey, are you okay?"

She shook her head a little, and snapped, "Bijon, what is it?"

He looked at the table setting for two and asked, "Are you having someone over tonight?"

"No," she said, bothered by his question and the interruption of her memories.

He looked at her and said, "Okay, just wanted to know." He turned and walked back toward his room.

She thought about how she had treated him over the years and said, "Are you?"

He spouted back, "Am I what?"

"Are you having someone over tonight?"

"No, I just smelled the food, heard the music, and now I see the table set. I thought maybe you were having company." He walked into the kitchen and asked, "What are you cooking?"

"Lasagna. It's almost ready," she yelled from the dining room.

"Smells good." He went back to his room and closed the door.

She checked on the lasagna and put the finishing touches on the salad. After sliding the garlic bread in the oven, she thought about Bijon. In the recesses of her mind, she heard her mom say, *you must give everyone a chance. Get to know them before you pass judgment on them.* Regrettably, she had done the opposite with Bijon. She didn't know for sure that he was a terrorist, she was just uncomfortable around foreigners. But she had to admit, he was a nice guy. She decided to put their differences aside and knocked on his door.

He opened it and said, "What's up?"

"Um...I was just wondering if you're hungry. I kind of made a lot of food, and I can't eat it all by myself. There's no sense in letting it go to waste."

His stomach growled, but he said, "Uh...I appreciate the offer, but I think I'll pass."

"Come on, Bijon. It's not like I'm going to poison you," Lindsey said, smiling, but quickly noticed that Bijon wasn't smiling back. Instead, he was frowning.

Lindsey said. "I'm just kidding. There's a whole pan of lasagna and from the sound of your stomach, it sounds like you haven't eaten in days. Tell you what, I'll take the first bite. Surely, you don't think I'd poison myself."

He sighed, then raised his eyebrows and said, "You know, I'm not sure what to think about you. But I definitely don't think you're the suicidal type."

Lindsey said, "Please, I know I've been rude to you. Can you take this as a peace offering? Since it's been just you and me in the house for the whole summer, maybe we could start this next year off by trying to be friendly."

Bijon half-heartedly smiled, and said, "Okay."

They sat down and ate, both unsure of the other. They tried to make the most out of what had been a rocky relationship.

Lindsey said, "How does it taste?"

He said, "It's good, thank you."

She said, trying to make a joke, "I think it's just what the doctor ordered, what do you think?"

Bijon smiled.

32

It was senior year. Jackie was ready to take control of her life and get out of the business. First, she had to prepare everything for her last party. As she set out the trays of food, she decided to sample some of the fried mozzarella sticks. She took a bite, and the gooey cheese splattered down her chin. She closed her eyes and enjoyed the chewy delight while it melted in her mouth. Then, she pulled bottles of champagne out of an enclosed crate and placed them in a row on the table. It was at this moment that Jackie found herself sinking into another depression. Who was she kidding? How could she get out of this mess? She went upstairs to get dressed for her last party and to make sure her housemates were out of the house.

Jackie changed into her tight DKNY blue jeans and a cute, purple one-shoulder fitted top, with her Christian Dior black high heel lace up sandals that she bought over the summer. She sprayed her favorite perfume, Dolce and Gabbana's Light Blue on her neck and then her wrists. Jackie turned in the mirror admiring her shape. She sucked in her tummy a little and wondered if she needed a tummy tuck. Then she touched up her Berry Rich lipstick.

The doorbell rang and she headed downstairs to greet her guests.

One by one, they came in anxious to get their high. Like every other night, they waited their turn to snort a line and Jackie collected their money. Her heart was heavy. It felt like an anchor on a ship thrown overboard stuck and forgotten at the bottom of the sea. These people came here to make themselves feel better, and at the same time, their actions made Jackie feel worse.

The doorbell rang again. Jackie frowned wondering who it could be because she had checked everyone off the list. She opened the door, and it was Trina.

"Hey, girl," Trina said.

Jackie panicked. Lying on the buffet table and visible for all to see were lines of white powder and a square mirror. She tried to push Trina outside of the door, but she insisted on coming in.

"Hey...what are you doing here?" Jackie asked, scared to death that she would see what was going on.

"I came to support you, and maybe even buy some beauty products. I realize that I've never been to any of your parties before, and I should have by now."

Before Jackie could stop her, Trina walked past her and said, "Wow, Jackie! You've got a crowd."

Fidgeting with her hair and trying to block her view, Jackie said, "Trina, I need you to go."

Trina looked at Jackie in a bizarre way, and asked, "Why?"

A white guy called over to Jackie and made a joke, "Can I get a discount if I snort half a line?"

Trina walked over to him and stared at the lines of coke on the table. Her mouth dropped open. She yelled, "What's going on here?"

Jackie started flailing her hands and said, "I can explain. It's not what you think."

"Your part-time job is selling coke? Are you crazy?" She stormed past Jackie without saying another word.

Jackie followed, but before she could catch her, Trina opened the door and ran down the stairs.

Jackie chased after her screaming, "Trina, wait! I'm getting out. This is my last party."

Trina stopped and turned around with a baffled look on her face. "Jackie, how long have you been doing this?"

"It started a couple years ago, and I've been trying to get out. That's why I've been so upset."

"I don't know what to say."

"Please Trina, don't hate me. I really am trying to get out."

Trina shook her head with tears in her eyes. "Um... No. Of all the things to do. You know my brother was shot and killed in a drive-by by a drug dealer. How could you do this, I told you about all the misery me and Momma have been through?" Trina sighed and said, "I'm done." Trina ran home.

"Trina, please," Jackie yelled. "Trina! Trina!"

And just like that, Jackie lost one of her best friends. She went back into the house and hoped the coke was gone, because she was ready for everyone to go home.

For the rest of the week Jackie prayed. She prayed for herself, Trina, and the business meeting. She hoped that Trina would forgive her. Although, she really didn't think that was going to happen.

She called Trina, but she didn't answer, so Jackie left several messages. She went by her house and knocked, but she wouldn't answer the door. She remembered the first day she came to Karrington and met Trina. They were both in line to register for classes, and ever since then, they've been virtually inseparable. She was the only friend Jackie had, other than Brittany, and now she was gone.

Despite the setback with Trina, Jackie knew she had to press forward. Today was the big day and she prayed that God would show up for her. Jackie got to the business meeting at the hotel, hoping to talk with Ursula before it started. She knocked on the door, and Ursula answered.

"You're early. I told you; you didn't have to help setup."

Jackie smiled, somewhat relieved that she and Ursula had worked out their differences and were cool again, but she knew that wouldn't be the case for long.

Anxious to talk to Ursula, and a little scared of what she might say, Jackie said, "Oh, I know. I just wanted to talk to you. Are you here by yourself?"

"Yeah. Leslie is on her way to help me set up. Why, what's up?" Ursula walked back to the table where she was preparing the plates and silverware for the meeting.

"Well, we're seniors now, and I'm ready to get out of the business. You said you were getting out when you graduate."

"Sh...sh." Ursula pushed Jackie into the back bedroom. "I don't want anyone to know that."

"What? You said no one was here."

"They aren't, but I don't want that out."

"Well, it's time." Jackie put her hands on her hips with a sense of resolve.

"Jackie, after graduation, not now."

"Well, I can't wait. I want out now, and I'm telling Nita today." Jackie walked out of the bedroom into the living room.

Ursula grabbed her arm and swung her back into the bedroom. "Jackie, are you crazy?"

"No, I'm tired of having parties and watching people get high. I'm tired of worrying if someone will OD in my house, or if they'll have an accident on the way home."

Tears filled Jackie's eyes and flowed down her cheeks.

"I can't watch drug addicted babies suffer anymore. I'm sick of hearing about drug deals gone bad. I'm tired of hiding." Jackie's voice cracked. "I'm tired of hoping no one finds out what I'm doing. I'm worn out. This is it. I'm not doing any more parties. I don't care what she does to me. She can beat me up. She can put a knife to my throat again. I don't care."

"She can kill you! Do you care about that?" Ursula yelled.

Jackie wiped the tears from her eyes. She whispered, "Actually, Ursula, I don't."

Just then, they heard someone opening the door. She motioned to Jackie to act like nothing was wrong. Ursula pushed Jackie into the living room and followed behind her.

Nita came in and greeted them in an upbeat mood, "Hello, girls. How are you?"

Jackie stepped forward and said, "Nita, I need to talk to you."

Ursula interrupted and said, "Jackie wants to talk with you after you set your things down. I know you need a chance to review your quarterly reports."

Jackie sighed while Ursula threatened her with her eyes.

"The two of you act so strange sometimes. Is there a problem?" Nita looked at Jackie's tear-stained face. She could see where the smeared mascara had left a trail down her cheeks.

Ursula added, "No, everything's fine. Your shrimp cocktail is on ice in your room and there's champagne too."

Nita eyed both and said, "Thank you." She inspected the living room of the suite and said, "Is this the right room? It looks a little small. Ursula, call and make sure. It's been a while since we had a meeting at this hotel." Once again, she observed their behavior and closed her bedroom door.

Ursula pulled Jackie's arm and led her into the other bedroom on the other end of the suite. She then motioned for her to be quiet. "I'm going to ask you again, have you lost your damn mind? Do you remember what happened to us two years ago?"

Jackie pleaded, "Yes, but we are seniors. You said—"

"Shut up. I know what I said, but now is not the time." Ursula raised, and then lowered her voice to just above a whisper, "Listen, you can get out of the business when I get out. I'll put a plan together, but until then, just wait."

"No, I can't wait. I'm telling her, and I'm leaving." Jackie then darted to Nita's bedroom and knocked on the door, before Ursula could stop her.

"Nita, it's Jackie. Can I come in?"

The voice from behind the door said, "Sure, just a minute," and a moment later, the door opened.

Within seconds, there was another knock, but this time it was coming from outside of the penthouse suite door. They all looked at each other, and Nita said, "Ursula, be a dear and take care of that while I talk to Jackie."

Jackie said a short prayer, *God, please help me,* and walked through the door. Nita sat on a brown cloth chair by the window while enjoying her shrimp cocktail and champagne. Jackie swallowed hard before she spoke because she knew it might be her last time. "Nita, I'm leaving the business. I can't do this anymore."

Without looking at Jackie, Nita dipped her shrimp into the cocktail sauce, took a bite and chewed. "Jackie, you know you're really starting to bore me with this. How many times have we had this conversation?"

Jackie had a large lump stuck in her throat, but she persevered and said, "Many, but this is the last time." Her heart stopped and then galloped to a full sprint like a horse running towards the finish line at the Kentucky derby.

Nita tilted her head in Jackie's direction and said, "Do you remember what happened the other times we had this conversation?"

Losing some of her resolve, Jackie said, "Yes."

"Okay. Do you remember what I said I would do to you if we ever had this chat again?"

Now fearfully reluctant to continue with Nita, Jackie's eyes moved from side to side, looking for a way out. She could still feel the steel blade of Nita's knife against her neck from the last time they talked. The "Yes," she eked out was barely audible.

Free flowing tears ran down Jackie's face again as she said, "I'm begging you, Nita." She got on her knees, "Please let me go. I've done everything you've asked me to do. I got a little over fifty-six thousand dollars saved. I'll give it all to you, just please let me out of this."

Nita grinned at Jackie and said, "That's how you should always be in my presence, on your knees. You should be bowing down thanking me for all I've done for you. Instead, you are begging me to get out." Nita stood up and yelled, "You stupid bitch!" She slapped the left side of Jackie's face with the back of her hand and Jackie collapsed to the floor from the force of the blow. Her face stung as she cried in anguish over being unable to penetrate Nita's steel heart.

Nita walked over to the closet and removed a gun from the top shelf. She came back and pistol-whipped Jackie across her face with the butt of the gun. Jackie's face bled and swelled fast. She knew she had a black eye. Holding the left side of her face with her hand, Jackie looked up at Nita and something in her said, *Stand up.* Jackie remembered a song she heard at church that talked about standing. She stopped whimpering. Tears continued to stream down her face and she stood up.

Nita stopped and stared at Jackie inquisitively. Nita hit her harder with the butt of the gun and yelled, "How dare you stand up to me? Who do you think you are? You ungrateful bitch!"

Every time Nita knocked Jackie down, she stood back up and let Nita hit her some more. Part of her felt like she deserved it, but the other part of her wanted to show Nita that she was serious.

"Where would you be today without me, and now you want to throw it all away? Well fine, go ahead."

With blood gushing from above her eye, Jackie looked down at her shirt and the beige carpet on the floor. They were both covered in blood.

Nita took the gun and told Jackie to open her mouth. Tears flowed in a steady stream down Jackie's face, and her body shook.

Nita took the safety off the gun.

"Nita, please, no! I'll do anything, please don't kill me."

"Bitch, I said open your mouth. I'm done playing this game with you."

Jackie opened her mouth, but she was unable to catch her breath. She whimpered as Nita put the tip of the gun in and pushed it forward. Jackie gagged on it, because Nita had it in so far. "How dare you disrespect me." Nita placed her finger on the trigger.

Terrified, Jackie knew this was it. It was over. She closed her eyes and said a silent prayer.

Just then, Ursula knocked on the door and said, "There's a mix up on the rooms. The hotel staff would like to talk to you. They gave us the Presidential Suite instead of the Penthouse."

No one answered her. Ursula opened the door and gasped at the sight of Nita holding a gun in Jackie's mouth and the blood covering Jackie's face, clothing, and the floor.

She cleared her throat and said, "Ahem...Nita, the person from the lobby is at the door and wants to talk to you. Nita, please don't do this." Ursula stepped in the room and closed the bedroom door behind her. She spoke in a whisper, "They are at the door now. Nita, please."

Nita clenched her teeth and seethed with anger. She inched the gun out of Jackie's mouth, but stared at her just to let her know they were not finished.

Crushed by Nita's intimidation, Jackie fell to her knees gagging from the gun. She threw up, placed her head in her hands, and screamed an agonizing cry.

Nita said, "Thank you, Ursula. Didn't I tell you this was the wrong room?"

Nita took her time putting the gun back in the closet. She adjusted her clothes, brushed imaginary lint off her outfit, and said to Jackie, "You are as good as dead to me."

Nita walked out of the bedroom like the incident was the cost of doing business on a normal day at the office.

Ursula ran over and knelt by Jackie, "Oh, what did you do?" They could hear Nita talking to the person at the door and then the suite door closed.

There was so much blood mixed with vomit; Ursula didn't know where to start. She ran to the bathroom for towels and then said, "Let's get you cleaned up." After seeming to control the bleeding, she walked Jackie into the bathroom.

"Damn, I left my bag on the other side, let's go over there." Ursula peeked out of the bedroom door to confirm that Nita was gone. Then she walked Jackie into the living area, and over to the bedroom on the other side of the suite. Jackie leaned on Ursula but said nothing.

The beating left Jackie's face black and blue. As she stood frozen in front of the bathroom mirror Ursula wet towels and wiped the blood from her face. In shock and in extreme pain, Jackie looked at what had become of her. Ursula called the front desk and got a first aid kit delivered to the room. She took the bloody shirt off Jackie and removed the rest of her clothes. She turned on the shower and helped Jackie climb in. Jackie stood under the water unable to move or speak. Ursula bathed her and pulled clothes from her own overnight bag and dressed her. She applied ointment and bandages from the kit to Jackie's wounds. Next, she took out a prescription bottle filled with Valium, took two tablets out, and handed them to Jackie with a glass of water.

"Take these. They will make you feel better."

Jackie still didn't speak but followed Ursula's instructions and took the pills. Frightened and in pain, she was unsure of what just happened and what would happen to her next. Unable to think clearly, the shock of this event had yet to connect in her mind. Ursula walked her over to the bed and helped her lie down. She found two cold compresses in the first aid kit and placed them over Jackie's face.

"Jackie, I'll be back. Do not come out of this room. After the meeting, I'll drive you home. Okay?"

"Alright."

Twenty minutes went by, Ursula came back and told Jackie that they moved the meeting to the penthouse on the east side of the hotel. She gathered all of Nita's belongings, including the gun.

"I put this room on my credit card, so you don't have to leave. You can stay as long as you need. Rest, I'll be back after the meeting," Ursula said.

Jackie nodded and when she did, she felt loopy. She didn't have control over her head. It felt like it was still moving even though she willed it to stop. Her face still ached from where Nita hit her with the gun repeatedly, but she was proud that she stood up to her. For the first time in her life, Jackie had made her own decision and stood up for what she believed, even if it almost cost her life.

She stayed in the suite for a whole week and missed all of her classes. Ursula checked on her daily, bringing her clothes and other necessary items. It took that long for the swelling in her face to go down and the cut to partially heal. The purple bruising that was there at first was almost gone. Ursula was the only person who knew where Jackie was, and she was proving to be a good friend after all.

33
———

LaJuana rose early Saturday morning to follow Ms. Evil, the nickname she gave the woman who ruined her life. She waited outside of her house, and after three hours, she watched her get in her black Jaguar and peel out of her driveway. LaJuana followed in her old red Chevrolet Cavalier that her uncle bought her. It barely passed inspection, but at least it got her to and from work. In addition, it gave her the means to spy on the one she hated most of all.

Ms. Evil parked on the street and ran behind an abandoned graffiti covered building. The windows were boarded up so there was no way to see what was inside. LaJuana wondered where she was going and why? In all the weeks she spent watching her every move, she knew this wasn't her typical pattern or a place she usually went.

~

Back at the row house, Jackie pulled a glass down from the cabinet and poured herself some orange juice, this time with no alcohol. It had been two weeks since her latest encounter with Nita. Each day,

Jackie walked in fear, constantly looking behind her and waiting for the moment that Nita would kill her.

Yesterday, Jackie received a call from Isabella, one of her four reps. Isabella wanted to get together and find out the details about what happened at the penthouse. Jackie planned to convince her to get out as well.

Jackie finished her orange juice, checked her watch, and then grabbed her purse as she rushed out the door for their lunch date. They met at a restaurant in southeast D.C. called Sensations, and Valerie, one of Jackie's other reps, came along with Isabella. They all hugged each other and sat down at a table. They told her about Nita's announcement that Jackie would no longer be in the business anymore.

The server came by with three waters. "Are you girls ready to order?"

Isabella said, "No, can you give us a minute? We're still deciding."

Jackie asked, "She didn't say anything else?"

Valerie said, "No. I thought it was odd, but no she didn't."

Isabella said, "Ursula told us what Nita did to you."

Jackie's cell phone rang, and she looked down at the name on the phone, "Hold on, it's Ursula."

Isabella and Valerie looked at each other, puzzled.

"Hey, Ursula. What's up?"

Ursula screamed in the phone, "Get out of there! They are going to take you to Nita!"

"What?"

"Leave, it's a setup! They are setting you up. They plan to kill you."

"What?" Jackie looked at Isabella and Valerie. Without a word, Jackie hung up, grabbed her purse, and headed for the door, quickly scanning the room looking for Nita, but she didn't see her. She ran out of the restaurant toward her car. But before she could get there, Valerie and Isabella caught her by the arms, and Isabella stuck a gun in her lower back. Jackie couldn't see it, but she could feel it.

Jackie struggled to get loose, but Isabella tightened her grip and whispered in her ear, "Jackie, listen closely, because I'm only going to say this one time. We're going to walk quietly to the back parking lot, and you're going to act like nothing is wrong. Then, you're going to get in Valerie's car. Do you understand?"

Jackie didn't answer her, partly because she couldn't believe that Isabella was turning on her, and partly because she was trying to find a way of escape. Isabella nudged the gun deeper into the small of her back. Jackie flinched, and Isabella asked, "Do you understand?"

Hesitant, Jackie replied, "Yes." Her heartbeat fast, and she could hardly catch her breath. What were they going to do? She wondered if this was how her life was going to end. She closed her eyes and prayed to God, asking Him to come to her rescue.

"Now, if you can't follow these simple instructions. I will shoot you, and you know I don't want to do that, but I will," Isabella said, imitating a stern and familiar voice and tone. If Jackie didn't know better, she would have sworn Nita was the one behind her.

Jackie stood still. She knew that Isabella was very ambitious, so she took her seriously. That was one of the reasons Nita wanted her to become a rep. They walked her around the back of the building to Valerie's grey Honda Accord. Valerie opened the door, and Isabella reminded her, "Remember what I told you. Get in." Isabella got in the back with Jackie, while Valerie locked the doors and drove off.

"How can you do this to me? I thought you were my friends," Jackie said as her voice trembled.

Isabella pointed the gun at her and said, "Jackie, I am your friend. This is not personal, think of this as career advancement."

"What? You want my position?" Jackie looked at Isabella confused by the way she was behaving.

"Jackie, I've always wanted your position. I was just waiting for you to step aside. Now, it's my time."

Jackie peered out of the window and saw what appeared to be an all-around normal day, except in the car. A transvestite walked down the street with a long, blonde ponytail and red high heel pumps. Kids ran through water from a broken fire hydrant, and a homeless woman pushed a shopping cart full of old clothes, papers, and empty soda cans.

Beginning to become frantic, Jackie asked, "Where are we going?"

Isabella raised the gun a bit. "Quiet, we'll be there soon enough."

Valerie said, "Jackie, we don't want to do this, but we don't have a choice."

Isabella yelled at Valerie, "Shut up and drive!"

They arrived at a street that looked familiar, but Jackie couldn't see the name of it because the trees were covering the sign. Valerie turned down the street, and immediately turned into the driveway of what looked like a graffiti splattered abandoned apartment building. She drove around to the back of the building and parked. Liquid fear pulsated through Jackie's veins.

Meanwhile, LaJuana watched from a safe distance as a grey car raced by and turned into the driveway of the building.

Isabella told Valerie to open her door, and then yelled at Jackie to get out. Jackie did as she said.

"What are you going to do to me? Please, I just want out." Jackie cried so hard that she hyperventilated.

Isabella yelled at her, "Stop crying! You knew what you were getting into when you started."

Jackie caught her breath and said, "No, I didn't. I had no idea that throwing a little party would lead to this." She was nervous about what would happen next.

"Blah, blah, blah. Get down on your knees and put your hands behind your back." Isabella walked in front of Jackie, proud of her newfound power. She pointed the gun at Jackie's head and said with an attitude, "I've always wanted to do this, not to you, but you know, in general."

"No, no, I'm begging you, no!" Jackie said while her tears blurred her vision. "Please, I'll do anything, please don't shoot me."

LaJuana now saw a black BMW race up the drive burning rubber toward the back of the building.

In one motion, Ursula put the car in park and jumped out. She walked up with her gun pointed straight at the side of Isabella's head. "Let her go."

Isabella said, "Are you crazy? That's not the plan."

Ursula yelled, "Having her on her knees was not the plan either. Get up, Jackie."

Jackie looked at both, as Isabella lowered her gun. Almost afraid to move, Jackie used her hands to brace herself on the ground, lifting one knee up and then the other to stand. She darted behind Ursula and listened to them argue the details of her murder in broad daylight.

Isabella said, "You're such a fool. Ursula, put the gun down, now!"

Ursula continued to point the gun at Isabella's head. "No, not until yours' is down first."

With the coldness of the gun against her temple, Isabella sneered. "I can't wait. Nita is going to kill you, and I will be glad when she does."

Annoyed, Ursula said, "Bitch, put the gun on the ground. You let me worry about Nita."

Isabella shook her head and placed the gun on the ground. With a smug look on her face, she said, "You're gonna pay for this."

After watching the disappointing display, Nita walked out from behind the dark green dumpsters that lined the parking lot, wearing black riding pants, a black jacket, black leather boots, and black gloves. The outfit was fierce, but so was the situation.

Everyone turned and looked at her. With gun in hand, Nita walked up to the girls and said, "I've already seen and heard everything."

It was a cool, sunny day, but the air was still and tense, filled with the extreme fear that they all had of Nita. Jackie thought about her plight and realized that she would soon be reduced to just another dead drug dealer found on the streets of Washington, D.C. The entire predicament was hard to imagine, given where she came from, a little girl brought up in a good family with private schools, designer clothes, and a family business to inherit.

As Nita approached Ursula and Jackie, her glare pierced them like a knife and her eyes dripped with contempt for them both. She paraded around them like a lion surveying its prey, ready to pounce if anyone moved. Jackie wished she were anywhere but here, sharing this moment with her fellow sisterhood of drug dealers, and only seconds away from death.

Nita moved to the side of Ursula and Jackie, shaking her head back and forth while she paced. She said, "Ursula, Ursula, Ursula, what is it with you and Jackie? Are you lovers?"

Ursula pressed her lips together and held her breath, while aiming the gun at Isabella.

Nita raised her gun to her own head and used the muzzle to scratch her temple, "You know, I thought you learned your lesson. But no, you keep letting Jackie get you into trouble." She placed the gun to her side and walked up close to Ursula's ear, then asked, "Ursula, why are you here?"

Ursula stared straight ahead at Isabella with her hand shaking as Nita intimidated her.

Nita screamed louder, "I can't hear you! Why are you here?"

Ursula flinched because the scream hurt her eardrum. She said, "Because this is my fault. I knew Jackie wasn't ready for this. But I wanted her to see what real life looked like. I was wrong, I shouldn't have done that."

Astonished, Jackie looked at Ursula. She thought she knew her but realized that she didn't know her at all.

Ursula turned to her friend and said, "Jackie, I'm so sorry." And then she looked at Nita. "Please, Nita, please don't do this. Jackie doesn't deserve to die."

"Really, she doesn't deserve to die. That's not what I think. I think she does, and I should have finished this back at the penthouse." Nita stepped back and paced around whirling the gun at the other girls and asking them, "What do you girls think? Because I think anyone that doesn't follow my instructions should die."

Valerie and Isabella nodded in agreement with Nita.

"Isabella, move over there with Valerie," Nita demanded.

Isabella scrambled over to Valerie, and Ursula lowered her gun.

"Girls, can you remind Ursula what my instructions were?" Nita said as she stood in front of Ursula with her back facing the other girls. She punished Ursula with her eyes as Isabella explained the instructions, and then told how Ursula changed them at the last minute. Then she got to the part where Ursula told her to let Jackie go, and she did because Ursula was pointing a gun at her. Nita interrupted Isabella and asked, "Did I tell you to let Jackie go?"

LaJuana got out of her car and tiptoed to the side of the building where she saw Ms. Evil rush behind earlier. It had been several minutes, so she peeked around the corner and saw Nita with a gun talking to a girl while another girl held a gun. She watched and listened, and then she saw Jackie.

Isabella answered, "No, but—"

Nita said, "Exactly," and immediately turned around and shot Isabella in the chest. Isabella fell to the ground. The girls screamed, and Valerie ran, Ursula grabbed Jackie's arm and restrained her from running too. Jackie tried to jerk away, but Ursula's grip was too strong.

LaJuana gasped, and then her shock turned into anger. Pissed off, she ran back to her car as fast as she could, panting for air. She opened the glove compartment, and took out the pistol her grandmother gave her for protection.

Meanwhile, Nita shot Valeria in the back. "That's for running, I didn't tell you to move."

Nita stopped and complimented Ursula. "Very good, Ursula. At least you can follow that direction."

Tears trickled down Ursula's face.

Nita said to her protégé, "You see, when I give instructions, I expect them to be carried out to the letter. Now Ursula, drop the gun."

"No, Ursula. Don't drop it!" Jackie yelled.

Ursula whimpered, "If you had just waited, we could have gotten out together."

Nita strutted toward Ursula, holding her gun at her side. Ursula raised her gun and pointed it straight at Nita. Nita didn't flinch, instead she grunted, "Oh really? That was your plan? So you were leaving me too, even after I gave you the key to Ostentatious?"

Fearful of Nita, Ursula's arm shook vigorously.

Nita regained the composure she lost by adjusting her clothes and brushing off the imaginary lint. Calm and calculated, she asked, "Well, when were you going to tell me about this?"

"Nita, I just needed this to get me through school. Please don't hurt me, please!" Ursula cried.

Nita squared her shoulders and gritted her teeth. "After all I've done for you, and you were using me all along. I don't think that people who use me deserve to live either."

Without another word, Nita raised her gun, aimed it at Ursula, and shot her in the chest. Ursula and her gun fell to the ground, and Jackie ran. Nita fired her gun at Jackie and hit her in the back, near her right shoulder. Jackie fell face forward to the ground and passed out.

LaJuana stayed out of sight and watched the entire situation unfold.

Jackie came to, felt the burning and throbbing in her shoulder, and saw her blood. She was almost able to get herself up on all fours despite the pain. Desperate to get away, she crawled using her left arm to move herself forward. She looked back and saw Nita walking toward her.

Jackie cried, "Please don't, please."

LaJuana sprinted behind Nita and pointed the gun at Nita's head.

Then Jackie heard another voice. "Don't move or I'll blow your head off." She laughed, "This is great. I've been waiting for this moment for a long time."

Jackie didn't know if an angel had come to her rescue or what, but the voice sounded strangely familiar. She thought maybe she was just imagining it, or maybe she was hallucinating. Jackie struggled to look behind her because she was certain that she knew the voice. Finally, she saw LaJuana standing behind Nita pointing a gun directly at Nita.

LaJuana laughed because she was finally able to confront Nita, a.k.a. Ms. Evil. "Ooo-oo, when I saw you at the row house two years ago, I knew that we had met before. But it took me a while to remember where. And then it hit me. I said, I gotta pay that bitch back."

"Okay, calm down. I think you've got the wrong person here.

There must be some mistake," Nita said in her most high society voice. "Why don't you put the gun down so we can talk about this."

"No, heifer there's no mistake. I've been following you for almost a year, just waiting on the right opportunity to meet you. Now, drop the gun or I'll shoot!" LaJuana smiled and cocked the gun.

Nita didn't move, so LaJuana yelled, "I'm not going to ask again!"

This time Nita complied, but said, "You're going to be very sorry for this."

Jackie made her way to her feet and walked over to LaJuana and Nita, holding her arm. She reached over, snatched Nita's gun with her good hand, and stood next to LaJuana. "What are you doing?" she asked.

"Jackie, this is a private matter. But I could ask you the same question. What are you doing here?"

Nita said, "She works for me."

Jackie, shaking from the pain in her arm, barely managed to point the gun at Nita and yelled, "I don't work for you!"

Nita saw something in Jackie's eyes that she also saw after she pistol whipped her, courage. She said, "Okay, okay. You don't work for me, but I need you to listen to me very carefully. Okay? Jackie, give me the gun."

Jackie responded, "Are you crazy? I hate you! Why would I give you anything?"

"Jackie, I've done nothing but tried to help you. Look at all the money I given you."

"You haven't given me anything but sleepless nights and anxiety attacks. I ought to shoot you just for that."

LaJuana yelled at both. "Shut up!"

Nita said, "Jackie, think about it. You were a little country girl from Texas who had no friends. I made you popular, gave you confidence, and showed you some style. Be grateful, you half-breed bitch."

Wincing through the pain, Jackie replied, "I don't need you to have confidence. That comes from within. And yeah, maybe I had some issues, but I don't anymore. You thought I was weak, and you preyed on that. How does it feel now to be on the other side of the gun?"

LaJuana interrupted and said, "Don't shoot her! This is my chance, and I'm not letting anyone spoil it. I'm going to shoot her myself."

Despite the burning sensation in her arm, Jackie felt her adrenaline kick in and she was ready to kill Nita. Jackie said, "LaJuana you have no idea what she has done to me. How she has made my life a living hell."

"A living hell? Jackie, you have no idea, what a living hell is. Nita, look at me." LaJuana tighten her grip on the handle and then aimed the gun at Nita's forehead. "You don't even know who I am, do you?"

Nita looked at her.

LaJuana said, "You need to answer me. I've got a short fuse."

Nita said, "Honestly, I don't know who you are."

"My name is LaJuana Williams. My momma named me after her first love, marijuana. That's the first drug you gave her. My momma's name is Lisa Williams. Now, get on your knees."

Nita bent one knee down and then the other, wondering how this low-class girl found her. "Yes..." Nita stuttered a little bit, "I do know her."

LaJuana ordered, "Jackie, take this rope and tie her hands behind her back." Jackie was still not sure if she was dreaming or not but she looked at LaJuana in complete bewilderment.

"Um, LaJuana, do you see me bleeding over here? How am I supposed to do that with one arm?"

"Okay." LaJuana put the gun down and said, "I'll tie her up. If she moves, shoot her in the leg, but don't kill her. That's my job."

Jackie did her best to hold the gun with her good arm, while Nita gave her a threatening look before she said, "Look, I was right in the middle of some business with Jackie. Can we talk about this at another time?"

LaJuana said, "Do you think I care about you or your business?" She tied the rope in a knot and picked up her gun.

Valerie was face down on the ground and moaning in pain

because of the gunshot wound to her back, but Ursula and Isabella remained silent and motionless. While LaJuana faced off with Nita, Jackie fought hard not to give into the pain in her shoulder. Instead, she went over to Ursula to see if she was okay.

LaJuana continued her speech. "But marijuana wasn't good enough. You turned her on to heroin, and then cocaine. You really did a number on Lisa in Baltimore, didn't you? Do you have any idea how my childhood was?"

Nita answered with an attitude, "No, I don't."

"Well, I'll tell you. It was hell. Do you know how many foster homes I went to? Better yet, do you know how many times I was raped in those foster homes? I betcha don't know that my momma tried to sell me for a dime bag of cocaine. You didn't know that did you?" LaJuana slid the gun down Nita's forehead and placed it right between her eyes.

Nita hated to hear excuses. Bold and determined, she said, "You're not the only one that had a hard life. I had a hard life too. So, what, suck it up! You don't see me wallowing in it."

Jackie put her gun down and pulled her cell phone from her pocket. Barely able to move, she squatted down and dialed 911 as she leaned over Ursula, trying to make sure she was okay. "LaJuana, I'm calling the police."

"The hell you are! Jackie, hang that damn phone up. This bitch is going to pay for how my life turned out."

"What? I'm bleeding. Look at Valerie, Isabella, and Ursula. They need a doctor."

LaJuana said very calm, "I'm sorry about your arm and your friends, but I don't want the police called. I've dreamed of this moment, and now I want to live it out just the way I planned."

Jackie said, "Oh my God, are you serious?" The situation was mind-boggling, but she couldn't focus on LaJuana because Ursula was making a gurgling sound like she was having trouble breathing. "She is going to die, if we don't call an ambulance." Jackie looked at LaJuana, "LaJuana, please, I'm in pain, let me get some help."

"I said, no!" LaJuana turned around and pointed the gun at Jackie.

"I want Nita to feel complete numbness, because you know what, that's how I feel. I learned to stop feeling a long time ago."

Jackie yelled at her, "Don't point that gun at me! Look, I don't know everything she has put you through, but I'm hurt and I'm calling the cops. Let this bitch rot in jail, that's real revenge. Killing her is the easy way out."

LaJuana pointed the gun back at Nita and said, "Nope, I can't do that. It's not good enough. I'm going to put a bullet in her for each year of my life that was taken from me."

"LaJuana, don't. She is not worth that." Jackie put the phone back in her pocket, picked up the gun and pointed it at LaJuana. "Damn it girl, put the gun down. LaJuana, you are trying my patience. I'm not trying to shoot you. Put it down."

LaJuana pointed the gun back at Jackie and screamed, "Jackie, let me take care of this!"

As Jackie and LaJuana debated, Nita was able to untie herself and pull out a small pearl handled switchblade from inside her boot. She flicked it open and threw the blade at Jackie but missed. Startled, Jackie and LaJuana immediately turned their attention back toward Nita and fired at the same time. Nita fell over.

Moments later, the cops rushed in. "Both of you, put your hands up and drop the guns," a police officer motioned as other officers surrounded the bloody scene.

Jackie put the gun on the ground and tried to raise her hands up in the air, but she couldn't lift her right shoulder.

LaJuana said still standing over Nita and without turning around, "Officer, I need you to leave me alone."

"Ma'am, I'm only going to ask you one more time to drop the gun and put your hands up."

Jackie said to LaJuana, "Put the gun down. You know D.C. cops will shoot you."

LaJuana said, "Okay," but quickly fired a fatal shot into the middle of Nita's forehead.

Without hesitation, a countless array of shots filled the air, and LaJuana fell to the ground.

34

It was Sunday morning and once again, Brittany was throwing up. This had happened off and on, for the last two months. She realized that she couldn't keep ignoring the fact that she might be pregnant. She went into the bathroom, took the test, placed it on the sink, and waited for the results. Her heart pounded with anticipation. Part of her wanted it to be negative, because she knew that things hadn't been the same between her and Charles for a while. But the other part of her wanted a positive result, hoping that a baby would reignite the love they once had and make them a real family.

While in Africa over the summer, she tried to spend as much time with him as possible. They made love every time they saw one another; each time she tried different ways to pleasure him. In her heart, she hoped that he would miss her and long for her, the way she missed and longed for him. But troubling thoughts rolled around in Brittany's head.

Someone knocked on the bathroom door. Brittany was startled at first, but yelled, "Yes."

DeMarcus called out, "How long are you going to be?"

"I don't know. Clear off. Use the loo downstairs."

"Brittany. Come on."

"DeMarcus, not now. Leave me alone."

DeMarcus shook his head and ran downstairs headed for the other bathroom.

Brittany held her breath and looked at the results. Two bright pink lines appeared in the window of the test. It was positive. She sunk down on the toilet seat with her head in her hands. What was she going to do? She sobbed because she didn't know.

Finally, after an hour, she got up and walked to her bedroom to call Charles.

"Hey, it's me."

"Hi, Brit." She could tell he was not excited to hear from her.

"I have some news."

"What's up?"

"I'm pregnant."

"What? Again?"

She rolled her eyes at his indignation and said, "It's not like I tried to. We were at it almost every day."

"Well, what do you want me to do?"

"Why are you flying off the handle at me? This is not all my fault."

"Of course it is. I thought you were on the pill. If I had known you, weren't I would have used my jonny's."

"We've never used jonny's before and I never told you I was on the pill." Brittany felt like their conversation was going downhill fast.

"Well, get another abortion," Charles shouted.

"I don't want another abortion," Brittany fired back at him.

"Well, you certainly can't keep it."

Brittany took a deep breath and decided to reason with Charles. "Why can't I? Maybe this is our second chance. I know things haven't been right between us for a while, but maybe we should make a go of it, for the baby's sake."

"We're not making a go of it. I didn't want to tell you this before, but I'm dating someone else, and it's gotten quite serious." He paused. "It's not you, Brittany. It's just that you're so far away. I missed you for so long, I had to find a way to fill the pain."

"But I can come home and we can take care of the baby together."

"Brittany, your parents will never allow it. It's better for everyone if you have an abortion."

"I thought you wanted our baby before."

"I did. But I think your parents were right; we're not ready. We're too young."

Brittany sniffed, trying not to break down again. She took several deep breaths to calm herself.

"Please, Brit, have the abortion. You don't want to bring shame to your family again. And frankly, I've moved on. It's better this way, don't you see?" Charles pleaded with her.

"No, I don't, but thanks for your advice. You don't have to worry about me contacting you anymore. I'm sorry I troubled you. Please enjoy your life." Brittany hung up the phone and cried into her pillow.

Just then the phone rang, and Brittany thought it was Charles calling her back. She sat up and answered the phone ready to accept his apology. She wiped her tears and said, "Hello."

"Brit, what's going on? I just got a call from Karrington University Hospital. Jackie was shot yesterday." The voice on the other end of the phone sounded frantic and rushed. It was Jackie's mother.

Brittany's heart dropped in her stomach. "What? Mrs. Jones? Oh my God! What are you talking about?"

"Jackie's in the hospital. They did surgery last night." She could hear Jackie's mother crying and trying to be strong at the same time. "You don't know anything about this?"

"No, I didn't even know she was in the hospital."

"Can you go and be with her until we get there? They say she can't talk. Something about an allergic reaction to surgery. Please tell her we're catching the next flight out."

"Absolutely, I'm on my way to the hospital now. Travel safely."

"Thank you, dear, and Brit, please pray for her."

"I will." Brittany pulled her jacket off the hanger and ran downstairs to leave. When she opened the door, there were two police officers standing on the porch.

One of the officers said, "We have a warrant to search LaJuana

Williams' and Jackie Jones' rooms. We will also be searching the rest of the house."

Brittany asked, "Why?"

The other officer said, "Official police business."

Brittany let them in, showed them the two rooms, and then headed to the hospital.

35

Jackie woke up groggy from what seemed like a long slumber. She looked over and saw Eve standing by the bed and Lydia reading a magazine by the window.

Eve said, "Good, you're finally awake. We don't have much time. We need to talk about what you're going to tell the police."

Unable to completely follow Eve's words because of her drowsiness, Jackie gave her a strange look.

Eve said, "Jackie, stay with me." Eve looked at Lydia and said, "I think she is falling asleep again."

Lydia walked over and stroked Jackie's hand, trying to keep her awake. Eve tapped Jackie on the face. It felt more like a slap. Jackie frowned. Still disoriented, she stared at Eve, not completely understanding what was going on.

Lydia said, "What are you doing? She just had major surgery. Are you nuts?"

Eve said, "I need her to wake up. This is important."

Jackie didn't say anything, she was worn out. She tried to swallow, but it hurt her throat to do so. Her body was too weak and exhausted to talk to Eve. She closed her eyes and prayed that when she opened them again, Eve would not be there.

Lydia shook Jackie's arm a little and said, "Come on, Jackie. You've got to wake up."

Jackie opened her eyes and looked at them. Eve said, "The police asked us if we knew Nita, Ursula, Isabella, and Valerie. We told them we didn't. Then they asked why we were in the parking lot of an abandoned building. We told them that we were walking to the store, heard the commotion, and came over to help, even though we were hiding in the building and saw the whole thing. They are going to ask you too, so just make up something. But don't tell them about the business, how it's run or anything. They could bring you up on charges for partic- ipating."

Jackie's memory was fuzzy, like she was dreaming, but it was all starting to come back. She remembered the police reading her rights, but she couldn't remember for what. She wanted to know more about the nightmare, but first she wanted to know where Ursula was. In a barely audible voice, she uttered her name the best she could, "Ursula?"

Lydia looked at Eve, and then back at Jackie. "I'm sorry, Jackie. Ursula didn't make it. She died shortly after they brought her to the hospital."

Jackie's heart sank to the bottom of her stomach. She tried to speak again, but she couldn't get a sound out. Tears plummeted down her face because she knew that Ursula's death was her fault.

Lydia said, "Don't cry, Jackie. Calm down. You're making the monitor beep faster."

A nurse walked in to check on Jackie and saw that she was crying. "Is everything okay?"

"Yes, we were just explaining what happened, and it's making her sad," Eve said.

The nurse responded after checking Jackie's monitor, IV bag, and pulse. "You're raising your blood pressure. Try to rest."

Jackie nodded.

The nurse snapped, "Perhaps you should talk about something else." She eyed Eve and Lydia, then walked out of the room.

Jackie was visibly shaken because her friend was dead. She raised her head and said, "Nita?"

Eve answered, "Oh, she died too. Don't you remember, you and that girl shot her?"

Jackie's eyebrows raised up. So far, she had only recalled bits and pieces, but she hadn't remembered it all. She listened to the callous way Eve informed her of Nita's death. Her nonchalant attitude reminded Jackie of TV news anchors reporting the news with no emotion. This seemed strange to Jackie, because she always saw Eve kissing Nita's ass. Now she was talking as if Nita's death meant nothing to her.

Jackie eked out, "Isabella?"

This time Lydia responded in haste, "In surgery, and so is Valerie, although they don't know if Valerie is going to make it. It's touch and go." Lydia talked hurriedly to get to the real reason they were there. "This is our chance to get out, so you can't say anything to them about the business."

Eve corrected her and said, "What she means is we have to lay low for a while. We still have our supplier, but we just have to wait until things cool down."

Lydia said, "Be stupid if you want to. I'm out."

Eve said, "You're just freaked out right now. It's only a setback. Jackie, if you want back in, it's okay because the supplier had several complaints about Nita from other territory managers."

Jackie couldn't believe the conversation she was hearing. First, how did Eve know the supplier? She thought no one knew the supplier except Nita.

Eve looked at Jackie's, and then Lydia's expressions. "Listen, I was sent in to spy on Nita's operation. I work for the supplier, not Nita. So, I'm telling you, everything's fine. He wants all of us to stay in."

Jackie thought, *Like hell. I'm not getting back in. Stupid bitch, didn't she know I was trying to get out?* Amazed, Jackie rolled her eyes and then closed them, trying to fall asleep.

Lydia said, "Maybe she is too groggy to understand what you're saying, but I'm not. This is it. I'm done. I'm not getting back in."

Eve said, "You're probably right, she is tired. Let's come back. Listen, Lydia, Nita made some mistakes, but that doesn't mean you have to quit."

Lydia ignored Eve's pleas.

Eve leaned down and whispered in Jackie's ear, "Don't forget what I said. Don't tell, think of a lie. I will be back tomorrow to see what you come up with."

Jackie wouldn't tell her anything. The only reason Eve was at the hospital was to protect the business from the police. She couldn't care less about Jackie.

Brittany looked puzzled as she passed Eve and Lydia coming out of Jackie's room.

She rushed to Jackie's side and said, "Oh my God, Jax! What is going on? Your parents just called and told me you were shot. They are catching the first flight out of Dallas. They'll be here soon."

Jackie said nothing; she just looked up at Brittany and cried.

A nurse interrupted them to check Jackie's vitals again, because the machine continued to beep. She also made sure that the morphine drip flowed on a consistent basis. She placed the morphine pump button in Jackie's hand and told her to push the button when she felt pain.

Without any hesitation, Jackie pushed the button.

The nurse then turned to Brittany and said, "She is on a lot of medication, so she probably won't be much company today. You may want to come back tomorrow."

Brittany said, "Thanks, I don't mind." She sat with Jackie for several hours.

While Jackie slept, Brittany went downstairs to the cafeteria for saltine crackers to settle her stomach.

A police officer approached after she left Jackie's room. He asked her about how well she knew Jackie. She told him. Then he asked her if she knew Ursula Mendez, Nita Lockheart, Isabella Samuels, Valerie Tolbert, or LaJuana Williams. Brittany explained that she didn't know any of the people he named, except LaJuana. He asked more questions, which Brittany couldn't answer, and then he told her that

LaJuana was killed. Brittany gasped in disbelief. Before she continued to the cafeteria, she sat down in the surgical waiting room trying to process it all. Fifteen minutes went by, and her stomach churned. She got up and called Bijon's cell phone as she made her way to the cafeteria.

Bijon answered, "Hello."

"Bijon, its Brittany. I have some bad news." She told him what had happened and explained that she would be home as soon as Jackie's parents arrived.

Bijon was shocked by the news and zoned out for a moment. Brittany raised her voice, noticing that he was not listening. He came back from wherever he was, and she told him that she wanted him to get all the housemates together for a meeting. He said he would.

Still in a daze, Bijon meandered into the kitchen and took out a glass. He saw a bottle of vodka on top of the fridge. He opened it, filled the glass to the rim, and went into the dining room to sit down. He drank the vodka straight and then called Sean to come over.

Jackie drifted in and out of consciousness, almost like she was floating. She saw a police officer standing over her bed. For a moment, she thought she was seeing things. But the officer said, "Ma'am, I just have a few questions." Jackie didn't respond. She closed her eyes and fell back to sleep.

She heard people screaming and yelling, but she couldn't tell how far away or how close they were. She just knew that she was exhausted and could barely keep her head up. In her dreams, Jackie saw flares on the ground with yellow and black police tape all around the area. She laid on the damp, hard ground but she couldn't tell if it had been raining or if she was lying in a pool of her own blood. She looked over to her side and gasped as she realized it was, in fact, her own blood.

Emergency vehicle sirens swirled in the air; bright lights illuminated the sky as police officers worked on the crime scene. Unfortunately, she was so out of it, she really couldn't understand what the paramedics were saying, nor was she able to answer them.

She kept praying to God that it would be over soon. She just wanted to go home and get in her bed. Her arm bled, and she started to feel dizzy, almost like she was going to faint. As the paramedics worked on her, she glanced over at Nita's body. Never in a million years would she have thought that this would have happened. Nita's body laid there, still and bloody.

36

Jackie's parents arrived at the hospital. After a quick greeting, Brittany left and headed back to the row house.

When she walked into the den, the concern on her house-mates' faces was evident; and the mood of the house was somber and serious.

"Hi, everyone, I just wanted to give you an update on Jackie. You guys know about LaJuana." Brittany put her head down, still in shock herself. "It's hard to believe that LaJuana's dead, and Jackie's lying in the hospital."

Everyone was quiet as the turn of events left them speechless, especially Bijon. He was drunk and still unable to process the whole thing. He stood up to go to the bathroom but threw up on the carpet instead. Everyone looked at him and turned their nose. His friend, Sean said, "I'll clean it up," and helped Bijon to the bathroom.

Brittany gagged after seeing Bijon toss his lunch. She tried to lighten the mood and said, "Jax is doing better. She had surgery last night and is groggy from the anesthesia. She is in shock and not talking right now. If you can, please go by and visit her. She needs to know that we all care about her."

DeMarcus asked, "What hospital is she in? And what's the room number?"

Brittany answered with compassion, "Karrington University Hospital, Room 317." She knew that Jackie and DeMarcus have been sleeping together for quite some time. And for the first time, she saw that DeMarcus cared about her friend.

DeMarcus grabbed his hoodie and headed out the door.

Brittany yelled, "I'm not finished yet!"

DeMarcus was almost to his car by the time he heard Brittany.

At the hospital, Jackie's family hovered over her. They all tried to comfort her, and she was so glad to see them. But, as the afternoon progressed, they each separated to their own corners thinking about this disaster and wondering what had happened. Everyone wanted answers. But no one asked Jackie any questions.

Jackie watched her mother sit in the chair beside her. She smiled at her and held her hand. She knew her mom didn't care what happened. She was just glad that her daughter was alive.

The nurse came in to check on Jackie and explained why she was unable to talk. She had a bad reaction to the endotracheal tube inserted during surgery.

Jackie was relieved to be excused from talking because her throat was very sore and raw. More importantly, she wanted to remain quiet until she could come up with an appropriate lie for this tragedy.

DeMarcus entered the room and introduced himself to the family. Her parents and brothers decided to go downstairs to the hospital cafeteria for something to eat. They explained to him that Jackie couldn't talk because of an allergic reaction to the surgery.

Alone with Jackie, he walked closer to her bed and looked at her. He leaned down and kissed her on the edge of her mouth. Jackie closed her eyes and felt the coolness of his lips touch hers.

He said, "You're going to be fine, and I'll be here as long as you want me to be." As he was talking, Lindsey came in. DeMarcus explained to her what Jackie's parents told him about her inability to talk.

Lindsey told Jackie about Bijon getting drunk and throwing up. But all Jackie could think about was her pain.

She reflected on the pain she inflicted on all the drug addicts she sold to. She also thought about the anguish those boarder babies would feel for the rest of their lives. And, if that weren't enough, she felt guilty about Ursula and LaJuana—both were now dead because of her.

Her heart was heavy from all the agony that surrounded her. It ached for her to breathe, let alone laugh at what DeMarcus and Lindsey said to her. As Jackie lay there, she noticed something deeper in each one of them. She saw that they too were in misery.

DeMarcus' pain stemmed from something that went very wrong early in his life. She still didn't know what it was, but it made him so angry that sometimes he acted as if he could kill. Lindsey did a good job of masking her pain. But now, Jackie could see a glimpse of her loneliness as she recognized that Lindsey had no one who really cared about her. She even thought about Bijon, a kid born in the United States of Indian descent. He was poor but trying to live the American dream and be true to whom he really was, a gay Indian American medical student.

Jackie's face was wet from the tears of sorrow she cried for them, and the sorrow she felt for herself. This quiet time allowed her to consider her choices. Jackie realized that we all can choose right from wrong. Unfortunately, she chose wrong; however, she ultimately did the right thing and got out.

A cop said to Jackie, "Ma'am, are you okay? Can you hear me?" Jackie had been daydreaming in her own world for some time. She saw the cop and heard him talking to her, but no one else was in the room. She guessed DeMarcus and Lindsey left or went to the cafeteria.

She looked up at him because she was still not sure what lie she was going to come up with.

Just then, the door swung open, and Lindsey stepped back in.

The officer said, "Ma'am, can you come back later? I need to ask Ms. Jones some questions."

Lindsey said, "Officer, I believe I can help. As you could see, Jackie's still in shock and recovering from the surgery. She can't talk because of some allergic reaction. But, before all of this happened, she told me everything."

In complete amazement, Jackie's eyes bucked wide open as Lindsey continued, "You see, Jackie needed money, and she met this older lady."

"You are probably talking about Nita Lockheart."

"Yeah, I think that's her name."

"Now, I don't know where they met. But anyway, Nita wanted to act as Jackie's pimp and prostitute her out."

Jackie's eyes grew bigger, and more intense as Lindsey went on. She tried to speak, but all she could get out was "No." Lindsey and the police officer looked at Jackie. Lindsey patted her arm, like she was comforting her, and carried on with her lie.

"I know, Jackie, it's embarrassing, but we have to tell the truth now. Nita promised Jackie lots of money if she performed certain acts. So, Jackie decided to do it. But when it came time for her to meet her first client and service him, she got cold feet and left the client in the bed naked and upset. Nita of course was angry and tried to make Jackie pay her back or service another client, but she wouldn't. So, Nita threatened to kill her."

The police officer responded, "I'll bet. We pulled her rap sheet, and it's a mile long. You name it, and she has just about done it. But go on."

"Anyway, Jackie feared Nita. She told me that she didn't know what Nita was going to do to her. So, the only thing I can figure was that Nita must have been stalking her and just waited until she could get her alone to shoot her."

The cop pondered the idea. "Interesting, but that doesn't explain why the other girls were shot. Or why both Ms. Williams and Ms. Jones shot Nita Lockheart?"

"Well, knowing Jackie, that must have been self-defense." She looked at Jackie, "Right? Because there's no way Jackie could hurt anyone."

Jackie didn't know what to think or do, so she nodded in agreement.

The officer asked, "What about the other young ladies who were injured?" He looked his notepad and asked, "Who are Ursula, Valeria, and Isabella?"

Lindsey looked at Jackie and asked, "Aren't those your friends?" She looked at Jackie hoping she answered yes. Jackie finally nodded, not knowing what Lindsey was up to. Lindsey said, "Only thing I can think of is they were going to meet Jackie there, and just were at the wrong place at the wrong time."

The cop said, "It still doesn't explain why they were at an abandoned building?"

"Now that part, I don't know. You'll have to ask Jackie when she can talk."

Intrigued by her response, the officer said, "What about LaJuana Williams?"

"Well, she was one of our housemates, but I don't know why she was there."

The cop said, "She and Jackie both shot Nita."

Lindsey gave her two cents. "Well, I don't know about that, but if you ask me, LaJuana has always been strange. If you know what I mean."

The cop eyed both suspiciously and said, "We searched LaJuana's room and found a poster board with information about her mom and drugs linked back to Bonita "Nita" Lockheart in Baltimore, Maryland. She also kept a diary explaining her plan to murder Nita. Do you all know anything about that?"

Lindsey and Jackie both looked surprised and shook their heads.

He looked down at Jackie and said, "It sure is ironic that LaJuana lived in the same house with you. And both you and LaJuana had connections to Nita. I searched your room too."

The officer waited for a response from Jackie, but she didn't give him one. She maintained her poker face, especially since she knew there was nothing in her room to connect her to drug activity.

"Well, Jackie, is this true about the prostitution?" Jackie looked at the cop and then at Lindsey. She was so tired of lying, but what else could she do?

Lindsey said, "I think she is still a little embarrassed, even though she never did anything."

The cop said, "There's nothing to be embarrassed about. There will be no prostitution charges filed."

Jackie sighed and as best as she could said, "Yes, it's true," which caused her throat to ache more. She started coughing. Lindsey poured some water in a cup and placed the straw in Jackie's mouth.

The cop said, "Well, ladies, thank you. Jackie, I'll have some more questions for you later, after we get the autopsy reports back."

Jackie nodded and Lindsey said, "I think she gets out of the hospital in a couple of days, and then she'll be back at home."

"Thank you so much for helping me," the police officer said.

"You are so welcome. Anything to help you guys protect and serve."

"By the way, what is your full name?"

Lindsey was flattered at spark of interest she saw in the officer's eyes.

"It's Lindsey Reeves. Do you need my phone number?"

The cop smiled and said, "That would be helpful."

With a flirtatious smile, she gave it to him.

"Thanks."

Lindsey said, "It's my pleasure. Let me walk you to the door." She wrapped her arm around his and escorted him out.

Jackie closed her eyes as they left. She thought, *More lies. When will they ever end?*

37

Monday morning peeked it's head just above the clouds, as Trina awoke to the fact that she had overslept and was late. She hurried around the room throwing her clothes on, brushing her teeth and locking the door. She was sad because she usually walked to school with Jackie, but she didn't see her. Maybe Jackie was upset with her since she hadn't returned any of her calls or maybe she left on time. Trina wanted to call her friend but decided not to. Besides, Jackie had been lying to her for more than two years. She couldn't get past the drug thing, especially after everything her family had been through. She couldn't help but wonder why Jackie would do that.

Trina had longing gaze. It was the way she felt anytime someone close betrayed her. She disconnected herself from the person and vowed never to forgive them. It took time, but she eventually forgot about them like they never existed. Even though Jackie and Trina had been friends since freshman year, she knew she would soon forget Jackie too.

She walked into her microbiology class with slumped shoulders and a limp posture. Once she found an empty chair, she plopped down. The professor said, "I don't know if you heard the news last night, but the university is saddened today because two of our students died Saturday night and a third one was just released from intensive care. Ursula Mendez and LaJuana Williams were both shot and killed. We don't know what happened, but the third student, Jackie Jones, is still in critical condition at the university hospital. Please bow your heads for a moment of silence."

Trina looked at the professor in complete horror. She gathered her books and raced out the door. She darted down the hill fast and crossed the street in front of passing cars. She heard the screeching of brakes and horns honking. She raised her hand and said, "I'm sorry." She ran as fast as she could, praying that her friend was all right. Thankful that the hospital was close by, she sprinted and ran right to the information desk in the lobby.

Out of breath and a bit disoriented, Trina said, "Can you tell me what room Jackie Jones is in?"

The volunteer said, "Calm down, let me check."

She scanned her patient record, flipped a couple of pages, and then said, "She was in intensive care, but now she is in room 317."

Trina ran to the elevator and pushed the up button. It seemed like the elevator took forever. She paced back and forth wondering what happened and why. She looked up at the elevator and saw the numbers on top descending, 4-3-2-1.

Finally, the doors opened and three people walked off. Trina was in such a hurry that she rushed into the elevator without allowing the others to get off. She apologized and pushed the number three. An old black man walked onto the elevator using a walking cane and moving like a snail. Trina tried to be patient, but she couldn't wait, so she helped the man into the elevator. He said, "Thank you. I need to go to the second floor; can you push two?"

Trina said, "Yes." She pushed two and when the doors opened, she helped the old man out of the elevator and pushed the close door button.

The elevator arrived on the third floor. Trina rushed to find room 317 but no one was there.

She ran to the third-floor nurses' station and asked, "Is Jackie Jones in room 317?"

The nurse looked at her chart and said, "Yes, sort of."

"What do you mean? Where is she? She's not in her room."

The nurse asked, "Are you a relative?"

"No, I'm her friend."

"Well, I'm sorry. I can't discuss her care with you. But you are welcome to wait in the waiting room." She pointed to the door down the hall marked *Waiting Room*.

Trina asked, worried, "Can you tell me what happened? Please. Is she going to be, okay?"

The nurse saw the extreme panic in Trina's eyes and motioned for her to come closer. In a soft voice, she said, "I can't give you details, but they had to take your friend back into surgery. She started bleeding internally. They think the bullet caused damage to an artery."

Trina said, "Oh my God, that's awful!"

The nurse looked down at her chart, raised her eyes from above her glasses, and said, "She also coded, but they brought her back before they took her into surgery."

The nurse put her hand on top of Trina's, looked in her eyes, and said, "Pray for your friend." She then walked over to the room where Jackie was staying and used a dry eraser to remove Jackie's name from the board.

Trina followed the nurse with tears in her eyes, and asked, "You don't think she'll make it?"

"Oh honey, I pray that she does. But after surgery, she will go back to recovery before she is placed back on a floor. And chances are, she won't be back in this room. We have to give this room to someone else. General surgery is on the second floor, they have a waiting room down there as well."

Tears rolled from Trina's eyes down her cheeks. She asked, "Are her parents here?"

"Yes. The hospital called to notify them of the change in their daughter's condition. They are on their way."

Trina looked at the elevator. She didn't know what to do. She decided to go to the second floor waiting room. Trina looked at her watch and wondered how long Jackie would be in surgery. She said a prayer to God asking that Jackie be healed.

A few seconds later Trina's cell phone rang, and she answered. It was her boyfriend. He asked, "Trina, did you hear about Jackie?"

"Yes, as a matter of fact, I'm at the hospital right now. She's in surgery."

"Oh?"

"I haven't seen her. I'm so worried. The nurse said that she started bleeding internally and her heart stopped. They had to restart it. This is a nightmare," Trina cried.

"Okay, baby, calm down. What part of the hospital are you in?"

Trina stopped crying enough to say, "I'm on the second floor in the general surgery waiting room."

"Okay, I'm on my way."

"Okay."

Trina couldn't believe what was happening. She sat in the waiting room thinking about the whole saga. She really wanted her friend to live. She knew Jackie's parents would have questions, but she didn't know what to say. She just hoped that Jackie made it through the surgery. Trina's world had been unexpectedly interrupted. Two weeks ago, life was perfect. Now, she didn't know if her friend would live or die.

She thought, *it's as if Jackie had two separate lives—one for college and one for crime.* The more she thought about it, the more she didn't understand. There had to be a good explanation, but what was it? It couldn't be just about money.

Trina made up her mind, she didn't care what Jackie had done. She had already forgiven her. She was tired of trying to forget each person that had ever hurt her, because the anger and bitterness that came with that overwhelmed her and caused her ulcer to act up. Trina decided to call the person that started this unforgiving train, her father.

After twelve years of not seeing or talking to him, she flipped her cell phone open, located his name, and dialed his number. She would start forgiving today.

38

Lindsey came downstairs with the newspaper under her arm. She laid it down on the dining room table while she went into the kitchen for something to eat.

DeMarcus came in from his Anger Management class. He walked through the dining room on his way to the kitchen. He stopped at the table because he saw pictures of girls on the front page, one being Jackie. He picked up the paper and a familiar face smiled back at him. He recognized the smile instantly and the warmth of her eyes. He exhaled. He found her. Finally, he had found his long-lost love, Ursula. He read the headlines and then the words in the story. Silence surrounded him.

Lindsey came out of the kitchen with a bag of chips and said, "Oh, I guess you see Jackie made the front page."

DeMarcus didn't say anything, he just kept reading. Lindsey watched him because his eyes got bigger and then he fell to his knees. Concerned, she reached out and offered to help him. What she didn't know was that no one could help. Everything he prayed for, everything he hoped for was now gone.

"Oh God, no!" He closed his eyes, trying to will what he read in the newspaper to be wrong. He screamed, "God, no, not Ursula!"

DeMarcus spent months traveling back and forth to New York searching for her; the person he really loved. He had no idea that all along she was right there at Karrington. He tried hard to recall if he had seen her on campus before, but he couldn't.

Did I see her and not recognize her? Did she recognize me? These thoughts skipped through his mind, but the prevailing thought that overshadowed all of them, was the fact that she was dead. Gone forever, unable to reunite or rekindle the love they once shared.

He screamed at the top of his lungs and cried uncontrollably. Lindsey didn't know what to do. She called out to see if anyone else was in the house, but no one was there. She had never seen him like this before. He had always been the macho bully; now he was a poor defenseless child who desperately needed his mother.

Overwhelmed by shock and pain, he couldn't believe that after all these years, she was right here under his nose. The article said that her apartment was plastered with pictures of a little boy that looked to be about seven or eight years old, but they had yet to find him. They urged people if they had seen the boy to contact the authorities. Ursula seemed to have no family, and so they were holding the body, waiting for someone to claim it. DeMarcus quickly did the math in his head and wondered if the child they mentioned was his.

Finally able to get him to calm down, Lindsey helped him to the couch. He clinched the newspaper in his hands. He sat on the couch sobbing quietly. She put her arm around him to comfort him. When she did, he fell into her lap like a scared child.

DeMarcus hadn't fallen apart like this since his mom died. Just like then, he didn't know where to turn or what to do, so he just continued to cry.

Lindsey sat there holding DeMarcus for what seemed like hours. Neither of them said a word. Finally, after almost two hours of silence, DeMarcus' cell phone rang in his book bag. He didn't move, he just lay in her lap. Lindsey reached down, picked up his bag, and found a silver cell phone at the bottom. She picked it up and handed it to him, but he didn't move. She decided to answer it herself. "Hello."

The voice on the other end of the line said, "Hello, is this Marissa?"

Lindsey snapped back, "No, this is not Marissa. Uh...this is one of DeMarcus' housemates, Lindsey. May I ask who's calling?"

"Oh, it's his aunt."

Lindsey told DeMarcus, "It's your aunt."

He took the phone and barely got out, "Hello."

Big Mama said, "What's wrong, baby? Are you okay? You sound like you're crying."

"I am."

"Tell Big Mama what's wrong."

DeMarcus tried to talk, but he couldn't breathe "I...Ursula."

"Well, baby, that's what I was calling you about. Ursula has been at Karrington going to school just like you, and she's graduating. I just got a lovely letter from her in the mail."

DeMarcus started crying uncontrollably all over again.

Lindsey saw the girl's name beside her picture and started reading the article about her.

Big Mama said, "I'm starting to panic, because I know you wouldn't cry unless something awful had happened."

She said, "Baby, you have to tell me what's wrong. You're scaring me. I can't help you if I don't know what's wrong." Big Mama just heard him sobbing on the phone. She asked again, "DeMarcus, why are you crying? What's going on, son?"

DeMarcus tried to explain, but couldn't, so Lindsey took the phone and explained that Ursula was dead.

Distressed, the aunt paused and said, "Oh Jesus. No, that's not possible. There must be some mistake. I just got a letter from her telling me how much she loved me. She was just like one of my children." Big Mama screamed and cried, "Oh God, no!"

Lindsey said, "I'm sorry for your loss, but the newspaper said she was shot."

She gathered her composure quickly. "Okay, tell DeMarcus that Big Mama's on her way. I'll call my son, and we'll get on the first flight out of California. Lindsey, I know it's a lot to ask, but can you stay with him until we get there or at least until Marissa gets there. I have Marissa's number; I'm going to call her and ask her to come over."

Lindsey said, "I'm fine. I can stay with him until she comes. But, if you can't find Marissa, I'll stay until you get here."

DeMarcus said, "Don't call Marissa. We broke up, I don't want her involved."

Big Mama heard him talking to Lindsey and said, "Okay, I won't call her. Thanks so much, darling, for staying with him. We'll be there as soon as we can."

DeMarcus couldn't believe this. Everything he was hoping for had vanished. He dated and loved, but held back his real love for Ursula, and only Ursula. No other woman ever seemed to compare to her. But now Ursula was dead, and he felt as if he was dying inside too.

Lindsey hung up the phone and looked down at DeMarcus. She took a tissue from the tissue box on the end table and wiped his tears away. His eyes were now bloodshot red. He couldn't seem to stop crying.

Lindsey asked, "Who is Ursula?"

But DeMarcus didn't respond, he just cried.

For the first time since they lived in the row house, she didn't despise him, and she didn't dislike him. Instead, she felt sorry for him, and he was the one person in the house that she thought she could never feel sorry for.

39

The doctors told Jackie that she should make a full recovery, after extensive physical therapy. However, she had to stay in intensive care for a couple more days before they planned to move her back to a regular room. Jackie was thankful that she was alive. She felt like God had given her a second chance to make things right in her life, and she planned to do just that.

Intensive care was a little boring, because none of her friends could visit. Her mom decided to tell the nurse that Trina was Jackie's sister, hoping that would cheer Jackie up. She was glad to see Trina. In fact, Trina came to the hospital every day since Jackie's second surgery. She brought Jackie magazines, books, and everything she needed. She even snuck in candy corn, which was Jackie's favorite candy.

After being in the hospital for more than two weeks, Jackie was finally discharged. She was busy packing her things in her suitcase, when she heard the door open. It was Broderick. They both stared at each other in silence. Jackie was shocked that it had taken him this long to come and see her. She knew that Trina told him that she was in the hospital.

He came in holding a newspaper under his arm and closed the

door. Without saying anything, he sat down in the chair beside the bed. Jackie thought, as she watched him, *No kiss, no smile, no nothing.*

He finally broke the silence and asked, "How are you doing?"

Before Jackie answered, she saw the disappointment in his eyes. She responded, "Fine. What about you?"

He said, "I've been better. That was before I found out that my girlfriend was involved in a prostitution ring while we were dating." He held up the newspaper and said, "Is this true? Prostitution?"

Jackie read the story earlier, and explained, "No. I wasn't part of a prostitution ring."

He said, "All of those times I couldn't find you, or you wouldn't answer my call, were you servicing your clients?"

Jackie screamed, "No! I would never do that."

Frustrated with her explanation, he said, "Jacqueline, think about it. We hardly ever went out on Saturday nights, only during the week and a Friday here or there if I was lucky. Why?"

She said, "Because I had things to do. Besides, we studied together during the week. I wasn't prostituting, you have to believe me."

The conversation with Broderick got old fast. She had already had it with her family. They were very disappointed. But she reassured them that she had never had anything to do with prostitution. Her mom and Jackson believed her. The jury was still out on her dad, Jarrett, and now Broderick.

Broderick quickly retorted, "Well, I'm confused about you." He rubbed his hand over his face. "I love you, but there are parts of you that I just don't understand or trust."

Jackie couldn't believe that she heard him say he loved her.

"Are you listening to me? I'm not sure what to do about you. I can't have people knowing that my girlfriend was prostituting or was thinking about prostituting. This article said they are still investigating."

Jackie put her head down, she was beside herself. She couldn't believe that she had gone through two surgeries, almost died, and he was only concerned about his reputation. She listened to him and watched him scan parts of the newspaper article. He probed her for answers about everything listed in the piece.

Exasperated, she stopped him. "Well, you know what, Broderick, you're right; I've made some mistakes in my life. So, I fully understand." She kept packing her things, so she could go home. "I'm sorry that I'm not the person you thought I was. I'm sorry that this whole ordeal has caused you so much pain. I'm sure you came here to break up with me." She paused, took a deep breath, and a tear fell on her suitcase. She said, "Well, let me do it for you. You're unhappy, and right now, I'm unhappy. Let's call it even. It just didn't work out."

She picked up a pair of jeans and a shirt and walked into the bathroom to change her clothes. She hoped that Broderick would get the hint and leave. Only she forgot she had one mobile arm.

He sighed heavily, upset with Jackie.

She came back into the room, holding her clothes in her hand, as she was unable to change without help.

Broderick was still there and angrily, he looked at her and asked, "What's wrong?"

Jackie darted her eyes toward him, barely lifted her sore arm, and winced in pain. She tilted her head at him and said, "Duh."

For the first time since he'd been there, he looked at her arm and realized that she was hurt. He said, "Do you want me to help you?"

"No. I'll call the nurse."

Tormented by the newspaper article, he pleaded with her, "Jacqueline, I just need you to tell me the truth."

She said, "What difference will it make? You're so worried about your precious reputation. You couldn't care less about me. I told you that I didn't prostitute myself and you still don't believe me."

Jackie pushed the nurse's button, and the nurse asked, "How can I help you?"

"Ah...when you get a chance, I need a little help getting dressed."

The nurse replied, "Okay, give me a few minutes, and I'll be right in."

"I asked you; do you need help? You didn't have to call the nurse," Broderick raised his voice and said, "I'm standing right here!"

Jackie snapped, "Apparently I did," while placing her toiletries in her cosmetic bag.

"Okay, Jacqueline. If you didn't have anything to do with prostitution, then what did you do?" He raised his voice and said, "Three people are dead. One of them was your housemate and another was a girl we were in class with last year."

She ignored his question and said, "I've said all I'm going to say right now. I'm just waiting on my parents to come get me."

He stood up and said, "That's the problem. You haven't said anything. Is this how you want it to end?"

"Obviously, that's what you want, so yeah." Deep down Jackie loved him, but after all she had gone through, she didn't care anymore. She was tired of trying to be what everyone else wanted her to be. She was just going to try to be Jackie for a while.

He walked over to her and grabbed her good arm. "No, I want you to tell me the truth." He peered into her eyes. "I know you, and I know you're lying. What happened?"

Jackie jerked away from him, trying to free her arm, but she couldn't. "Let go, and just leave," she screamed.

The nurse walked in, ready to help Jackie change, and saw their heated confrontation. She said, "Jackie, are you alright? Do I need to call security?"

Jackie said, "No. Can you just give us a minute?"

The nurse gave Broderick a threatening look and said, "Okay, I'll be right outside."

Broderick let Jackie's arm go. She wanted to tell him the truth, but she knew he would break up with her anyway. So she saved him the trouble.

"Broderick, it's over. I'm done. You don't trust me, and I'm tired of trying to make this work."

"Okay, fine. But this is it. I'm through playing this game of dating, breaking up, and getting back together. I'm no longer putting my life on hold because of you. If I walk out this door, I'm moving on, and I'm never coming back. So, do you want to tell me what happened, or is this the end?"

Jackie paused because she knew this was it. She said softly, "I'm sorry it didn't work out. Maybe it was never meant to be."

Broderick picked up his newspaper and slammed the door behind him.

Jackie fell on the bed and cried. Because of her choice to lie, she had lost the only real boyfriend she ever had.

40

After leaving the hospital, Jackie's parents took her back to the row house. They opened the door and called out to see if anyone was home. She was thankful to find the house empty. Her housemates were probably in class, and Lindsey most likely spent the night with one of her male friends.

Jackie asked her family to sit in the den because she needed to talk to them. More importantly, she knew her father needed to vent. This entire time, he had spoken very little to her, but she knew he was anxious, ready to lecture her, and find out what happened. Outside of standing up to Nita and being shot, she felt like this was the second hardest thing she ever had to do.

She got enough courage to say, "Dad, I know—"

Swift to cut her off, her father said, "You know what? Our entire trip to D.C. was spent sitting with our hearts in our stomach, not knowing what kind of condition you were going to end up in. Do you have any idea what that felt like?" He paused, waiting on her response, and then said, "Do you?"

Jackie looked down, deeply saddened to hear about their worry.

"Daddy, I'm so sorry."

He sat on the edge of his seat with his eyes focused on her every word and movement. His tone was sharp and elevated. Jackie thought that at any moment, he was going to get up and attack her.

"You've worried your mother and the rest of the family half to death. We sent you up here to get an education and graduate, not to get caught up in some God forsaken mess like this. I want some answers, and I want them now."

Before she could answer, he continued his tirade.

"And all you could say is 'I'm sorry'? What about this newspaper article and prostitution?"

He held up the newspaper and shook it at Jackie, just as Broderick had done earlier.

Jackie was scared. She didn't know what to do. She felt like her pain medications were wearing off. She put her head down again and pitifully said, "Daddy, the police will clear my name, because I didn't do it."

"Okay, let's start with why the police were involved. What the hell went on that cops were questioning everyone you know and searching this house for the past three weeks? What the hell did you do?" He stood up and raised his hand to Jackie. "You have disgraced yourself and our family name. There's no telling what I'm going to do to you."

Her mom yelled to him, "Honey, please! She just got out of the hospital. Let's hear her out."

He paused, and then looked at Jackie waiting for an explanation.

No one moved, and no one said anything. They all knew when he got upset his eyes changed from olive green to an almost gray color. And right now, they had changed colors. But he wasn't the only one upset. They were all upset. Her mother could barely look at her.

Jackie felt bad and took a deep breath. She said a silent prayer, and then started at the beginning. She told her family everything. By the time she finished, their mouths were agape with amazement, and her mother cried softly. Her father sat, astonished at the actions that she described, and the people involved in her parties.

Jarrett said, "You're definitely going to need some counseling after this."

Jackie said through her tears, "Daddy, there's nothing that you can do to me that I haven't already done to myself. I'm sorry for my mistakes, and I take full responsibility for my actions. But I don't want to go to jail, and I don't want you to lose this house. Please, let me make this up to you, and the family."

Her father rubbed his hand back and forth over his forehead, and after a few seconds, he spoke. He looked like he had been to hell and back, and he'd taken the whole family with him.

"Jackie, did this start before or after Ruby died?"

"Before."

"And you kept doing it after she died?"

"Yes, but I was trying to get out."

He yelled, "I don't believe you," and glared at her like she was a stranger.

"Daddy, I'm sorry. I want to make it up to everyone."

"Jackie, how in the hell are you going to make this up to anybody? I don't know what to say..." He shook his head. "You've outdone your-self. Out of all the things to do, you could have picked up the phone and called us at any time. But you chose to sell drugs?"

Agitated, he sat down and hung his head low. Then he glanced at her mom and said, "Where did we go wrong?"

Jackie's mom looked at him, and then at Jackie. She sniffed and said, "We built the business. It took time from the kids." She wiped her tears with a Kleenex. "And we stopped going to church. I've always felt guilty about that, and I would take it all back, if it meant that we didn't have to face this day."

He gave Jackie a strong but cold look. "No, this is not about us. This is about Jackie. You're a totally different person. You're not the Jackie we raised."

Jackie fought back tears and stood tall, hoping she would somehow find the strength to explain.

"You're right, Daddy. I'm not the same. I'm different from the Jackie you knew. My life in D.C. has been different from most college students, and there's nothing I can do to change that. But, Momma and Daddy, I made choices – some bad choices. I did the wrong things, and I should have known better. That's on me. But you didn't teach me how to make my own decisions."

He stood up and said in a stern voice, "Now hold on, there's no way this is our fault. It's okay for me and your mom to analyze and question how and why this happened. It's another thing for you to try and blame us." He yelled, "Who do you think you are? Jackie, you are old enough to make your own decisions. No one has to teach you that, it's a part of life."

Jackie stood firm and got louder herself. "No, it's not! You didn't teach me how to love myself. I've spent my whole life trying to fit into everyone's world except my own. None of you know what's it's like to be in my skin, for people to look at you and not know if you are black, white, or what."

"What are you talking about? Jackson and Jarrett have the same problem, but they didn't go out and sell drugs," her dad said, but gave a judgmental glare to Jackson because Jackson had tried drugs and disgraced himself and the family.

"Daddy, look at them, and look at me. I'm the lightest of your kids, and I'm a girl. It never occurred to you or Mom that self-image counts more when you're a girl?"

Her mother responded, "It did, and that's why we took Brittany in as an exchange student."

"Brittany's my friend, but she couldn't give me what I needed. No one taught me to accept me and embrace being from two different worlds. No, you didn't have time for me. You spent all your time on your precious business."

Her Dad said, "Now look here. That 'precious business' you're talking about is what pays for the two-million-dollar house you grew up in, all the designer clothes you had to have, and the car you have at home. What does your color and our business have to do with you selling drugs? All our time was spent so you and your brothers would have the best in life. It's a far better life than your mother and I ever had when we were growing up."

"Well, look at me." Jackie pointed to her shoulder in a sling. "Is my life better? No, Daddy, it's not. And my color and your business have everything to do with me selling drugs. You didn't equip me. I've had poor self-esteem since I was born. So yeah, when it was time for me to make my own decisions, I couldn't do it, because I didn't believe in me. I let other people make my decisions because I didn't trust myself. That's on you and me."

"How dare you sit and accuse me, like I put the cocaine in your hand."

"I'm not saying that. But instead of addressing my problem, you put me in Jack & Jill and moved Brittany in, hoping that I would learn how to make my own decisions and somehow find my "blackness." Well, I did. But not the way you wanted me to. In the end, I took responsibility for what I did, and with God's help, I got out."

"You leave God out of this. He had nothing to do with your decision to sell drugs."

"Yes, he did," she yelled back at him. The entire family was shocked at Jackie's behavior toward her father.

"Girl, are you out of your damn mind? I promise, somebody better say something or do something, because I'm about to knock her out."

"Daddy, please listen," she said in a calmer voice. "God tried to stop me several times. He tried to warn me, but I didn't listen. He taught me an important lesson that if I accept me for who I am, it doesn't matter what anyone else thinks about me, including you. It only matters what he thinks about me." She looked at her father with determination. She wanted him to know she was serious.

Her father raised his eyebrows at her as she continued talking.

"I created the deception in this row house, while I was supposed to be working on my degree. This is where I lied and dealt drugs. I'm ashamed of snorting cocaine and having sex in your house. I realize how much I've disrespected you, and I'm sorry. I really was trying to get out, but Nita wouldn't let me. And then the coke parties made me feel important and gave me friends. For once in my life, people accepted me for me, and I liked it. I realize it was false acceptance, but a piece of me needed that, to be accepted no matter what."

No one said anything, they just stared.

Not knowing what to do, Jackie broke the silence and said, "And I do want to make it up. I'm hoping that the police don't find out about the coke parties, but if they do, then I'll face the consequences. If I can walk away from this with even partial use of my shoulder and arm, then I will be forever thankful to God."

"But I believe that He's going to let me walk away with much more. I had a lot of time to think about the Karrington University Boarder Babies program. After I graduate, I want to take this house and create a facility called "Forever Home," with your permission, of course. If not, then I will buy my own building. Those babies need a place to call home, a place where they can be taken care of, and a place to play. I plan to hire nurses and teachers to take care of them. So, if you're okay with that, I'll write a grant to the state for funding. You had to see these drug addicted babies left in the hospital. It's not their fault, but someone needs to care enough to do something about it. It's the least I can do, considering all that I've already done."

She could tell her father was listening, but he and the family seemed lost and dismayed. Maybe it was the sudden change of subject, or it could have been her plans for the house. Jackie wasn't sure if her plan sounded horrible, or if they thought that she couldn't pull it off. Either way, she knew her father had a different plan for her.

Her mom smiled and said, "Jackie, you seem to have a plan for what you want to do with your life. And you've even thought about grants and hiring nurses. Are you sure about this?"

"Yes, because I realize something, I have to stop trying to fit in and be accepted by everyone. That's why I'm not coming back home to work for the family company, and I'm not going to law school. This is what I want to do with my life. At church I learned that Jesus took a stand, he never tried to fit in, so I'm not going to either." Jackie was confident that she had made her point.

Her mom clarified, "Baby, that's all we've ever wanted was for you to make your own decisions. And when you didn't make them, we thought we needed to make them for you. You have changed, you've matured." Jackie's mom stood and gently hugged her daughter.

Jackie again turned her attention to her dad, because she knew he was really the one she had to win over.

"Daddy, I know that you want me to come back to Dallas and help run the business, but I don't want to do that. I'm tired of being told what to do with my life. It's time that I start making my own decisions. I want to stay here in D.C. and help the boarder babies. For the first time in my life, I want to do something that has some meaning. I'm not saying that the business doesn't have meaning, but it's not what I need to do."

His expression was much softer than before. Jackie thought she saw a bit of remorse in his eyes and believed that he heard her and understood.

"I don't know if I can trust you to stay in D.C. by yourself. You've done some terrible things, and you're going to have to prove to me that you're trustworthy. I'm not sure you can do that."

"I'll do whatever you want me to do. I'll have a curfew and call you every night at the same time. Just tell me, and I'll do it. I want you to know that you can trust me again. I don't want to lose your trust." Jackie started crying. She knew that this whole ordeal had severely damaged her relationship with her father.

Her tears seemed to touch him, but he didn't comfort her. Instead, he said, "You'll need to put together a business plan and include all of the necessary research."

Jackie's face erupted with excitement and a big smile. "Okay, Daddy. Thank you!"

Her father crushed her enthusiasm. "I'm not saying yes, because I'm not sure if I'm going to let you even stay at Karrington. I know this is your senior year, but I don't really care."

Disappointed, Jackie said, "Whatever you say, Daddy."

Jackson said, "I know of someone that can help you write the grant, and of course, I'll help you with the contracts and liability issues involving these children. The house is up to code, but I don't know if it's ready for a daycare."

"It wouldn't be a daycare. This is where they would live, until they were old enough to leave."

Her Dad said, "After we review your plan, your mom and I will think about it. We will also decide where you will spend the rest of your senior year."

"Okay, thanks, Daddy." Jackie knew not to push him any further.

Afterwards, her parents left and returned to their hotel. They would come and check on Jackie the next day before they returned to Dallas. In the meantime, Jackie decided to go to her room and lie on her bed. She thought about her future, wondering if she would go to jail, or if she would finish her studies at Karrington. She really wanted to create "Forever Home." But, more than anything, she was amazed at how she stood up to her dad.

After about two hours, someone knocked on her door, and Jackie called out, "It's open."

Lindsey came in, sat in Jackie's chair, and began thumbing through one of Jackie's magazines. "Hi, Jackie. How are you feeling? You gave us quite a scare, you know?" she said, laidback, like she really didn't care about Jackie or how she was feeling.

Jackie said, "I'm fine," wondering what she really wanted and knowing that Lindsey wouldn't have made up that lie for the police, unless there was something in it for her. She sighed and waited to hear more from Lindsey.

"Well, I wanted to come by so you could tell me 'Thank you.'"

Jackie frowned at her.

Lindsey continued to talk, "You know, for helping you out with the police."

"How did you help me out with the police?" Jackie didn't remember the whole conversation because she was still woozy from the pain medication, but she remembered the lie about prostitution.

"You remember. I told them that you were involved in prostitution, but I could have told them about the drugs."

"Hum...And why did you do that?"

"To help you, of course. Come on, Jackie, we both know you were dealing drugs in the house, but I have a proposal for you."

"Really, what would that be?" Jackie wasn't sure what she wanted, but she had become hip to Lindsey's games.

"I am planning to have my lawyer draw up the real estate papers for this house, and I want you to sign it over to me."

Jackie immediately sat straight up in the bed and moaned because it hurt her back. Wincing, she said, "What! Are you crazy?"

"As a matter of fact, I am, but that's beside the point." Lindsey laughed. "I found out from my lawyer that if drugs are sold or done in a residence, the residence can be seized by the court. So, if you sign the house over to me, I'll keep your secret. The courts won't seize the house, and you won't go to jail."

Jackie collected her thoughts while looking at Lindsey, because she was correct. In a calm voice she said, "Well, I guess if you contact the police about that, then I'll have to let them know that you filed a false police report explaining a made-up prostitution ring. I took criminology last semester, and I can't remember if that offense is punishable by a year in jail and a two thousand, five-hundred dollar fine, or a year in jail and a four thousand, five-hundred dollar fine. I can't recall. Anyway, we'd both be in jail, wouldn't we? And then, there's the credit card fraud you've been doing. You know, the Visa, MasterCard, and American Express cards you've been getting in the mail. Let me see, what were the names, oh yeah Mia Smith, Norma Walker, NaTasha Bolden...You want me to keep going?"

Lindsey didn't say a word, but the expression on her face was all Jackie needed to put the icing on the cake.

"I have a few of those envelopes in my safety deposit box at my bank. Would you like me to get them for you in the morning? Really, it won't be a problem."

"You opened my mail?" Lindsey yelled.

"Well, technically, it's not your mail. You were opening someone else's mail or creating someone else's mail. But let's not get bogged down with the details. I never opened the mail, that would be mail fraud, and I'm pretty sure that's a felony too." Jackie looked up at the ceiling, searching for the answer. "Well, I know credit card fraud is. How many envelopes did you have? My last count was around ten, so that's ten counts on each charge. I'm not sure, but you'd probably serve at least ten to twenty years in prison. Since this is my first offense, I'll probably get out sooner for good behavior. But, wow, the charges against you, I don't know, there's so many."

Beside herself with anger and rage, Lindsey stormed out of the room and Jackie got up and followed her. "I've got a question. Out of all things to blackmail me with, why the house?"

Lindsey turned around and yelled back, "It's my mother's house! Your parents bought it from my mother. Why do you think I was the first one to rent a room here? It has sentimental value."

"Lindsey, you're confused. My parents didn't buy this house from your mother. They bought it from a lady named Ms. McKinsey who had—"

Lindsey finished her sentence before Jackie could. "Bone cancer. She had to sell the house to pay her medical bills. I'm Lindsey McKinsey. That was my name before I got married. Why do you think I've been waiting on my employment settlement? I needed that money to buy my mother's house back. I did all that work, and I still didn't get any money."

Stunned, Jackie couldn't believe what she was hearing. It was all starting to make sense. Lindsey was always so particular about the kitchen and about things scratching the buffet table. And although Jackie never believed the company would give Lindsey any money for her bogus lawsuit, she persisted with it.

"You're not getting the house. Did you fake the harassment claim, too?" Jackie questioned.

"Of course, I did. I thought if I offered you enough, you and your parents would sell me the house."

"Damn, Lindsey. You're worse than I am!"

Lindsey walked up the stairs to the third floor and slammed the door.

Jackie was speechless. She knew Lindsey loved being at the house by herself in the summers, but she had no idea about her connection to it.

This was Jackie's first time ever blackmailing anyone. She shocked herself by how well she was able to do it, but she was done letting people push her around. From now on, she was taking charge of her life.

~

The next day, Brittany knocked on Jackie's door. When Jackie answered, Brittany walked in and closed the door. She asked, "Okay Jax, seriously, what really happened?" And just like she did with her family the day before, Jackie proceeded to tell her the whole story.

Shaken and confused, Brittany said, "I have my own confession to make." She started sobbing.

Jackie asked, "What's wrong with you?"

She told Jackie about the pregnancy and Charles' response to it. Jackie didn't see that one coming. She consoled her and then discussed Brittany's options. Still unsure of what she would do, Jackie listened and advised as best as she could. For Jackie, it felt good to be the one giving advice instead of always receiving it.

Jackie walked downstairs to get Brittany some water. Through the front door window, she saw a police car drive up and park in front of the row house. She stopped on the stairs, and her heart dropped in her stomach. *Why are they here? Are they going to arrest me?*

She raced into the kitchen, trying to decide if she should run out the back door and down the alley or stay and face the inevitable. Just then, Bijon walked into the kitchen with his friend, Sean.

Bijon asked Jackie, "How are you doing?"

She said, a little nervously, "Fine."

Bijon introduced Sean to Jackie as his friend. Sean gave him a strange look, but said, "Nice to meet you." They left and returned to Bijon's room.

She heard the doorbell ring and said, "Damn." She thought fast. If she ran, they would catch her. But, if she didn't answer the door, then one of her housemates would, and they would tell the police she was home.

Jackie took a deep breath, swallowed hard, and walked slowly to the door, as the doorbell chimed again. She opened it, and the officer from the hospital stepped in. He said, "Hi Jackie, hope you're feeling better. I just had a couple more questions."

She said, "Yeah, I'm doing better, thanks, uh...please come in. What questions do you have?" Trying not to appear scared, she hampered her fear and stayed calm. She walked over to the couch, sat down, and motioned for him to have a seat.

He said, "Thanks. Well, we checked on the prostitution allegation, and it checked out."

Surprised, she said, "What? It did?"

The officer gave her a suspicious look.

Jackie took back her words, "It's just that...I didn't think Nita would leave any evidence. She prided herself on being smarter than the police."

He said, "Every criminal thinks they're smarter than we are. You didn't think we would catch her, did you?"

Jackie thought to herself, *good save, he bought it.* "Uh...well I knew it would catch up with her eventually. Nita was a scary person. But I promise I didn't have anything to do with the prostitution stuff."

The officer laughed a little. "Relax, we know you didn't. We think there was a drug ring too."

Jackie nodded, because she knew he had her now.

He rationalized, "Although, we couldn't find any evidence of a ring, but we have our suspicions. We did some further research, and Bonita Lockheart's rap sheet had convictions for drugs, prostitution, and burglary rings. She was in prison twenty years ago for a burglary ring she ran on the upper east side of New York."

"What? I didn't know that. She was an ex-con. My God, what didn't she do?" Jackie wondered how that could be. Nita always said that no one could catch her, especially the police. She should have known Nita was lying.

Seeing the confusion on Jackie's face, he told her, "People are very deceptive. You have to be careful who you associate with. We know that you bought a couple of outfits from her boutique. We ran the transactions from the store for the last five years. We believe that's where you met Nita. Is that correct?"

Jackie had no other choice but to answer his questions. He'd done his research and was about to slam her. She watched this scene play out a hundred times in the movies.

Hesitant, she responded, "Yes, that's where I met her."

"Well, I'm sure you already know that Ostentatious Boutique was a front for her prostitution ring. She had six sales associates working each day. Their shift schedules were on a huge board in the storage room along with the johns they serviced. The girls at the store confessed that it provided them extra money on the side. Most were teenage runaways that Nita supposedly rescued from the streets. When we interviewed them, apparently Nita had told them that the sex with strangers was okay as long as you wore a condom." He chuckled a little. "Talk about gullible. I still can't believe they bought that one."

He took out a package of cigarettes and asked Jackie, "Mind if I smoke?"

Jackie shook her head in a daze, unable to comprehend everything he'd said. She sat in silence trying to remember all the times she had been in the boutique. If nothing else, it explained why all the sales associates were so gorgeous. Did she see any men there? Did she see anything that looked like prostitution?

He asked her again, "Hey, uh, mind if I smoke?"

She said, "Oh, no."

He lit his cigarette with a pocket lighter and said, "Nita seemed to play a lot of games on naïve girls. The storage room in the back had been converted into two separate suites or more like love palaces. They both had candles, mood lighting, and all the liquor and cocaine one could ever want. Oh, and the autopsy report came back. Your gunshot Nita in the leg. It was the gunshot to the head that Ms. Williams fired that killed her. So, you're off the hook. I think we solved this one. We were able to get some good information from Ms. Williams' room."

The whole time the officer talked, Jackie held her breath. She started turning pale, and the officer asked, "Are you alright?"

Jackie nodded.

He said, "You don't have to be afraid of Ms. Lockheart anymore. She is dead, and that's for sure. She can never threaten or hurt you again. I'm familiar with this kind of fear when someone's been victimized. Here is a card for a victims' advocate at our precinct. Give her a call, and she can help you get past your fear."

Jackie took the card and said, "Thanks."

"You know, I do have one question," the officer said as he eyed Jackie. "Your parents' credit card had a lot of transactions on it for liquor and food, mostly from high end restaurants. Twice a month? Who was all that for?"

"Well, you know. I have a lot of college friends, and we throw parties. Plus, I go to a lot of parties, and so I buy food for them."

"I guess that's not too strange. Over the years, I've seen a lot of Karrington students spending a great deal of money on all kinds of things."

The officer left and Brittany came down the stairs, wondering what happened to her water. As they walked into the kitchen, Jackie told Brittany about the officer's findings and the details of Nita's operations.

They took the water and headed back upstairs. Jackie reflected on how her life had drastically changed over the last two and a half years. She had lived and almost died. She made some mistakes and even lost some friends along the way. She had learned to accept the girl she was, and even more, the woman she had now become —a beautiful, intelligent African American woman. Acceptance can be the most devastating, but also the most rewarding journey imaginable.

SEQUEL SNEAK PREVIEW

Excited for what happens next?
Read on for a preview of Kimberly Thacker Webb's sequel
Degrees of Deception: City Secrets

Coming soon from
Emerald Pen Publishing in 2025

1

Despite the whispers and sneers from the people in the church, Jackie walked down the center aisle toward the shiny, burgundy casket. She needed forgiveness from her friend, but more than that she needed to forgive herself.

A lady stared at Jackie as she passed the pew. "What is *she* doing here?"

Jackie heard the stinging comment and paused her gait while leaning on the pew in front of her. She swallowed hard and inhaled deeply, determined to keep walking down the aisle.

Again, the lady scoffed and picked up her fan, waving it in front of her face that wore an expression laced with disgust. The woman sitting next to the lady said, "Prostitutes...in the house of God? It's a wonder that lightning doesn't strike her down."

Hearing the comments made Jackie feel like a low-life hood rat. Deep down she knew the ladies were only responding to what they read in the newspaper, but their words felt like verbal daggers. Trina walked beside Jackie, watching her friend's reaction to the words foes were spitting at her. Jackie stopped, closed her eyes, and placed her hands over her ears in an attempt to drown out their opinions. It seemed like the entire crowd was watching Jackie's every move.

Trina faced Jackie and pulled her hands down from her ears. "Don't pay attention to them." Trina then turned around and gave the two ladies a glaring look as she nudged Jackie to keep walking. Jackie continued toward the casket containing her friend, Ursula. A picture of Ursula wearing a grey and blue horizontal striped sweater sat next to the casket. Ursula always said it was her favorite sweater because it made her boobs look perky. Jackie smiled a little at the thought of this sentiment and Ursula's quirky personality. As Jackie walked, she focused on the photo even more. Despite everything they had been through, she could still feel the love in Ursula's eyes for her and their friendship.

Another lady spouted off, "She got some nerve showing up here."

This time Trina turned and approached the lady. She said with a despised tone, "You need to mind your business and keep your opinions to yourself. You don't even know what happened, and besides, I thought this was a house of God."

Jackie swallowed hard because she didn't deserve to be there. She didn't have any hate or animosity toward the ladies in the congregation because she agreed with them. While the lady argued with Trina, Jackie reached the closed casket holding her dear friend. In an unhurried motion, she laid her hand upon the casket and spread her fingers over it. Her heart sank into the pit of her stomach as her eyes glazed over the top of it.

People continued to whisper, and Jackie felt the eyes watching her. Their sneers and glares told a story of judgment and disgust. Trina saw Jackie out of the corner of her eye and hurried back to her side.

Jackie looked down at the casket and stroked it like she was petting a kitten. She thought, *How could this be happening? Ursula looked out for me. Ursula was there for me when things didn't go well with Nita. And even at the end, she was again trying to save me, and because of me...she's gone forever. Why didn't I just wait for her to come up with a plan to get us out?*

Tears ran down Jackie's face as she remembered her friendship with Ursula. The good and the bad times were ever present in her mind. Even at its worst, their friendship always remained intact, and now she would never see her again. Memory after memory flooded Jackie's mind as she stared at the casket. She felt queasy as a pool of stomach acids churned into a mound of despair. Her head lowered, and muffled sobs came forcefully as her legs buckled.

In one instance, Trina caught Jackie. "Are you alright?"

Jackie hung her head low. "No." She closed her eyes and took in deep breaths. She would never understand how her life had changed so quickly.

Jackie whispered, "You don't understand. Ursula was more than a friend. She was in some ways my hero. She took care of me in the hotel after Nita beat me up."

Trina looked around making sure no one heard Jackie. "Let's find a seat and talk about this later."

Jackie stood still. She remembered the first day she met Ursula, a beautiful, hip Puerto Rican girl who knew exactly what she wanted out of life. She even remembered how Ursula divided the lines of coke with a razor blade on Jackie's dining room table in the row house. Jackie remembered it all. Suddenly, she gasped for air.

Trina leaned over and whispered, "Okay, we're going to sit down, now," and then guided Jackie away from the casket and back down the aisle. But before Jackie could take a seat, she saw DeMarcus and an older lady seated on the front pew. Jackie and DeMarcus made eye contact and with a quick turn of his head, he shifted his gaze away from Jackie.

The older lady noticed DeMarcus' rudeness and gave a comforting smile to her. Jackie wondered why DeMarcus was sitting on the front pew. That was reserved for family or someone close to the deceased. He told Jackie that he knew Ursula and they had a special friendship, but she thought he meant like Jackie and DeMarcus' friendship. In one motion, Trina pointed Jackie in the direction of the row she selected and motioned for Jackie to follow. After they both were seated, Trina looked around and then whispered into Jackie's ear, "Look at this church, it's beautiful."

Without trying, Jackie's eyes were immediately drawn upward

toward the ceiling where she was welcomed by the regal architecture. On the ceiling was a mural of Mary, the mother of Jesus Christ wearing a white flowing dress with a navy-blue scarf wrapped around her waist and arm, looking down on the audience. Little chubby white babies with wings were beside her and underneath her. Beautiful white puffy cotton clouds sat above Mary's head, and an ever-ending blue skyline covered the entire background of the painting. Trina tried to talk to Jackie, but the tranquility of the blue horizon caused Jackie to tune out Trina's voice. She couldn't take her eyes of the painting. Every corner of the church seemed to contain a majestic mystery, as though there was some secret hidden in the art that was too important to miss. This was the first time Jackie had ever been in a cathedral like this before.

Not many people were in attendance. Most were church members. There were a few students, two professors, DeMarcus and possibly Ursula's family members. Unfortunately, Jackie missed LaJuana's funeral because she was still in ICU when it took place, so she was at least grateful to say goodbye to Ursula.

As a few more people filed into the church and the organ played, it was obvious that the small gathering was swallowed up by the massive height and depth of the Catholic cathedral. Part of Jackie was glad that clearance to release Ursula's body took so long. Unfortunately, they were unable to find a family member in Puerto Rico or New York to claim the body or pay for the funeral. So, an anonymous alumni donated money to pay for the funeral and burial expenses.

Jackie sat in silence next to Trina, as others began to seat themselves on their pew. Despite the ups and downs of her friendship with Ursula, Jackie could still hear her laughter and see her fun-loving smile. But now those moments were gone. They were all one-by-one fading away, because Ursula wouldn't be laughing anymore.

The priest asked the congregation to stand and read from the printed program. Jackie stood and stared at a picture of Ursula on the front page. Trina took the program and opened it to the order of service. They both listened to the priest while he read phrases, and the audience repeated sayings written on the program after he spoke.

Jackie's reading of the phrases lagged as she reflected on her life. She felt an emptiness inside like someone dug a hole to remove all her secrets, but instead, they left it uncovered with a hollow opening where her soul was supposed to be. The only sign of life in Jackie was the pain from her shoulder and the sound of her breath. That was how she knew she was alive. Everything else seemed to be moving in slow motion, like a reel from an old black and white movie. When she thought about selling drugs, having sex with two different men, and being a part of a murder, she pondered how far she had truly fallen. This was not her life. In fact, she didn't recognize herself or this life anymore.

Everyone in the church was sitting except Jackie, while the priest continued to speak. The priest glared, and Trina pulled Jackie down to her seat.

Trina whispered, "Jackie, why didn't you sit down?"

Jackie whispered back, "I thought he was still talking and we were responding."

"You didn't hear him say please be seated?"

"No. I guess my mind was elsewhere."

Trina shook her head and pointed to the section of the program where the priest was speaking.

Jackie continued with the thoughts in her head. *Although I'm glad the nightmare with Nita is over, I'm not sure if I deserve to be alive.* At the age of 21, she had seen so much death. She could hardly put her thoughts into words. Standing up to Nita, shooting Nita, two surgeries where she almost lost her life, facing her parents, lying to the police, explaining her friendship with Ursula to DeMarcus and losing her boyfriend had all taken its toll. She'd been able to fake being much stronger than she really was to others. But she still didn't know why someone hadn't committed her to an insane asylum, because if they knew the torment that she was going through... they would.

Jackie scratched her forearm, and then dug her nails in breaking the skin until droplets of blood appeared.

Trina whispered, "Jackie, stop!"

Jackie gave Trina an inquisitive look.

Trina said just above a whisper, "What are you doing? Look at your arm." Trina grabbed her purse to retrieve a Kleenex and handed it to Jackie.

Jackie heard Trina, but she couldn't respond. Her thoughts held her hostage and the only thing she could focus on now was the casket. She didn't feel the pain or see the blood until Trina took the Kleenex and wiped the blood herself. Jackie awoke from her daze and pushed the Kleenex on top of her forearm near her wrist to stop the bleeding.

The priest had the congregation stand again for the continuation of the read and response part of the program. Jackie stood with the bloody Kleenex covering her arm. She tried to follow along, but instead memories of Nita's and Ursula's bloody bodies lying on the hard, bloodstained concrete washed over her mind. This vision haunted her day and night. No matter how she tried to block these images, they showed up out of nowhere. And if the images weren't bad enough, sometimes sounds would accost her as well—gun shots going off in her ear as if the incident was happening all over again. Without warning, her mind would thrust her back to the crime scene, watching while LaJuana's body fell to the ground not even ten inches away from her. When the priest finished, he asked the audience to be seated. This time Jackie heard him and sat down.

I've got to get control over my mind. I have to get these thoughts out of my head before I crack up.

Even now, as she sat in the church with its stain glass windows, hearing the audience singing and the sounds of sadness and tears floating through the air, Jackie still couldn't get the image of Nita's face out of her mind.

The priest said, "We are going to change our program slightly. At this time, the family would like to ask if anyone in the congregation would like to offer brief words of encouragement to the family."

A blonde lady wearing a black pinstriped suit stood up with a folder in her hand and walked to the podium. She opened the folder and faced the family members on the front row.

She said, "Good morning. My name is Professor Emily Shannon, and I am the dean of the business school." And then she turned the page in the folder and read, "On behalf of Karrington University, we want to extend our condolences to the family of Ursula Mendez. Ursula was a business major, and I had the pleasure of having her in one of my classes. She was a studious young lady, and I'm very sorry for your loss. She was scheduled to graduate this May, and I know she was very excited about graduating."

Jackie remembered conversations with Ursula where they talked about how much Ursula wanted to graduate, move away and leave this life. She was so determined to do it, and Nita would never know. Jackie sat quietly clutching her purse with her one good arm and trying to breathe. She felt each breath become more labored than the previous one.

Ursula is never going to be able to live the life she wanted. Why should I get to live mine? Who am I fooling? How can I pick up my life from these ashes?

Jackie's life had been a whirlwind, and she was not quite sure how to turn it around. She'd learned a lot from her near-death experience. She tried to fake confidence in herself, with Ursula and with Nita, but deep-down buried underneath all the misery and fear was a little girl who was afraid of everything and everyone. She had done a good job convincing her parents and the university that she was fine, but Jackie knew she was far from fine. In fact, the silent storm that was raging inside was about to erupt, if she didn't get a hold of her emotions.

Jackie failed to hear the rest of the professor's words. When she raised her head again, the professor had taken her seat, and DeMarcus now stood at the podium.

He said as he fought back tears, "Ursula was my first love."
What?

Trina covered her mouth while Jackie's eyes widened as they sat still listening to everything he said. Jackie and Trina looked at each other.

He paused as he put his hand under his nose to wipe away his snot. His aunt got up and walked to the podium to hand him her handkerchief. She then took her seat.

He said, "Thank you, Big Mama. Ursula had been through a lot, and we had that in common. We both have been through a lot. We met when we were young and our relationship continued out of our pain and attraction for each other." He chuckled a little, "She was crazy sexy. Can I say that in church. right?"

Big Mama said, "Yes, baby. Say what's on your heart."

"Well, I just want to say she was my confidant. She was the only person I told all my secrets. We lost touch after my aunt moved, but I've always loved her, and she will always be my first and only love."

Jackie listened as DeMarcus talked about his relationship with Ursula. She had no idea he felt this way about her. She wondered why he had been so mad at her after she got back from the hospital. He asked her how she knew Ursula and that was it. He hadn't said anything to her not even glad you are better or so glad you didn't die. She thought he was just in one of his moods, but it was more than that. He missed Ursula. She couldn't put it together before, but now it all made sense. He was mad at her because Ursula was gone. Jackie could tell from listening to him and watching his body language. He not only used to be in love with Ursula, but he was also still in love with her.

She watched him step down from the podium. His eyes protruded in Jackie's direction and his nostrils flared before he sat back on the front pew with his aunt.

She thought back to the number of times Ursula came over. How was it that they never saw each other? And then at the university, the business school was on the other side of campus, so it was possible that he and Ursula never ran into each other. But Ursula came to the house. *How did they not see each other there?* It didn't matter now, Jackie felt responsible for Ursula's death, and now, for DeMarcus not being able to be with his one and only love.

Jackie felt unwell. Her heart was racing and her forehead dripped with sweat mixed with the tears streaming down her face. All of a sudden, she stood up. Trina pulled her good arm, trying to get her to sit back down. She whispered to Jackie, "You have to follow the program. It's not time to stand up. The priest is starting the homily."

"What? Never mind, I can't stay. I need to get out of here. I can't do this right now." The members of the parish looked at Jackie once again, but this time DeMarcus and his family also peered at her.

She said to them, "I'm sorry, I can't."

Jackie sprinted through the church doors and outside into the parking lot. Trina picked up the bloodstained tissue that fell to the floor, grabbed her purse, and ran after Jackie. Just like that, Jackie left Ursula's funeral hoping to put her past behind her once and for all. She paced up and down in front of the parked cars looking for her car.

Trina caught up with her and asked, "Jackie, why did you run out of the church?"

"I can't take it anymore. It's too much or me."

"Okay, we can leave." Trina watched how Jackie was searching inside her purse for something.

"What are you doing?"

"Looking for my car keys, I don't remember where I parked my car. I can't find my fob to sound the alarm."

Jackie dumped the contents of her purse on the ground. She knelt trying to find her keys amongst the other items in her purse.

"Jackie, stop it. You don't have a car anymore. Don't you remember? You got rid of it last year before you left for the summer. You haven't had a car for months." Trina knelt to pick up Jackie's items from her purse. Jackie closed her eyes and threw her head back.

"Oh shit, that's right. I'm losing my mind."

Jackie stood and looked up to the sky, sighed hard and remembered that she had gotten rid of the car at the same time she got rid of any and everything that reminded her of Nita. They had a car service pick them up for the funeral.

Trina stood and handed Jackie's purse to her with everything back in place and then said, "Don't worry I'll call a car." She pulled out her cell phone and made the call.

Jackie didn't say a word. She knew that little by little she was losing her grip on reality and there was nothing she could do about it. She felt like time was standing still, and yet it was moving. Everything was happening so fast. She couldn't catch up with the movement of life.

She and Trina walked back to the church and sat on the steps to wait for the car.

Trina said, "Jackie, I know this must be hard on you, going to Ursula's funeral and hearing about how DeMarcus feels about Ursula. But the worst is behind you. You've just got to pick up and focus on school."

Jackie narrowed her eyes and crossed her arms over her chest as she shook her head and sighed. She thought, *Trina wants me to focus on school. Is she serious? I just ruined two people's lives. How could I focus on school or anything else?*

"You don't have to look at me like that. I'm not crazy."

"After everything that's happened to me, how can I focus on school?"

"Well, you have to, Jackie. Your parents want you to do what's best for you. They want your top priority to be graduation."

"How do you know what my parents want?"

Trina put her head down and exhaled.

"Jackie, you just need to focus on school. It will help you get your mind off everything else."

Jackie gave Trina an inquisitive expression. "No, answer the question. How do you know what my parents want?"

Trina shook her head, her eyes darted back and forth.

Jackie pressed further, "Did you talk to my parents?"

"Yes."

Jackie stood up. "About me?"

"Yes."

Jackie looked down at Trina and cocked her head before she said, "Why are you having secret conversations with my parents about me? Did you talk to them while they were here?"

"Look Jackie, I don't want to get involved."

"Involved? Answer me!"

Trina stood up trying to diffuse the situation. "Yes, I talked to them while they were here. They just asked me to keep an eye on you and let them know if there was anything they should be alarmed about."

Jackie looked Trina up and down and then laughed. "Oh, so you're my babysitter. Wow, didn't see that one coming."

"It's not like that. They know we are close friends."

"Yeah, a close friend would have come to me and said, 'Hey I talked to your parents, and they want me to keep an eye on you.'"

"Jackie, you're making this more than what it is."

"No, I'm not."

"Jackie, you were in some serious shit. You just got out of the hospital, and you're struggling mentally, and we all know it."

"So, when were you going to tell me?"

Jackie looked at Trina and could tell she hadn't planned to tell Jackie anything.

"Well, ain't that a bitch. You weren't going to say anything at all. You were just going to spy on me and report back to them?"

Jackie thought back to the conversation she had with her parents. Her dad's exact words were, "And the first thing you have to do is graduate."

The problem was that concentrating on school really had been the last thing on her mind, and now she also had to worry about her friendship with Trina.

Trina interrupted her thoughts, placing a hand on Jackie's good shoulder. She looked in her friend's eyes and said, "Look, I'm not the enemy. I'm just concerned— just like your parents. No one's trying to hurt you."

"I'm not so sure about that. It doesn't help that my best friend is talking to my parents behind my back."

"Okay, that's fair. I shouldn't have agreed to that behind your back. I'm sorry. Do you accept my apology?"

"That depends. Are you going to call my parents after every little thing?"

"No, I'm not going to call your parents unless it's an emergency."

Jackie glared at Trina.

Trina said, "And I talk to you first," trying to convince her fried to trust her again.

After a few awkward moments, Jackie finally gave Trina a look of approval.

"I have other stuff to think about, now that I know DeMarcus and Ursula had a relationship."

Trina said, "You can't dwell on that."

Jackie sighed with exacerbation.

"I'm just trying to help."

"I know you are, but you can't. So just let it go."

"Jackie, maybe if you talk about how you feel, it will—"

"I have talked about it, and it still doesn't help."

The door of the church swung open, and people dispersed down the stairs heading to the All-Saints Hall for refreshments. Jackie and Trina moved off of the steps because they were blocking the exit. They stood off to the side watching the people walk across the parking lot to the hall.

Trina continued, "You talked about what happened, but you haven't talked about how all of this is making you feel, especially this new information."

"Yeah well, I don't feel anything other than a complete failure for ruining everyone's life."

"Don't say that?"

"What? It's true."

"No, it is not."

The car arrived. Jackie and Trina hopped in the backseat as the car sped out of the parking lot, up the street towards the beltway.

In a low tone, Trina asked, "Did you give any more thought to talking to the university psychologist?"

"Nope."

"Maybe you should."

"Maybe so."

"Are you going to call them?"

"Look, what I need now is to just be alone. There are a lot of things I need to figure out, and I can't do that and deal with a shrink. Just let me get myself together first and then maybe I'll call them."

Trina raised her voice because she didn't think she was getting anywhere. "Jackie, that's what they are there for, to help you get yourself together."

Jackie turned and yelled back at Trina, "Dammit, why can't you catch a clue and just drop it?"

Trina looked at her friend. This wasn't the Jackie she knew. Jackie had changed almost overnight. Trina threw her hands up and said, "I'm not going to drop it."

The driver asked, "Is everything okay back there?"

Jackie rolled her eyes.

Trina said, "Yes sir, we're just talking."

Jackie took a deep breath and let her hands slide vertically down her face. She said in a calm voice, "Look, today has been a rough day for me. Not to mention the surprise I just got." Jackie lifted her hands surrendering to Trina with tears in her eyes, "I need you to let it go. Can we just ride home in peace?"

Trina sighed hard, worried about her friend. She looked at Jackie and finally said, "Fine."

They both sat in silence for the next twenty minutes as the driver drove them home. Jackie looked out the window as tears rolled down her face. Trina looked over at her friend and held her hand.

DISCUSSION QUESTIONS

1. The main character, Jacqueline (Jackie) Jones failed to manage her money, and that was an expensive decision with devastating consequences. Why is it difficult for college students to manage their money? What factors motivate their behavior?

2. If you were in Jackie's shoes, and calling your parents to get more money was not an option, would you have tried the one-time gig to recoup your funds? If not, what would you have done?

3. Brittany, Jackie's housemate, flew her boyfriend to DC from Africa because she wanted to see him, and it served as an act of rebellion against her parents. What act(s) of rebellion have you secretly performed that your parents don't know or didn't know about?

4. Physical and mental abuse come from layers of mistreatment, cruelty, hurt and fear. What do you think was the origin of DeMarcus' abuse toward Marissa?

5. Brittany's statement to Bijon, "We say in Africa, if you can't make it in America, then you can't make it anywhere." What was your perspective of the world view conversation

between Bijon and Brittany regarding the financial state of Americans? What surprised you about their exchange?

6. Ursula, Jackie's friend offered to help Jackie get a job with her company. Do you think Ursula was sincere in her efforts to help Jackie with a job? Do you think Ursula had ill will for Jackie and her upbringing?

7. After the cab driver robbed Jackie at the Wellington Rome Hotel, Jackie heard a still small voice saying, *it doesn't have to be this way.* Why didn't she listen? Was this God speaking to her? How often do you hear God's voice and ignore it?

8. The business meeting at the Wellington Rome Hotel revealed the inner workings of the cocaine party empire. What were your observations on how Nita structured her business?

9. What caused Nita to develop self-hate? Why do you think Nita wanted to be white?

10. Why did Nita adjust her clothes and brush imaginary lint off her clothes on a consistent basis?

11. What made Nita think that Chase Winters was going to leave his wife? Do you think it's common for a married man leave his wife for his mistress?

12. Karrington University consisted of a diverse campus population where professors and staff members demonstrated care and concern for their students. In what aspects did Karrington University act as a parental figure to Jackie?

13. What aspects of the cocaine party did Jackie enjoy? Have you ever attended a cocaine party or found yourself in another type of potentially illegal or compromising environment for which you knew you didn't belong?

14. Why do you think Ursula regarded Nita as a mother figure?

15. Jackie had feelings for both Broderick and DeMarcus. How do you think she separated her feelings between two

of them? Have you been in love with two men at the same time?

16. Why was Bijon afraid to have a relationship with a female? Why did Bijon want to keep his relationship with Shaun a secret?

17. Why did LaJuana want and need to exact revenge on Nita?

18. Nita had a celebratory lunch prepared at her home for her chosen one, Ursula. How did Nita's plans make Ursula feel? What was the significance of the Rhododendron floral centerpiece and what symbol does it represent? What did Ursula want to do with her life?

19. What was Jackie's drug of choice?

20. Why wasn't the drug overdose and death of Jackie's aunt Ruby a turning point for Jackie? How many other occurrences are found in the novel that were turning points for Jackie to stop selling cocaine?

21. Losing the trust and support of family is hard for anyone, but especially when you lied and deceived others. How did Jackie defend herself to her father?

22. How do you think decisions of the characters in this novel will change and/or shape them in the sequel?

23. Why do you think Lindsey's blackmail attempt to gain the rowhouse back didn't phase Jackie?

24. The sermon "How Big Is Your God," spoke to Jackie in a special way. Have you ever attended a church service, and it spoke to your situation? Do you believe God speaks directly to you?

25. The theme of this novel is choices and consequences. Do you think the appropriate consequence was given to Jackie?

RESOURCES

Degrees of Deception is a work of fiction, however the characters in this novel deal with an array of real life challenges. If you or someone you know is facing some of these challenges and needs information, please see the resource list below.

National Helpline for Mental Health, Drug, Alcohol Issues
Substance Abuse and Mental Health Services Administration
5600 Fishers Lane
Rockville, MD 20857
1-877-726-4727
1-800-662-4357 (HELP)
https://www.samhsa.gov/find-help/helplines/national-helpline

Suicide & Crisis Lifeline
Call or text 988
https://988lifeline.org/

National Domestic Violence Hotline
P. O. Box 90249

Austin, Texas 78709
1-800-799-7233 (SAFE)
Text "START" to 88788
https://www.thehotline.org/

www.ingramcontent.com/pod-product-compliance
Lightning Source LLC
Chambersburg PA
CBHW021955130726
47903CB00014B/1416